LITTLE SECRETS

VICTORIA GOLDMAN

To Hollie

Thank you for taking part
in my blog tour

Best wishes

Victoria x

THREE
CROWNS
PUBLISHING

First published in the United Kingdom by Three Crowns Publishing UK in 2025
www.threecrownspublishing.com
www.vgoldmanbooks.com

Cover design by Mark Swan (kid-ethic.com)
Criminal in jail silhouette icons created by Freepik – Flaticon:
https://www.flaticon.com/free-icons/jail
The Panbrook Prisongate Map drawn by Thomas Ziegel

Paperback ISBN: 978-1-7396954-5-3
eBook ISBN: 978-1-7396954-4-6

LITTLE SECRETS

Friday, June 18, 1999
Published at 22:45 GMT

[FRONT PAGE]

Prison on lockdown

HMP Panbrook (also known as The Brook) is currently on lockdown. Five ambulances have been seen entering the prison gates.

The Category C prison in Hertfordshire was originally due to close on Wednesday, June 16. Five prisoners remain on the premises and are waiting to be transferred.

More to follow.

The Panbrook Prison Hotel
Granger Road
Chelmsworth
Hertfordshire
CH3 5GV

21 January 2019

Dear [Name]

Congratulations!

Thank you for entering The Panbrook Prison Hotel Tenth Anniversary Lottery.

We are delighted to inform you that you have been selected from hundreds of entrants to attend our celebrations, which will take place from Friday 21 June 2019 to Sunday 23 June 2019.

Your weekend stay will include:

- two nights in our premier prison-themed hotel rooms with luxury en-suite facilities
- prime access to The Panbrook Prison Hotel and its extensive grounds, including our kitchen garden
- complimentary meals in The Lock-Up, our award-winning restaurant and bar

- a visit to Panbrook Prison Museum, including the *Panbrook Prisongate* exhibition
- the opportunity to speak to our VIP guests – Fiona Trayton (former HMP Panbrook governor), Dr Bryan Land (former HMP Panbrook prison doctor) and Thomas Benson (former HMP Panbrook prisoner)
- an exclusive invitation to our anniversary party on the Saturday evening

We are looking forward to welcoming you to The Panbrook Prison Hotel. To confirm your place, please email Celebration-Time@Panbrookhotel.com.

Yours sincerely,

Derek Taylor
Owner and M.D., Charter Group

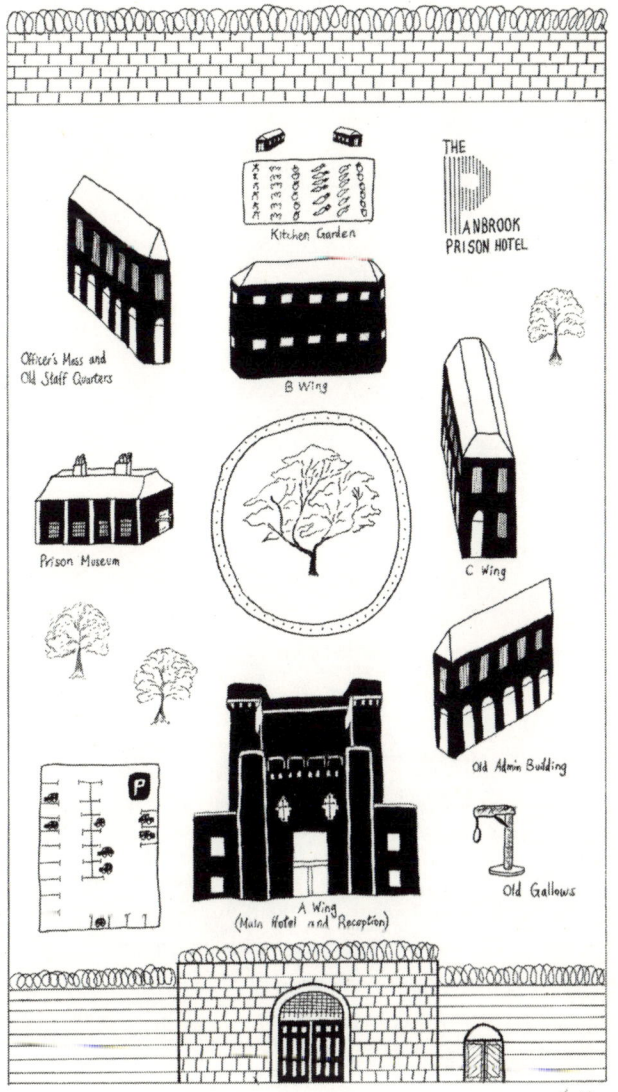

MADDIE

NOW

FRIDAY
1.30 p.m.

Anna Kendall was guilty

The words on the lift mirror are as crimson as fresh blood. As I trace each letter slowly with my finger, the writing leaves a faint sticky residue on my skin.

My stomach feels tight, as if clenched by an invisible fist.

Who could have written this ... and why?

I gaze at my reflection as if that holds the answer. Worry creases my brow, and my lips are pressed tightly together, emphasising the faint crow's feet framing my eyes.

My thirty-year-old self would never have believed that one day I would be here at Panbrook. My fifty-year-old self is struggling to believe it too. It's astonishing where the universe can take you – and the curveballs it throws.

Just three months ago, I was in charge of a tiny, boutique

hotel in the hills of southern Spain, living a quiet life away from the tourist hub. Now, I am the manager of a bustling hotel premises that has been at the heart of a true-crime controversy for twenty years.

And just six months ago...

Tears are beginning to prickle my eyes. I shake my head to waft away the memories before they overwhelm me.

My hand trembles when I pick up the damp cloth to scrub some more. Just as well this isn't a permanent marker pen. Red letters merge into one, as glistening drops of pink water land on the floor.

The lift shudders when I take a step back to assess my handiwork. I shudder too as stabbing sensations ripple across my skin. A doctor said my nerve pain is triggered by fluctuating hormones. A counsellor told me it's due to grief. But I suspect it's caused by guilt, over promises broken – and maybe fear of what's to come.

The fourth word has now been reduced to a pale pink smudge.

Anna Kendall was

Anna Kendall was what? A hard-working prison nurse? A loving mother? In the wrong place at the wrong time? Or, as many seem to believe, a scheming young woman?

A cool draft ripples the chiffon scarf around my neck, carrying with it a faint woody scent. I gaze beyond my reflection and through the open lift doorway to inspect the empty landing behind me.

These third-floor bedrooms aren't being occupied by guests this weekend – just by senior staff to get some sleep or freshen up if they need to. A reward for all our hard work, Derek told us, but it's really to make sure we are on site at all times.

'I don't tolerate tardiness,' my boss told me in his pompous voice on my first day.

The prison may have been closed for twenty years, but these buildings are still governed with an iron fist.

Not that I will be getting much sleep. I don't at the best of times, lying awake for hours staring at the ceiling as a cruel cocktail of pain and heartache plagues my dreams. But this weekend, there will also be too much to do and too much to think about.

A creak comes from behind me, followed by three faint knocking sounds. I take several slow, deep breaths to calm the fluttering sensation in my chest. I deliberately brought the lift up here to keep this handwritten message away from the guests and other staff, even placing out-of-order signs on the floors below. But perhaps that was wasted effort.

I turn around, tiptoe to the edge of the lift and peer left then right. Relief stirs in my gut as I inspect the parallel landing opposite – it is also empty.

Sunlight beams down through the high atrium-roof windows onto the plush black-and-cream striped carpet that stretches out ahead of me, shimmering like an optical illusion. This long zebra crossing leads to a tall window at each end of the landing. The left side overlooks the hotel's car park, and the right overlooks the remains of the old gallows.

A door slams below. Dulled footsteps pad over soft carpet, followed by the babbling of enthusiastic voices. The sound drifts upwards, leaving a faint echo hovering around me.

I peer over the handrail again. The original wrought-iron staircases are blocked off from the narrow walkways with a panel of reinforced glass. Health and safety didn't matter when the prison was bustling with sweaty men packed into filthy cells. But now it is everything.

From each walkway, you can see all the way down to the ground floor. When guests say the hotel's prison layout makes them feel queasy, I stifle my amusement. They should visit southern Spain, stand on the *Puente Nuevo* bridge in Ronda and gaze down into the deep *el Tajo* ravine. Then this view wouldn't seem so bad after all.

I spy the couple from Room C19 on the floor below and duck my head. A middle-aged man wearing a navy NYC cap is walking towards the other lift, accompanied by a woman with a baby-pink cardigan draped over her arm, taking photographs of the original green cell doors. A silver bangle wrapped around her slender wrist glints under the strip lighting.

As their voices drift away, I check the time on my watch. Nearly two o'clock. I need to get on. The welcome reception is scheduled for two-thirty in the courtyard garden.

The lift creaks as I step back inside it. When I reach the mirror, I grip the cloth and rub it against the remaining scarlet letters.

A deathly silence hangs in the air, and the hairs at the back of my neck twitch. Another cool draft ruffles my scarf. I shiver and use the back of my hand to push away a loose curl that has fallen across my eyes.

This building was once filled with death, disease and the dregs of society. I don't believe in ghosts, yet I still sense something lurking here: an eternal sadness maybe.

I can recite the prison's chequered history to hotel guests for hours, backwards if I need to. I have studied the neat displays in the museum, researched the archives and examined the extensive photographic collections. Yet I still often wonder what it was really like back then. Not just twenty years ago, but going back fifty years, even one hundred. I want to experience how it felt, how it sounded, how it smelled, not just how it looked.

It certainly wasn't like this: soft cream-painted walls, a faint hint of jasmine in the air, and sunlight illuminating the sparkling clean surfaces.

Sometimes when the hotel is reasonably quiet, I shut myself in an empty bedroom – each one crafted from three former cells. I close my eyes to their luxurious fittings and prison-themed accessories, and imagine who once lived in them: their crimes, their stories, the people they left behind.

Another cold draft. On my face this time, like an icy kiss caressing my cheek. Yet the windows on this landing are closed.

I glance down at my phone on the steel lift floor, feeling the urge to call someone, anyone, remind myself that I'm not alone, that the hotel contains other staff and guests this weekend.

But instead, I press the damp cloth against the mirror. I don't have time for anything else right now.

Just two words to go.

Anna Kendall

If only scrubbing out her name would scrub out the past. This nation is obsessed, even twenty years on, loving stories of the macabre, of murder and mystery. Anna has been the subject of three television documentaries this year already, the last one on BBC2 only three weeks ago. She is mentioned thirty-five times – I counted – in the small museum in the grounds of this hotel.

I have an opinion about what happened that weekend in June 1999 – of course I do, everyone does – but staff aren't allowed to divulge anything in here. Hotel guests are encouraged to make up their own minds about the events of that tragic Friday evening. We even ask them to fill in a feedback form before they leave.

- Did you visit Panbrook Prison Museum during your stay? **YES or NO**

- Did you take one of our guided tours of the hotel premises? **YES or NO**
- Did you read all of the available evidence from June 1999? **YES or NO**
- Do you think Anna Kendall was guilty? **YES or NO**

Derek believes this enhances the visitors' experience, giving them the notion that their opinion matters. Yet it doesn't. It won't change anything – nothing can change anything – and we may never know the full truth.

These words must be meant for someone here this weekend, though. Probably that journalist who arrived at lunchtime, with a large overnight bag in one hand and a laptop case in the other. As soon as I passed him the key card to Room A28, he scurried off to our first floor, head down like a sewer rat, and I haven't seen him since.

I recognise him from 'then', of course; Lloyd Palmer, the young news hack who covered the Panbrook Prison murders on the *Herts Life* website soon after it broke on the BBC for the first time. He has aged over the years – haven't we all – but still has the same dark, shifty eyes.

He wouldn't miss another opportunity to delve back into the past, dredge up all of the dirt ... and in a prison, there's always a tonne of dirt.

It has been hard to forget him, his television interviews and his book that was published nearly ten years ago, soon after the prison was renovated. *Panbrook Prisongate* was a *Sunday Times* bestseller, remaining at the top of the charts for twelve weeks, boosting his illustrious career into the fast lane.

Some people accused Lloyd Palmer of cashing in on the tragedy and the mystery surrounding Anna Kendall. Yet others were grateful that someone was finally bringing justice for the five prisoners, since the case never reached the courts.

Anna's family has retained dignified silence for all these years. But trial by media can be worse than trial by jury, even after death.

And now the story has returned to public scrutiny on the back of the hotel's tenth anniversary celebrations this week-end. Should Lloyd Palmer be dredging this all up again? Or twenty years on, shouldn't he finally be putting the story to rest?

As I scrub the mirrored surface more vigorously, the ache in my wrist travels towards my elbow. So when my phone pings, I welcome the interruption.

I step away from the wall and crouch down to peer at my phone screen, leaving more pink watery tears glistening on the floor beside me.

A WhatsApp message: *HELP! I need you! NOW! Disaster!*

Ellie.

I shake my head slowly, a smile flickering across my lips and a warm sensation rising in my chest. Nate and I used to call her our 'unexpected ray of sunshine', until she became a teenager, when 'stormy weather' seemed more appropriate. Now our shy, nervous little girl has blossomed into a self-assured young woman about to embark on the biggest adven-ture of her life so far.

This was the right time for me to return to grey, overcast days and traffic jams, although it was a struggle to leave my Spanish life behind. I miss the cloudless blue skies, the relaxed way of living, the '*mañana, mañana*' philosophy. But my precious child has been living here in England for the last two years, and fate has now brought me back.

I wipe a tear from my cheek. This isn't the time for senti-ment. The bride-to-be will have to wait for my reply, and I will have to wait a little longer to find out more about her latest drama. I shouldn't use my work phone for private matters, but Ellie is my exception. She has *always* been my exception.

A rogue thought pops into my head. *Maybe these graffitied words are directed at me.*

I gaze at my damp hands, then at the residues of paint on the mirrored surface. Four letters remain.

Anna

As I scrub away her name, my phone pings with a message from Derek's new P.A., Rosalie. Her one word – *Problem* – sends a shiver down my spine. My shoulder muscles tense, and those stabbing sensations return, rising into my neck and towards my jaw.

I stare at the damp cloth in my hand, the faded lettering on the lift mirror, and the pink tears on the floor.

Everything has to be perfect this weekend. Everything has to flow smoothly.

This is what I promised Derek when I accepted his job.

This is what I promised myself when I came to work at Panbrook.

And this morning, while I was packing my weekend bag, this is what I promised the five dead prisoners and Anna Kendall.

MADDIE

NOW

FRIDAY
2.55 p.m.

I step under the cream gazebo canopy and lean against the table. My bare arms are tingling in the warmth of the June sunshine, my throat craves some water, and my skin needs some shade. But most importantly, there's only so much tedious, superficial small talk I can take.

One hundred hotel guests have gathered here for our welcome reception, sipping from champagne flutes and wine glasses, and snacking on crudités and pastries. The women are dolled up in swanky dresses and flashy jewellery. The men are wearing chinos and shirts with open collars. Derek is mingling with the crowd, while Rosalie trots behind him like a faithful Spaniel puppy, holding her hotel iPad close to her chest.

This circular area is where inmates used to take their exercise during an allotted time each day. By the time the prison closed, it was an overcrowded rabbit run, with prisoners walking around on the spot, unable to find any open space. The exercise track is now made from gravel rather than the original cement, and Derek has brightened up the central grassy area with a red acer, ready for al-fresco dining on dry, summer days.

Yet it still feels claustrophobic out here, thanks to the hotel's tall, stone Victorian buildings.

Goosebumps fizz over my skin as I imagine thousands of eyes watching me. Murderers, drug dealers, gamblers ... all were incarcerated here at some point over the years. What have these former prison blocks witnessed? What dark secrets do they hold?

If only they could tell us what really happened in this prison on that fateful night.

A manky-looking brown pigeon pecks at a grassy patch beside the table leg. I attempt to shoo it away with my foot, but it stands firm and gazes at me with defiant, beady eyes. The hotel sits in its own grounds, still enclosed by the original stone perimeter wall, miles away from anywhere. It's no surprise that rats of the ground and rats of the sky are the only wild creatures brave enough to congregate here.

I flick away stray pastry crumbs before placing my iPad down on the silver-coloured cloth. Holding the heavy crystal jug, I fill a glass tumbler with icy mineral water flavoured with fresh lemon slices and mint leaves. The Bucks Fizz looks tempting, as does the Pimms and lemonade, but I need to keep my wits about me this weekend.

As I search the courtyard garden for familiar faces, I also examine the features of strangers.

One of these hotel guests must have written that message on the lift mirror. But who? Some were invited specifically by Derek – VIPs, local dignitaries and the media – but most entered the newspaper lotteries to win their coveted places. The couple I saw earlier are standing in the shade; she's still carrying her baby-pink cardigan, but he has removed his NYC cap, exposing his bald head. Her wrist is now bare.

One lottery winner hasn't checked in yet – Oliver Hodgson. Rosalie has been trying to contact him before our boss discovers that not everything is going to plan – that some aspects of this weekend will be out of his control.

Across the gravel, Derek raises his glass to his lips and slugs back more Pimms. He rakes his fingers through his thinning, grey hair, and swallows sharply as if to clear a lump in his throat. Then he strides over to the metal lectern and taps the microphone.

'Hello.'

Voices go silent as everyone turns towards my boss.

'Welcome to The Panbrook Prison Hotel's tenth anniversary weekend.' He raises his glass. 'While you're not serving a life sentence, you're certainly staying for a life experience.'

As laughter fills the air and Derek puffs out his chest, I curb the urge to roll my eyes. My boss spent hours slaving away at his computer trying to perfect his opening lines, and I still think they're clichéd and ridiculous. Are the guests laughing with him rather than at him? It's hard to tell.

'For those who don't know me, I'm Derek Taylor, owner and managing director of Charter Group.' He grins at the crowd. 'It's wonderful to see so many familiar faces here today, as well as new inmates joining us for the weekend.'

The door to the main building opens and a couple in their sixties hover in the doorway. Derek drums his fingers on the lectern as they step into the courtyard and join the other guests. The man gives Derek an apologetic smile and fiddles with the lanyard around his neck. This can't be our missing lottery winner – like most of our guests this weekend, Oliver Hodgson will be checking in on his own.

'As you'll know, ten years ago today, our state-of-the-art hotel opened its doors. We are delighted to welcome Fiona

Trayton, former Panbrook governor, Dr Bryan Land, former Panbrook doctor, and Thomas Benson, who was a ... a resident here before the prison closed.' Derek nods towards the front row. A stocky elderly man resting a wooden walking stick between his legs bobs his head in return. 'We are also delighted to welcome a last-minute special guest – journalist and author Lloyd Palmer. I'm sure you saw the exciting announcement earlier this month that Mr Palmer is researching an update to his bestselling book, *Panbrook Prisongate*. I expect he will be asking some probing questions this weekend – and maybe some big reveals are on their way.'

A few people clap but there are also some quiet boos. I look around but can't spot the culprits.

Derek taps his microphone and clears his throat. The crowd quietens down again. 'Every inch of this hotel is steeped in history. HMP Panbrook was a Category C prison, with several Grade II listed buildings. If this is your first visit, you'll see that we have retained many of the original Victorian features to preserve the heritage of the site, while giving the renovated buildings a modern, luxurious twist.'

He takes a swig of Pimms, swirls it around in his mouth and swallows. 'No part of Panbrook that was originally used for corporal or capital punishment has been converted into guest rooms, you'll be pleased to hear. So you should have peaceful nights – although some of our rooms are believed to be haunted.'

Nervous laughter surrounds me as a wicked smile plays on Derek's lips. A few people clutch their glasses more tightly as they glance at their companions and then at the nearby buildings.

'Seriously, though, we hope you enjoy your experience here and that it will be one you never forget.' Derek nods at me. 'And now I'll pass you over to our hotel manager, Madeleine Batten.'

As my boss steps off the podium, I step forwards. This is my chance to fool everyone into thinking I'm confident and composed, when I am really a bundle of nerves inside. For years, I have worked behind the hotel scenes rather than on the frontline. I like to fade into the background as much as possible. But when Derek offered me this job nearly three months ago, desperate for a favour, I couldn't refuse.

I rest my iPad on the lectern. 'Hello. And welcome to The Brook. Hopefully by now you'll have had time to read through your welcome pack, but I'll give you a brief summary of the site so you don't get lost during your stay.'

I wake up my iPad and, using my index finger, open up my Notes app. 'The main prison building straight ahead of you across the courtyard – behind me – also known as A-wing, is where you'll find The Lock-Up restaurant and bar. C wing – where many of you are sleeping this weekend – and the old admin block are on your left, and that's the old B wing behind you.' I point out each building in turn, tensing my forearm muscles to stop my hand from shaking. 'There's a hotel map in your welcome pack, hand-drawn by a talented graphic designer and illustrator called Thomas Ziegel, who stayed at our hotel last year.'

Now I have come to the part that I've been dreading the most.

I take a deep breath to steady my voice. 'As you'll all be aware, twenty years ago HMP Panbrook closed its doors for the final time under a melancholy cloud.'

A faint sniffle comes from the back. As I glance around the crowd, Rosalie's eyes catch mine. She shrugs and gives me a weak smile, and nudges Stella, head of Housekeeping. Stella responds with her trademark scowl and tugs at the O-shaped pendant hanging from a thin silver chain around her neck.

I return to my notes. 'The facts about the ... tragedy ... are presented in a special exhibition in Panbrook Prison Museum, which is on your right. The museum will be open every day between ten-thirty a.m. and one-thirty p.m. You'll find more details in your welcome pack. Some of you have signed up to hear our honoured guests speaking briefly tomorrow about life here at the prison before it closed. Mr Lloyd Palmer has agreed to be available for questions as well.'

As the journalist in the front row gives me a brief nod, I shuffle on my feet. There's so much I should be asking him this weekend, yet reticence holds me back. I have learnt over the years that you should never ask questions if you are afraid of the answers. But sometimes timing and destiny means you can no longer wait.

'Tomorrow, Derek will be taking a group of journalists into B wing.' I stare at the building looming above us. 'If you're on the press list, you'll find the ticket in your welcome pack. Dinner this evening will be at seven o'clock in The Lock-Up. I look forward to seeing you there.'

My skin tingles with excitement.

Finally, my real work begins.

**Excerpt from the Introduction of *Panbrook Prisongate* by
Lloyd Palmer – published by Spotlight Books, August 2009**

What actually happened that evening at HMP Panbrook in June
1999? Why did those prisoners die – and who was really responsible for their deaths?

The Panbrook Prisongate murders have remained in the
public eye. Various people have given their opinions about the
events of that evening, and also about the possible motives of
the suspect. Yet all we have are the limited facts released by the
police to the media in the few weeks before the case was
closed.

In my book, you will meet all five victims through the words
of people who knew them best: **Steven 'Fingerling' Fisher**;
Lucas 'Hulk' Somers; **Jonathan 'Cock' Roach; Raziq 'Razorhead' Ahmed;** and **William 'Pills' Owen**. And, of course, you
will meet **Anna Kendall**.

To discover the truth about that night, we need to delve back
into the past…

Lloyd Palmer, August 2009

6

ANNA

APRIL 1995

'Welcome to The Brook, Nurse Kendall.' Kellie Wyndham steps away from the desk and shakes my hand. Her firm grip warms my palm. 'I hope you got through security okay. It's a right faff at the best of times. It's easier once they know who you are.'

The head of Healthcare is around double my age – and double my height. Okay, maybe that last point is a slight exaggeration. But I'd kill for long legs like hers. 'Kill' probably isn't the best word to use round here, though.

'It was fine. I'm just so excited to be here.'

Kellie raises her eyebrows. 'Excited?'

My cheeks burn. I want to give a good impression on my first day. I'm a trained health professional, after all, and I need to keep her onside. I imagine I'll need a strong ally in a place like this, surrounded by all these blokes.

'I mean ... I've been so looking forward to working here.' I give her a broad smile. 'Though I'm not sure the officer who checked my I.D. found my joke about *Porridge* very funny.'

'*Porridge*?'

'You know, that old TV show. My dad loves it ... He's been telling me the best way to smuggle a file inside a cake, and—'

'I know what *Porridge* is.' Kellie taps her foot on the floor. 'But I don't recommend joking about that sort of thing in here unless you fancy a strip-search.'

I can't work out if she's serious or not, so swallow back a laugh just in case. I'm babbling again. Bloody nerves. *Time to shut up, Annie.*

'So, um ... where do I get my uniform?' I pull my hem further down over my knees, wishing my dress was another inch or two longer.

'No need to worry about that.' She gives me the once-over and nods in approval. 'Just don't wear anything shorter, and nothing that'll attract attention, especially when you're climbing stairs or on the landings. Here...' she hands me a piece of paper '...read this. You'll find the rules and regulations listed on there.'

It looks like I'll need to go shopping on the weekend. This is the longest dress I have, and the only plain one. It would be easier to wear a uniform, like at the hospital. I eye her navy suit. Maybe I can wear trousers. I'll go through the list – I don't want to drive her too mad with questions on my first day.

She grabs a clipboard from her desk. 'Right, I'll give you a short tour. Then leave you in the capable hands of Dr Land for the morning.'

Her eyes light up when she says his name. Interesting ... Some of the docs at the cancer unit seemed pretty fit – 'til I got to know them better.

'Bryan's one of the few SMOs who've lasted long enough to get to senior position,' Kellie continues. 'You'll be shadowing him for a few days.'

'Lasted long enough?' I cringe at the slight wobble in my

voice. *Annie, get a grip.* 'What happened to them? I know you've had some stabbings, and—'

'Oh, nothing like that.' Kellie chuckles. 'It's just easy to burn out here. Not everyone can hack the pace. It's survival of the fittest.'

The Brook may look like a grand Disney castle on the outside, with its stone walls and tall turrets, but it's certainly no fairy-tale inside. Everything looks so grey and miserable, even though it's bright and sunny out here today.

We're standing in the prison courtyard. It's empty right now but if I shut my eyes I'd think it was heaving, with all the shouts, swearing and wolf whistles coming from four rows of small, cracked windows in the building in front of us.

And it reeks out here.

'This will certainly be a total contrast to your last place.' Kellie checks the piece of paper on her clipboard. 'The hospital's cancer ward, wasn't it? Must have been hard for you.'

'It probably seems a bit crazy to come here.' I give a half-shrug. 'But I fancied a new challenge.'

And I've certainly found one.

Piles of rubbish are dotted around the yard, over the muddy grass and exercise track: rotting food, filthy clothes, scrunched-up newspapers and dead pigeons. As if on cue, a plastic bag floats down from a top window and lands on a pile. Bluebottles swarm into the air. And is that a rat peeking out? *Gross.*

A deep, husky voice shouts 'Bullseye!', followed by whoops and howls.

When I look up at the building, bright sunlight stings my eyes.

I switch my attention back to Kellie, who's telling me

about the prison layout. 'So here at The Brook we have three wings, each one in a separate building. We've just left A wing. That's B wing straight across, and there,' she points to the right, 'that's C wing. Each wing has four floors. Ground floor is called 'The Ones', first floor's 'The Twos', all the way up to 'The Fours.''

'Any chance of a map?'

She laughs – 'You'll get used to it' – and points to a narrow, concrete path between B wing and C wing. 'Keep going down there and you'll come to our kitchen garden, storage sheds and the path to the entrance of staff quarters.' She taps her clipboard. 'You'll be staying there?'

'Yeah...' I shuffle on my feet. 'Just during the week ... for now anyway. 'Til I find somewhere local. A small flat or something, I guess.'

'Just be careful here, Anna.' She gives me a kind smile.

She's thinking I'll be an easy target, of course she is. With all these blokes in here, locked up for years. Dad thinks I'm asking for trouble too. He keeps handing me *Daily Mail* news cuttings about prison fights, trying to scare me. But no one will put me off this job. Now I've made up my mind, nothing's going to change it.

'I'll be fine.' Those wolf whistles seem to be getting louder. 'I can handle the prisoners.'

'I wasn't talking about them.'

Oh. 'You don't need to worry. I can look after myself.'

Kellie rests her hand on my shoulder. 'Well ... if you have any problems with officers or patients, come to me or Bryan. You'll soon learn who's on your side here – and who to avoid.'

Kellie unlocks the next metal gate and waits for me to follow her through. 'You'll find it easier once you get your own keys. We'll sort that out this afternoon.' She slams the heavy gate shut and locks it back up. 'Don't dilly-dally at the gates, as you've got around thirty seconds to get through before the alarm goes off.'

As we head back to Healthcare, I'm trying to remember the route, counting my steps, looking for landmarks, but every grey wall looks the same. And I can't think straight for all the wolf whistles and shouts, cat calls, purring sounds ... and something that sounds like mewing.

'Is it always so loud here?'

'Only when they see there's new pussy in town.' Kellie stops walking and raps on the grubby wall with the back of her clipboard. 'Oye, you lot, quit it!' Her expression turns sour, like she's bit into a lemon.

The noise stops.

Bloody hell – she's good. At least I now know how it's done.

I stare through an open viewing flap into one of the cells and spot some blue-and-white striped shirts. Several pairs of eyes leer at me. Two or three blokes must be crammed inside. I try to edge away, but the landing's so narrow there's nowhere to go, except closer to the big gap on the other side of the metal railing. I don't fancy falling down there, even with the suicide netting stretched across it.

Kellie's nearly at Healthcare – she walks so fast, I'm almost sprinting to catch up with her. I really don't want to get lost on my first day.

'You new?' A prison officer nudges my arm. Shit, where did he spring from? He's a big bloke with a round owl-like face and large, unblinking eyes – so not someone who's going to hide easily. His plump belly quivers over his black leather prison belt.

'Yeah, just joined Healthcare. I'm Anna ... one of the nurses.'

He looks over his shoulder. 'Best get in there then.' His

keys jangle in his hand. 'You won't want to be out here in around thirty seconds, when all them cells open.'

Being honest, I don't fancy it. But he probably thinks I'm going to freak out, and there's no way I'm showing my nerves.

'Well, I—'

'Anna?' Kellie pokes her head out. 'You coming?'

'On my way. Just chatting to—'

'You'll soon get used to this place.' His gaze glides over me. 'If you don't, you won't last long ... Most don't.'

My back twinges and my legs ache, but my brain's buzzing and I feel ridiculously upbeat. It's been a long and busy day, and I didn't end up looking like an idiot after all. So that's a bonus.

I wrap the blanket around me like a cocoon. It's April but still chilly, and the blanket makes me feel safe.

I've learnt so much already. My staff induction and key training. Lunch with officers in the mess. Watching Dr Land do a bunion inspection on grubby, stinking feet. Staffing the meds hatch, with bolshy patients demanding drugs. Handing out counselling booklets. I'm learning the prison patter too – it's a whole new language. Though I bet I'll have nightmares tonight, after all those leering eyes and cat calls.

I snuggle deeper under the covers and shut my eyes. The 'Back for Good' tune springs into my head. It was the last song on Dad's car radio this morning.

'You sure this is what you want?' Dad was driving me up the winding road to the prison gates. 'You could always say you've changed your mind.'

'I'm sure I'll be fine.' I gazed out of the window and swallowed back a lump in my throat.

'Your big brother will look after me, don't you worry.' It was like Dad could read my mind. 'And if he doesn't, I'm sure you'll have words. Your mum would have been so proud, Annie. Looking after people, no matter who they are or what they've done. Making a difference ... We always knew you would.'

When I got out the car, he handed me a spanking new BT phonecard and a huge bag of 10p's to make sure I keep in touch.

I didn't want to admit it, but it's going to be hard for both of us. Me shut in The Brook, and Dad living in the house on his own. It's the longest we've been apart since my uni days.

He'll have to get used to it though. Me too. I'll be looking for a flat this weekend, and some wheels. A rusty old banger, no doubt, judging by my pitiful bank balance. I don't want to stay at the staff quarters for longer than I need to.

My room here is bigger than I thought it would be, to be fair. Not like a hotel – not even a basic one – but it smells alright, and the bed seems comfy.

'The Brook's in the middle of nowhere, so there's no pub nearby,' Kellie told me. 'Some officers have parties in the staff quarters on the quiet. Everyone likes to have a pint and let off some steam, so we need somewhere to crash.'

Not many people live on-site, so the kitchen was empty tonight; most just sleep over when it suits them. It's certainly convenient, but it's so close to the prison that I feel like I'm being watched all the time. I need my space.

Maybe I am a bit crazy after all – switching from a safe and sterile hospital to this filthy building full of dangerous blokes.

But whatever Dad says, I know I'm doing the right thing. For now, this is where I'm meant to be.

7

MADDIE

NOW

FRIDAY
4.15 p.m.

I lean back against the bench in the courtyard garden with my phone on my lap, soaking up the hazy sunshine and welcoming the light breeze against my cheeks. After the reception party, I visited the kitchen to make sure everything is on track for dinner, and then came out here to confirm the arrangements for the party tomorrow night. I should be doing this in my office but it's too hot and stuffy inside to concentrate, even with the fans on at full blast.

So far, I have emailed the gazebo company, the caterer and the band, but now I'm enjoying a short break. One advantage of working in this large hotel is that I get to delegate. When I was working in Spain, nearly everything was down to me. Plus, Derek has insisted that I mingle with guests at every opportunity this weekend since I know so much about the 'Anna Kendall scandal' – his words, not mine.

But I'm really only interested in speaking to the VIPs this weekend.

Some guests are currently taking selfies or reading the brass information panels on the front of the stone buildings; others are wandering around our kitchen garden or the rest of the three-and-half acre site.

Derek wanted to organise a packed schedule – he doesn't like to relax – but I explained that our guests will need some downtime. I'll need it too, being used to hotel visitors having long, late lunches, Spanish siestas and lazy afternoons.

'You messaged.' Stella sits down next me, her gaze scanning the courtyard. 'Saw you from inside. Derek still in The Lock-up with the VIPs?' She raises her liver-spotted hand to her face and rubs at the wrinkled skin around her eyes, then lowers her head when a couple of guests walk past. Like me, she isn't comfortable among the crowds.

'Yes, they're all tucking into tea, cake and biscuits.' My mouth floods with saliva at the thought of crumpets and scones, fairy cakes and muffins – afternoon tea wasn't part of my routine for over twenty years. I thought I had everything I wanted and needed in Spain, but now that I'm back, I'm gradually realising what I have missed.

I squint at Stella, holding up my hand to block out the sun glaring over her right shoulder. 'You didn't have to come out here. You could have messaged … or called.'

'Nah … Figured it's a good time to get some air. Clear my dodgy lungs.'

Stella is the oldest member of staff, in both length of employment and in age, but she doesn't like to be reminded of the latter. She has been working in Housekeeping ever since the hotel opened. Derek jokes that she came with the building, one of the fixtures and fittings in the prison sale, and at times I can believe it.

Not that Stella expects to be here for much longer, she tells me whenever Derek piles on the pressure, which, she also tells me, is far too often. She smokes like a chimney, coughs up her guts several times a day and has a dodgy heart, so perhaps she's right.

I lean back against the bench. 'I need someone to give the inside of the A-wing lifts a scrub as soon as possible. Maybe Radha can do it. Earlier, I noticed one of the mirrored walls was covered in fingermarks.'

'Fingermarks? Seriously?' She snickers. 'Who's going to notice?'

'Derek will, Stella. Me too.' I ignore her eye-roll and give her a placatory smile. The previous manager was less fastidious than I am – everyone here now knows that I won't tolerate sloppy work. 'That's not a problem, is it?'

'Not at all, Madeleine. Whatever you want.' She touches the O-shaped pendant around her neck as if it is a magic charm. 'How did the mirrors get so dirty?'

I glance at the A-wing entrance, where a flicker of movement has caught my eye. 'I have no idea.'

Fiona Trayton steps out of the building, followed by Thomas Benson and Bryan Land. She points at the red acer and mutters something to her companions. When the doctor laughs and gestures towards the gravel track, and then at B wing, the former prison governor shakes her head at him. Thomas Benson leans on his walking stick and gazes around the courtyard.

Stella stands up and turns around. 'Best get back inside before the boss realises I'm not in Housekeeping. Just need to check something in the kitchen garden and then I'll speak to Radha.'

As I watch her marching around the side of the building, I can't get that handwritten message out of my mind: *Anna Kendall was guilty*. Hopefully it was just meaningless graffiti –

one of the guests poking fun. I swallow back the niggling feeling it wasn't.

Some true-crime bloggers have been protesting about this weekend on social media, calling it 'distasteful' because this is also the twentieth anniversary of the five men's deaths. Not only have those prisoners maintained a devoted following over the years, but Lloyd Palmer's book also has a substantial fanbase, with various Facebook groups, website forums and podcasts devoted to the case.

True-crime treasure hunters flock here, desperate to see where the deaths occurred. Photographs are rarely enough. Some attempt to steal 'souvenirs' – old library books, loose bricks from the courtyard, and plant pots from the kitchen garden. Last week, I caught a guest trying to break into B wing, looking for a memento from one of the five prisoners' cells.

Derek doesn't want any trouble this weekend so he has micro-managed the guest list, trying to keep these adventurers off the hotel site. Security is even stricter than usual, with everyone checked in at the front gate, just as they were in the prison days.

My boss called his competition 'a lottery', but it wasn't random at all. He wanted to celebrate the hotel's auspicious milestone while maintaining control over who would be here, keeping those armchair detectives off the premises.

The previous manager organised adverts in the local newspapers and national press. Each entrant was asked to complete a form and include a prison-themed selfie. Derek chose his favourites, and then each lottery winner was carefully vetted by private investigators before they received the invitation.

I watch everyone milling around the grounds. What if one of the crackpots has sneaked in anyway and is determined to cause trouble with our VIPs? Derek certainly won't be happy, and my own plans this weekend may become more challenging.

My phone pings with a new message from my boss, speak of the devil.

Contact Oliver Hodgson. Rosalie told me. Find out where he is.

Followed by a red angry-faced emoji – the only one he ever uses.

I pick up my iPad and open up the guest-list file to search for Oliver Hodgson's mobile number. There's no answer when I call him, so I leave a message asking him to phone me back. With the hotel's history being so high profile and room prices usually so pricey, this weekend's free lottery places have been highly sought-after. So why hasn't Mr Hodgson turned up?

As I lean back against the bench for an extra dose of sunlight, a figure casts a shadow across my lap.

'You work here?' The voice is loud and brash, with a Scottish accent.

A young woman looms over me, tottering on uncomfortable-looking stilettos. Her nose wrinkles as if an unpleasant odour hovers in the air, yet all I can smell is jasmine and lavender from the nearby flowerbeds. A pink-cheeked older woman hovers behind her, gazing at the ground.

'You work here?' the young woman says again. She pulls at a pretty pearl pendant on a rose-gold chain around her neck.

'Yes, I do.' She clearly didn't pay any attention to the welcome speeches. I stand up to stop her looking down on me, physically at least. 'How can I help?'

'The loos. Where are they?' Her tone remains icy sharp.

Some guests seem to forget that hotel employees are people too, that we are not simply slaves to cater for their needs. Others look through us as if we are ghosts drifting between the hotel walls. This does have its plus sides though, and I have been privy to some fascinating 'private' conversations between guests over the years.

'Go through this doorway,' I point at the entrance next to me, 'and they're on your right.'

'Come on.' The woman takes the older woman's arm and pulls her towards A wing.

'You're welcome,' I whisper under my breath as I watch them walk away.

Mother and daughter. It isn't difficult to work out that relationship; they have the same dark brown hair and vivid hazel eyes. Though I know from experience that there is far more to a maternal bond than matching looks.

Ellie didn't answer her phone when I called her back, so I left a message, being careful not to speak in a concerned tone after her WhatsApp earlier.

Everything's fine, I reassured myself. *It won't be anything serious.*

Nate and I both lost our mums when we were young, which may be why I have tended to smother Ellie over the years. In her angry adolescent phase, she accused me of being a 'helicopter parent'. Obviously I denied it at the time, although I knew in my heart that she was right. And now she is getting married, and still so young, I'm finding it hard to break the habits of close to a lifetime, especially since I am doing all of this on my own.

'Ooph, hot out here today.' Thomas Benson stands in front of me, gripping his walking stick. His arms are speckled with tattoos.

My breath catches in my throat at the spiderwebs etched over his elbows and a handgun inked over his left wrist. Reminders of his dangerous, criminal past.

'Question for you, but tell me to bugger off if you don't want to answer.' He gives me a broad grin, exposing a mouthful of yellowing, cracked teeth: probably a consequence of poor dental care during his prison days.

'Not at all. Fire away.' I have met hotel guests like him many times before: lonely, older people desperate for conversation. Though after his extended stint in prison, he's probably used to being on his own.

I shuffle up on the bench and offer him a seat.

'If I sit down, may not get up again. Not so young now – my legs don't work so good.' He chuckles loudly, his eyes twinkling with mischief, and leans heavily on his stick. His shirt gapes open, revealing a clock face tattooed onto his chest. 'I were wonderin' why's B wing not renovated, like A and C?'

'It's partly due to planning regulations blocking Derek's intentions, but also because of what happened in there.' I nod towards the stone building. I have been working here for two months and still haven't yet managed to persuade Derek to let me inside. 'Pressure from the prisoners' families to keep it preserved, and Derek didn't want to encourage treasure hunters.'

A couple of other guests wander past, chattering loudly.

I gaze at Thomas. 'My turn to ask you a question or two, if you don't mind.'

'Course. Anythin' you want.'

'You left here a couple of weeks before the prison closed. How well did you know those five men?'

'I knew some of 'em more than others. Fingerling were a smackhead so I kept out of his way. Hulk were a snitch, and Pills and Razorhead both liked a good fight. They had to be tough, you know. You had to be a lion in here, not a lamb, or you'd never survive one night.'

'And Jonathan Roach?'

Thomas wrinkles his nose. 'We all called him "Cock", you know. Was always sucking up to the screws. Ruled the roost here, he did. Well-to-do. Figure lots of people would want to do away with him. You know, some believed he were havin' an affair with that nurse what did it.'

A nerve sparks between my shoulders, and I shrug gently to ease it away. 'Do you believe that?'

'Dunno what to believe.' Thomas moves his fingers up behind his ear and fiddles with a hearing aid. His plain silver ring twinkles in the sunlight. 'Cock made it clear there were someone, mind. But so many stories flyin' round, even more so after she ... you know.'

My fingers tighten around my phone. 'Did you know her well? Anna Kendall, I mean.'

'Saw her a few times in Healthcare. When my back were givin' me gyp, she offered drugs when I need 'em.'

'Drugs?'

'Meds for the pain.' He gives me a long hard stare, his eyes narrowing into a glare. 'Never had time for them smackheads – steer clear, I did. And she once helped me out when I were really sick. So I never believed anythin' those coppers said about her.'

'Do you know if she was close to anyone in here in particular?'

'Close? How should I know? But she were well-liked, if that's what you're askin', by us cons, the screws ... and I don't think any of them had a bad word to say 'bout her. Until them coppers got involved, that is, after that night, after what happened in there.'

He raises his stick towards B wing, swaying to keep his balance. 'Always thought this place were cursed, mind. You know, some folk think their ghosts still haunt them landin's.'

I gaze up at the building with its barred, glazed windows glinting in the sunshine. When we go in there tomorrow, will it be an empty shell? Or will we sense the tragedy around us: the pain, the desperation, those five men's final breaths?

8

MADDIE

NOW

FRIDAY
5.00 p.m.

Derek has asked me to meet him in our ground-floor staff room. I was a few minutes early so made myself a small mug of coffee and downed a couple of paracetamol capsules to ward away a brewing headache. Now, I'm sitting on one of the black-and-white striped tub chairs, which are arranged in a half-circle. Perhaps this will be a good time to discuss the new cleaner, Radha, with my boss: my reservations about her work – and her conduct.

My phone vibrates in my pocket. I try to ignore it, but it keeps on vibrating. Then it stops and the caller tries again. This time, I place my mug down on the glass table, pull out my phone and answer it.

'Hey, Mum.' Ellie sounds reasonably calm – a good sign after her end-of-the-world message.

'Sorry I couldn't chat earlier.' I speak quietly, even though the staff room is currently empty. You never know when someone will creep in, and I don't want Derek to realise I am taking personal calls. 'I had my hands full with—'

'You'll never believe what's happened.' Ellie's voice rises in pitch and volume. Damn – not as calm as I thought.

'I mean,' she continues, 'I can't believe it myself, so there's no way you'll believe it either. We must be the unluckiest brides in the universe. And now Viv and I don't know what to do, and it's all going wrong, and...' She lets out a loud sob.

'Ellie, calm down.' I wish she was here so I could give her a lingering hug, run my fingers over her blonde corkscrew curls, the way I used to when she was little. 'Whatever it is, we can sort it out. But you'll need to tell me what's happened first ... or I can't help.'

'The venue. Hampton Hall. They've cancelled on us. Two months to go and they've bloody cancelled the booking, leaving us in the lurch. For urgent building work.'

Frustration bubbles inside me. This is the last thing I need right now, when I have no time to make things better, for not just one but two distraught brides in the lead up to their wedding day. No one else can help them, with Viv's parents living abroad, and at moments like this, I miss Nate's hands-on approach to parenting the most.

My own mother was too busy working to spend much quality time with me; my father disappeared soon after I was born. Mum was in charge of Housekeeping at a large country hotel and took me to work with her in the school holidays when childcare wasn't available. I would sit behind the Reception desk for hours, pretending I was in charge, and play in the extensive gardens, imagining they were mine. Sometimes Mum would sneak me into the bedrooms, where I would admire the luxurious décor and immaculate surroundings, and the posh clothes and shiny trinkets belonging to hotel guests. It's no coincidence that I chose to work in hotel management, following in my mother's footsteps. And after she died, when I was fourteen, I vowed that I would be a better mother one day – putting my child's needs above my own.

'Mum, are you still there?' Ellie's voice tremors as if she's stifling another sob.

A reminder that she's relying on me, has always relied on me, and I have never let her down.

'Leave it with me. I'll think of somewhere. I may not be able to sort it out now, but...'

A rattling sound comes from the wall nearest me, then faint rustling. It must be the old water pipes again. Pete, our caretaker, is rushed off his feet but will need to inspect them when he has a moment.

At the other end of the phone call, a voice murmurs in the background: deeper than Ellie's, with a hint of an Aussie twang.

'Actually, don't worry, Mum.' Ellie sniffs, and I hear more muffled talk. 'Viv and I ... we'll make some calls and keep you updated. You need to concentrate on this weekend. Will speak to you tomorrow. Love you.'

I smile as she ends the call. Ellie has always been a fiery, excitable one; Viv, the calming influence she needs to get through her crazy life. The perfect match.

I cast my mind back to the first time Ellie's hand clutched mine ... her big round eyes, the softness of her skin ... I hadn't thought I was truly ready to be a mum, yet from that moment my whole world felt complete.

'I'll always be here for you,' I remember whispering in her ear. 'I'll always protect you.'

And I have done so ever since.

The rattling sound comes again, now from above. I send a message to Pete. Apparently the last time the hotel had this problem, he discovered field mice scampering through the wall cavities. He'll need to remove them before any guests make a complaint – poor reviews on TripAdvisor are a major hazard of my job.

The staff room door slams open and Derek strides in, holding an unopened bottle of whisky in one hand and a half-full glass of Pimms in the other. Rosalie scurries in behind him. I reckon she's a similar age to Ellie, but her mousy brown hair is swept back in a taut ponytail, making her seem much older. And she doesn't smile much.

Despite the air conditioning unit whirring above us, damp patches stain the underarms of Derek's pale-blue shirt. His hair is slicked back with sweat, and his cheeks are flushed.

When I stand up quickly, as if I have been caught slacking, my knee knocks the table leg, and coffee sloshes around in my mug.

Derek's sharp gaze digs into me as he places the whisky bottle down on the glass surface. His gold signet ring glints in the harsh fluorescent lighting, due to the large cluster of diamonds in its centre.

'None for me, thanks.' I raise my mug in the air. 'I don't drink on the job.'

'It's not for me, either.' Derek downs the rest of his Pimms, then raises his eyebrows at his P.A. 'Coffee would be nice though.'

Rosalie trudges over to the Nespresso machine on the countertop. She presses a few buttons and brings back a full mug, as well as a plate of chocolate muffins.

Derek grabs the drink from her without saying a word. That Scottish woman isn't the only one here who has trouble saying 'Thank you'. Hopefully the coffee will neutralise some of the alcohol flowing through his veins.

'Madeleine, anything to report?' Derek doesn't do polite greetings either.

I shake my head emphatically, as my thoughts return to the

writing on the lift wall. 'Everything's going to plan.' Any discussion about Radha can wait.

'Well, that's good news.' Derek takes a sip of coffee and lets out a loud sigh. 'Rosalie, I said I like *two* sweeteners – did you forget again?' He hands the mug back to her.

'Sorry.' She plods back to the coffee machine, trying to avoid my gaze.

The poor girl won't last long if this is how he intends to treat her. Perhaps once the pressure of this weekend is over, he'll be more amenable – though I doubt it. Various staff members resigned before I arrived, including the previous hotel manager at short notice. Several have threatened to sue Derek for undue stress, discrimination at work and all manner of misdemeanours – I have seen some of the threatening letters and eavesdropped on irate phone calls – but so far no one has taken their complaints any further.

When Rosalie returns, she clatters the mug down on the table. A few droplets of murky, brown liquid spurt out onto the glass. This time, I detect a hint of defiance in her eyes. Perhaps she will last longer than I thought.

I resist the urge to wipe up the split coffee. It isn't my job to clean hotels – that was my mother's role. I'll ask Radha to come in here after we leave.

Rosalie offers us the muffins. Derek grabs one from the plate and takes a hefty bite, but I shake my head and take a step back.

'I'm allergic to nuts.' I point at my silver allergy alert pendant, the most expensive choice on the website, of course – I don't do tacky and cheap.

She scrutinises the muffins, twisting one around on the plate, her eyes crinkling in the corners as she prods at a chunk of chocolate. 'It doesn't look like this contains nuts.'

'I'd need to inspect the ingredients first, or just one bite could kill me.'

Rosalie raises her eyebrows and puts the plate down. She may think I am exaggerating, but one tiny chunk of nut could make me uncomfortable at best – an itchy tongue, a puffed-up face, a stuffy nose – or need emergency medical attention at worst. I finger the medicines pouch strapped around my waist, containing an Epipen adrenaline autoinjector, asthma inhaler and antihistamine tablets. I learnt the hard way over twenty years ago that it isn't safe to take risks – and to trust no one – after unintentionally eating some pine nuts. Since then, I like to confirm the ingredients myself.

'Did you manage to speak to that missing lottery winner?' Derek directs this at me, but Rosalie butts in before I can answer.

'He called Reception. Said he was stuck at a work meeting all afternoon and couldn't get away, but he's hoping to arrive in the morning.' She blushes and looks down at her feet. 'I said that would be fine.'

'It may be fine with you, but it certainly isn't fine with me. He had better turn up tomorrow.' Derek runs his fingers through his few strands of hair and presses his lips together tightly. 'Madeleine, one of the guests on the first floor has made a complaint about his room. A disturbance. It should have been attended to by now, but you need to give him this.'

He picks up the whisky bottle and shoves it into my hands.

I turn it over to read the label: Glenmorangie. 'Who is this for?'

'Mr Palmer, if you don't mind.' That should be a question but I know it isn't. Derek leans back in his chair, picks up his coffee and takes another sip – this time he nods at Rosalie, and I even detect the hint of a satisfied smile. 'Make our apologies and show our appreciation.'

Appreciation? For the second time today, I have to stop myself rolling my eyes at my boss. No doubt Derek wants to make sure the hotel gets good publicity, but appreciating that journalist is just one step too far.

'I'll give it to him.' Rosalie grins at Derek. 'Madeleine has so much to do. Really. I'd be happy to—'

'I've asked Madeleine to do it.' Derek scowls at her. 'On behalf of hotel management, since she's the most senior member of my team.'

As Rosalie lowers her head, sighing with disappointment, I pick up the whisky bottle, realising I have no choice.

It's time to formally introduce myself to Mr Palmer.

9

MADDIE

NOW

FRIDAY
5.20 p.m.

I hover outside room A28, facing the heavy iron door with the *Do Not Disturb* sign dangling from the handle. Trepidation rumbles in the pit of my stomach as I hold the whisky bottle against my chest. The cells' original viewing flaps were sealed up during the renovation work. I wish I could prise this one open and see what Lloyd Palmer is doing inside.

I can already imagine his critical words: *The Panbrook Prison Hotel prides itself on its superior luxury and excellent reputation, but can't get its ambience and service right.*

I suspected the journalist would be a challenging guest this weekend. Tough-nut news hack was his nature twenty years ago, and he can't have changed much over the years.

Derek referred to a 'disturbance' up here. That couple I saw earlier taking photographs didn't seem noisy or disruptive to me. I inspect the landing around me: the black-and-cream carpet, the neat row of closed green doors, artwork on the walls...

The large painting looks a little out of line. I walk over and tip the base gently to the left to straighten it. Derek commissioned several original canvases when he furnished the hotel. This one depicts a silhouette of a man looking out through prison bars into a rose garden. Scarlet flowers provide a splash of colour in the otherwise greyscale.

As I walk further along the landing, I spy wisps of grey feathers on one of the cream carpet stripes, illuminated by the bright sunlight shining down through the atrium roof. These feathers have probably been brought in on the underside of someone's shoes, which means Radha hasn't been doing her job properly – again. I scrape off the flakes with my fingernails, then walk towards Mr Palmer's room.

I knock on his door and wait for a response. When there isn't one, this seems to be a good excuse to give up and leave, but the bottle weighs heavy in my hand as a reminder of what Derek is expecting me to do.

I let out a sigh and knock again, loudly and more abruptly, and call out, 'Mr Palmer, it's the hotel manager.'

As I pull out my phone to ask Reception to call his room, the door opens. He stands in front of me, slightly out of breath, running his fingers over his raven-black hair. A cold shiver trickles slowly down my spine as I gaze into his dark eyes for the first time.

He still doesn't say a word; just folds up a pair of wire-framed glasses and slots them into his shirt pocket. Voices blare out from the bedroom behind him.

'Derek Taylor asked me to bring you this as an apology for any inconvenience.' I shove the whisky bottle into his hands. 'I understand there's been a problem.'

'Inconvenience isn't quite how I would describe it.' His

voice is as deep as I remember from the television interviews, and just as arrogant. 'Someone was in my room while I was downstairs at the reception event.'

'How do you know someone was in there?'

The journalist grips the whisky bottle with both hands. 'It stank of smoke when I came back.'

'Are you sure you didn't leave the door open? Or unlocked?' I try to peer behind him, but he's obscuring my view.

His eyes narrow into a glare. 'I put the *Do Not Disturb* sign on the door when I left, to make sure Housekeeping didn't come in.'

'Is anything missing?'

'My sanity, it seems.' His mouth twitches into a wry smile. 'Do you quiz all of your guests like this?'

My cheeks flush with warmth. Most people's voices rise when they're irritated, but I notice that his voice gets even deeper. The hectic preparations for this weekend are clearly taking their toll on my manager-customer relations skills – or perhaps this man simply rubs me up the wrong way.

'I can move you to a different room, if that's what you'd prefer. One guest hasn't arrived so we do have a spare in C wing, but it's smaller and doesn't have a desk.'

He shakes his head, furrowing his brow at the potential inconvenience. 'No, it's fine. The odour's gone now. But please check with Housekeeping that no one has been in my room, and remind them not to come in here over the weekend.'

'Of course ... but can I come in and take a look anyway, to check everything is as it should be? Derek expects me to be thorough.'

'If you must.'

As Mr Palmer pushes his door further open, the voices inside get louder. I create a mental image of my spreadsheet, my eyes travelling down the guest list row by row. He's supposed to be here alone this weekend, but has he been getting to know our other guests already? He always was a charmer, yet this would be speedy work. He once had a wife, a lawyer called Nina; a few years ago, the tabloids informed the public that they were getting divorced, as if anyone cared.

'Actually, please give me a moment to tidy up.' He turns around and paces into his room. I hear a series of hasty movements, a shuffling of papers, what sounds like the opening then closing of a drawer. 'You can come in now.'

I look around the landing before walking inside and shutting the door behind me.

Lloyd Palmer's room is indicative of the others in the hotel. Two original cells have been knocked together to create the sleeping area; the other cell has been converted into the bathroom. My nose twitches at an overpowering sweet, spicy aroma as Freddie Mercury belts out 'Under Pressure' at the top of his voice.

The journalist's overnight bag is open on the bed, with clothes and toiletries spilling out onto the plain cream bedding. Four black-and-cream striped cushions are stacked up neatly on one side. The small bedside table is topped with the hotel's digital radio (a luxury brand, of course), Mr Palmer's *Panbrook Prisongate* book and Derek's whisky gift.

The journalist presses a button on the radio and Freddie's voice fizzles out.

'I assume you're otherwise happy with the accommodation?' His room looks comfortable enough, but Derek ordered me to get some feedback.

A plush cream rug is bordered by a narrow strip of wooden flooring. The free-standing wenge furniture is minimalist: a double wardrobe with chrome handles, an office desk with a small leather chair, and a chest of drawers with the top drawer slightly ajar and a piece of lined yellow notepaper peeking out.

'Yes, it's very ... prison-themed.' His laugh is tinged with sarcasm. 'The smoky smell was strongest through there.'

He leads me into the bathroom, where black-and-cream striped towels are hanging on the chrome towel rack, and Molten Brown travel-sized toiletries are lined up neatly by the sink.

I inhale deeply a few times, while his dark eyes scrutinise me. 'I can only smell aftershave.'

'Well, I did spray it everywhere. I'm a smoker myself, but that doesn't mean I want to smell it in my room all night.'

'The hotel is a no-smoking venue, Mr Palmer, although guests and staff sometimes sneak a cigarette where they think they won't be seen. Maybe smoke drifted in from outside.'

The journalist leads me back into the sleeping area. He points at the closed barred window, which is framed with black-and-cream striped curtains that match the carpet on the landing.

'I've kept it closed ever since I arrived, Ms Batten, so there's no chance of that. But thank you for the suggestion.'

A pigeon lands on the window ledge. As it preens itself, I press my fingers together, wincing at what's probably lurking under my fingernails from those feathers on the landing. 'I assume you didn't see any pigeons outside your room earlier? They sometimes venture into the building.'

His jaw tenses. 'Pigeons? Are you suggesting one may have come in here while I was out? Birds can't slip through locked doors and windows. And they don't smoke – do they?'

His raised eyebrows suggest he's expecting a response, but I keep my mouth shut. Arguing with guests is against all hotel management rules, unless they are being particularly rude or obnoxious, and this conversation hasn't quite reached those depths yet.

He strolls to his bedroom door and opens it. 'Someone was definitely in here. As I said, please make sure no one else from Housekeeping comes in without my permission.'

Walking towards him, I realise I'm not quite ready to leave. So many questions have filled my head for months – no, make that years.

'Are you doing more research this weekend?'

'Yes, that's right. I have the opportunity to speak to Bryan Land, Thomas Benson and Fiona Trayton again, and it is very kind of Mr Taylor to give me access to the museum archives tomorrow. As Derek explained earlier, my publisher has asked me to update my book. A second edition. That's why I decided to come after all.'

A muscle in my neck spasms. 'What are you looking for?'

'I'm not sure exactly. But no one has found out who was on the premises that weekend. I'm sure there must be a list somewhere, or maybe someone will remember something. I think that's the key to discovering the truth.'

'The truth?'

'Yes, whether or not Anna Kendall was guilty.'

My neck muscle twinges again as I recall the handwritten message on the lift mirror. Maybe those words were meant for him after all.

'In your book, you concluded she was. Guilty, that is. Are you planning to change your mind – about what happened that night?'

'The jury's still out on that one, but I'm certainly keeping an open mind. Depending on what I find, of course. And what about you, Ms Batten?' He raises his eyebrows. 'Do you think Anna was innocent or guilty?'

I think back to those promises I made this morning, to the five men and to Anna Kendall. And to the promises I made in the past.

'Does it matter what I think?' My words are more abrupt

than I intended, and I wish I could take them back. Derek won't want me upsetting any of the guests – and especially this one. 'Anyway, I need to get on. I'll see you at dinner, Mr Palmer ... Enjoy the whisky.'

I leave the room before I say anything else I'm going to regret.

10

MADDIE

NOW

FRIDAY
5.45 p.m.

I push open the door to room C19 and peer in. When I reached the ground floor after seeing Lloyd Palmer, I met that lottery-winning couple heading outside. They said they were going to explore the hotel grounds and mentioned a creaky drawer in their wardrobe.

I would usually send Pete to deal with these complaints, but I noticed in the files earlier that the husband, Dave Etherton, is celebrating his fiftieth birthday today. Handing the whisky bottle to Lloyd Palmer gave me the idea of asking the kitchen to make up a complimentary fruit platter. Why should the journalist be the only guest with extra treats this weekend? He's certainly no one special, despite his arrogant manner and author name on a book.

I place the fruit gift on the desk and write out a congratulations note. Then I nudge the silver platter right into the centre of the leather surface. My years of hotel experience have taught me that these little details are so important, distinguishing 'luxury' from 'ordinary'. I pull a pair of vinyl gloves out from my pocket and slip them on – my mother always used to carry a supply – and rub away some smudges on the leather.

Inside the wardrobe, everything has been folded neatly on the shelves. The guests have left a laptop, wallet and jewellery roll in the top drawer under Mrs Etherton's frilly knickers and his Calvin Klein boxers. The drawer feels and sounds smooth to me, but I send a message to Pete anyway, asking him to inspect it when he has a spare moment.

My mother taught me that you can tell a lot about people from their possessions. 'Wealthier guests tend to have higher expectations of hotel staff, but they usually leave better tips,' she would say, 'so they need special attention – freshly laundered towels every morning, and an extra mint on their pillow in the evening.'

Cash tips are unusual these days, but it's hard to break that habit. And I still like to know who I'm dealing with.

After my conversation with Mr Palmer, I look inside the bathroom as well. It smells fresh and clean, with a lingering aroma of floral body spray. But the couple's his-and-hers toiletries have been left in disarray along the shelves, with smears of her foundation soiling the glass.

I jump at a knock on the outside door, followed by the sound of a key card in the lock. I remove my gloves, shove them in my pocket and step back into the bedroom.

'Hellooo?' Radha peers around the door, waving her key card in the air. 'Oh ... sorry, Madeleine. I didn't expect anyone to be in here. Mrs Etherton asked Reception for a spare towel – to dry her hair, I think. Everything okay?'

'Yes, all's fine. I was just bringing her husband a birthday treat. It looks delicious, doesn't it?' I jerk my chin towards the fruit basket. 'We used to do this for hotel guests in Spain for special occasions. I thought it would be a nice touch, and maybe encourage them to come back again next year.'

'Ooh ... fancy.' She backs out of the room and returns with a white face towel. 'I'll leave her this.'

'Actually,' I stifle a smile, 'while you're here, please can you straighten up the toiletries and give the glass shelf a polish in the bathroom. It's looking a little smudged. And can you make sure the wardrobe drawers feel smooth when they're opened. The top drawer in particular. The guests made a complaint. It seems fine to me, but it would be good to have a second opinion.'

'Of course, Madeleine. I'll do it all now.' As she steps towards the bathroom, her trouser pocket gapes, revealing a rectangular cardboard packet stuffed inside.

'What are those?'

She halts and swivels round. 'What are what?'

'Those cigarettes in your pocket. You know our policy here.'

She pulls out the scrunched-up packet and grips it tightly. 'I found them on a radiator near the lift. I was going to give them to Stella.'

I hold out my hand. 'I'll take those, thank you. The staff room table also needs a wipe. And, by the way, did you go into A28 earlier? The guest made a complaint, that it stank of smoke in there.'

She shakes her head as she passes me the packet.

On my journey back downstairs, staring at my reflection in the now sparkling-clean lift mirror, I finger the cigarette packet – Marlboro Gold. I've contacted Stella, and she has no record of any member of her team going into Mr Palmer's room. Maybe

Radha was lying to me. But if she was, why would she have gone in there?

The journalist certainly seemed to be hiding something when I went to see him, not allowing me in there straightaway. He claims he's keeping an open mind this weekend ... seeing what he missed when he originally wrote his book. But why would he change his view after all these years?

Following the last-minute announcement that he would be attending our anniversary weekend, the press has been hounding us, along with emails from strangers – some *for* Anna, some *against* her. Meanwhile, Lloyd Palmer will be making good money with a second edition of his book, boosting his own reputation while thrusting Anna's family into the spotlight all over again.

Now the journalist is back on the premises, scrutinising the archives, the clock is well and truly ticking.

The pressure is on.

When I leave C wing, I spot Pete opening up a small storage shed at the side of the museum. 'There you are.'

This is the first time I have seen our caretaker all afternoon, his one-word answers to my messages being the only sign he is still on the premises. He always seems ageless, though I suspect from the wrinkles at the corners of his eyes that he is older than he looks. His hair is currently covered with a large black cap, and his bushy beard looks like a grey ferret has curled up over his chin.

A brown pigeon pecks in the dirt near my foot, its tubby body strutting around on thin, short legs, with manky feathers speckled with dust and grit.

I resist the urge to nudge it away. 'I was wondering if you're avoiding me.'

'Never. Just busy as usual.' Pete wipes his hands on his jeans. 'Checking the pipes later. And that bedroom drawer. Both on my list.' He taps his empty shirt pocket. His long

VICTORIA GOLDMAN

sleeves, as always, are cuffed around his wrist. Meanwhile, I'm sweltering in my sleeveless dress. 'First, I need to do a few bits for Derek. Can't keep him waiting.'

'One of the VIPs, Mr Palmer, has complained about a smoky odour in his room. There haven't been any other complaints, but can you make sure the air conditioning's working properly.'

'Sure.' Pete taps his pocket again.

I walk over to the museum entrance and unlock the padlock. My hand brushes against cobweb threads as I pull the door shut behind me and flick down the light switches on my left, bathing the room in a soft glow. The dim, recessed floor lights create an eerie atmosphere along the wooden walkways, and strategically placed spotlights shine more brightly around the displays.

The museum was the hard labour house until the Criminal Justice Act in 1948, and then became the prison's segregation unit. Even now, it always feels cold and damp in here, no matter how much I turn up the heating. Sometimes I imagine hearing faint cries of the past, as if the prisoners' pain and anguish lurk in the shadows.

In Victorian times, prisoners were forced to walk a treadmill. The wheel revolved slowly to grind corn – ten minutes on, five minutes off, every hour for around ten hours a day. Other prisoners turned a crank, with a set number of turns every day – usually several thousand – earning them their meals. Derek has installed modern replicas of these old torture devices in the museum for visitors to try; staff, too, if we desire a workout.

A light flickers in the next room, which is where we keep the main exhibits. Each room leads into the next through a narrow doorway. Visitors usually browse the museum displays and exhibits in around forty minutes, slightly longer if they choose to read all of the small print.

A creaking sound comes from further inside.

'Hello?' My keys jangle in my shaky hand. 'Rosalie?'

Our museum curator called in sick yesterday – a bad case of summer flu – which prompted an hour-long rant from my boss. It was too short notice to find a replacement, so he has asked me and Rosalie to step in when we open the building up to guests tomorrow. This isn't ideal, as I have so many other things to do, but at least it means I'll be able to keep an eye on Mr Palmer.

In Room Two, I pause at the life-size resin mannequin that Derek found in an antique emporium several years ago. With a lick of paint and Victorian costume, it became Isaac Cane, who stole a loaf of bread in 1873. Derek says the mannequin looks authentic but it makes me feel queasy. Paint has flaked off Isaac's waxy face, leaving an oval scar on his cheek. His glassy eyes seem to follow me around the room.

The creaking comes again, this time from the back of the building.

'Rosalie? Hello? It's Madeleine.'

Still no answer.

A faint draft cools my cheeks, probably from the old windowpanes flexing in the gentle breeze outside. Pete keeps saying that Derek will get around to replacing them some day, but I won't hold my breath. My boss doesn't spend money unless he needs to – and he likes to keep the old features of the original prison as a tourist attraction.

Room Three is devoted to the events of 1999: our *Panbrook Prisongate* exhibition, its name taken from Lloyd Palmer's book. Six wooden cabinets contain photographs and information about the prisoners, Anna Kendall and the limited evidence that was made public. The journalist agreed to the exhibition featuring his title as long as the hotel stocked his book in the museum shop and promoted it in one of the cabinets.

Five prison mugshots hang on the wall. Five pairs of eyes watching me as I stride past – inquisitive and accusing. A headshot of Anna hangs beside them, her blue eyes pleading her innocence. I shake my head and turn away.

As I reach the first cabinet, the overhead lights flicker and then thrust me into darkness. *Keep calm, Maddie.* This isn't the first time a fuse has blown in here – this is an old building, after all. But I can't afford for it to happen with hotel guests inside. Something else to add to Pete's 'to do' list.

The switch on the back wall is on a different circuit, but which way is it? I take a step forwards and stretch my hands in front of me, trying to find anything that feels familiar. But there just seems to be an empty space.

The creaking sound starts up again. Once. Twice. Three times. Followed by a faint squeak of what sounds like hinges.

A draught cools my skin, and a smoky odour wafts into my nostrils. The hairs on my skin ripple with unease, as my imagination toys with me.

'Hello? Who's there?'

I take a few more steps forwards until I welcome the familiarity of smooth wood against the palms of my hands. Once I shuffle to the right of the cabinets, my fingers catch hold of the steel handle of the old storeroom door. I wiggle it but not surprisingly the door is locked – Derek told me that the key was lost years ago, long before he took over the hotel, and he has never bothered to replace it.

If this is the door handle, it means the light switch should be...

I reach up and flip the knob. The main lights flicker on, then off, then remain on. White streaks glow in front of my eyes, and I have to blink a few times to adjust my vision. When I can finally see clearly, I glance around. The room looks the same as always, except for wispy pigeon feathers trailing along the floor towards the glass cabinets containing the *Panbrook*

Prisongate exhibits. Just like the feathers I saw on the upstairs landing in A wing.

I peer around – nothing looks out of place.

How did these feathers get in here? A determined pigeon, perhaps, sneaking in through a cracked pane of glass or an open doorway?

I listen carefully. All is silent.

Unless ... those creaking sounds, that faint draught, that whiff of smoke ... Maybe I interrupted someone. Maybe they sneaked in just before I arrived. But how – and who?

My jaw aches, and my ears buzz with disbelief. Has one of those true-crime junkies gate-crashed this weekend after all?

11

ANNA

JULY 1995

'Miss! Miss! Need my jacks.'

It's Evans, my last patient of the morning. He wriggles his nicotine-stained fingers between the rusty bars of the meds hatch gate. I shiver. They look like brown worms trying to get in.

'Here you go.' I pass his anxiety meds and a small plastic cup of water through the gap. Once he's gulped down his pill, I tick him off my list and sign his meds chart. 'See you tomorrow.'

'Fanks.' He gives me a big toothy grin. His breath stinks of fags, and I try not to gag. 'I'll bring ya flowers. What d'ya like? Roses? Daffs?'

'Tulips. Pink and yellow. Just don't be late next time.'

We both laugh. There's as much chance of him entering that new National Lottery.

Most of the patients act like right prats. But a few are so charming, it's easy to forget why they're inside. Though every bloke in here is still a threat – even the entertaining ones.

'Don't give away anything personal – about your family, where you live, your age ... even your shoe size,' Kellie warned me on my first day. 'But remember – you're still expected to care. You just have to set boundaries.'

Evans tips an imaginary cap and hands over his empty cup.

'Move ... now. Get your arse back to your cell,' an officer bellows from the end of the corridor.

Talking of prats ... This one's a small bloke, with a rat-like face and lots of bite in his voice. Rat Face treats the patients like dirt, and doesn't approve of us nurses, who are here to care rather than tell the prisoners off. Bryan insists we treat them like human beings, and even bribes them with posh sugar packets so they behave when we examine them. Someone has to keep an eye on these blokes' health – and it won't be most of the officers.

I leave the meds hatch, lock the door and head to the consult room.

Bryan looks up from the desk when I stroll in and pull the door shut. 'Morning, Anna.' He smooths down his wavy blond hair. He wears it long, but it could do with a trim. When he ties it back, he looks a bit like Brad Pitt. 'Kellie said you pulled at the pub on the weekend.'

I nod with a sigh. 'Except he turned out to be a right loser. Came back to my place and disappeared first thing without leaving his number. I can't even remember his name.'

'Maybe you'll have better luck at the party here next week – I hear Kellie's dragging you with.'

'Have you seen all the officers? No chance of that.' I roll fresh blue tissue over the couch and smooth it with my palm.

Bryan flicks through a stack of brown folders next to him. Each IMR contains a prisoner's medical notes, and all appointments are listed in the healthcare ledgers. We have a computer too, but Bryan says he doesn't like mod cons, so I always log everything on the database for him.

'So, are you ready for sick parade?'

'Of course.' I lean against his desk and fold my arms. 'What's on today?'

Sick parade's like a lucky dip. If patients want to see a doctor, they fill in a scrap of paper and pop it in a box. But some bastard officers just stick the notes straight in the bin instead.

Bryan runs his fingers down the list. 'Looks like a busy morning. Guess the patients know their favourite nurse is on duty.'

I roll my eyes. 'They just think I'm a pushover. That if they're nice to me, they'll get what they want. But I don't take any nonsense, you know that. So who's up first?'

'It's Mance with his dodgy knee.'

Ah ... Mance. He's a lifer – murdered a lawyer in cold blood – and one of the oldest prisoners here. Probably has arthritis, but it's been hard to diagnose, even though he's in constant pain. Bryan's booked him in for tests and scans at the hospital but they keep getting cancelled. It's like working in the Dark Ages.

'Not much more I can offer him.' Bryan shakes his head in frustration. 'I've told him to keep moving the joint, but there's little chance of that with just one hour's exercise in the yard. And paracetamol isn't cutting it. I can't give him anything stronger, or he's likely to sell it.'

He points at a pile of counselling booklets next to him. 'I managed to bring in a new range of these today. Updated advice, and new questionnaires for patients to fill in so we can monitor them better. Can you hand them out? I've earmarked these ones for specific patients – there's a list on top – and there's a smaller pile over there for the library.'

Bryan's radio crackles into life. *Code Blue on B wing*. Then comes the request for Healthcare. He slams his burger down on his plate. 'Guess that's the end of lunch.'

Talk about bad timing. I've been desperate for a sandwich all morning. Finally get one, and shit hits the fan. I take one last bite, as it won't be here when I get back.

We both stand up and grab our medical bags. Or rather, I heave mine up and follow Bryan out of the officers' mess. His shoes slam down on the metal landing as he strides ahead. My size four feet are probably half the size of his – two steps for every one. Working in this maze is certainly keeping me fit.

Bryan unlocks the prison gates; I slam them shut behind me. We've now done this together so many times. It's amazing the difference a few weeks makes. I've stopped panicking whenever an alarm goes off, though I still always wonder what we'll find.

We cross the yard to B wing. Bryan, babbling away. Me, imagining all the worst-case scenarios. Our keys rattling on our belts. Code Blue is serious, the most serious it can be.

Stabbing? Overdose? Suicide? It could be anything.

As we rush to The Twos, more radios spring to life and officers shout around us.

'Lock them away.'

'Get him back in his cell.'

'Clear the landings.'

Something big's happening...

The first-floor landing's empty when we get there, other than a couple of officers twisting keys in locks, and a third standing outside an open cell like a sentry.

'Alright, Miss.' Blokes cat call and wolf whistle through their cell flaps. 'Looking good, Miss.'

Then 'Bat Out of Hell' blares out and fists slam on cell doors in time with the beat. It's never quiet here for long.

'Thank God, you're here,' a gruff voice calls out from the open cell. 'What took you so long?'

Bryan pulls two surgical gloves out from his trouser pocket and drags them over his hands.

'Fucking stabbing again,' the voice carries on. 'Not looking good.'

Bryan steps inside. There's no room for all three of us, or four if I count the patient, so I just peek in. It reeks of B.O. and pee.

A young bloke, a similar age to me, is slumped against the wall next to a mouldy sink. He's not moving, and his eyes are closed. Blood dribbles out of a large wound in his side.

Bryan kneels down and checks for a pulse. He shakes his head at the officer, then in my direction.

Shit. My mouth goes dry. We've had three stabbings at The Brook in just two months. The other blokes survived, but it's too late for this one. He's covered in track marks and scars. Probably fighting over drugs again. This is no way to die, but also no way to live, so maybe he's now in a better place after all.

I shake myself out of it and start behaving like a professional. 'Anything I can do, Bryan?'

'Sadly not.'

I take a closer look at the man on the ground. 'Hey, didn't he come to sick parade this morning?'

'Yes, he did. You're right.' Bryan jots down notes in his report book. 'I gave him two paracetamol – complained he had chest pain. Didn't want me to examine him at first but then agreed. It's all in the IMR file.'

I shift aside so the officer can come out. He reeks of fags.

'Still here, then.' It's the officer from my first day. The big bloke with the owl-shaped face who saw me outside Healthcare. I hadn't recognised him in the cramped, dark cell.

'You didn't think I'd last, did you?'

The officer chuckles. 'Wee lamb like you? I was worried you'd thrown yourself to the lions. But I hear from the cons you can hold your own.' He winks. Not in a creepy way, more like Dad when he's teasing me.

'Nearly done here,' Bryan calls.

Owl Face mutters something into his radio, then clicks it back on his belt.

'Wassup, Miss?' Pairs of eyes gawp at me through the nearest viewing flaps, but it doesn't bother me now. They're locked in, and I'm not. The prisoners treat me with respect – well, most of them, most of the time.

I spot some movement on a landing above me, just as Owl Face walks over. A woman in a black suit is watching us through the netting, gripping the handrail with both hands. Her light brown hair is poker straight and stops at her shoulders. She turns away when she sees me staring.

I nod in her direction and whisper, 'Who's that?'

'Tin Man. I mean, Gov Trayton.' Owl Face's eyes narrow. 'Hard as nails, that one. She'll expect a full briefing. Won't want this happening again ... though it will. Kellie's clashed with her many a time.'

'Clashed? Why?'

'Trayton's one of the reasons I can't get Mance the tests he needs.' Bryan walks out the cell and smooths down his hair. Just as well he remembered to peel his gloves off first. 'She blocks my request every time – blames budget cuts and prison regs. It's the constant battle with some of the govs and officers. Present company accepted, of course.' He grins at the officer next to me.

Owl Face chuckles. 'Some of these cons ... they're just normal blokes when you get to know them. One stupid mistake brought them inside. No reason why we shouldn't help them, though some can't ever be released. Too dangerous to society.' His radio crackles. He takes it off his belt and holds it to his ear. 'I'd best get on.'

I watch him tread over to the opposite landing.

Kellie told me to look out for the good officers. Ones I can trust. Maybe I've found one.

It's my turn on clinic this afternoon. The minor stuff Bryan doesn't need to deal with. I look down my list. Skin infection, back pain, toothache, dodgy tummy ... It's hardly surprising the prisoners get ill, crammed together in grimy cells all day.

I flick through the pile of booklets I still need to hand out. 'Sensible Drinking'. 'All about HIV and AIDS'. 'Healthy Eating'. 'Say No to Drugs'. Bryan means well, but I'm not sure any of the patients actually read them, let alone fill out what's inside – literacy certainly isn't their strong point.

I'm still thinking about that Code Blue at lunchtime. The patient slumped on the floor, and all that blood. Owl Face was right. Ending up inside could happen to anyone – wrong place, wrong time. Pub fight getting out of hand. Speeding after one-too-many pints. But lots of the blokes in here have done something much worse – GBH, murder, rape... – and will never belong on the outside. They'll probably die in here anyway – and maybe that's not such a bad thing.

An officer knocks on the consult-room door, with Roach, my first patient, in tow.

I need to psych myself up for this one, as Roach gives me the creeps. He's always watching me, trying to sneak up close. On the outside, I'd call him a stalker. At least here, he's mainly locked in a cell. Though delivering Bryan's booklets to the library means I can't avoid him completely.

As usual, he swaggers in holding a tatty piece of prison-issued lined yellow paper, which he must have bought with his canteen money. 'Miss ... Anna ... I've got an itchy dick.' He scratches his crotch and lies down on the couch, creasing the fresh blue tissue.

'Nurse Kendall to you. Anything else?' I make a note in the ledger, then in his IMR file. 'Sore when you pee? Signs of a rash?'

'Why don't you take a look, Nurse Kendall?' Roach doesn't talk like most of the prisoners. Sounds a bit posh. Comes from money, I reckon. 'Have you ever read Shakespeare? You'll like this one. I can get you a book from the library if you want. Special rates.' He winks, holds up the paper and starts to read out loud: '"Shall I compare thee to—?"'

'I'll book you in with Dr Land.'

I've very little patience left after the day I've had so far. And this is the third day in a row with Roach's mystery ailments. Yesterday he said he had a lump on his lip and asked if I'd snog it better. I was tempted to report him but didn't want any extra paperwork.

'Nah, I don't need to see the vet today. He can give me the usual another time.' As he flutters his long, dark eyelashes, I cringe at that word the prisoners use for the doctor, as if we really are treating animals in a zoo. 'Come on, it won't take long, Nurse Kendall. I just need something for it. A good scratch might do it.'

'I'll certainly give you a good something.' Kellie strolls in holding a plastic bag of syringes and waves it in the patient's direction. 'Now get out of here, Roach, before I slap your cock with this. It'll do more than itch by the time I'm done.'

Roach shifts off the couch and swaggers out the consult room. Then he turns back and blows me a kiss. I wait for him to go before I roll my eyes.

'Next time, book him in to see me or Bry.' Kellie unlocks

the supplies cupboard and sticks the spare syringes on the top shelf. 'He's trouble.'

'Who's trouble?' Bryan wanders in clutching his medical bag. He's been doing cell checks this afternoon. 'Not me, I hope.'

Kellie blushes. 'We were just talking about Roach.' Last week, she had her hair styled into 'The Rachel' – all layered and highlighted. It suits her. Shame Bryan's married – they'd make a smashing-looking couple.

Bryan gives me a sympathetic look. 'Ah ... Cock.'

Most of the prisoners and officers call Roach 'Cock', but no way am *I* going to do that. He'd give me even more bother.

Kellie updates Bryan on today's shenanigans.

'That one's definitely trouble and probably sees Anna as a soft touch.' Bryan puts his medical bag down carefully on the desk, avoiding the open files, lidless pens and half-filled mugs. 'Erm, Anna?' He points at the couch.

I turn around. That bloody patient's left me his tatty bit of paper.

'Anna, how's your new flat?' Kellie locks the supplies cupboard. 'I've been meaning to ask you.'

I scrunch Roach's poetry into a ball and throw it at the wastepaper bin near the door. It drops straight in. *Bullseye.*

'Anna?'

'It's ... fab.' *Not.* 'Just need to spruce it up a bit. Cool pictures. Extra furniture.'

I change the tissue on the consult couch.

'I can give you a hand if you want.' Bryan's eyes light up. 'One weekend, when we're both off duty, I can take you to that new furniture shop in Chelmsworth.'

Oh God. He's trying to help, I know he is. But there's no way he's coming round to my place, and that shop's far too pricey. I haven't even let Dad visit yet. He sent me a new Tefal kettle and box of PG Tips in the post as a hint. I rang him from the staff payphone to say thanks, and when he asked, I said I'd run out of 10p's and had to go.

The problem is, my flat needs more than just a few cool things. It's teeny and cramped, with paper peeling off the walls and mouldy grouting in the bathroom. Not quite what I planned for my first home, but needs must.

'I'll tell you what...' Bryan picks up some files and stands up. 'We can—'

'Knock knock!' Thomas Benson pokes his head around the door, his blue-and-white shirt gaping open at the chest, revealing a clock-face tattoo. 'Here to see you, Miss.'

Saved by a lifer. This one could do with a scrub and a shave – I spot a lump of potato stuck to his beard – but, God, am I glad to see him.

Excerpts from the 'Meet victim #1 – Jonathan "Cock" Roach' chapter in *Panbrook Prisongate* by Lloyd Palmer – published by Spotlight Books, August 2009

"I spent a fortune on private education to give my son the best start in life. What a bloody waste of money that was. With top grades at school and a first-class law degree, Jonathan could have had it all. But while he was studying hard, he was also playing hard, and his bank balance was attracting the wrong sort of attention."

> — GORDON ROACH, FATHER OF
> JONATHAN ROACH

"Fast cars and loose women were Jonno's two main loves at uni. I've never met another man with such an inflated ego. Then there were the drugs – cannabis mainly, an occasional line of coke – and Jonno loved to gamble."

> — SUSAN DENHAM QC, WHO WAS AT
> LAW SCHOOL WITH JONATHAN
> ROACH

"Gordon was concerned about his son's wayward behaviour, so as a favour I gave Jonathan a job as a trainee solicitor when he graduated. The boy was very enthusiastic, always volunteering to visit my clients in prison. I thought it was a positive trait at the time. Looking back, this was an indication something wasn't quite right."

— ANTHONY ROBINSON, FAMILY
FRIEND AND CRIMINAL LAWYER

"Anthony told Jonathan he could take over the law firm one day when Anthony retired. Unfortunately, my son was in a shitload of debt. I don't know why he didn't come to me for help. But he was too bloody-minded to ask."

— GORDON ROACH

"Someone in the firm was siphoning off client money. Only small amounts at first, but it was slowly escalating. I had my suspicions but hadn't mentioned it to anyone else. I must have asked too many questions, however, as the boy guessed I was onto him. And then the bastard was plotting to kill me. Can you believe it?"

— ANTHONY ROBINSON

"Jonathan asked to borrow a significant amount of money, saying he wanted to get clean. I assumed he was paying off his debts so didn't hesitate to hand it over. I had no idea what he was really up to, the bloody fool. Hiring a hit man through one of Anthony's clients … seriously. I didn't even know they existed in the real world. My son handed over ten grand in cash, promising a further ten grand once the job was complete."

— GORDON ROACH

"I had a tip-off from a former client: let's call him Bob. Bob had introduced Jonathan to an … associate, let's call him... But then Bob had a change of heart – because he realised the police were onto him, no doubt – and Jonathan and this associate were arrested. Just as well, or I wouldn't be here today. That's when Gordon wiped his hands of Jonathan – the boy was on his own."

— **ANTHONY ROBINSON**

"When Cock arrived at The Brook, he were loud and brash – kept tellin' us he were loaded. After a while, we realised it were all bullshit. He had connections but no cash. His posh voice made him a target so he were desperate to be liked. Heard rumours he were gettin' smack and coke in through the library, but I never saw nothin', you know. He were always spoutin' poetry. Romantic shit, it were. Told us it were for the love of his life. We thought it were probably all talk, but there were always some doubt. What if he were havin' it off with a screw chick? And before you ask, it could even have been that Kendall nurse."

— **THOMAS BENSON, FORMER PRISONER AT PANBROOK PRISON**

"We all heard rumours about Roach getting drugs in through the library, via books ordered in, but the officers couldn't prove it. That was the problem with dealing with a lawyer – especially a banged-up, crooked one with contacts on the outside. Officers were afraid of him. Prisoners too."

— **DR BRYAN LAND, FORMER PANBROOK PRISON DOCTOR**

13

MADDIE

NOW

FRIDAY
8.00 p.m.

The Lock-Up restaurant is situated on our ground floor, close to our offices and the staff room. Tall wooden bookcases still line the sides of this former prison library, with hundreds of original books piled up in arty formations behind locked glass doors. Derek has kept the books as an authentic feature, wanting to retain some sense of the former prison life.

In one of our museum cabinets, we feature a list of the most-read prison library books at Panbrook – at the top is *Papillon* by Henri Charrière. I find it astonishing that prisoners would want to spend their sentences reading about other people's incarcerations, although perhaps they found it comforting to learn about those even more unfortunate than themselves.

Occasionally I flick through the dusty book pages to check for any hidden gems. I have discovered photographs, poetry, love letters, old counselling booklets and other forgotten relics. I even came across an anonymous death-wish list, written in black ink in a crumpled copy of Stephen King's *The Green Mile*. I place everything I find in the museum, to preserve these fragile documents of the past, except for a love poem written by Jonathan Roach to Anna Kendall on prison-issue lined yellow paper. I've kept that one as a souvenir. No one is going to miss it after all.

I finished my meal quickly to give me enough time to wander around the room, on Derek's orders. We created a table plan for the guests, trying to group them according to their postal address. I feel like Hercule Poirot, ready for a big reveal speech, with everyone now gathered together for a final reckoning.

Which one of you wrote that message on the lift wall? I ask them in my head. *And which one of you managed to break into the museum?*

But the only question I ask out loud, as I visit each table in turn, is: 'I assume everything is to your satisfaction?' Everyone nods and smiles and compliments me on today's menu: herb-roasted chicken, salt-baked Jersey Royals and Parmesan broccoli, all served on a stainless-steel mess tray as a throwback to the past. Our chef creates her culinary delights using fresh herbs and spices from our award-winning kitchen garden.

The Ethertons are sitting with two other couples and one woman on her own. The single guest, broad-hipped with a blonde bob, is reading Lloyd Palmer's book. I glance at the journalist on the VIP table, wondering if he has noticed, but he's too busy tapping away on his laptop. His glasses are perched on the bridge of his nose, giving him the air of an absent-minded professor.

One place at this table is noticeably bare – Oliver Hodgson's. I forgot to ask the kitchen staff to remove his chair before dinner.

I sit down on the empty black, velvet seat next to Mr Etherton. 'I hope your creaky drawer has been fixed.'

'Yes, and thank you so much for the fruit. It was delicious.' He rubs his stomach.

His wife fingers her empty wrist. 'Where do I report lost property?' She has wrapped her cardigan around her shoulders to ward off the evening chill.

'Lost property? You can report it to me if you want. What's missing?' I wake up my iPad and open the Notes app.

'My silver bracelet.' She presses her lips together tightly. 'I can't remember if I left it in my room, or maybe I dropped it somewhere outside.'

'What does it look like?'

'It's a bangle, with a little sun at one end and a moon at the other, with tiny diamanté sparkly bits. Dave bought it for our first anniversary – because of my name, Celeste.'

Mr Etherton squeezes his wife's knee. 'Cost me a fortune, but she's worth it. Not sure I'd find a replacement now.'

'Well, it certainly sounds beautiful. We must find out where it's gone.' With a sympathetic smile, I type out the details. 'I'll speak to Housekeeping and our caretaker, just in case they've found it.'

Stella is fastidious about security and takes missing property very seriously. I've already mentioned my concerns about Radha, who hasn't been here for much longer than I have. During the two months I have been working at the hotel, a few guests have reported missing items from their rooms – a few valuables have turned up in lost property, but others haven't been found.

My boss is sitting with our other VIPs, deep in conversation with Thomas Benson. The former prisoner was given a life sentence for shooting a man during armed robbery, then awarded early release for good behaviour just before the prison closed. Fiona Trayton probably signed his paperwork. She and

Bryan Land are currently eating in silence. They worked here at Panbrook at the same time, but their stiff postures suggest that there was no friendship between them.

Lloyd Palmer's seat is now empty. I spot him on the other side of the room, near the kitchen, browsing the bookshelves.

Placing my phone down on the table wrinkles the grey tally marks printed on the cream cloth. I smooth them out with my hand.

'I hope you're enjoying your stay so far.' I direct this at Fiona Trayton. Her red-and-white wrap dress is smart and sophisticated. She must be in her early seventies – at least – but her skin remains flawless and her silky grey hair sits neatly on her shoulders. 'I guess the prison looks very different from when you were here last.'

'It certainly does, and the food tastes a lot better.' She gives a deep laugh.

'And you, Doctor?' I turn to him just as he stuffs a piece of chicken into his mouth. Like Fiona, the doctor has aged well. His lengthy white hair frames a taut face. 'I hope you're enjoying your meal.'

'Call me Bryan.' As he wipes his mouth with his napkin, a strand of chicken lands on his yellow shirt. 'And I agree with the gov.'

Fiona raises her eyebrows in surprise.

'I couldn't even compare this with the grub I had here at The Brook,' the doctor continues. He stabs a small potato with his fork and twirls it around on his mess tray until it's fully coated with gravy. 'Then, it was a greasy burger and limp chips in the officer's mess, or a stale sandwich. I don't miss this place one jot.'

As he stuffs the potato into his mouth, I turn back to Fiona. 'Leaving here can't have been easy, especially in those circumstances. I read that you were at the party that night.'

'Yes, but I wasn't here for long.' She prods her fork into a stray sprig of broccoli on her tray. 'Anyway, it was years ago. I barely remember what I did last week.'

Bryan clears his throat to attract my attention. 'I wasn't here that night at all – sadly my late wife was taken ill. I knew the prisoners, obviously, but Annie treated most of them more than I did, so I didn't need to be here.'

'Annie?'

The doctor smiles at me. 'All her friends and family called her Annie. Everyone she was close to. Obviously I didn't at first, but we all became good friends in Healthcare.'

I lean forwards and steeple my fingers. 'So which prisoners did you see the most?' I glance at Lloyd Palmer to make sure he isn't eavesdropping on our conversation.

'Lucas Somers and, unfortunately, Steven Fisher. Fingerling drank drugs like a fish, and often badgered Healthcare for them.' The doctor looks down, grimacing, and flicks the chicken strand off his shirt.

I turn back to Fiona. 'I've always wondered why those five particular men were the last ones in the prison. Did something link them together?'

'Just a coincidence, as far as I'm aware. Wasn't it, Dr Land?' She frowns as the doctor shakes his head and stabs at another potato. 'Steven Fisher didn't even know the others. They just happened to be the last prisoners left here that weekend.'

I tap my fingers on the table as more questions fill my head. 'The police believed Anna was bringing drugs into the prison, possibly collaborating with Jonathan Roach. Do you think—?'

Raised voices interrupt me, coming from the other side of The Lock-Up.

Silence blankets the room.

One of the waitresses is scurrying away from Lloyd Palmer towards the kitchen, her shoulders hunched in a huff. The journalist is hugging his closed laptop against his chest, staring at her retreating back.

The room begins to buzz with noise as conversations start up again. A waiter carries a tray of drinks from the bar, and another begins to clear some empty mess trays. Dr Land stuffs the potato into his mouth, Fiona Trayton stares at her manicured nails, and Thomas Benson coughs loudly.

My phone buzzes with Derek's name on the screen. Across the table, my boss is glaring at me and pointing towards the journalist.

When I reach Lloyd Palmer, he nods at me as if we are old friends meeting for a coffee.

I give him a piercing stare. 'Is there a problem *again*, Mr Palmer?'

He raises his hands and takes a step backwards. 'It seems I'm getting a reputation for difficult behaviour ... or maybe I already had one.' He offers me a wry smile.

He can certainly be a charmer when he wants to be, trying to extract personal information from family members, former prison staff and old friends of Anna twenty years ago. This is all outlined in his book, clear enough for anyone to see. But in my mind, he's also a troublemaker.

'So there wasn't a problem with your meal?'

He shakes his head. 'It was top class. That waitress and I ... We just bumped into each other when I stepped backwards, that's all it was. I—'

A vibrating sound comes from my trouser pocket. I scold myself in my head for forgetting to turn off my notifications.

I pull out my phone, just in case it's urgent. It could be Oliver Hodgson to confirm his arrival tomorrow.

Ellie's profile picture greets me on the screen. It features a photograph of the two of us with Nate, taken last year. Her blonde curls were tied in pigtails, making her look much younger. By then, Nate's face was so grey, drawn and drained that he looked like a man in his seventies rather than in his early fifties.

Warm breath irritates my ear.

I turn around to find the journalist staring over my shoulder.

He pushes his glasses up the bridge of his nose and gestures towards my phone. 'Derek told me you moved here from Spain to take this job, soon after a family bereavement. I'm sorry for your loss.'

I swallow back a rising lump in my throat as I stare at my boss. He's currently talking to Dr Land. I hope he isn't sharing more of my personal information.

The journalist peers at my phone again, his eyebrows raised. 'Good-looking family. Your daughter looks a lot like her dad.'

'Thank you, Mr Palmer.' I clench my fists to dampen down my rising temper. My family is none of his business. I was right: he hasn't improved over the years, and his sweet talk won't change my opinion of him. Once a sewer rat, always a sewer rat.

'I'll see you at the museum in the morning, Ms Batten.' He gives me a mock salute. 'Looking forward to going through the archives and then into B wing. Everyone wants to know what really happened that night in 1999, don't they?'

As I walk away from him, I sense his eyes following my every step.

1 4

MADDIE

NOW

FRIDAY
9.30 p.m.

I lean back against the black-and-white striped cushions and close my eyes, welcoming the opportunity to take the weight off my feet. I sprayed some perfume onto my wrists earlier, and the oriental scent lingers in the air. I chose this particular room for some peace and quiet. It's away from the hustle and bustle of the staff areas, but located next to the third-floor lift so that I can easily access the rest of A wing and other key parts of the hotel.

In 1963, part of this room was home to Shaun Goodwin, who was beaten to death by his cellmate following an argument over their choice in music. Hotel guests who have slept in here have reported a faint odour of urine, orchestral music and shuffling sounds in the early hours. Derek once called in a paranormal investigation team, who recorded a series of footsteps and a shadowy figure in the bathroom. Yet I've spent several hours in here, eyes open, eyes closed, daytime, night-time, but have yet to see or hear anything – or anyone – remotely supernatural.

Today has been more full-on than I ever imagined, and now it seems so much later than nine-thirty. My eyelids feel heavy and my forehead aches at its midpoint. But I can't afford to sleep tonight. A few months ago, I made a promise that I have yet to fulfil. And I fear the ghosts my dreams will bring, rather than the ghosts believed to be festering in this building.

I smooth my hands over the cream bed sheets on either side of me, appreciating the warmth and softness of the fabric, and the...

I open my eyes.

I must have drifted off, just for a few moments according to the time on my watch.

I can manage a short while longer to replenish my energy levels, but then I *must* recap on the arrangements for tomorrow and beyond – I can't afford for anything to go wrong. There's the museum, the B wing visit, and the grand anniversary party that will showcase the hotel's excellence, ignoring the tragic events of the past.

If only they could be ignored, though. Six faces haunt my days as well as my nights. What happened, Anna? Did you do something so unbearable and unforgivable that you felt you had no choice but to leave your life behind?

My phone lies on my side table, resting on my dog-eared copy of *Panbrook Prisongate*. I have read this book so many times, scrutinised the words, the scant evidence and the journalist's conclusion that Anna Kendall was guilty. Yet a deep voice in my head still insists she wasn't.

I pick up my phone. Scrolling down my contacts list, I stop when I reach Ellie's name and gaze at her profile picture: the photograph of me, Ellie and Nate. My hair was longer then, lighter too, dark brown curls falling softly around my ears onto my neck. When I gaze into my past-self eyes, I detect the sadness behind them, the knowledge of what had gone on before and what was still to come.

Nate had been complaining about lower back pain for several months, blaming his office chair, the sagging sofa seat, the intense Spanish sunshine, an overdose of sangria and churros, reaching his fifties ... Eventually I drove him to a doctor's appointment, assuming he would be given some ibuprofen tablets and perhaps a physiotherapy session or two. Instead, the doctor sent him for an MRI and other tests, and not long after that the bad news arrived. They had found a tumour in his spine, too close to the cord, too dangerous to remove. We were tugged into a nightmare of hospital appointments, challenging treatments and difficult decisions, until his health deteriorated further and there was nothing else that the doctors could do.

I grab a tissue from the cardboard box on the bedside table and wipe away the tears trickling down my cheeks.

Nate insisted on having a family portrait before he was forced to say his goodbyes, so we booked a morning session and dressed up in our party clothes. This is my favourite of all of the pictures: Nate finally giving the photographer a broad smile, fighting through his pain.

I trace his jawline with my finger, and then I trace Ellie's: the same heart-shaped face, almond-shaped blue eyes and button nose. Ellie looks so much like Nate, although he always insisted she is more like her mum. We tried to give her a younger sibling – she wanted a sister – but it wasn't meant to be. Unexplained infertility, the clinic called it.

Two failed attempts at IVF soon took their toll, as we struggled through grief, guilt, anger and melancholy at the loss of what could have been. Until we focused again on what we already had – Ellie – and learnt to count our blessings.

A dripping sound comes from above. I look up, where

there's nothing beyond the ceiling other than the eaves and the great outdoors. According to the Met Office, it's due to pour with rain tonight, after five days of glorious sunshine. We're hoping to hold tomorrow's celebrations in the courtyard garden, but it's impossible to plan for anything with the inclement British weather.

I call Ellie, and this time she answers her phone straightaway.

'Hey, Mum, I was just thinking about you.' Her voice is faint, drowned out by background noise – loud music, laughter, a clinking of glasses.

'Where are you?' I have to concentrate hard to hear her. 'It sounds busy.'

'Hold on...' I hear footsteps, followed by the slamming of a door. 'Better?'

Her voice is clearer now. I nod, and then remember she can't see me. 'Yes, where are you?'

'The Horse and Cart.' Her local pub. 'For Ben's thirtieth.'

'Ben?' She's mentioned his name before, but I can't place him right now.

'Mum ... I introduced you to him at our engagement party. He's one of the physios working with Viv.'

'Ah, yes. Brain fog moment.' Now I remember him: a short guy with a scruffy mop of reddish hair. 'You called me earlier, during dinner. Is everything okay?'

'Sorry, I forgot to check the time. And yes, it is. You're worrying again, aren't you?'

My cheeks grow warm.

'Viv and I had an idea about the venue change,' her voice rises with excitement, 'but we'll talk about that later. It's not important now ... So, how's it going? Is that journalist causing trouble? Everything going to plan?'

I laugh at the barrage of questions – typical Ellie, ever since she learnt to talk. 'Nothing I can't handle. And yes, everything's going exactly to plan.' The same lie I told Derek.

'Is there *anything* you can't handle?' Ellie laughs too, with Nate's laugh – soft, low and melodic.

I swallow back a lump in my throat. If only he could be here to see our daughter walk up the aisle, to be the support I need, to help with everything I have to do.

'Sure you can't slip me in tomorrow?' She laughs again. 'I'd really love to take a look around the hotel.'

'I said no, and I meant it. It's not a good idea. I'm really busy, and you'll—'

'Okay, okay … I get the message. I'll just be in the way.' She gives a weary sigh. 'I'd better get back into the pub. I don't want to miss last orders.'

After we end the call, I gaze at the phone in my hand. I know how much Ellie would love to be here. She has been begging to join me this weekend, but I told her it wouldn't be appropriate. I couldn't bear to be shadowed by family members, worrying about her at every moment.

I have to concentrate on what needs to be done.

15

MADDIE

NOW

FRIDAY
10.00 p.m.

When I arrive at The Lock-Up, Fiona is stumbling away from the bar, swaying gently as she grips an unopened bottle of Pinot Noir. I had already tried her empty room and figured this was the next logical place to look. Lloyd Palmer is sitting in one of the booths chatting to Derek and Bryan Land. I wish I could stay and listen to their conversation, but I have other plans.

'Ms Trayton.' I tap Fiona gently on the arm, causing her to startle. 'Ms Trayton, I wondered if I could have a quick word in private.'

'Now? I'm going back to my room.' Her sour breath wafts towards me. She looks longingly at the bottle in her hand, and then back at me with disdain. 'I suppose you could join me for a quick drink.'

I cast one last glance at the journalist, the doctor and my

boss, still chatting and laughing, then follow her out of the bar.

Fiona stays silent all the way up to the first floor until we step out of the lift.

'It feels so strange to be back at The Brook. I certainly never expected to be on The Twos again.' Her eyes flicker around as we pace to her room. 'I mean, it still *looks* like The Twos. The landings and galleries, staircases, cell doors ... The only thing missing is the suicide netting.'

I detect a hint of humour in her voice. To be fair, our hotel decor was once her reality. While she may never have slept in one of these former cells, she spent her working life locked inside a prison building, mainly *this* building.

Fiona's room is next to Lloyd Palmer's, on the other side of the large painting. She beckons me in as though she is welcoming me into her home, gesturing towards the leather chair by the desk and urging me to take a seat.

She's staying here for only two nights but has certainly made herself comfortable, perhaps because Panbrook was once her second abode. On her side table, she has placed a small silver photo frame, along with a hardback thriller, empty tumbler and folded pair of reading glasses. Her navy wheelie bag rests against the wardrobe door, and a small floral toiletry bag lies on the chest of drawers.

I sit down in the chair, not intending to stay long as I'm conscious of the time, while also hoping that we can talk for a few minutes at least. She pulls a corkscrew out from her wheelie bag and opens the wine bottle like a skilled mixologist. Then she picks up the empty tumbler from her side table and fills it.

'You can pour one too if you want. There's a spare glass in there' – she waves her hand in the direction of the bathroom – 'or don't you drink while you're on duty?' She raises her eyebrows as though this is a challenge.

'Not tonight, but thank you.'

Fiona perches on the edge of the bed, wrinkling the cream bedspread, and crosses her legs. Her wine tumbler jiggles in her shaky hand. 'So what did you want to discuss? About the museum visit tomorrow? I told Derek I would be happy to talk to guests about life at The Brook.'

'Thank you. But I actually wanted to ask you a few things away from the crowds. About that night in June 1999.'

'I told you earlier, I don't remember much. I popped in to say goodbye to Eric at the party and left here just before...' she curls her hands into fists, 'before it happened.'

A glistening of tears in the corners of her eyes reveals a fragility I hadn't noticed earlier. Being a prison governor must be challenging at the best of times, with a constant need to be in charge and not show any emotion, something I can relate to well, but even more so when a major incident happens on your watch.

I glance at the open wine bottle on the desk. Being back at the scene of the crime must be evoking strong memories. 'Did you know Eric Martin well?'

'Yes, he was one of the best and most senior officers I had. He died five or maybe six years ago. His wife and I still keep in touch.' She gazes into her glass. 'I didn't know about his party at first. They didn't want me to know. But things always filtered back eventually. Those parties weren't really my scene anyway, a bit raucous, but I decided to put in an appearance at this one.'

'Why this one?'

'Eric had been a loyal member of staff, and I wanted him to know that. Being an officer wasn't an easy job.'

'So...' I lean forwards, 'you must know exactly who was here at the prison that night. The staff members, I mean.'

'As I have been saying ever since then, I don't remember the details. That journalist was quizzing me earlier in the bar.'

She downs another generous measure of wine. 'Not that I could tell him anything he doesn't already know.'

'What was Mr Palmer asking you?' My skin prickles with a mixture of excitement and irritation. Perhaps he has found some new information already, something that isn't in his book, something I've missed.

'He asked who was here that night, just as you're doing now. The only thing I am certain of is that those five prisoners were here, along with Anna Kendall.' She shuffles on the bed, wriggling backwards in a restless manner. Wine sloshes around in her glass.

I should offer her the chair but don't want to stem the flow of conversation. 'The prison staff didn't sign in at the gate, which was against procedure. Surely you took action afterwards.'

'There were twenty, thirty officers, maybe more, many just popping in for a moment.' She shrugs as if their names are of no importance, as if forgetting that those five men died on her watch. 'Most didn't bother to sign in and out as officially the prison was closed that weekend. They didn't expect to still have prisoners here, and junior guards were slacking on gate duty. By that stage, I didn't see the point in enforcing it. If it hadn't been for that transport failure, the prisoners would have been long gone. I didn't expect any problems that night. None of us did.'

'Yes, the transport failure. The person who cancelled the transport for those five prisoners was a woman. Anna Kendall, it's always been assumed. But surely that would have been too obvious, focusing all eyes on her.'

Fiona takes another gulp of wine. 'The call was made from a payphone near her daughter's nursery. So it seems logical to assume it was Anna – that she planned what happened in advance.'

'But—'

Fiona bangs her hand on the desk. 'Ms Batten, whoever made that call was certainly someone who knew the prison procedures. Someone who knew there was no chance of arranging new transport at such short notice, once the error was realised. With everything that happened afterwards – the poisoned cakes, what she did when she ... Who else could it have been?'

I raise my eyebrows, but she doesn't take the bait – the police never considered the governor to be a suspect. 'Okay, so assuming it was Anna, this means she had a grievance with one of those five men, maybe more of them. Otherwise why would she have killed them? Which then means it can't have been a coincidence that at least one of them remained here that weekend.'

The main light flickers. Fiona places her tumbler down on the side table and reaches over to a chrome switch next to the bed. She flips it up and down a few times until the light stabilises.

My skin prickles with unease. Surely not another power surge.

'As I told you earlier – and that journalist – and the police many years ago, it really was just a coincidence.' Fiona picks up her glass again, tipping it to the side. The berry-coloured liquid sloshes precariously close to the edge.

I squint at the bedcover, costing up the laundry bill for wine stains in my head. Derek would blame this on me, no doubt. 'Do you know why she may have targeted one of them?'

'As I also told you earlier, I didn't know any of those men particularly well. Governors didn't tend to see much of the prisoners unless there was a problem.' As she shakes her head, I detect the hint of a scowl. 'Although I admit that Jonathan Roach has always stuck in my mind.'

'Was there a particular problem with him?'

She raises her right hand and rubs her chin with her index finger. 'There were a few altercations, mainly between him and William Owen. That I do remember. Those two men didn't get on with one another at all. They were sharing a cell at one point, but I had to split them up.'

'Do you know why they argued?'

'No, I was never told.' She gulps down more wine, her eyes brightening with fresh alcohol flooding her bloodstream. 'And Steven Fisher, he was trouble as well, as Dr Land told you at dinner.'

'What about William Owen? What was he like? Was he a troublemaker too?'

She stares into her glass before looking up again. 'Sorry ... what did you ask?'

'About William Owen. Was he a troublemaker?'

'All the prisoners were trouble, or they wouldn't have been at The Brook, Ms Batten.' She chortles ominously, and a cold draft trickles down my spine. 'I wanted to move him once. That didn't go well.'

'I read that he wanted to be near his family, with his little girl so ill. Is that why you let him stay?'

'Everyone seemed surprised I had a heart. You think I didn't know they called me Tin Man behind my back?' Fiona sniggers. 'I saw his girls when they visited once. Two peas in a pod, except one didn't look too healthy. It was all very sad, I admit. The remaining child must be in her twenties by now. Similar age to my granddaughter.' She directs a tender smile towards the photograph by her bed.

'So you did know the men fairly well after all.' I ignore the glint of disdain in her eyes to plough on with some of the questions buzzing around my head. 'What do *you* think happened that night?'

Fiona stands and tops up her glass, the wine bottle shaking

in her hand. She sways and staggers, as if she's balancing in a small boat caught in a riptide. 'Why Anna did what she did?'

My hands twitch. 'You clearly believe Anna was guilty.'

'I—' She stares into my eyes. 'Look, I've read Lloyd Palmer's book – haven't you? He outlines the case against her very well.'

'Except it wasn't the case against her. It was just his own personal ramblings, based on a few scant facts and conversations. The case never reached the courts, and the police never released anything into the public domain.' I lean back and take a deep breath, trying to calm my hammering heart. 'Let's say Anna didn't do it. Who else is a possibility? What about the prison staff?'

'I didn't know most of them very well, other than Eric.'

'And Anna?'

'I didn't really have many dealings with her. I was told she was proficient at her job and seemed well liked by the staff, but clearly there was a problem, or she wouldn't have done it.' She yawns and puts down her glass.

'Some people think she was getting drugs into the prison, and—'

'Ms Batten, it's late.' Fiona staggers to the door and opens it.

'Do you know who she was particularly close to in here, apart from the other Healthcare staff? Could she have been in a relationship with any of the officers?'

'Ms Batten, please … enough of your questions. I know what happened back then is on all our minds this weekend, but I wasn't expecting to be interrogated by the hotel manager. And as I said, I hardly knew Anna at all.'

She sounds convincing with her sharp, efficient tone.

Except I know she's lying.

16

ANNA

SEPTEMBER 1995

'No files in these, I hope, Nurse Kendall.'

Bloody hell, Kellie's got a good memory. I'd forgotten about that – my first-day blunder. Dad's still watching those old episodes of *Porridge*. If he stopped, maybe he'd worry about me less.

She lifts up the Tupperware box and eyes the contents: fairy cakes I've baked for her fiftieth. A beam spreads across her face.

I wheel my desk chair as far back as I can go in the cramped Healthcare office. 'You can't have a birthday without cake.' I made these ones all fancy for her, with piped pink icing and those little silver balls that crunch when you bite them.

She grabs a cake and pulls it apart, then sticks a piece in her mouth. Her eyes light up as she chews and swallows. 'Mmm ... I'll have to have a birthday more often.' She stuffs the rest of the cake in her mouth, then glances at the desk. 'Anna ... um ... something's beeping.'

Oh shit. I look down at the computer and press 'save' before it crashes. Our dial-up connection is really crap in here.

Kellie keeps asking Trayton to upgrade the system, but management blame everything on budget cuts.

'Are you logging Bryan's appointments on the database again.' Kellie sticks the Tupperware lid back on. 'He should be doing that himself.'

'He says he doesn't—'

'I know, I know. He likes the old ways. None of the mod cons. Blahdie blahdie blah.' She giggles so loudly, someone might think I snuck booze into her cakes. 'Maybe we should buy him one of those new flip phones. Have you seen the price of them? Can you imagine even carrying a phone everywhere you go?'

'Oh God, I'd never get any peace and quiet.' I'm giggling now too. 'Dad would be calling every day – actually, make that every bloody hour – checking I'm okay. My brother's got a mobile phone for work – says Dad drives him loopy.'

'Has he got a new girlfriend yet?'

'Yeah … He met this English girl in Paris a few weeks back. Cherry, she's called, and apparently, she's *the one*. She's much younger than me – nineteen, I think – works behind the bar. I mean, seriously?' I roll my eyes. 'I can't see it lasting.'

'And what about you and that bloke in the club last week?' Kellie raises an eyebrow expectantly. She's desperate for me to 'find love' – her words, not mine. 'You were all over each other. Have you seen him again?'

'Nah. He handed me his number, but I'm just having a good time – letting off some steam after work. I'm not looking for anything steady right now.'

'Is Bryan in?' Eric Martin peers round the door. His grey hair gets whiter every time I see him. He's the oldest officer at The Brook and once told me he can't wait to retire, but he's got nearly four years to go.

Kellie shakes her head. 'He's still in the clinic next door

with Somers. He'll be another ten minutes or so. Can we help?'

Eric steps into the room. 'It's Benson. B2-35.'

'Bryan saw him last week for his knee pain.' I search for the prisoner's IMR in the pile next to me. It would be so much easier if everything was computerised. Bryan may not believe it, but mod cons do have some benefits. 'Is it bad again? Tell him to come in tomorrow.'

Eric shakes his head, pressing his lips firmly together. 'Can't see that happening. He says he has belly pain and threw up some blood ... and he doesn't look good. He can't even—'

'Anna, *you* go?' Kellie unlocks the storage cabinet and hands me my medical bag. 'But let Bryan know, in case he wants to cut Somers short.'

'Somers? That wasn't in the appointments' ledger.' I tut my disapproval. 'He really does need a secretary.'

I knock on the consult-room door and peer through the glass.

Bryan waves me in. 'Everything okay, Nurse Kendall?' He leans back in his chair.

Lucas Somers is sitting on the couch looking thoughtful, as if I've interrupted something important. This patient's huge, even sitting down, with chunky legs pulling at his jeans, and a thick neck poking out his shirt. I've not had dealings with him yet as he always sees Bryan, but Kellie calls him a gentle giant. Paint him green, and he'd look like his nickname, Hulk. He's clutching a box of booklets and a library book about counselling techniques, as if these are precious goods. At least he's enthusiastic about his prison role.

'Just heading to B2 to check on Benson. Apparently he's got belly pain and won't get off his bed.' I shush Bryan down when he grabs his medical bag and starts to stand up. 'Don't worry, I've got a bodyguard with me,' I point behind me at Eric, who pulls his shoulders back and sticks out his chest.

'Gov Trayton, this is Nur—'

'I know who you are.' Her phone voice sounds just like she looks – official and business-like. 'What do you want, Nurse Kendall?'

I've not spoken directly to the gov before, but Kellie and Bryan are too busy right now. 'It's about Thomas Benson, B2-35. He's not in a good way.' *Now there's an understatement.* 'Severe abdominal pain, vomiting blood and looks anaemic. It could be an ulcer. He's been taking high-dose ibuprofen for weeks. He needs to go in.'

'I've got no escort staff. He's probably just messing around.' She sighs, like I'm a real inconvenience. 'You'll have to manage it in Healthcare.'

The receiver goes silent, then a dull tone. Bloody hell, she's cut me off.

I call through to the gov again. I've a bad feeling about this. Call it 'nurse intuition'. I don't think Benson is pulling a fast one.

My hands are shaking when I put the phone down. Ten minutes later, she storms into the Healthcare office and stops by my desk. I swivel the chair round to face her. She rests her hands on her hips, elbows out, like she means business.

'I said I don't have the escort staff.' She gives me a condescending look. 'Just keep monitoring him. That's what we pay you for, isn't it?'

I take a deep breath to steady my nerves. 'If it's an ulcer and he isn't treated properly, he could die in here. But I'll write on his IMR that you're taking clinical responsibility for him, and then you can sign it. No problem.'

She glares me and taps her foot as if she's thinking about what to say. I feel myself wobbling again. *Annie, don't show it.* I open the IMR file and pick up my pen.

'Okay ... you'll get your escort.' Her hands are back on her hips. 'But there had better be something seriously wrong with him.'

Twenty minutes later, Kellie and Bryan walk into the office, just as I'm about to take a break.

'Well?' Bryan opens the Tupperware box and pulls out one of the birthday cakes I made for Kellie.

I can't stop myself grinning. 'Ambulance is on its way. But I never want to go up against Trayton again. I can't believe I did that.'

'Well done, Anna!'

As Bryan stuffs the cake into his mouth, I stand up and take a bow.

'Are you joining us for drinks, Bry? We can do a double celebration.' Kellie gives him one of her pleading looks, but as usual Bryan doesn't seem to notice. *Bloody men*. 'We're crashing at the mess tonight – I brought in a load of booze.'

'I can't tonight. Sorry, I know it's your birthday...' he actually looks upset for a change, 'but I need to get home. My Faye had a funny turn over the weekend so the hospital's running some tests. I can't leave her on her own.'

Poor Bryan. His wife's so unwell, he never seems to have any fun. Somehow we'll get him to party with us one day.

'I'll give you a penny for them.' The bench creaks when he sits down. He offers me a ciggy.

'Nah, I'm good. Only at parties. I'll stick with this for now.' I raise my plastic cup of water. 'You staying?'

He shakes his head as he lights up. 'Not really my scene.' The bench creaks again as he leans back and blows a smoke ring into the air. 'But I'm sure you'll have a good time, as always.'

Ever since that Code Blue on The Twos, Owl Face and I have met in the kitchen garden at the back of B wing after our Tuesday shifts, catching up on the week we've had. It's like chatting to Dad, but without all the drama and worry.

The kitchen garden is always buzzing with prisoners and officers, like a giant beehive full of workers, but it's still a bit of calm in all the madness of The Brook. The benches are surrounded by bright flowers and fragrant herbs and spices, so it looks and smells gorgeous.

Some prisoners are working the beds, some control the drying machines in the big sheds at the back, and others package up the herbs and spices for the market. The Brook makes some dosh, the prisoners learn new skills and earn a few pennies, and the officers like being outside. It's hard work, and prisoners are prone to heatstroke, frostbite and accidents – lots of them come into Healthcare. But let's face it, anything's better than being on the landings all day. Wins all round.

As one of garden orderlies bends down, sweat dribbles down his shirt. He rips out some dandelions from the herb bed and tosses the yellow flower heads into a wheelbarrow. His trousers slip a little, revealing a green-cross tattoo on his back.

'Hey, you're not doing that right, Pills.' My hand trembles as I put my cup down on the bench. 'If you don't get the root too, it'll grow back again. What tools have you got?'

Pills throws his head back and lets out a deep laugh. 'What tools? You're fucking joking, right? You're asking the wrong bloke.'

I turn to my bench companion – 'Back in a sec' – and lead the orderly into the shed.

When we return – Pills holding the pointed trowel I've chosen for him – Bryan wanders through the gate at the back of B wing. Carrying his medical bag – as always – he crosses the garden to the concrete path and waves at me. He must be on his way home. His hair's tied back with an elastic band to keep it off his face. He's refused my offers to attack it with a pair of surgical scissors.

I show Pills how to pull out the whole dandelion with the trowel, so the long roots come out of the soil too, then return to the bench.

Owl Face blows another smoke ring into the air. 'I'm impressed. I spend all afternoon out here watching these blokes and know nothing about gardening. Then again, I don't think Pills does either.'

'My mum used to garden, and I used to help her. She even won a few local prizes.' I raise the cup to my lips and sip some water. 'That's probably why I like being out here. Feels familiar, somehow.'

'The prisoners like it out here too. Gives them some freedom, or as much as they can get. And they like being part of something big – something productive.' As he taps his ciggy against the bench, lumps of ash fall onto the concrete path. 'Hope Pills appreciated your help.'

'Well, I told him if he's going to do a job, he may as well do it properly.'

'You've got a kind heart, Anna.' Owl Face nudges my arm. 'I heard what happened with Tin Man today.'

'What? How—?'

'Anna, *everyone* knows what happened with Tin Man Trayton.' He chuckles. 'Talk of the mess, it was. The prisoners too, knowing someone's got their backs. Not many officers fight for them, not enough. We'd all be called soft if we—'

'Just doing my job. That's what nurses do.'

I jut my chin towards Bryan. One of the prisoners has stopped him for a chat. 'Why's Somers out here. I thought he's on woodwork.'

'Hulk was put on gardening today because Benson's off. They needed more help before market day. Woodwork can wait.'

Somers raises his hands as if he's on edge. I lean forwards but can't hear their conversation. I hope Bryan's alright – I've heard rumours Somers has a short fuse when something riles him.

I turn back to the prison officer at my side. 'Somers was with Bryan in the clinic for ages this morning.'

'He's trained as one of the Listeners, so I expect he's reporting back. Maybe one of the other prisoner's been self-harming or talking about suicide.'

Somers finishes chatting to Bryan and heads towards the gate into B wing. One of the officers lets him through.

'Doesn't that make Somers a grass rather than a good guy?'

A smoke ring hovers in front of me. I wave it away with my hand.

'Nah ... the prisoners trust him. We all do.' The bench creaks as Owl Face shifts forwards. 'Suicide's a big problem at The Brook. They tell Hulk things they won't tell us. Could save their life one day.'

Pills is standing up now, chucking herbs into a plastic crate. He grins at us and takes a bow.

'Oye, Pills, get back to your work,' a female officer shouts at him.

My cheeks warm in the fading sunlight. 'Maybe I should teach all of these prisoners how to garden properly. Then they'd be more productive.'

My bench companion chuckles. 'Healthcare's certainly been busier since you started at The Brook. If you're out here too, they'll all be wanting a transfer to gardening duty, and not just 'cos it pays well for inside. Most men would kill to do this job ... though some already did.'

**Excerpts from the 'Meet victim #2 – Lucas "Hulk" Somers'
chapter in *Panbrook Prisongate* by Lloyd Palmer – published
by Spotlight Books, August 2009**

"Lucas towered over the other children at school so stuck out like a sore thumb. But no one dared bully him for it. In fact, he was such a popular child. The others were always sharing their sweets with him, buying him lunch and helping him with homework. So I was shocked when I heard what he'd done."

— MRS EDITH BELL, LUCAS'S FORMER ENGLISH TEACHER

"All the teachers thought the sun shined out of Luc's arse. But he was the class bully behind the scenes. He tripped me up in the playground if I didn't give him my tuckshop money. Not just once, but every week. I was too scared to report him – and too scared not to comply. No one said 'no' to Lucas."

— GRAHAM EADEN, LUCAS'S FORMER CLASSMATE

"We met at work, a small carpentry firm. Luc was working on cabinets, and I'd just joined as junior secretary. Love at first sight, it was. Love at first sight. He was so kind and generous, and everyone else loved him. Always doing things for him. Nothing was ever too much. Nothing."

— MARGARET SOMERS, LUCAS'S WIFE

"I never had issues with Lucas's work, but one of the apprentices said Lucas was getting aggressive if they didn't do things the way he wanted. When I confronted Lucas, he denied it, saying this apprentice had it in for him – jealousy, probably. He got quite upset, so I told him to take a few days off to calm down – he shouted at me, grabbed his tools and left."

— DANIEL INGLEWORTH, LUCAS'S FORMER EMPLOYER

"We were driving back from a rare night out when it happened. Nothing raucous – just a meal in the local Italian, it was, and Luc only had a pint. He said he'd had a bad day at work, but didn't spill the beans when I asked. When a young bloke started making vulgar gestures at me from the next car, I said it was nothing, but Luc got all upset."

— MARGARET SOMERS

"I was driving Paul home after the pub. He blew this pretty woman a kiss, that was all. Just harmless fun. Then when we stopped at the lights, the other bloke hopped out and banged on the window. He was huge. Towered over Paul. Intimidating, you know? Paul apologised, I heard him. But the other bloke was in his face. Next thing I know, he's holding a screwdriver and stabbing Paul in the chest."

— IAN STANTON, FRIEND OF THE VICTIM PAUL MACK

"Luc must have been provoked, must have been. Never heard him raise his voice, not to me, the kids, not once. Someone in the other car was screaming, and another bloke was shouting. When I got out, there was blood everywhere. Everywhere, it was, and Luc on his hands and knees trying to save this other man's life. I know Luc ended up in prison, but whatever happened wasn't his fault."

— **MARGARET SOMERS**

"Hulk packed a powerful punch, and everyone knew he didn't take no shit. You have to be liked inside, or you get beat up, and he used that. Became the peacemaker on the wing, but it were really 'cos no one dared mess with him. And we'd all tell him things, you know – confide in him our deepest darkest secrets. If I'd known it were all goin' back to Healthcare, I'da killed him myself – the bastard were dobbin' us in."

— **THOMAS BENSON, FORMER PANBROOK PRISON PRISONER**

"Somers wanted to train as a counsellor for troubled teenagers when he was finally released. Shame, as he could have been a great asset to society. I encouraged him to train as a Listener – a peer-support counsellor. He was a regular visitor to Healthcare, but we generally kept it all hush hush. Sometimes he was worried about a prisoner's mental health or the behaviour of some of the officers. That week, the week they died, he said he had something important to tell me before the prison closed. I never found out what that was. But maybe that's why he was murdered. Maybe someone wanted to silence him before he revealed their secret."

— **DR BRYAN LAND, FORMER PANBROOK PRISON DOCTOR**

"Our kids never really got to know their dad. All my Luc wanted was to do his time and get back to us. Make it up to the kids, you know? Be a proper family again. He could never truly forgive himself for what they said he did. That nurse, that Anna Kendall, she ruined our lives. Ruined us. We hope she's rotting in Hell."

— **MARGARET SOMERS**

18

MADDIE

NOW

FRIDAY
11.00 p.m.

Back at The Lock-Up, it's closing time and our guests are trickling out of the bar to return to their rooms. Several stumble past me reeking of sweat and beer, their cheeks flushed and their spirits high. There is no sign of our VIPs or Derek, so I assume they have already gone to bed.

Inside, the bar area smells clean and fresh. Derek is a firm believer that if hospitality areas smell enticing, guests will linger for longer, spending more money on food and drink. Natural essential oils of jasmine and lavender are diffused through Panbrook's HVAC system to help our guests unwind. It certainly seems to be working tonight, judging by the numerous used glasses and empty beer bottles littering the tables.

As soon as the bar area has been cleared, cleaned and sanitised for tomorrow, our bleary-eyed staff leave The Lock-Up and head to the car park to travel home.

I take the lift back to my room, mulling over my conversation with Fiona. She seems so uneasy here at Panbrook, so why did she agree to join us this weekend? Perhaps she thought she could cope with the memories that now seem to be overwhelming her. She's hiding something, I'm sure of it. She certainly didn't like me asking questions about that night. Even with alcohol surging through her bloodstream, she wasn't prepared to divulge much about the past.

As I stare out of the window overlooking the courtyard, a flicker of movement catches my eye. A hunched figure is creeping out of the building.

Lloyd Palmer.

I pull on my navy cagoule and grab my key card, hotel keys and phone to head downstairs.

Creeping along the perimeter of the courtyard garden, careful not to crunch the gravel, I follow the journalist in the distance. A breeze flares up, and droplets of rain splash along my sleeves. I zip up my cagoule until the collar nestles tightly around my neck. My damp trousers cling to my legs.

My muscles flinch at every sound – scuttling noises, rustling leaves, hooting owls – and goosebumps prickle along my arms. I'm shivering with the cold and the damp rather than fear, despite drawing my cagoule hood over my head to keep the pounding rain off my face. Static crackles in my ears. After all these years in Spain, I have forgotten how wet British summers can be.

When Lloyd Palmer stops at B wing, I skulk into the shadows of the gazebo, hiding behind the canvas, peering around the side. He rattles the main doors. When they don't open, he rattles them again. Why would he think that B wing is open tonight?

Eventually he gives up and turns towards me. I pull back and freeze, barely taking a breath until he walks past, and watch him head back towards the main building. Once he's inside, I need to find out what he's up to. No one should be going into B wing tonight – certainly none of the guests.

As I take a step forwards, a flicker of light on the first floor of B wing catches the corner of my eye. It flits from window to window like a will-o'-the-wisp, bobbing high then low against the dark backdrop until it fades away. A torch? A flame? Just a trick of the light, maybe, or perhaps the reflection of lightning in the distance. Yet the fluttering sensations in my gut tell me it wasn't.

Has Lloyd Palmer arranged to meet someone inside B wing tonight? But why not speak to them in the daylight at a respectable hour? Unless this is someone who shouldn't be at the hotel this weekend – someone who doesn't want to be seen.

My heart pounds as my mind drifts back to my museum visit and those wispy pigeon feathers on the floor. Was someone inside there with me? Perhaps it was one of the true-crime fanatics searching for clues.

If I can find my way into B wing, who – or what – might be lurking in its shadows? The building is claimed to be haunted by the spirits of women and children who were once crammed into lice-infested cells. The prison was well known for its hangings, and it's believed that the burials took place within these grounds.

During the eighties and nineties, several prisoners killed themselves in their cells, some through drug overdoses and others by whatever means they could find. Perhaps they were victimised by staff and other prisoners, or perhaps they preferred to have no life at all rather than the one they imagined ahead of them.

Inmates reported eerie happenings at night, hearing mysterious footsteps and chilling cries, even glimpsing the ghost of a young boy dressed in rags.

I look up at the window and shake my head in despair. My imagination is taking over. There are no ghosts – they don't exist. But I do need to find out who Lloyd Palmer was supposed to be meeting in B wing. After all, I'm the hotel manager in charge of these premises – and Derek expects me to do my job properly and efficiently. I do, too.

First, I need to work out where this person managed to get into the building. As the journalist has demonstrated, it can't have been through the main doors.

I follow the contour of the building to the right, stopping at each entrance and trying to open them, until I reach an unlocked gate partially hidden by a large jasmine bush, facing the kitchen garden. Its old hinges creak and drag as I nudge the heavy gate towards me. *Bingo*. Once it swings open wide enough, I sneak in through the gap.

I take my phone out from my cagoule pocket and switch on the torch. Dust motes dance in the beam ahead of me like tiny sprites guiding my way as I tiptoe forwards and drag the gate closed.

B wing's prison landing stretches out in front of me. Its wrought-iron staircases are dulled and rusting: poor relatives of their polished counterparts in A wing. My phone torch casts long flickering beams and shadows along once-white walls that are now flaking and yellow. An Emergency Exit sign above me is spattered with dark patches of mould and mildew.

I was under the impression that B wing had been cleaned and sanitised when the prison closed, but perhaps this is how any building would look after twenty years of abandonment.

The air inside feels cold and damp, with a musky odour mixed with a faint scent of bleach. Clumps of weeds grow through tiny cracks in the floor, sprinkled with mouse droppings like small black rice grains. Over the years, Derek has preserved the building by carrying out only essential repairs, too tight-fisted for anything below the surface, other than spraying with disinfectant before tomorrow's visit with our journalist guests.

I direct the light beam upwards, towards the central atrium. The glass roof looms high above me, with remnants of suicide netting still strung tightly across the gaps between the landings. Rain patters against the panes of glass, and lightning flashes in the distance.

As my footsteps echo over the rickety walkway, my skin crawls with unease. Whoever is in here will now realise they're not alone. How will they respond when they discover I'm not Lloyd Palmer?

I'm tempted to turn back and return to my cosy room, even if I can't get a decent night's sleep. The more I delve deeper into the past this weekend, the more I realise I'm not quite as brave as I hoped I would be. Not a detective or an explorer, not even a true-crime enthusiast – I am just a middle-aged, probably perimenopausal, hotel manager totally out of my depth, but I once made a promise that I need to keep.

Clenching my phone tightly, I realise what this also means. Whoever is in here must have keys to this building, fitting into locks that haven't been used for two decades. Could this be a former prison officer – or even a former prison governor? Did Fiona arrange to speak to Lloyd Palmer tonight away from the other guests?

Something rustles further ahead. I shine my phone torch in the direction of the noise, then trail it back towards me. There's no sign of life, but large shoeprints lead towards the staircase. Someone has definitely been in here this evening – and recently. They're not a figment of my imagination.

Forcing myself to walk on, I then pause again as the rustling returns, and with a shaky hand direct my torch beam towards the base of the staircase. A sour taste spills into my mouth. A large grey rat is snuffling around a scrap of paper next to the bottom step. The grimy rodent stares in my direction, its eyes fixed on mine, before scarpering off.

I breathe a sigh of relief, for the monsters of my imagination have been replaced by creatures of flesh and blood.

I walk up the staircase towards the front of the building where I saw that light from outside. The air seems even cooler here. A faint smoky odour lingers in the air, and that rustling sound starts up again. I swallow back the urge to scream. Ghosts don't exist, I know they can't. Nate and I discussed so many times about whether I would feel him once he was gone. I have had no indication that he is contacting me from the other side. No voice begging me to take care of Ellie and keep the vow I made – just a smattering of memories ingrained in my head and my heart.

My torch beam reveals a series of faded blue doors, as I walk down one narrow corridor, then another. Each Panbrook prison wing was designated its own colour: A wing was always green, B wing blue, and C wing was red.

None of the doors are locked, so I peer inside each dilapidated cell, trailing my torch beam around. Cobwebs cling to rotting window frames, and an occasional scrap of rug lies on a grimy floor. Walls are dotted with fragments of faded pictures featuring Page Three girls. Metal bed frames are propped up against the sides of the cells, alongside empty shelving units, broken sinks and toilets. I shiver as I try to imagine being locked inside such a tiny room for up to twenty-three hours a day.

A pattering sound comes from a cell further up the row. If there are any shoeprints up here, I can't see them as the floor is too filthy. I walk slowly along the landing, my heart thumping, until I reach the mould-spattered door. The cell number is still visible: Cell 135. Inside, rain is pounding against the window-pane and pouring in through a crack in the grubby glass.

This was Jonathan Roach's cell, where his life ended, where he took his final breaths. In the summer of 1999, the five men's cells were emptied once the forensic teams left the building. Their furniture and their belongings were all considered to be part of a crime scene that the police were struggling to fathom out.

Except this cell isn't currently empty.

A solitary object lies on the floor: a brown cardboard box, around the size of a shoebox, with 'OPEN ME' written in black ink on the lid.

I reach into my cagoule pocket and pull out fresh gloves – as my mother always told me, you never know when you'll need them. Inching closer to the box, I kneel down and whip off the lid with trembling hands. An intense metallic odour wafts in my direction, and an icy finger trails down my spine.

Inside the box is a dead pigeon cradled within an open plastic bag. Congealed blood has spattered over the edges, and its putrid guts are spilling out.

I slam the box lid down and lean backwards. My hands itch as I recall those four words I scrubbed off the lift wall, *Anna Kendall was guilty,* and the grey feathers on the carpet outside Lloyd Palmer's room.

Someone is playing games this weekend. But who – and why?

19

MADDIE

NOW

FRIDAY
11.30 p.m.

A flash of lightning rips through the night sky, illuminating my surroundings, and more rain pours in through the crack in the glass, pooling on the floor.

As I pull my cagoule around me, my nose wrinkles at the faint rancid odour hovering in the air. I can't leave this pigeon here to rot, not when our guests will be visiting this building tomorrow. When I pick up the box, a small wad of folded papers peeps out from beside the plastic bag. I lay the package down and pull them out. The papers have been placed inside carefully to avoid any splashes of blood. Unfolding them reveals a newspaper cutting and a passport-sized photograph of a woman with long blonde curls.

I focus my torch beam on the newspaper first, expecting it to be faded and yellow, a remnant of the prison's past, yet it is crisp and cream, dated just a few years ago. Next, I shine the torch beam on the photograph.

'Anna.' I stare into her familiar blue eyes as I whisper her name. 'If only you were here to tell your story. If only you could tell me who—'

Thunder booms outside, followed closely by more flashes of lightning strobing the cell, as though I'm trapped in an old black-and-white horror movie. I clench the small photograph tightly, the four sharp corners digging into my hand.

A creak comes from the landing above me.

I jerk upright. 'Anna?' Then I shake my head at my stupidity, tension throbbing in my ears. Whoever has been in here tonight certainly won't be Anna.

Doors creak, and rusting hinges squeak. This is just the storm whipping up outside, I remind myself; rain slamming against the roof and the windows, rather than the emotions of lost souls entrenched in the fabric of this building.

Yet my heart hammers in my chest and I'm struggling to swallow. I can't inhale enough air into my lungs and feel like I'm going to pass out.

I need to get out of here.

I pull off my gloves and shove them into the cardboard box, then stuff the newspaper cutting and photograph into my back trouser pocket. Holding the box under my arm, I tiptoe back through the maze of silent corridors and lifeless cells, through the open security doors, until I reach the main prison landing.

The air is now brimming with a faint woody scent, mixed with jasmine and lavender. Air must be seeping in from the grounds and gardens outside. As I trail the torch beam over the floor to confirm my path is clear, I discover a set of footprints heading in the direction of the open gate. My skin feels clammy, and a cold sweat trickles down my back.

I creep to the gateway and peer across the courtyard garden. All I can see are puddles glistening in the moonlight.

I pull the small gate shut behind me and stroll across the courtyard, no longer sticking to the shadows. My nose twitches at the sweet odour of the summer downpour that's dwindling to drizzle. Something else I have forgotten – and missed – during my two decades living in the Spanish heat. I shove the box containing the pigeon into the rubbish bins as I pass them.

On A wing's ground-floor landing, damp footsteps trail across the polished floor to the emergency exit and fade away at the base of the staircase.

I lean against the nearest wall to regain my breath. As my heart rate slows, I shove my fingers into my back pocket, feeling the newspaper cutting and photograph inside it. Proof that tonight's events really happened, that I haven't been hallucinating.

Someone left these items for Lloyd Palmer. But if they have proof of Anna's innocence or guilt, why not just hand it to him, rather than leave sinister gifts?

I visit the nearest restroom to wash my hands. Then I hang my rain-drenched cagoule on the peg behind my office door so it can dry by the morning.

As I walk towards the lift, footsteps sound above me. I hide in the shadows and look up.

A small, stumbling figure is wandering along the walkway.

'Should ... have ... back here.' Their slurred words fade in and out as they turn around, as if to face someone, and their voice gets louder. 'I've ... quiet ... time.'

I flinch at a clap of thunder, just as someone tumbles over the top of the safety screen.

20

MADDIE

NOW

FRIDAY
11.55 p.m.

Fiona's right leg is bent at an unnatural angle and her eyes are closed. Her cream, satin pyjamas are streaked with blood, which is weeping slowly from a large cut on her elbow, creating a red patch on a white carpet stripe.

I crouch down beside her and gag at the odour of stale alcohol. 'Fiona?'

Her eyes flicker, followed by a faint groan.

'Ms Batten?' I jump at the deep shout from above me, and look up.

Lloyd Palmer is peering over the handrail, dressed casually in grey joggers and a navy hoodie. 'Don't move her. I'm coming down.'

The lift behind me whirrs and creaks, then whirrs again.

I pull out my phone and call an ambulance. Then I call Derek.

'What?' His voice sounds groggy, his tone abrupt. Well, he wanted this to be a weekend to remember – just be careful what you wish for.

'Derek ... you need to come downstairs to the ground floor. I've already called an ambulance.'

'Ambulance?'

'Yes, and you'd better get Dr Land.'

Lloyd Palmer is leaning against the wall by the lifts, next to a small crowd of guests in various states of undress. His intense, dark eyes are watching the events unfolding in front of him, making mental notes for the update of his book, no doubt. Every so often, his eyes flicker in my direction and he gives me a reassuring smile.

The journalist arrived down here shortly after I called Derek. 'I heard a scream.' He sounded genuinely concerned. 'Is she—?'

'I've called an ambulance.' I stared at his dry, white trainers. 'You weren't with her just now?'

He narrowed his eyes. 'Why would I be? I was in my room.'

Looking at him now, do I believe him? He was supposed to be in B wing tonight to find that pigeon with the newspaper cutting and photograph. I saw him come back into this building, but that doesn't mean he returned to his room. Was he the person Fiona was shouting at before she fell? Perhaps she left the package for him to find and then realised it was me instead. If so, this means she has a set of old prison keys. If not, this means someone else does.

Fear stabs at my chest as I lean against the wall to steady myself.

Dr Land is crouching down with his hand curled firmly around Fiona's wrist. A large doctor's bag, with scuffs and scratches marking the brown leather, sits beside him. His long navy T-shirt is scrunched up over checked cotton pyjama bottoms as, like everyone else, he has dressed in a hurry, pulled from the depths of slumber.

Rosalie hovers over him, her cream blouse looking out of place over a pair of baggy shorts. 'Have you checked her blood pressure? And what about her breathing?'

Dr Land scowls at the interruption. 'You can see she's still breathing, and I don't have the right equipment here to do a full assessment. Let's wait until the ambulance arrives.'

Pete is inspecting the top of the staircase with his back to us, still wearing his cap and a long-sleeved shirt. There's no sign of Thomas – maybe without his hearing aids he can't hear the commotion. No sign of Stella either.

When everyone sees the ambulance crew arriving, with Derek leading the way, they part down the centre like a split-ting of the Red Sea. Bryan grabs his medical bag and stands up to speak to the leading paramedic – an Asian woman with her black hair scraped into a ponytail. The second paramedic, a young man with large plastic glasses, bends down to take Bryan's place.

Now that the main drama is over, some of the onlookers stroll over to the lift and press the buttons to return to their rooms.

Lloyd Palmer wanders over to me, reaches inside his hoodie pocket and brings out a small box of sweets. He raises it towards me and flips the lid. 'Mint? Might help with the shock of it all.'

I nod slowly and unfurl my hand. He drops a small, white sweet into my palm, glancing around as though he is dealing drugs.

As I slip the mint into my mouth, I silently will the jour-nalist to walk away, but instead he hovers just out of reach.

I turn to Bryan. 'How's Fiona doing?'

'It doesn't look great, though it's hard to tell. I suspect she's broken her hip for starters, and there must be some internal damage. Most prisoners died if they fell from a landing, so it's a miracle she survived, although it was only one floor fortunately. It will be a difficult night for her.' The doctor gives a slow shake of his head, his lips thin with disapproval. 'And she still reeks of booze, even after all these years.'

Fiona is mumbling to herself while the male paramedic measures her blood pressure and listens to her chest with his stethoscope. His partner speaks to Rosalie, who straightens her blouse and tiptoes carefully over the carpet as though she's afraid to wake the dead.

'Madeleine?' Rosalie says my name softly. 'Apparently Fiona is asking for you. Are you up to going over?'

'Yes, I'm fine.'

The male paramedic moves away when I crouch down beside the ex-prison governor and take her cold, pale hand in mine.

'Fiona?'

'Closer-come.' As she slurs her words, her unfocused eyes flicker around the hotel staff and guests. 'Pops...'

'Pops?'

'He...' She lowers her eyelids as a grimace of pain passes across her face.

The paramedic returns. 'We need to take her now.'

21

MADDIE

NOW

SATURDAY
1.00 a.m.

Derek claps his hands. 'Can I have your attention? Everyone ... please...'

After the paramedics took Fiona away to Hertsfield General Hospital, my boss insisted on gathering in the staff room for a briefing with his senior team. There are only five of us in here, but the way Derek raises his voice, you would think we were an army.

'Obviously we haven't been able to keep this from the guests.' Derek frowns and rubs his forehead. 'It wasn't what you would call a discreet incident. But we must carry on with the rest of the weekend as planned.'

I blink back the tears that have been brimming ever since I watched Fiona fall. Stella has wrapped a blanket around my shoulders, the kindest gesture I have ever known her to make. She didn't look too happy earlier when I knocked on her door to wake her up – Housekeeping needs to clean the landing before the morning – but she's now chatting quietly to Pete.

Derek may be able to ignore what has happened, but I haven't stopped shaking. Right now, it feels as though I may never be able to stop, unable to wipe the image of Fiona's harrowed face from my mind.

I have been in charge of thousands of people in hotels over the years, and no one has ever been seriously injured on my watch. A few cuts and bruises, heatstroke, suspected heart attacks and asthma attacks ... but nothing like this.

I think back to when I saw Fiona last, clutching that wine bottle and pouring yet another glass. How much did she drink after I left her room? And, more importantly, why did she leave it? I certainly hadn't warmed to her, yet somehow I still feel responsible for tonight's events.

Derek claps his hands again. 'Just to reiterate, the paramedics confirmed that it was an unfortunate accident so there's no need to call the police.'

'An accident?' The memory of Fiona's words throbs in my ears. 'But—'

Derek holds his palm up to silence me. 'Fiona Trayton had been drinking heavily, we all witnessed that in the bar.'

His eyes fix on mine, accusingly, as if I forced her to take that wine bottle back to her room. Perhaps as hotel manager I shouldn't have encouraged her to keep drinking, but Fiona didn't seem to be someone who would appreciate an intervention, any more than my boss would.

'And Madeleine, you've already said you didn't see anything before she fell.'

'I didn't see anything definite, but I thought she was talking to someone.'

'Or just mumbling incoherently, Madeleine?'

I understand why Derek doesn't want the police involved. If the press learn about Fiona's fall, this weekend will generate publicity of the unwanted variety. But shouldn't we make sure she wasn't pushed?

'Maybe this *is* a police matter.' Pete nods at me, as if he can read my thoughts. 'Not easy to get yourself over that safety glass without help – or a push. The glass isn't damaged in any way.'

Derek glares at him. 'But Madeleine didn't see any signs of help, and it's not impossible, especially if alcohol had lowered her inhibitions. Men threw themselves off the landings all the time when this place was used as a prison, Dr Land told me. I bet Ms Trayton saw it happen many times, too.'

Pete looks like he wants to say something else, but Stella nudges him into silence. We all know that once Derek has made a decision, it's impossible to change it.

When we stand up to leave the room, Derek grabs my arm.

'Oh, and Madeleine ... please remember to chase that guest who hasn't arrived. I expect Oliver Hodgson to be here at lunch tomorrow, or we'll be sending him the bill.'

Gazing at a bookcase in The Lock-Up, I gulp down the ice-cold orange juice. I can't face any alcohol, but I also can't face going to bed. I feel steadier, but my mind is still too active after tonight's events.

My copy of *Panbrook Prisongate* lies on the bar in front of me. *Pops.* What was Fiona trying to say? Someone's name, maybe, but I don't recall seeing it anywhere in the prison archives, nor in any news reports, and I can't find it in the journalist's book.

'I hope there's alcohol in that.'

I look up at the source of the voice.

Bryan Land is dressed in the same navy T-shirt as before but now with a pair of beige chinos. 'Where can a hotel guest get a drink at this time of night? I'd have a smoke too, if that was allowed in here.'

'Well, the bar is officially closed, but I'm in charge so you're in luck.' I wriggle off my seat and walk around the back of the counter. 'What can I get you? It's on the house.'

'A whisky would be good. After all the drama.'

I grab the nearest whisky bottle, pour him a shot and nudge the glass along the bar towards him. 'I assume you saw a lot of drama here over the years. You and Fiona used to work together, so that can't have been easy to see tonight.'

The doctor grimaces as he picks up his drink. 'I haven't seen her for twenty years. We weren't what you would call friends – colleagues, maybe – but she was good at her job. Couldn't fault her over that.' He slugs the whisky in one go and places his glass back on the counter. 'We all called her Tin Man behind her back. No hint of emotions. She liked her wine in those days too, but no one dared mention it.'

'Dared?'

'None of us wanted to risk losing our jobs.'

I lift the whisky bottle towards him, raising my eyebrows, and refill his glass when he doesn't decline. 'It must feel strange to be back here this weekend, but perhaps no stranger than the weekend you left.'

'I've always wondered whether I could have done something if I had been here that night. Taken charge, rather than leave it to Annie to deal with. Seen what was going on and saved those men's lives. I've always been surprised the gov allowed Eric's leaving do to take place, since we still had prisoners here.'

'Fiona said earlier that no one was expecting trouble that night.'

He raises his eyebrows. 'Really? She was never one to talk.'

'I guess the alcohol must have loosened her tongue.' *Though still not enough.* I pour myself another orange juice.

'She seemed to think Anna was guilty. Do *you* think Anna did it? Do you think the stress of the job finally got to her?'

'The police put the facts together, not me, so it doesn't really matter what I think. But whether they came to the right conclusion...' Bryan stares into his glass, swirling the whisky around inside it. 'Someone killed those men, and the police pointed the finger at Annie. Who could argue with them?'

Her family did, I want to point out. But no one listened then, so why would anyone listen now.

'The police didn't have much evidence. That's all in here.' I point at Lloyd Palmer's book. 'Kellie Wyndham, the other nurse here, she vanished after the murders, didn't she? That's why Lloyd Palmer couldn't interview her. Maybe there's a reason why she's never been found.'

'Kellie was a trusted member of our team.' The doctor stares into his glass, his mouth twisting into a frown. 'I don't know what you're suggesting.'

I swallow sharply. 'I'm not suggesting anything. I just— So okay, let's say Anna didn't kill those men, and nor did Kellie Wyndham ... Who do you think it could have been instead?'

'Sadly it doesn't matter anymore.' He shakes his head slowly. 'Annie overdosed and no one could resuscitate her. The police saw her death as a sign of her guilt and the case was closed.'

'But what about her motive? If she was targeting one of the prisoners, which one do you think it was? You must have known all of them.'

'Of course. I was the SMO.' He picks up *Panbrook Prisongate* and flicks through the pages. 'I don't think there were any prisoners I didn't see from time to time. Of the five, Steven Fisher was the one I saw the most, obviously.'

'Obviously?'

'Steven was always wanting drugs or pain relief.'

'I read he was off drugs when he died.'

Bryan waves the book in the air. 'That's the official line, but you shouldn't believe everything you read. Most of it's trash, but I wouldn't tell the author that.' He smirks, then places the book down and picks up his glass. 'Fingerling, Fisher, was off the harder stuff thanks to our detox programme. But he still smoked cannabis when he could get it. The odd line of coke too. He was increasingly paranoid and unstable.'

'So he was dangerous?'

Bryan gives me a patronising smile. 'All of the five men were dangerous, Ms Batten. That's why they were in here.'

He sounds just like Fiona...

Fiona.

Nausea rises in my throat as I recall her lying there, her silence after she fell as if resigned to her fate. If I had arrived a few minutes earlier, perhaps I could have stopped it. I flinch – these are similar words to the ones Bryan just used about June 1999. A counsellor once told me that it's unhealthy to dwell on the past.

'Even if the men didn't arrive dangerous, being at The Brook was an education,' Bryan continues. 'Though not the education the prison system wanted it to be. I'm sure you're aware that drug addiction was widespread in the prison, and there were always fights and stabbings. Not the safest place for anyone, especially not a young nurse.'

Anna.

'You and Anna were very close, weren't you?' For years, the media speculated over how close they were. The doctor was over twenty years her senior but a good-looking man, even now. 'She had a little girl, didn't she? You must have known her. Lily, was it?'

A smile flickers across his lips. 'No, Lucy. So sweet, so innocent ... Losing her mother at such a young age and in those circumstances, it was just tragic.'

I place the whisky bottle back on the shelf. Even if the doctor wants another drink tonight, after Fiona's incident I won't be encouraging it. 'I assume Lucy went to live with her father after Anna died. Did Anna ever tell you who he was?'

His eyes meet mine. 'Why do you want to know?'

'Just being nosy. Like you, I hope she's happy. That little girl has been in my thoughts ever since. I have a daughter too, of a similar age.' Ellie's face hovers in my vision, bringing a smile to my lips and a sting of tears to my eyes. 'Lloyd Palmer never mentioned Lucy's father in his book. I always wondered if Anna was in a relationship with one of the officers.'

'Annie once told me Lucy was conceived during a one-night stand. She always did love to party.' He rubs his chin. 'It's possible it may have been one of the officers, but she said she didn't know who Lucy's father was.'

'Her arrest must have been a huge shock for you ... for everyone.'

'It was, of course.' He grips his glass. 'She was so young, so fragile ... I felt I needed to protect her at times. From all the danger in here.' His eyes glisten with tears. 'Unpredictable and aggressive patients. Constantly having to watch our backs.'

'But Anna got on well with the prisoners, didn't she? Thomas said they liked her, respected her.'

'They did. Well, most of them.'

'Any prisoners in particular who didn't?'

'Well, there's Fingerling.' He shakes his head slowly. 'She never talked about what happened in the consult room that day. When she had to see him again, give him his meds – a week or so before the men died – I know she felt very uncomfortable.'

I eye the doctor. 'How uncomfortable?'

He exhales slowly, 'Well, according to the police at the time, uncomfortable enough to kill.'

22

ANNA

OCTOBER 1996

'Need your eye on something.' Estie pops her head around the door. Her greying brown curls are tied back into a ponytail, exposing her plump cheeks.

Estie's one of the few older female officers I respect and like. She cares about the patients but also doesn't take any nonsense, and she's good company on a night out. Right now, though, she's staring at me like I've grown a unicorn horn. She raises her eyebrows and tries not to laugh.

'I've got a beastly headache, okay?' I take the wad of damp, blue tissue paper off my forehead and throw it in the bin.

Estie's gaze flickers around the consult room. 'Was Pills in here again this morning? Heard he'd bashed his foot with a spade this time. Talk about accident-prone. Maybe you need to offer him a Healthcare season ticket.'

I massage the sides of my forehead with the pads of my fingers. The pain finally seems to be easing, but now I feel a bit sick. Kellie reckons I ate a dodgy kebab last night. Bryan says it was the cheesy pop music at the club I went to with some old hospital workmates. At least the cold compress seemed to be helping.

Estie gives me a sympathetic smile. 'Look, I know Pills wants to transfer to Healthcare from gardening. He doesn't stop talking about it. If he's driving you crazy with all his pestering, send him to Bryan or Kellie in future. You know what he's like. Eye for the ladies, that one. And we need to keep him away from temptation – all these medicines.'

She's right. Pills was a pharmacist in another life. A dodgy one, of course – otherwise he wouldn't be inside. He thinks his professional skills will be more useful in the clinic. But him working in here would be far too dangerous.

'It's fine. I can handle William Owen. So what do you need me for?'

'Not what – who.' She presses her lips together and lowers her voice. 'It's Fingerling.'

Bloody hell, this is all I need today. Steven Fisher's a smackhead. He's twitchy and unpredictable, constantly on report. Bryan's the only one who can keep him stable.

'Bring him to the clinic later. Bryan'll be back then. He's on cell checks in C wing right now.' I know dealing with difficult prisoners is part of my job, but it doesn't mean I have to like it. 'Bryan always gets Fisher to behave by bribing him with a sugar packet. They're much sweeter than the ones on the canteen list, apparently, but I don't have any in here right now.'

'Sorry, Anna, but it can't wait. Fisher's cut himself. Nothing too bad but it may need stitching.' She rubs her chin with her finger, like she's wiping away a smudge of dirt. 'He was a little riled up earlier but seems calmer. Eric's with him.'

My forehead throbs again. Now I wish I hadn't thrown away my makeshift compress. It's never easy to deal with smackheads. They can't think clearly, you can't trust a word they say, and they're always so persistent.

'Okay.' I let out an irritated sigh. 'I'll see him. Just give me a minute to get ready.'

When Estie brings Fisher in, he's rocking slowly from side to side and muttering to himself. His cheeks are red, and his eyes are like pinpricks. So much for prison detox. He always has enough smack to give him an intense high, but it's never enough to kill him. His left arm's dripping with blood just below the wrist from a jagged line on his skin.

'How'd he get that?'

Estie inhales deeply in disapproval. 'They're looking into it. No sign of a fight. He's calm now so shouldn't be any trouble. Cuff him though?'

'No, it'll aggravate the wound. And I'll find it harder to deal with.' *But the sooner he's out of here, the better.*

Estie stands next to Fisher, gripping his other arm tightly, while I grab a swab and a bottle of disinfectant from the small storage unit near the door.

'Right, Fisher, this may sting, but sit still in the chair and I'll just—'

'Nah!' He leaps forwards, shoves Estie into the corridor and slams the door shut behind her. Then he drags the cupboard across the door to block it off.

What the hell?

My heart's thumping rapidly. I back away from him until my bum rests against the desk.

Annie, concentrate. Think... I take a deep breath. *You need to talk him down.*

'Fisher, what are you doing?' I try to keep my voice low and steady.

Keep facing him. Get yourself nearer the door.

'I want to see the vet! NOW!' His eyes flash with fury as he throws the disinfectant across the room. The bottle smashes against the sink, pieces of glass and droplets of liquid flying everywhere.

'Whatever the problem is, we can talk about it. That's what I'm here for.'

'Fisher ... open this NOW! FISHER!' Estie thumps on the door and pushes against it but it doesn't budge. 'Code Blue in Healthcare.' Her radio crackles with each of her words.

Footsteps running. Voices shouting. It's a Code Blue panic, and I'm right at the heart of it. Nausea bubbles in my throat.

Estie bangs on the door again. 'Fingerling ... Fisher ... They'll send you to seg for this. OPEN. THIS. DOOR. NOW.'

'NAH. Don't-give-no-FUCK.' He's slurring his words. Must have been a whopper of a dose this morning. 'Where is he? WANT. MY. JACKS.'

'Dr Land's not here, as you can see.' I inch towards the back of the room. 'He's out on C wing – you'll have to come back later.'

'WANT. MY. JACKS. Vet always has 'em ready. Said he would.'

'You had your meds this morning.'

He was off his head then, too, but quieter ... calmer. What's set him off? Could he have been planning this? Is he capable?

As his gaze drifts towards an empty medical bag on the floor, I grab a pen from my desk and shove it in my pocket. 'All of the meds you get are logged. Dr Land doesn't give you any more than you need.'

'WANT. MY. JACKS.' Fingerling puts his hand down his trousers and pulls out a toothbrush.

My head throbs again and my heart beats rapidly. So he *has* been planning this.

He steps forwards and waggles the toothbrush in front of him. The end is sharp and pointed and glistening with blood.

I glance at the jagged cut in his arm, reach into my pocket and grip the pen tightly. Not just for comfort – for power. If he goes for me, I'm ready.

He's not much taller than me, but his bulging biceps flex and glisten under the harsh lighting. Heroin hasn't deprived him of muscle strength – yet.

'Don't wanna hurt you, Nurse. Just want my FUCKIN' JACKS.' He waves his hands in the air. 'Need them ... NOW.'

'I don't have any drugs, not the ones you want.' My eyes sting, and my tummy churns.

Annie, get a grip. Take back control.

'Not a divvy. I know you're stallin'. What 'bout in there.' He points at the cupboard where we keep all the supplies, the unit he pushed against the door.

'I don't have the keys.' The weight of my lie rests on the belt around my waist. I pull down the hem of my jumper to cover them.

Fisher thumps on the wall next to him, then kicks the cupboard with his trainers. He keeps kicking it until the wood begins to splinter. He sticks the toothbrush horizontally in his mouth, gripping it in place with his rotting teeth, then crouches down and rips the door apart with his bare hands. Blood's no longer just dripping down his arm, but from his fingers too – bright red smears along the pale wood and down his blue-and-white striped shirt.

He yanks out some of the sundries – gauze and pads, anti-septics and wipes – and throws them around like a toddler having a tantrum. I hold my breath as he clutches some syringes and stares at them, then shakes them, holds them up to the light.

'FUCKIN' EMPTY.' He grabs the medical bag and shoves it at me. 'GO ON! FIND. MY. JACKS.'

'This bag's empty too, Fisher. But maybe I can find something for you down here. You'll just have to be patient.'

I put my pen back into my pocket, bend down and rummage through the pile, then through another, so it looks like I'm doing something useful. I'm facing him at all times, remembering my training. I need to keep him calm until the cavalry arrives.

He moves onto the next cupboard, following the same routine. Kick. Kick. Rip the wood apart. Pull out the supplies. Order me to check through them. He even shakes Bryan's posh coffee jar and Kellie's pack of mixed herbal teas.

'Fisher, let Nurse Kendall go.' Bryan's voice. 'You don't want to hurt her. You know she's there to help you. You like Nurse Kendall, remember?'

Thank God. Let's hope he can talk him down.

I try to stand up but Fisher shoves me back.

As he leans in towards me, his sour breath makes me gag. 'NEED. MY. JACKS.' He waves the toothbrush in the air again, this time closer to my face.

I press my hand against my belly and take slow, deep breaths, gripping the pen in my other hand. How far will he make me go?

'You'll get them,' Bryan shouts through the door. 'I don't have any ready, but we'll sort it out. Let Nurse Kendall go.'

'NAH!'

I hold the pen in front of me where Fingerling can see it shaking in my fist. I don't want to have to use it. I'm a nurse – I shouldn't need to stab my patients. But if he gets any closer...

Three sharp bangs on the door and it slams open. Two officers in riot gear grab Fingerling and drag him away from me, then push him face down on the floor. Another officer leads me around him and out of the room.

As soon I'm in the corridor, I can't hold back any longer. Salty tears flow down my cheeks.

Bryan wraps his arms around me. 'You're safe now, Annie. You're safe.'

'You alright? Heard there was trouble with Fisher. That little shit.'

I jump at the deep voice and look up.

Sweat drips down his front, dampening his blue-and-white shirt. He turns around, revealing the cross tattoo at the base of his spine, and pulls some lavender spikes off the nearest shrub. 'Meant to be good for stress.'

My fingers tingle in the autumn sunshine as he hands over the soft, purple buds. I hold them under my nose and inhale. The scent feels comforting, calming. As I lean against the back of the bench, my throbbing headache begins to ease.

'See, this is another reason why I should be in Healthcare.' He curls his hand into a fist and thumps his knuckles into his other palm. 'I'd be more than happy to—'

'Oye, Pills, get on with your work.' Estie gives him a nudge to move out the way. 'Stop hassling Nurse Kendall. I heard you were in there again this morning. Foot all better now, is it?'

After I was debriefed, Estie brought me out to the garden. She wanted to take me to one of the private offices but I needed some fresh air. And being in this area of the prison, surrounded by the beauty of nature, always makes me feel more relaxed. Since then, Estie's been standing next to me like my personal bodyguard.

Some of the prisoners have been hovering a bit too close, to be fair. I'd like to think a few of them care, but most just want excitement and gossip.

'You alright, Miss?' Ahmed this time. He comes across as tough, but I've also seen his softer side. Rumour has it he's in here for stabbing someone in a club, though he denies it, of course. They all do, don't they? Bryan's right – you can't always tell. No one's going to admit to the sordid truth. That they're a killer, a murderer, a conman, a drug dealer, a common thief...

'Get on with your work, Razorhead.' When Estie takes a step towards him, Ahmed picks up a pair of secateurs to prune the climbing roses. He cuts back the dead stems and ties the longer shoots to the trellis behind them, just as I taught him.

This is the only area of The Brook where prisoners have access to potentially deadly weapons. So each bloke is vetted carefully before they're given this job. Ahmed seems to be a natural.

'Not surprised you spend so much time out here. It's got a great view.' Estie nudges me as she eyes the prisoners. 'All this wildlife.'

I can't help but laugh, despite the rumblings in my tummy.

Bryan strides over, holding his medical bag, and hands me a plastic cup of water. 'Are you sure you're okay? That little shit—'

'Bryan, I'm fine.'

'Well, you don't look fine. You're trembling, and you're as pale as a ghost. And why are you out here anyway?'

He shakes his head at one of the prisoners who has inched a little closer and is flexing his fingers like he wants to say something.

'Not now.' Bryan scowls. 'This isn't a bloody stage show.'

The prisoner jiggles on his feet – probably one of the smackheads. 'Need to see you about—'

'Put a note in for sick parade tomorrow. I'll deal with it then.' Bryan sits down next to me. 'We need to get you out of here, Annie. Ready?'

'I'm fine.' I roll my eyes at him. 'I'll just go back to Health-care. I don't need any fuss. I need to finish typing up your notes, and then clinic, and—'

'You're in no fit state to work. Kellie's told me to get you home and she'll take over. My notes can wait.'

I shiver in a sudden gust of wind, and saliva drains from

my mouth. Those bloodshot eyes leering at mine. The sharpened toothbrush in his fist. That was a close call. What if he...?

I raise the plastic cup to my lips and gulp down some water. 'Where's Fisher now? Why was he asking for jacks? We don't keep drugs in Healthcare – not the type he was looking for.'

Estie rests her warm hand on my shoulder and gives a gentle squeeze. 'Fisher's confused as usual. He's gone to seg on a GOAD charge. You're safe.'

I rub my forehead with my shaky hand. I need to stop thinking about it. About him.

Bryan stands up and picks up his medical bag. 'Right, you're going to your dad's place. It's all arranged.'

'You called my dad?'

'Yes – and no arguments.'

'But—' I double over and throw up on the gravel.

I'm sitting on my old bed, hugging a hot water bottle.

'Annie, can I get you anything.' Dad hovers next to me, his forehead creasing with worry.

He's wearing the yellow jumper I bought him for his birthday. He says it reminds him of sunshine and sunflowers. It reminds me of all that too – and Mum. Her gardening tools are still lying in the shed, now covered in cobwebs and dust.

He's not left me alone for more than one minute since I arrived here – three hours ago. 'I can whip you up an omelette. Or a cheese-and-pickle sarnie. Or how about a choc chip muffin – your favourite? I bought those fresh today.'

I stifle a yawn. 'To be honest, I just want to get some sleep. It's been a long day.'

'Of course, love, you need your rest.' Dad puts his arm around me and gives me a gentle squeeze. 'I spoke to Doc

Singer earlier. She said she can prescribe something if you can't sleep. I'll be out here if you need me.'

When he leaves the room, he keeps my door open just a crack. I feel like I'm twelve again and on my sick bed with flu. Except flu would be easier to deal with.

I'm sure I'll be fine. These things happen, I know they do. I knew it when I took the job. And Fingerling's a nothing, a nobody. He's not worth my thoughts. I've other things to think about and concentrate on now.

A sour taste swirls in my mouth, and an ache radiates from the centre of my forehead. I know it's not from a dodgy kebab or banging club music.

I lean over and nudge my bedroom door shut, then reach down and open my bag. I pull out the wand with the two thin blue lines. The test I did in The Brook's staff loo this morning, just before Estie and Fisher turned up.

I press my hand against my belly and imagine a fluttering of life inside it.

'It's okay, he didn't hurt us,' I whisper. 'No one will. Ever.'

Excerpts from the 'Meet victim #3 – Steven "Fingerling" Fisher' chapter in *Panbrook Prisongate* by Lloyd Palmer – published by Spotlight Books, August 2009

"Mam always said Stevie were a mistake. Used to bash us all, but he got it worst, being the smallest. The runt, she called him. Maybe she bashed his brains out – would explain why he turned into such a little shit. Though maybe he were just born that way, like his dad who were always inside."

— BELINDA MARSONS, STEVEN'S ELDEST HALF-SISTER

"Steven was trouble soon as he could walk. When he was eight, he nicked ciggies from behind my shop counter when I was out the back. Another customer spotted him. I wouldn't take no shit so called the cops. He was kicked out of school for smoking weed, but he were never there anyway. Always stoned and swearing on the high street."

— ALISHA REDDY, ONE OF STEVEN'S FORMER NEIGHBOURS

"Steven Fisher was convicted of drug offences as a teenager. He was already addicted to cannabis when he arrived at HMP Panbrook, but was soon introduced to cocaine and heroin by other inmates. He was often sent to the segregation unit, 'seg', after clashes with officers.

He was usually watched very carefully and kept cuffed, except that one time in Healthcare."

— **FIONA TRAYTON, FORMER PANBROOK PRISON GOVERNOR**

"Fingerling was a right bugger. Okay, let's call him a little shit. He was a menace. Always badgering me for methadone. I assume you know what happened to Anna in Healthcare that time? I always wondered if she was taking revenge on Fingerling that night – if she did it, of course. I still don't believe it."

— **DR BRYAN LAND, FORMER PANBROOK PRISON DOCTOR**

24

MADDIE

NOW

SATURDAY
9.30 a.m.

Last night's pounding rain is just a distant memory shimmering in the few remaining puddles in the courtyard garden. A relief for all of us hotel employees, as we will be holding tonight's celebrations out here. The gazebo survived the heavy downpour, astonishingly, and its canopy is being decorated from midday. Although we still have The Lock-Up on standby, just in case the weather takes another turn for the worse – the pitfalls of relying on British summer weather.

I shove my key into the rusty lock of the museum and try to turn it, but the mechanism doesn't respond. Pushing open the door, I'm greeted by muffled conversation.

'Hello?'

'In here.' A deep voice comes from the next room.

I walk through the narrow doorway into Room Two where Mr Palmer is sitting on a plastic chair next to Isaac

Cane, resting a large book on an open glass display cabinet. One of the old prison ledgers dating back to the early nineteenth century.

He looks up as I enter, pushing his glasses further up his nose.

'How did you get in?' I look around for Derek. 'Please be careful with the records.' I scrunch up my nose when he turns a page rather too quickly for my liking.

'I let him in,' Rosalie strolls out of Room Three, 'on Derek's orders. I knocked on your door this morning several times. Decided not to wake you, after what happened last night.'

Pity flares in her eyes as warmth diffuses through my cheeks. 'I'm fine.'

Despite planning to stay awake all night, I flicked through some more of Lloyd Palmer's book, then fell asleep on the bed, dreaming of Anna Kendall and Bryan Land and inmates cutting their wrists with pointed toothbrush ends.

By the time I woke up, it was already seven o'clock, much later than I had intended. My damp pyjamas were sticking to my flushed skin, and my shoulders ached. I took a quick shower and chose a knee-length navy dress from my wardrobe and a matching chiffon scarf, clipping my medicines pouch around my waist as usual. Then I grabbed a coffee and a slice of toast in The Lock-Up kitchen.

During my walk over to the museum, I called the hospital to ask about Fiona. The nursing staff wouldn't provide much information as I'm not a family member, but they said that her condition remains critical. Judging by the nurse's serious tone, it doesn't sound promising.

I also left another message for Mr Hodgson, with a reminder that we are expecting him by lunchtime. I asked him to confirm if, or when, he intends to arrive, and included Derek's threat to send him the weekend bill. My boss certainly doesn't like tardiness, but his obsessive preoccupation with this missing lottery winner is wasting my time.

I point at the ledger in Mr Palmer's hands. 'You do know that's not related to the Anna Kendall case.'

'I'm aware, yes ... but it *is* interesting to understand the history of the prison.' He closes the book carefully and returns it to the cabinet. 'I assume you've read *everything* in the museum, Ms Batten ... several times, I imagine. My book too. I don't suppose you've found anything I missed the first time?'

I shake my head as despair drums in my stomach. After over two months here, I still haven't found my answers. Though I also feel a little smug that I discovered that box in B wing instead of him. Which reminds me – I need to work out why he was supposed to find that newspaper cutting and photograph.

Rosalie leads the journalist into Room Three like a Pied Piper, with him scurrying behind. I narrow my eyes when he stops beside one of the *Panbrook Prisongate* exhibits.

She unlocks the cabinet and waits while he carefully removes two books, before locking it back up. 'Anything else?'

He flashes Rosalie a smile. 'Not right now, but I'll let you know when I'm ready.' His glance at my face catches the end of my eye-roll, which twists his smile into a broad grin.

'What do you think you'll find in here?' I edge closer. He's pulled out two Healthcare clinic appointment registers and a wad of handwritten patient records. 'Surely you found everything while writing your book.'

'Just taking a fresh look after all these years.' He opens the top book and runs his finger down the page. His finger moves so quickly, I can't work out what he's looking for.

After a few more minutes, I decide to leave them to it. Mr Palmer is taking photographs of the registers and handwritten notes using his phone. Rosalie is peering over his shoulder, asking questions about what he's searching for, having already browsed William Owen's health records.

I'll ask her later if the journalist found anything of interest. Right now, I need to check all of the exhibits and prepare for the presentations before the other guests arrive.

In Room One, I confirm the treadmill and crank are working correctly, oiling the joints and mechanisms, and testing them just to be certain.

The motorless treadmill was specially commissioned by Derek from a bespoke fitness company when he renovated the hotel. The ladder-like machine is positioned at an angle, looking very similar to the treadmills of olden times. You grip its never-ending rungs with your hands as you climb, your feet on the lower rungs. The faster you climb, the faster the rungs move, controlled by a belt you wear around your waist.

I adjust the lighting in Room Two to make it bright enough to read the exhibits but low enough to create a sense of ambience. When these were the punishment cells, this room would have been dark and uninviting, and Derek doesn't want or expect anyone to feel too comfortable in here now.

Peering into each cabinet, I'm relieved to see that everything is still where it should be. Prison-issue bedding lies next to the uniforms of inmates, from grey gym gear to the blue-and-white striped shirts and jeans worn before the prison closed. Plastic bowls and cutlery, tubes of toothpaste used to stick pictures to cell walls, cigarette packets, counselling booklets and sugar sachets, gardening tools, and prison phone cards used as currency or bribery ... all items providing some sense of the former prison life.

At ten-thirty on the dot, the first batch of guests arrive. Rosalie stands at the entrance to welcome them inside and asks each one to write their name in the visitors' book, in keeping with our health and safety regulations.

Soon afterwards, Bryan and Thomas walk in with Derek

and some of the lottery winners. They follow me into Room Two, the room with the largest floor space, where we are holding our short presentation. Once Mr Palmer has joined us, I send Rosalie back into Room Three to make sure all of the archive cabinets have been locked.

I begin my presentation with a potted history of the prison, its gothic architecture and ghostly sightings, all written in advance by our absent museum curator. My voice drops to a whisper while I recount some of the blood-curdling stories from over the years: the prisoners who died here, those who got away, and the ones who are believed to have never left. I explain the background to the exhibits, and point out some of the original features, including the mesh steel windows covered in bars that let insufficient light inside.

'And now we come to the main reason why you're here this weekend. The Panbrook Prison murders. It's time for me to hand you over to our special guest, Lloyd Palmer.'

My throat tightens as the journalist talks through the details of the case, the backgrounds of all five men and Anna Kendall, and the events of that night. After my conversation with the doctor, I wonder about the accuracy of Lloyd Palmer's *Panbook Prisongate* book.

'That evening, each of the five prisoners is believed to have been poisoned by cakes supplied by Anna Kendall, the prison nurse. Her motive is still unclear. And then Anna took her own life while she was on remand.'

The journalist points at the photographs to give the men a face since he can't give them a voice. I imagine all five of them watching, shaking their heads in dismay when he stumbles over some facts, and nodding with relief when he gets others right.

Once he's finished, I encourage questions and ask for expert participation. Thomas gives his personal impressions of all five men, repeating some of what he conveyed at dinner.

Bryan explains that he's happy to speak to anyone afterwards, one to one, if they have questions about general prison life. My jaw twitches with disappointment that Fiona hasn't been able to join us.

Eventually, I invite our guests to peruse the museum exhibits and browse our small shop counter. The doctor makes a beeline for Mr Palmer, and the two of them slope off into the corner of the room.

In Room Three, I find Rosalie reading an exhibit about Jonathan Roach and William Owen. She's still clutching the visitors' book in her hand.

'Did you know the case?' I stand beside her and rub an itch at the back of my neck. 'You can't have been very old at the time.'

She nods slowly, staring at the pictures on the wall. The two men gaze back at us. 'My mum ... she was always talking about it.'

'You lived round here?'

'Not far in those days. But you couldn't miss it anyway.' She points at a display of newspaper cuttings in a black frame and gives a sorrowful laugh. 'It was the only thing people talked about, or it certainly seemed that way.'

I think of the journalist to blame, the man in the other room, who wouldn't let things lie even after Anna died. The man who wrote the precious bible that may not be quite so precious after all, and who now has access to these relics of the past yet again. How would the media respond if he did indeed find some new evidence, proving once and for all that Anna did – or didn't – kill those five prisoners? Shoving Anna, these five victims and all their families back into the spotlight.

When Rosalie moves in front of Anna's photograph, her lips curl into a grimace and she swallows sharply. 'They used to play prison poisoner in the playground.'

'Sorry? Who?'

'At my school, some of the older kids. They'd eat their lunch, writhe around and play dead. Then someone had to guess who killed them – which one was Anna. They thought it was funny.'

'But not you.'

'Death is never funny.' She says this with such a deadpan face that I can't decide if she is serious at first, but when no smile appears I realise she is.

Nate used humour as his way of coping right until the end. *You'd better label the backs of the photos so you and Ellie don't forget my face. You'll soon find someone else to nag instead.* I tried to laugh alongside him but cried when I was alone and have continued to cry intermittently ever since.

'Can I have a word, Ms Batten?' Mr Palmer is standing in the doorway, clutching his folded glasses in his hand.

'Now isn't the best time.' I pull out my phone so I look busy. 'Perhaps once I've finished in here ... after lunch?'

'In that case, I'm going to look at the Healthcare archives again for a while.' He winks at Rosalie. 'Derek said he'll open the cabinets this time.' Then he winks at me. 'Don't worry, I won't be unsupervised.'

As Rosalie brushes past me towards the shop till, I spot a sheen of tears in her eyes. This *Panbrook Prisongate* exhibition often has that effect on people, the whole museum does, triggering emotions in even the most dispassionate visitors. Such a tragic loss of life.

Soon afterwards, when Derek joins Mr Palmer in Room Three, I wander back towards Room Two and watch the guests as they continue to browse and read the information panels. Bryan leads a few people into Room One, seemingly eager to show them one of the exhibits.

One guest asks me for the directions to the Ladies. She's carrying a large brown paper bag from the gift shop, with some of our exclusive Panbrook herb and spice packets, along with a souvenir tea towel featuring the hotel logo. I leave the building and direct her to the nearest restrooms, then take the opportunity to fill my lungs with fresh air.

Watching a pigeon pecking around in the dirt, I recall its dead scrawny relative in the box in Jonathan Roach's cell. I still don't know who put it there – or why.

This pigeon looks well-fed – survival of the fittest, perhaps. Much healthier than the gaunt pigeons I'm used to seeing in Spain. After a minute or two, it gives up trying to find anything worth scavenging and flies off in the direction of the kitchen garden. It will certainly find tastier pickings there.

I lean against the stone wall of the museum and check my phone. I have no new messages, a good sign that there's no more pre-wedding drama – but nothing from Mr Hodgson either. I suspect he won't be arriving now, and imagine Derek sending him a bill, totting up the cost of the weekend room, the meals and more.

When the guest returns, we walk back towards the museum. She tells me how much she's enjoying her Panbrook stay and that she plans to bring her sister with her next time.

I pull open the museum door to let her back inside, then block her way. A wisp of smoke is drifting through the open doorway.

Someone shouts from inside, and the fire alarm goes off.

25

MADDIE

NOW

SATURDAY
11.00 a.m.

Panic squeezes my chest, but I need to remain calm.

'Please wait here,' I tell the woman, before rushing inside.

'Everyone out.' I herd our guests towards the door like cattle, with my ears throbbing at the fire alarm's high-pitched tone. Once we emerge in the fresh air, I instruct them to gather at the side of A wing. I count the lottery winners, and spot Thomas.

Four people are missing.

I run back inside and grab the fire extinguisher. Tendrils of smoke curl towards the ceiling like spectral fingers, carrying with them a smoky odour.

In Room Two, I find Rosalie covering her mouth with her hand.

'You need to get out. Call the fire brigade.' I look up at the ceiling. The sprinklers should have jettisoned into action by now. The museum's fire extinguishing system is considered to be state of the art to protect its priceless contents. 'Oh ... and take a register. Make sure everyone's there. You still have the visitors' book, don't you?'

'No, it's ... it's in there.' She gestures towards Room Three, where smoke is billowing through the doorway. 'I...' she coughs into her fist '...forgot to pick it up again after I pressed the alarm button. After I saw the smoke.'

'Have you seen Derek? Dr Land? Mr Palmer?' I pull my navy scarf over my mouth and nose and tie the soft chiffon behind my head to keep it in place. I could do with a bottle of water to dampen it down but this will have to do.

Rosalie shakes her head and coughs into her fist again.

I give her a nudge. 'Get out of here.'

While she scurries to the outside door, I head towards Room Three.

'Mr Palmer? Derek?' My throat stings as I call their names. My muffled voice sounds croaky behind my scarf. A smoky haze drifts in front of my eyes, and my vision blurs as tears stream down my cheeks. I wipe them away with the back of my hand. 'Bryan?'

The room is eerily silent. Smoke continues to swirl around me, obscuring my way like dense November fog and spiralling into my lungs. The fire extinguisher weighs heavy in my fist.

I call again and pause to see if there's any response, then I hear a rustling noise and a stamping of feet.

Two figures rush towards me under coarse blankets from one of our displays. Acrid smoke billows after them. They pull the blankets upwards, revealing Derek's silvery hair and Mr Palmer's dark eyes.

I tug at Derek's sleeve. 'Have you seen Bry—' My voice dissolves into a coughing fit.

Mr Palmer shakes his head. 'I'm sure he went outside.' He grabs my arm and pulls me towards the doorway.

I shake him off and peer back into Room Three. The smoke is too dense to see anything inside. My stomach clenches as I picture all of the records that will be destroyed. 'I need the visitors' register so I know everyone's out. Rosalie ... she said she left it—' Derek holds up the black hardback book. 'Okay ... let's go.'

The three of us scurry towards the outer door, a beam of sunlight guiding our way. When we reach the outside, I clatter the fire extinguisher onto the tarmac. A few guests jump in fright. I bend over and press my hands on my knees, coughing to dispel the smoke from my lungs. Derek and Mr Palmer remove their blankets and do the same.

With everyone crowding around us, I feel trapped in a smoke pit, unable to claw my way out. My pounding heart is trying to escape.

'Give her space.' A familiar voice. Mr Palmer's.

As I crouch down, my scarf falls away from my face. I close my eyes and concentrate on breathing slowly, in and out, in and out, feeling my heart rate calming down as I begin to relax.

'Are you okay?' Rosalie rests her hand on my shoulder.

I nod, welcoming the reassuring gesture, and clear my throat. 'Yes, I ... It's the smoke. Irritates my allergies. Have you made sure everyone's here? Bryan, he—' I cough again, unzip my medicines pouch and pull out my blue inhaler.

'Ms Batten...' The doctor gazes at me with concerned eyes. He unscrews the cap of the glass water bottle in his hand. 'I'm fine, as you can see. You, on the other hand...'

'But you...' I swivel my gaze towards the A wing entrance where Thomas is standing beside a large crate of water bottles. 'I thought you were inside. I thought—'

'I'd popped out for some fresh air and the Gents.' Bryan hands me the bottle. 'Take some ... slowly ... a few sips at a time. Use your inhaler first.'

I follow his instructions. The water eases the dryness in my throat and washes away the acrid taste. 'Derek ... the visitors' book?'

Derek opens up the register and flicks to today's date. He begins to read out the guests' names, but a piercing siren cuts him off and a fire engine screeches to a halt. Three firefighters jump out, clad in black jackets, fluorescent trousers and matching helmets. Two of them strap on breathing apparatus, unravel reels from the fire engine and run into the building clutching narrow hoses.

The third firefighter approaches us. 'Anyone left inside?' His voice is soft and high-pitched, a stark contrast to his broad, rugged appearance.

Derek calls out the names to confirm everyone is present, and nods as he closes the visitors' book. 'Everyone's here.'

I gaze at the old building. Smoke twirls and dances through the open doorway as if thrilled to be fleeing into the bright blue skies. Everyone says belongings can be replenished, yet not all inanimate objects are replaceable. The old records, the memories, the photographs...

A few minutes later, the two firefighters leave the building. They pack their hoses away and remove their breathing apparatus and helmets.

'Looks like someone left smouldering cigarettes in a wastepaper basket,' the tallest one tells us. His forehead glistens with sweat. 'Lots of smoke more than flames. It didn't spread fortunately.'

Derek draws in a deep breath of relief. I imagine my boss has been totting up the cost of repairs – always the business-man, even at times of crisis. 'But this means someone was smoking inside.' He turns to me as if I'm responsible – or to blame – for everything that doesn't go to plan.

'Not everyone takes notice of the "No Smoking" signs. Maybe this will act as a reminder.' I take another sip of water and wince at the raw feeling when I swallow.

What if the guests or staff hadn't been able to get out? What if all the evidence about the Panbrook Prison murders had been destroyed?

I shiver, swallowing back another rising cough. Perhaps this fire was started deliberately to get us out of the building. Mr Palmer had been trawling through the archives. Was it because of something he found – or nearly found? My skin prickles as I glance at everyone around us.

'Well, can we go back in now?' Derek checks his watch. 'The next batch of guests is due to arrive in five minutes.'

The firefighter shakes his head firmly. 'It will take a few hours for the smoke to clear, Mr Taylor, and then a few days for it to settle properly. It'll stink in there for a while and it's not good for the lungs.'

'We'll sort it out after the weekend then.' Derek gives a broad smile that doesn't reach his eyes. 'We'll just have to close the building to visitors. It's no big deal. It doesn't affect the rest of the hotel. Madeleine, I'll leave it for you to organise.'

My boss is probably more concerned about his party tonight. This museum visit was about other people's crimes and tragedies twenty years ago and beyond. Tonight is about Derek's own achievements, and no one should begrudge him that. He has worked intensely and relentlessly to ensure that this hotel has become such a triumph over the last decade.

I stand up, wander over to the museum and peer in through the doorway to check for damage. I turn back to the firefighter. 'Everything's behind glass so I assume it won't be affected by the smoke?'

'Should be fine, but you'll need to air the place – leave the windows open.' Sweat dribbles down his forehead towards his eyes. He wipes it away with the back of his gloved hand. 'I don't suppose there's another door you can leave ajar?'

I shake my head. 'Just an old storeroom at the back, and we don't have the key.'

Some of the smoke is already clearing from Room One. I squint into the darkness and spot a gap on the wall near the door. My head aches as I try to remember what was hanging there. 'I think something must have fallen down. A picture, maybe. Any chance I can pop in and pick it up so it doesn't get damaged?'

'Wait here.' The firefighter puts his helmet on and steps inside. He scrutinises the wall and picks something up from the floor near the desk, then saunters out again, holding an empty packet of Mayfair Green menthol. 'I suspect this is where the cigarettes came from. Looks like you'll need to have a word with the hotel guests. Nothing's fallen down, as far as I can tell. Maybe there's always been a gap there and you've never noticed it. The smoke's probably making your head fuzzy.'

'Ms Batten?' Mr Palmer nudges my arm. 'Can we have that word now ... if you have a moment?'

His face looks pale. His eyes are red and puffy from the smoke, and his expression serious. I bring my hand up to my own face – do I look the same?

'Mr Palmer, I—' I grasp the water bottle in both hands, trying to stop them shaking. 'Now isn't the best time to—'

'You'll want to hear this.' He leans towards me to whisper, 'You won't want this to be in front of anyone else, trust me.' I stifle a snigger at his suggestion that I could actually trust him. 'You see, I've worked it out, Ms Batten. I know. And I can't believe I've found her after all this time.'

My fingers twitch.

The glass water bottle falls out of my grasp and smashes on the tarmac.

26

MADDIE

NOW

Mr Palmer takes a while to unlock his room door, shuffling on his feet as he waits for the green light to appear.

I point at the key card in his hand. 'If that's not working properly, Reception can supply a replacement. I can sort that out for you.'

'It's fine.' When the door finally unlocks, he steps to the left so that I can enter first. 'I'll ask them later.'

Inside his room, a pale blue shirt is crumpled on the bedcovers, and one of the hotel's white bath towels, the embroidered logo in the corner, is scrunched up on the carpet.

'Sorry, I left in a rush.' The journalist brushes past me, his cheeks reddening, and picks up the towel. 'I would have suggested the bar, but I wanted somewhere more private. I suspected you would too.'

He drapes the towel over the rack in the bathroom, picks up his shirt and hangs it in the wardrobe. I lean against the wall by the door, watching him pottering about, ignoring my urge to help him tidy up. He seems calm enough. But what does he know – or thinks he knows?

Perhaps he's stalling deliberately, making me sweat it out.

If so, this is certainly working. Nerves buzz in my chest like a flock of flying ants about to swarm. I should just leave him here alone, as I have plenty of other things to do. But first I need to confirm that this really is nothing after all, nothing that will ruin the rest of the weekend or beyond.

He shifts two books off the chair onto the bedside table: a copy of *Panbrook Prisongate*, colourful Post-it notes sticking out the top, and an open Moleskine notebook. The top page is scrawled with black handwriting. My fingers twitch. I long to flick through the notebook to see what he has written.

'...drink?' His deep voice snaps me out of my reverie.

'Sorry?'

'Do you want a drink?' He opens the mini-fridge and grabs a couple of miniatures: an Absolut vodka and a Jack Daniels. 'I don't know which you prefer, but I think we both need one.'

'I— Just an orange juice, please.'

He returns the vodka to the fridge and pulls out a small can of San Pellegrino and two glass tumblers from the shelf above it. He pours the juice into one glass and hands it to me. Then he pours Jack Daniels into the other.

'Cheers.' He raises his glass and slugs some alcohol.

I gulp down a mouthful of orange juice. The sweetness washes away the remaining acrid taste of smoke, but the tart after-kick stings my throat.

'Does Derek know?' He swivels the desk chair around to face me, then sits down.

My skin prickles with anxiety. 'I should go. Get out of these smoky clothes before lunch.' I place the glass down on the nearest bedside table and turn towards the door.

'I still remember him.' The journalist's melancholy tone prompts me to turn back. 'I tried to find him when I was writing my book.'

'I have no idea what you're talking about.'

'He vanished after the murders.' Mr Palmer stares at me, his eyes narrowed in accusation. 'I did try to find him, many times ... and her. I just didn't expect a country change *and* a name change. Clever stuff.'

My mouth drains of saliva. I clutch my drink to calm myself down, the cold glass pressing against my skin.

'Earlier in The Lock-Up, when I saw your phone screen, I thought your daughter looked like your husband. They have the same eyes. But when I was browsing the photos in the museum just now, I realised she looks more like her aunt, with her curly, blonde hair, or perhaps I should say "her real mother".' He takes another gulp of Jack Daniels. 'When Anna was arrested, Nathan Kendall took Lucy in, I assume. He couldn't leave his little niece with nowhere to go. And then I'm guessing you must have adopted her.'

I lean back against the wall in need of some support. My head is beginning to throb. For all these years I have kept this secret to myself. Kept my daughter safe from the media ... from this journalist rat. It was easier to do while we were living abroad, although it has been impossible to totally escape the past, with those regular reminders on Netflix, YouTube and Facebook over the years.

And then Ellie decided to come back to England to study.

My daughter, Ellie.

Anna's daughter, Lucy.

My husband's niece.

'Why are you here, Mr Palmer?' I stare at the notebook on his bedside table. 'Please don't ruin my daughter's life.'

I think of all her wedding plans, her future with Viv. How can he do this to her now? I pick up my tumbler, craving another drink to wash away the tightness in my throat.

The journalist raises his glass towards me as if he's about to make a toast. 'Is that what you think of me? That I'm here to ruin lives?'

This is what everyone thinks of him, surely he should know that by now. Perhaps Anna overdosed so she wouldn't stand trial. Perhaps she died because of him, because of the media, because she was aware of all the stories about her, of all the lies.

'I just want to keep my daughter safe, that's all.' I picture Ellie's soft curls, her warm blue eyes. How much am I prepared to reveal in my quest for the truth? 'We don't call her Lucy anymore, we haven't since … since then. She's Ellie, as in L for Lucy, that was always her nickname. Ellie Batten.'

I grip the glass so tightly that I worry I'll crack it. 'But you're right, Nate took *my* name when we married in Spain. Using Kendall was a liability, for him and for Ellie, so it made sense at the time. Please don't ruin her life.'

I cringe at the begging tone in my voice as I repeat my plea.

Mr Palmer's eyes soften. 'I said I'm not here to cause trouble.'

'Then why *are* you here?'

'Here this weekend,' he trails his glass through the air, 'or here now?'

'Well, originally you declined Derek's invitation.' I stare at his notebook on the bedside table. 'And then two weeks ago, you decided to join us after all. Why?'

He lets out a heavy sigh. 'Netflix suddenly announced a new documentary about the prison next year. My publisher wants to bring out an updated edition of my book as soon as possible – they've asked me to find additional material. This weekend provided the perfect opportunity.'

'Perfect for you, maybe. But it caused us a lot of aggravation, having to rearrange many of our plans at short notice.'

'That was never my intention.' He shakes his head slowly. 'I declined my publisher's request at first too, if that's any consolation.'

I squirm. Perhaps I have been wrong about him for all these years. And if I was wrong about that...

No, I tell myself, *I can't be wrong about him. And I can't be wrong about her.*

I sit down on the crumpled bedcovers. 'Why don't you want to update your book? It's been very successful. Surely most authors would jump at the chance to be in the limelight again.'

He clutches his glass. 'Because that case destroyed my life. It's all I could think about for years. I lived it, breathed it ... It destroyed my marriage. My obsession did, I mean. I drank too much and—'

He lets out a sorrowful laugh, then slams his drink down on the desk. 'This place brings out the worst in me.'

I clench my fists to control the anger bubbling inside me. 'But what you did. All those news stories you wrote. For God's sake, isn't this all...? I mean ... Anna's dead, Mr Palmer. She couldn't cope, so she killed herself ... because of you.'

He flinches and draws in a breath. 'Well, now I'm looking for evidence I missed the first time. Maybe Anna was innocent after all.'

'Innocent?' I stare into his eyes expecting to see him mocking me, yet he seems genuine enough.

'Yes, innocent.'

'But you were convinced of her guilt twenty years ago ... even ten years ago when you wrote your book.' I point at the battered copy of *Panbrook Prisongate*, my finger outstretched like a gun ready to shoot a bullet through the cover. 'Why would you have been wrong?'

'When someone was in my room earlier, they left me a note. I was so sure it was you when I saw that photo on your phone ... when I realised who you were, who your husband was.' He furrows his brow in confusion. 'And you said House-keeping hadn't been in here. So who else could it have been?'

'What did the note say?'

'That Anna was innocent.' He stands up and walks over to the chest of drawers, placing his tumbler down on the wooden surface.

'It was almost a challenge.' He opens the top drawer, pulls out a folded piece of lined yellow notepaper and hands it to me.

I unfold it. As I skim-read the words, my skin prickles with goosebumps.

Anna Kendall was innocent. Come to B wing at midnight to find out why – find the pigeon.

I fold the note back up and place it on the bed, my hands shaking as I shove it towards him. 'This could just be a prank, of course.'

'That's true, and it probably was. I tried to get into B-wing last night, a little early, but the doors were locked.' He places the note back in the drawer and closes it with a firm shove. 'So I gave up and came back to my room. And then Fiona Trayton fell, and I forgot to mention it to anyone. But I *would* like to find out who that note's from.'

So would I. That dead pigeon I found. The picture of Anna and the newspaper cutting. Someone set it all up for him in advance – but they hadn't expected him to arrive at B wing so early.

The journalist clears his throat to attract my attention. 'Does Lucy … I mean, Ellie – you called her your daughter – does she know about her past?'

I nod. 'But she was very young so she doesn't remember anything. She was barely two.' Tears sting the corners of my eyes as I recall how my little girl cried day and night until the passage of time eventually dampened her memories. 'She doesn't remember Anna. She knows she's adopted and who her birth mother was. We never lied to her about that but—'

'You omitted the truth?'

I shake my head forcefully. 'She knows what her mother was accused of, and her links to Panbrook Prison ... and to this hotel. We told her when she was old enough to understand. But Nate promised that Anna was innocent, wrongly accused of a murder she didn't commit.' I clutch the glass tightly, my skin growing pale across my knuckles. 'And we told her to never mention any of this, and why.'

I imagine the publicity this will now generate once Lloyd Palmer rips the case open yet again, exposing the shadows of the past, and what this would do to Ellie and Viv. Of course Viv knows, Ellie told her once she was sure she could be trusted, but the media attention, the constant pressure ... We all know what happened to Anna, and I worry about how Ellie would cope with being in the public eye. She's not as strong as she likes people to believe.

The journalist squints at me. 'What was Anna like?'

I think back to the first time we met, and then the last time I saw her. 'We only met a few times. We were ... we were very different. She spoke her mind; I was much quieter. And she always seemed quite young for her age.'

'Despite the responsibilities of her job?' Mr Palmer sits back down and taps his fingers on the desk. 'So what about you? It can't be a coincidence that you're working here.'

'Ironically, Anna's the reason Derek hired me.' I glance at the journalist's book, recalling the hours I spent poring over the pages in Spain. 'He and I first met over ten years ago at a hotel managers' conference in Madrid. When I realised who he was, I deliberately sat next to him in the bar. I was intrigued to find out what they were doing to this place. He did most of the talking and most of the drinking, telling me all about the project. He was looking for someone local, efficient and organised; someone who already knew the history of the prison and had hotel management experience.'

'And you fit the bill perfectly?'

'Not exactly. I was never a local. I grew up in Surrey, then moved to Spain. But once I met Nate, I spent a lot of time around here whenever I came back to England. When I recited the backgrounds of the five prisoners and the prison nurse, Derek wanted to hire me on the spot. He was astonished that discussions about the Panbrook Prison murders had reached mainland Spain. But like everyone here in Britain, I had followed the news reports avidly. And I also had insider information, as you now know.'

'So why not take the job then?'

'I couldn't come back to England at the time; Ellie and Nate had to be my priority. We didn't want to bring her back. We...' My voice catches and my eyes sting. 'Before Nate died, he ... he made me promise I'd find out who killed those five men. He insisted his sister was innocent.'

A muscle twinges in my neck. That wasn't the only promise I made – and time is running out. I roll my shoulders to stretch the pain away.

'When Derek contacted me out of the blue, offering me the job again, it was ideal timing for me, as I was finally ready to return. And it was fortuitous for him that I agreed, as his manager had just quit. I wasn't going to say yes at first, but he mentioned this anniversary weekend. I realised this was the best way to access the museum, the buildings, any special guests ... to see if I could fulfil Nate's last wish.'

I wipe my eyes with the back of my hand. I had already promised to come back to England by then, handed in my notice, and Ellie was excited to finally have me nearby. I just hadn't realised that Derek was such a bastard to deal with.

'And what if Anna wasn't innocent?'

I clench my glass, aware that this is the flaw in Nate's plan. What if I find out the truth but it isn't the truth he wanted after all.

I point at the copy of *Panbrook Prisongate*. 'You certainly present a good case against Anna and not much evidence in her favour. She baked the cakes that killed them. Yet not even *you* could work out why. There were two prison guards on duty that night, and other people were attending the party, so someone must have seen something.'

'No one revealed the names of those prison guards to protect their identities in case there was backlash from the families. Because they were too busy partying to do cell checks.' He taps his glass with his finger. 'There were rumours that they were drinking on the job, and many people blamed the deaths on their negligence.'

'It's astonishing they were never prosecuted.'

'I think the police just wanted to shut down the case and move onto the next one. They had their culprit – Anna. And in those days, there was no social media pressure to keep the case open. But you're right, someone must have seen something. We need to find out who was here that night.'

We?

'At the museum, before the fire alarm, did you find anything? You were looking through the Healthcare registers.'

'I don't think so.' He stares at his notebook. 'But I'll have another look at my notes in the morning. I took some photos too. I keep going over and over why Anna might have done it. Who she may have been targeting. I assume Nate had no idea?'

I shake my head slowly as I think back. 'He said Anna would never have killed anyone. Whatever the police had on her was enough to charge her, though. So perhaps there's nothing else to find.'

He looks up at me, his eyes narrowed. 'Are you saying she did it after all?'

'No, I ... I'm—' The photo on my phone pops into my head. Ellie's blue eyes, Nate's strained smile. 'Of course not, Mr Palmer. I just feel totally out of my depth.'

'Then maybe we need to combine forces. Two inquisitive

brains are, after all, better than one, and maybe there's something you can remember about Anna that will help. What do you think, Ms Batten?'

The journalist holds his hand out towards me.

I inch my fingers forwards, then pause.

What would Nate think? What would he say? He told me to do whatever it takes but perhaps I am about to team up with the devil. Yet what if I don't? If Mr Palmer reveals my identity to Derek, I could lose my job. I need to know what this journalist knows, and I need to know what he has found so far. I don't really have a choice.

I reach towards him and grasp his hand. 'It's a deal, Mr Palmer.'

His grip is warm and firm. 'Call me Lloyd ... please.'

I force a smile, ignoring Nate's voice whispering *Traitor* in my head. I need to do this for Ellie. 'In that case, you may as well call me Maddie.'

27

ANNA

JUNE 1997

Lucy's intense blue eyes gaze up at me as I peer into her cot. *Shit*. Why isn't she fast asleep by now? I'm desperate for some kip. Maybe she'll drop off if I'm quiet.

She whimpers as I back away towards my bed. Her face turns red, and she clenches her fists. The baby manual Nate bought me said I shouldn't pick her up every time she frets or cries, or she'll never learn to settle. But my heart twinges with pangs of guilt.

I turn on the mobile above the cot, hoping it'll help to calm her. Five black-and-white embroidered birds flutter around a matching fabric nest. But her whimper grows into a desperate wail.

'Dad! Dad! There's something wrong with her, I'm sure of it.'

Footsteps head into my bedroom. Dad leans over me and rests his hand on Lucy's forehead, then her chest. She stops wailing and blinks at him. Maybe she has a fever. Why didn't I think of that? The nurse in me seems to have fallen asleep over the last few months.

As Dad straightens his back, he winces and presses his

hand against the base of his spine. 'She's a little hot, maybe. But it's a warm day, love. Maybe take her babygro off and let her sleep in her vest.'

Lucy's mouth turns down at the corners. She scrunches up her eyes and starts wailing again.

'But she might get cold.' I scoop her up and cradle her in my arms. She opens her eyes and puckers her mouth as she turns her face towards me.

'Guess she's just hungry, love.'

'I should know that by now, shouldn't I?' I hug her even closer. 'All I've done for the last month is change her nappies, feed her, bathe her, get her to sleep, and grab a few hours' sleep myself. Then start again.'

Lucy lets out a desperate cry, and her mouth roots against my T-shirt.

'And every time I think she's in a routine, she decides to change it.'

I hand her to Dad and choose a pink towelling bib from the top drawer of the changing unit. They follow me into the kitchenette at the back of the living room.

I open the fridge, pull out a baby bottle of formula milk – which I prepared this morning – and stick it in the bottle warmer. 'She didn't feed much earlier. She only took one ounce. Maybe I should get the GP to check her over.'

'Relax, love. She's fine. You're just doing what every new mum does. Worrying too much. It's natural.'

I shake the baby bottle and sprinkle a few drops onto my wrist. The milk feels okay, but what if it's not? What if it's too hot? What if it's too cold? I test it on my wrist again.

Lucy screams and arches her back, so I pull the bottle's lid off. Let's hope it's okay.

I sit down in the rocking chair and pop the teat into her mouth. She sucks vigorously and closes her eyes.

'Did Mum worry a lot when we were born?'

Dad chuckles. 'Of course she did. More about Nate than you, I guess. That's usual with a first baby, when everything's new. She used to joke that you almost brought yourself up. Weren't scared of anything.'

Lucy takes half an hour to drain the bottle, and then another half an hour to burp. She's still on a two-hour feeding cycle, so I'll be doing this all over again in an hour. Most babies go every three to four hours by now. It's no surprise I'm knackered, with little chance to catch up on sleep. So much for trying to get her into a routine. Or maybe her routine just doesn't suit mine.

After a final burp, her tiny eyelids flutter closed. Her chest rises and falls slowly and evenly in time with each breath.

I run my fingers over her soft, bare arms, and lean down to inhale her sweet, milky scent. She stirs and grimaces with a burst of wind.

Dad carefully lifts her out of my arms and places her over his shoulder. 'Let me take her for a while. It'll do you some good.'

'But I've got so much to do.' I stand up and carry the empty baby bottle into the kitchen. 'I need to sort out her bottles, do some washing, and I promised—'

'Love, you're exhausted, anyone can see that.' He sits down in the armchair with Lucy still on his shoulder, and gently rubs her back. 'Get some sleep while you can. You don't need to do all that baking later. We'll manage without it.'

I point at the bag of flour on the kitchen countertop. 'I promised Nate I'd make something fancy for tea. He said he's missed my fairy cakes. And I haven't baked any for ages.'

I can't say this to Dad, but I've been bored stuck here with Lucy in our poky flat, just the two of us, all day, every day. Maybe I'm just not cut out to be a full-time mum. Maybe I'm better at dealing with sick, murderous patients doing time than sweet, innocent babies in their first few weeks of life.

'A little birdie told me you're coming back to work next month.' Bryan rests Lucy against his chest like a natural, her little face staring at me. It's a shame he and Faye have never had kids.

'A Kellie bird, by any chance?'

He nods, gazing down at Lucy with a tender smile. 'I can't believe you're coming back already. I thought you'd want to spend more time with this little love.'

'I do, but I also need cash. Babies aren't cheap, you know. Can't sit on my arse all day.'

'You must get cabin fever in here, I guess.' Bryan attempts to hide his frown as he glances around my bedroom.

I've tried to make it cosy. Lemon-coloured wallpaper, a Winnie-the-Pooh picture on the wall and a multicoloured striped rug. But it still looks like a shithole. I'd love to move to a two-bed place but can't afford the extra rent. This is already a stretch, and we still need to eat.

I straighten my duvet cover. 'And this is why I need to go back to work. For my sanity, and Lucy's, and my bank balance. I know this sounds weird, but I miss The Brook. Even some of the patients.'

'I'm not sure I'd miss it.' His jaw clenches. 'We had a jumper last week. One of the smackheads. The netting caught him, but it was too late. He'd OD'd anyway.'

'Shit.' My heart beats faster. 'Anyone I'd know?'

He shakes his head. 'Look, if you need anything...' He gives Lucy a sniff and wrinkles his nose. 'Well ... *she* certainly needs something.'

I frown as I take my little girl off him and lie her down on the plastic mat on my bed. She's spat milk all down her front again. My fingers fumble with the stiff poppers as I remove her vest.

Bryan watches me, barking out suggestions as if he's still my SMO. 'I meant it, Annie. If you need extra money, I can help you out.'

'Nate has said he can help me too. But I want to do this on my own.'

Bryan raises his eyebrows. 'Are you sure? Because you've stuck her vest on the wrong way.'

I look down and fake a smile. I'm a trained nurse yet feel totally out of my depth as a new mum. I switch her vest around and do up the poppers.

'I'm serious though.' Bryan rests his hand on my arm. 'I want to help. If you won't accept money, I can buy some things for Lucy.' He looks around again and grimaces. 'Or help you do this place up.'

'We're fine. You've got Faye to think about. Kellie said she'd had another setback.'

Bryan nods as he rubs his eyes. 'She was in a lot of pain last week, finding it hard to get about. Breaking my heart to see her like that.'

'MS is a horrible disease. Faye's your priority, Bry. And this little munchkin is mine.' I gently kiss Lucy's cheeks and lie her down in the cot.

'If you come back to The Brook, what will you do about childcare?'

I turn on the baby monitor and gesture that we need to tiptoe out of the room. Bryan follows me, and I close the door behind him.

'Carol next door's a childminder. She's offered to have Lucy three days a week while I'm at work. I'll do her gardening for free and help her with her grandkids on a weekend if she needs me. And I'll bake her cakes as a thank you. Hey – maybe I could sell cakes for extra cash.'

'Ooh, talking of cakes.' Bryan opens up the Tupperware box on the living-room table. 'Sounds like you really *have* got it sorted. But if you're struggling at any time, I can help you. Just come and ask. Anyway, I need you back at The Brook.' He scratches his chin. 'My IMRs and appointment logs are a mess.'

'Are you still giving out those booklets?'

'Lucas says everyone benefits from them – lots of helpful things inside.'

I roll my eyes. 'Do you both seriously think any patients are actually reading them? They never fill in those question-naires. I used to find most of them ripped up and thrown on the pile with the dead pigeons.'

'Maybe they just like the pretty pictures.' The corners of his lips twitch. 'Certainly makes a change from Page Three. Anyhow, the gov's happy with the progress. And you know how hard it is to please her.'

He picks out a fairy cake and stuffs it into his mouth. I iced them carefully in white, with a cherry in the centre. Now I look at them again, I realise they look a bit like boobs.

'You're ... you're supposed to savour the taste.' I start to laugh, then remember Lucy's asleep and cover my mouth with my hand.

'Oh, how I've missed your baking.' Bryan licks his fingers. 'Kellie has too. Nice of you to make these for me today.'

As his fingers inch back towards the Tupperware, I snap the lid shut. 'I've made them for tea at Dad's place. He's picking me and Lucy up in an hour.'

'Oh yes, the big tea.' Bryan chuckles. 'So ... are you going to tell them?'

'Guess I'll have to. Dreading it though. I'm sure there'll be shouting.'

Bryan sits down in the armchair. 'If it's any consolation, some of the patients will be pleased to see you back.'

'Which ones?'

'Well...' he grins '...Cock certainly can't wait. He comes

into Healthcare once a week wanting to know where you are. He's been asking us to pass on his scraps of poetry ever since you left. I could have saved them all for you.'

I give him a dirty look. 'That's all I need. Roach in my life again. And the rest? Anyone left The Brook since I've been gone?'

'Prisoners or staff?' Bryan raises an eyebrow. 'None of the officers that I know of. Lots of prisoners don't come into Healthcare so much – I swear they came in just to see you. Not as many accidents in the garden either. Estie has put stricter rules in place – she told me to tell you that the orderlies are still following your advice. Plus, prisoners obviously come and go.'

My tummy begins to churn. I pick up a muslin cloth from the rocking chair seat and sit down. 'Who's gone?'

'Not the one you're hoping for.' Bryan purses his lips. 'But Pills and Razorhead gave Fingerling a tough time after what happened, so don't worry about him. He's off the scene, banged up in A wing now, usually 23/7. We'll keep him out of your way, I promise.'

The baby monitor crackles as Lucy lets out a faint whimper. What does a little baby dream about? Fingerling's shouts and cries still invade my sleep all these months on. I'll never look at a toothbrush in the same way again.

'Fisher's not the reason I didn't go back to work after what happened, you know. I just didn't want to risk anything, just in case— I wanted to keep her safe.'

'Oh, that reminds me. I've got *some* good news for you.' Bryan leans forwards, his eyes brightening, and steeples his fingers. 'Well, not exactly good news. But Pills has stopped asking to work in Healthcare. He's got other things to focus on now. One of his kids is really sick.'

'How sick?'

The baby monitor crackles again as Lucy wails. *Bloody hell*. She's not waking up already, is she?

Bryan runs his fingers through his hair. 'Well, the doctors are still doing tests, but it's not looking good. Kellie tried speaking to Pills about it, but he's clammed up. We thought he'd be more likely to open up to a nurse than an officer. So maybe it's good you're coming back now. You might have more luck.'

'Yeah, right. As if he'd open up to me. He knows I don't want him in Healthcare.' I scrunch up the muslin cloth in my hand, as memories of The Brook flood my brain. 'I know it's weird but I really miss the routine of that place. The meds hatch and sick parade. Even typing up your notes, and the Code Blues.'

Bryan chuckles. 'The Brook lurks under your skin, doesn't it?'

'You'll adore her, I promise.'

Nate looks tanned and happy. More relaxed than I've seen him for years. My big brother's finally back after six months in Spain, advising on a construction project, and he's trying to convince me he met the new love of his life in a hotel bar.

She's coming over to Dad's place for afternoon tea. It all feels a bit formal, and I'm worried she'll be a snob. In the photo he showed me, she's dressed up in a posh frock.

I smooth down my hair in the mirror, wishing I'd put on some make-up. Oh well, she'll have to take me as she finds me, post-baby fat and all.

Maddie turns up clutching a box of chocolates for Dad and a bunch of tulips for me – pink and yellow ones. Nate must have told her they're my favourites. My mind drifts back to Evans at The Brook. Is he still there?

Nate's latest flame isn't much taller than me, a bit plump round the middle, with lots of dark curly hair and a sparkly diamond necklace. She smiles at Lucy lying on the jungle play-mat in just her vest.

'Oh, she's so gorgeous. But isn't she rather cold?'

'Cold?' Dad stares at Maddie's thick, woolly jumper.

I do too. It's bloody June, for God's sake.

'Well, it feels freezing to me.' She flicks her curls away from her eyes. 'But then I guess I'm used to the heat. I live in Spain, didn't he tell you? I'm the assistant manager of a small hotel near Malaga.'

'Oh, I thought Nate said you were the chambermaid.'

A slight frown flickers on her lips. 'No, I—'

Nate nudges her arm gently. 'Ignore her. Annie's just playing with you.' He raises his eyebrows at me, and mouths, 'Be nice.'

'Must be exciting living in Spain.' Dad takes the chocolates and flowers from her. 'You planning on moving back here eventually?'

Maddie shrugs. 'Probably not. I'm thinking of applying for residency next year. I adore it there. The sun, sea and sand. We both do.' She reaches for Nate's hand and squeezes it gently.

Watching my brother, I can see he's serious about Maddie. The way he pulls out her chair when we get to the table and can't tear his eyes away from her. But is she really the one for him? She seems rather lah-de-da, with her posh voice and fancy jewellery. Well, it probably won't last. Nate's been through more women than I've seen patients at The Brook.

The Brook.

Looking down at my little girl, I blink rapidly to ward off tears. There's so much I want to do – need to do – with my life. Can I bear to leave her when I go back to work? She may not have been in my plan, but she's very much wanted and loved.

Maddie straightens the cutlery in front of her and rubs a speck of dust off her plate. I guess she's used to fancy restaurants. No wonder Dad's taken out the best china.

OK, so maybe I should try a little harder – for Nate.

'Would you like a fairy cake?' I offer her the platter. 'I made them fresh this morning.'

'They look great.' Maddie tilts her head and sniffs. Rubs her nose. 'What's in them?'

'Sorry?' I put the platter down on the table between us. 'They're just fairy cakes. Flour, butter, caster sugar...'

'Do they contain any nuts?'

Nate presses his hand to his forehead and frowns. 'Oh God, sorry, Annie, I forgot to tell you Maddie's allergic.'

I look down at my beautifully iced cakes. 'How allergic? They've got some almond essence in them but only a few drops. They're Bakewells – almond and cherry. Took me ages.'

'I'm allergic enough not to eat them.' Maddie picks up a strawberry from the fruit platter. 'I thought Nate said you were a nurse. You should know that. Maybe you need a refresher course after all those months off.' She raises an eyebrow.

Touché.

'Well, I certainly remember how to jab someone with an Epipen if they need one...' I wait for the fury on her face, but Maddie fakes a smile instead. 'Anyway, I'll be going back to work in a few weeks.'

Dad and Nate both talk at the same time, their tones equally stern.

'Annie, you can't.'

'What about...'

I raise my palms. 'It's sorted. Don't worry.'

Dad nudges my arm. 'But you can't stand that governor. Caused you lots of trouble last time? She still there?'

'She is, but I have to go back. I need the money.'

Nate's face clouds over as he pushes the platter to the other end of the table. 'It's about time Lucy's dad helped you out.'

'No chance of that.' Lucy's staring up at the ceiling, waving her little hands in the air as if she's batting away invisible flies. 'It was a one-nighter, I told you. I don't even remember his name.'

Maddie squeaks her chair backwards and stands up. 'Where's your restroom?'

Dad chuckles. 'Restroom? It's upstairs.' He points into the hallway.

Maddie grins at him. 'Sorry, too much time in a hotel dealing with American tourists.'

She's gone for ages so Nate asks me to check she's OK. Maybe he thinks this will be a chance for us to bond.

I find her in Dad's bedroom peering into the wardrobe. The top drawer of the dresser's slightly open.

'What the hell are you doing in here?'

She snaps the cupboard door closed. 'Sorry, I was looking for some tissues. The almond's making my nose itch.'

I point at the cardboard cube on the dresser.

'Oops, I missed them.' Maddie pulls out the top tissue and wipes her nose. Then she shoves another tissue up her sleeve and stares at me. 'Never know when I might need one.'

I watch her saunter out with her twitchy nose in the air as I nudge the dresser-drawer shut. I definitely don't like her – I just can't work out why. Let's hope her relationship with my brother doesn't last.

MADDIE

NOW

SATURDAY
2.00 p.m.

Derek leads the journalists into B wing through the main door from the courtyard garden. This entrance brings us straight out onto the lower landing.

After my conversation with Lloyd Palmer, I returned to my room and scrubbed myself in the shower for nearly twenty minutes, washed and dried my hair and changed my clothes, even my underwear. Yet a smoky odour still lingers when I inhale, mixed with a faint whiff of bleach that hangs in the clammy indoor air.

There's no hint of A wing's glamour in here, but the landings look less menacing than they did in the early hours, with daylight shining through dust-streaked windowpanes. The floors are splattered with dust and mould, and dead flies are dotted along the windowsills, their bodies stiff with thin legs pointing upwards.

While my boss gives a brief summary of B wing's layout, his words echo around us. Bryan Land stands on Derek's left side, gazing at the familiar surroundings with a faint smile. Thomas Benson, on Derek's right, leans on his stick, his eyes wide and his mouth slightly ajar. He has spent the last twenty years on licence, serving the remainder of his sentence in the community rather than in prison. Breaching his conditions would immediately send him back inside. Yet here he is anyway – standing in The Brook again.

As I gaze through the half-open doorways and iron gates that lead into the cells, a flicker of movement catches my eye. A grey rat, perhaps the same rodent I saw last night, is sniffing around fresh mouse droppings.

'I can't take you up to The Two's where the five prisoners died because it's against health and safety regulations.' Derek wipes sweat off his glistening forehead with the back of his hand. 'I do have insurance in place to bring you in here – but just no further than this. Well, not yet anyway. It gives me great pleasure to announce that Planning has just approved my updated blueprints for B wing.'

I snap my attention back to my boss.

'I've waited a long time for this. A press release will be going out on Monday, so this is embargoed until then. On The One's, we intend to add gym facilities and a luxury spa and beauty salon for hotel guests,' Derek continues. 'There will be an educational centre upstairs, preserving the prisoners' rooms as tourist attractions. Behind glass, obviously. We also intend to build another conference room down here for larger gatherings and functions. We know the public enjoys quirky celebrations: Halloween parties, spooky weddings, themed birthdays ... And just imagine the popularity,' he nods at me, 'of ghost tours and sleepovers.'

My stomach somersaults as I imagine the type of guests this would attract – tacky hen parties and stags, the noise and the mess, ruining the historic features of these buildings. Sweat trickles down my back until it dampens the waistband of my trousers.

'Then, towards the end of 2021, Mr Palmer and I intend to establish a true crime festival here, once all of the renovations are complete. We have CrimeFest in Bristol, Theakston Old Peculier Crime Writing Festival in Harrogate ... and one day we'll welcome you to PrisonFest at Panbrook. We already have some sponsorship in place from corporate donors and individual investors, some of whom will be attending the anniversary party this evening, but I will be looking for more over the coming months.'

The guests murmur with excitement, while I stare at Lloyd. He focuses on the floor, fiddling with his notebook and pen, as if he's too afraid to meet my eyes. A bitter taste swirls in my mouth. Earlier, he said that he doesn't want to be in the limelight – was that a lie? What other fibs has he told me?

We swapped mobile numbers to keep in touch easily. But can I trust this man not to reveal my secret – Ellie's secret? Was I a fool to admit to the truth, or at least some of it, but what choice did I have? I promised Nate that I would prove Anna's innocence, and I can't do this on my own.

At least I have held a few things back. I still haven't told the journalist what I found in here the other night – the photograph with the news report, and the dead pigeon, the clues he was meant to find.

When Derek finishes speaking, he introduces Thomas as the expert on daily life at Panbrook. 'Mr Benson was in here for nearly fifteen years, and since then has been volunteering with The Release Trust to help prison-leavers settle back into society. He contacted me soon after we announced our anniversary weekend plans and offered his expertise. How could I refuse?'

Beside me, the ex-prisoner leans heavily on his walking

stick and shuffles his feet. What does he think about Derek's plans to turn this building into a tourist attraction? More importantly, how will those five men's relatives react? Or has this already been leaked – perhaps they already know.

'So, Mr Taylor asked me to tell you 'bout the prison day.' Thomas's voice rises with enthusiasm. 'Supper were always served on The Ones at five every night, you know. We got trays from servery, then went to our cells to eat. If we were lucky, mind, we got to choose in advance what we had. Otherwise, it were pot luck. The night them men died, it were meat pie with fresh herbs from the garden, I heard. So it probably tasted less shit than usual. Lucky sods.' He chuckles. 'Well ... apart from the dyin' part, a'course.'

The former prisoner waves his stick in the air as he points out some of the landings' key features – the staircases, the safety netting and the metal walkways.

'After supper were Association for two hours. That's when the screws let us outta our cells. Hulk and Razorhead usually played backgammon or dominoes here on the ground floor. We'd be let into the yard for circuits. And then we'd be banged up at eight for thirteen hours or more. Could turn a guy mad, it could, unless we could get to the prison gym in the mornin' to let off some steam. Saw many a fight in here – took part in some too. But don't worry, I'm a reformed character now.'

He pulls out a gold pocket watch from his shirt pocket and waves it in the air. 'I saved up for this when I got out. Reminds me to stay on the right path. Prison robbed years off my life, and I've no plans to go back inside. So you're all perfectly safe with me.'

I eye Thomas's broad stature. He may now be in his seventies, but that doesn't mean he has lost his strength and stamina. Is he capable of pushing Fiona? I don't see why not – she was drunk, already off-balance, physically and mentally. Could he have climbed the stairs to leave the pigeon there the other night and rushed off ahead of me – is his stick just for show? What was his motive for contacting Derek about this weekend?

While suspicion nudges at me, the journalists are hanging onto Thomas's every word. I look around the group, then towards the doorway to the courtyard garden. Perhaps one of the family members is here among the guests. Did they vandalise the lift, push Fiona, sabotage the museum visit, as a demonstration against Derek's long-term plans? Maybe it was one of them arranging to meet up with Lloyd to share new information.

Tonight, the courtyard will be filled with more honoured guests. Those who helped to renovate the original building: the architects, the bankers and financial consultants, the surveyors and the lawyers. The local and national press, all wanting a good story, maybe even some gossip, and several of the local dignitaries. The mayor and her husband, MPs and everyone else who could be – and, in Derek's eyes, should be – involved in his next project. Is this really why he arranged this weekend – to invite them all as potential investors?

Someone with keys to this building left that package upstairs, so they must know this prison well. Could one of the potential investors be involved? Maybe some of them have been visiting these premises for months behind the scenes, behind my back.

Thomas raises his stick in the air again and directs every-one's eyes towards the narrow corridor that leads to Cell 135. 'Along there ... that's where them five was murdered.' His broad grin reveals his cracked teeth. 'You'd think with the screws partyin' out back that night, they'd get here quicker, mind. 'Specially with Fisher banging the cell bell – four times, I heard. But guess they had to climb all them stairs first – some were bladdered, they were. I heard rumours it were a right mess when they found them cons.

Puke smeared on the walls, all over the doors, all over the bodies.'

A few of the guests grimace, and I cough to hide a smile. Thomas told me earlier that he wanted to create some drama, give our guests a shock before they leave the hotel. I didn't realise that this is what he had planned. He's right, though: the news reports described the chaos, each poisoned prisoner locked in their cell, toilets overflowing, and no ventilation.

'Now let me tell you a story,' he calls out, 'about a con who loved nothin' better than to shit in his cell to get attention. His name were Fritz but we called him "Shitz". Felt bit sorry for the screws who had to clean him up after, mind.'

Derek scowls and steps forwards to intervene, but backs away when Thomas raises his stick, exposing his gun tattoo.

'Then there were the screw we called Pops.' The ex-prisoner's words send a shiver down my spine as I recall Fiona's words after she fell. 'He were a tough bloke, big, also liked his tattoos, kept us all in check. No one wanted to mess with him, mind. You must'er remember him, Doc?' Thomas gives Bryan a gentle shove. 'Popeye, we all called him. Never been sure'a his real name, though.'

The doctor clears his throat. 'Pops – I'd forgotten about him. Reputation as being bent as a nine-bob note. Seemed to hang around Anna Kendall a lot.'

Lloyd nudges my arm. 'Pops?' he mouths.

I shake my head. Until last night, I hadn't heard or seen the name 'Pops' mentioned anywhere. I didn't know he existed and had no idea what – or who – Fiona meant. But even if I had, would I have told the journalist? What if Pops is the man I'm searching for?

'Oh, them stories I could tell.' Thomas checks his pocket watch and turns to Derek. 'I got how much time?'

'Not long enough, I'm afraid, Mr Benson. But thank you so much for your interesting talk today.'

Derek steps forwards, grasping his hands together. Tension flinches in his eyes. He has arranged this weekend with military precision on an Excel spreadsheet and won't want to deviate from his timings. Fiona's fall and the fire incident at the museum will already have sent ripples through his plans.

My boss turns to Lloyd. 'And Mr Palmer, you stayed here several years ago, I recall?'

'Now there's a night I'll never forget.' Despite Lloyd's laugh, I detect a quiver in his tone.

'In what way?' The deep voice comes from the back of the crowd.

'I was here over ten years ago with a group of ghostbusters, just before A wing was renovated.' Lloyd chuckles when one of the other journalists – a man with his hair tied back into a bun – asks if he saw the Michelin Man. 'No green goo either, nothing like that. It was all very technical, scientific and very real.'

'And did they find anything?' I find myself asking. 'Did you see any ghosts?'

His eyes fix on me. 'Well, Ms Batten, that's hard to say. I guess it depends on whether or not you believe they exist.'

I flinch as a door creaks above us in the wind. *No*, I remind myself, *I don't believe in ghosts at all*.

'Anna?' One of the guests raises her hand towards the emergency exit. Her cheeks have drained of colour. 'Is that Anna Kendall?'

A cool breeze drifts through the room. Hairs rise at the back of my neck.

A petite figure stands in the doorway, glimmering in the daylight. She's clad in a nurse's uniform, blonde hair curling around a pale face.

29

MADDIE

NOW

Anna Kendall grins and giggles and twiddles her curls as lottery winners take photographs of her with their phones. Everyone appears to be astounded, perhaps even a little disturbed and confused, as though we really have summoned a ghost this weekend. And even I can almost believe we have, as her features and mannerisms are as authentic as they could be.

Derek is muttering to himself that 'ghost time' isn't marked on his spreadsheet, and looks relieved when some of the journalists appear to grow restless. He taps on his watch and calls for attention, then leads everyone towards A wing, with Bryan and Thomas trailing behind. A Panbook history documentary is scheduled to begin at three o'clock in the conference room, followed by cream tea.

Flint – one of the Reception staff – calls to Lloyd Palmer. The conversation seems rather animated, but I can't hear what they're saying. The journalist stuffs a small keycard envelope into his trouser pocket, stares at Anna Kendall for a moment and follows Flint into the main building.

Once we're alone, I grip the young woman's arm and pull

her to one side, out of everyone else's earshot. 'What the heck are you doing here?' I try to keep my voice quiet and calm.

'Sorry, I didn't think. I—' She notices my glare and bends down to pick up her small orange backpack.

'No ... you didn't.'

'Don't worry, I said I'm from an agency, an Anna Kendall lookalike.' Ellie gives me a lopsided grin and nudges me with her elbow. 'I said we'd arranged this as a surprise.'

I can't help but laugh at her audacity. Though I'm not sure whether to throttle her or hug her. 'The security guard shouldn't have let you through. You're not on the entry list.'

My stomach fizzes. *Who else has he let in today?*

'Oh, yes, about that...' Ellie gives me a sheepish shrug. 'I ... erm ... slipped through when he wasn't looking. He was standing outside having a smoke.'

'It sounds like I need to have a word with him. People don't normally try to sneak into a hotel, but then again, Panbrook isn't normal.'

I always tell people that Ellie has inherited her resourceful-ness and rebellious behaviour from me. I like to hope that maybe this could be more nurture than nature.

'Well, now you're here, I guess you may as well have a look round.' I take a step back and tut at her blue-and-white attire. 'Though I do wish you weren't wearing that.'

'The ward's a nurse down so I offered to do the later shift. Viv's gone to a work do 'til late and I was bored.' She smooths her tunic down over her trousers. 'Anyway, it makes me look more authentic.'

I bite back a smile. 'Except she didn't wear a uniform.'

Just as I followed my mother into the hospitality industry, nature has certainly won here too, with Ellie choosing the occupation that Anna chose, looking after the sick and comforting the needy – fortunately in a hospital rather than in a prison.

My office is too humid to sit in there for a chat, so we walk through to the courtyard garden to keep out of the way. It's currently out of bounds to hotel guests, with just a few staff members setting up tables, and an electrician fitting the stage lights. I move two white metal chairs behind the black LED backdrop, where no one will overhear our conversation. Although we won't have long, as the band, appropriately called Prison Rocks, will be setting up soon.

'This is so cool.' Ellie looks around, her eyes wide, jiggling her feet like a young child. 'Mind if I take some photos to show Viv?'

I laugh, constantly bemused by my daughter's social-media obsessed generation. 'But no posting on Instagram or Snapchat until Monday. It's all under embargo. And tell Viv this is for her eyes only.'

'Sure.' Ellie pulls out her phone from her bag, bounces to her feet and snaps photographs in all directions.

Derek had the final say on this evening's decor and enter-tainment. He wanted to create an impression, he said, some-thing theatrical that our guests wouldn't forget in a hurry. They certainly won't.

The gazebo canopy is now striped in black and cream like a prison uniform, and thin steel chains threaded with silver handcuffs hang down from the white metal rafters. Fake barbed wire trails around the top of its outer edges, giving it the appearance of a perimeter fence. We have also hired a medieval pillory, prison uniforms for the serving staff, and a photographer to record every precious moment.

Ellie sits down and rests her phone on her lap. 'This is such a fab place for a party.'

'It does look impressive. But my answer is no.' I gaze up at the B-wing windows, where dark panes of glass are reflecting the sunshine. Glints of light watching our every move. 'You are *not* having your wedding party here.'

'Oh, you guessed.' Ellie leans back with a heavy sigh. 'That's why I popped by. I wanted to see it all done up.'

'I'm not an idiot, Ellie. Of course I guessed. And before you ask again, my answer is still a definite no.'

A loud rumble comes from the stage area. I peer around the backdrop. A tall man in black jeans is heading towards us carrying a hefty keyboard, followed by a blue-haired girl holding a guitar stand and wheeling a metal case.

I straighten the curtain and lower my voice to a whisper. 'You didn't think I'd catch you here today, did you?'

Ellie sucks her lower lip and swallows sharply. 'Bad timing. But now I'm here, you can tell me all the details in person. How did yesterday go? Did you find anything out?'

'About your mum?' My chest tightens as memories of the past forty-eight hours flood through me.

'*You're* my mum, how many times do I need to tell you?'

'Ssh ... keep your voice down.' I shiver in a sudden gust of wind and rub my bare arms to warm them up. 'I love you, obviously. I brought you up because I love you ... and because she couldn't. And because Nate—'

Ellie interrupts me with a sad laugh. 'Surprising I've turned out so well really, when you look at my family set-up. My dad really my uncle, my birth father unknown, my aunt being my mum ... and my birth mum a killer.'

I know she's saying this to wind me up, it isn't the first time, but I still can't help rising to the bait.

'I promised Nate I'd prove she wasn't.' I curl my hands into fists. *But what if I can't?*

Now I think about it, this weekend is very much about my daughter, her past and, if she had her way for her wedding, even her future. She's more a part of the prison's history than I could ever be – than most of the guests this weekend.

I hate that Nate – Ellie's last link to her blood relatives – is now gone. Unless I can find the name of the man I'm searching for.

She clears her throat to break the silence. 'And the sewer rat?'

Lloyd Palmer with his dark, brooding eyes.

'He's ... he's helping me.'

Ellie leans forwards. 'What? But I thought—'

'This weekend has been full of surprises. You'll be happy to know he thinks she may have been innocent after all.'

But can I trust him, and is he right?

We watch the band setting up and listen to them jamming before the big event tonight. Eventually our break is over, as Ellie needs to be at the hospital for her shift and I need to get back to work before Derek catches me slacking with the hired help.

When we reach the foyer, Ellie squirms. 'Actually, I just need the loo. Long drive ahead.'

I lead her to the restrooms by The Lock Up and push open the door. 'I'll wait for you here.'

'I can find my own way out.' Her eyes flash with indignation. 'Mum, stop treating me like a child.'

'You're not on the entry list. I'd do the same if you were anyone else.'

Ellie pushes past me, clutching her backpack. 'What do you think I'm going to do? Steal the library books?' She rolls her eyes as she closes the door behind her.

I step forwards, my hand ready to push the door open again. But then I pause. Ellie is right, she's no longer a child. Though she is still *my* child, constantly triggering my urge to protect her, to hide her identity over the years. She's about to get married, soon belonging more with Viv than with me, and I need to learn to give her more space. Now would be a good time to start.

'Okay,' I shout through the door. 'Just call me when you get to work so I know you've arrived.'

30

MADDIE

NOW

SATURDAY
5.00 p.m.

Derek is holding court next to A wing, surrounded by a group of VIPs, giving them a potted summary of the original building renovations. Apparently, he will be providing more specific details once the remaining press and local dignitaries arrive tonight. I wish he had briefed me about his new plans in advance as I now feel totally out of my depth.

Thomas left the hotel half-an-hour ago. Flint carried his suitcase down to the hotel entrance, and I waited with the former inmate for his taxi to arrive.

When I asked Thomas again about Pops, he clammed up. 'Nothin' more to tell. It's all in the past.'

My stomach swirled with disappointment. 'Well, thank you for joining us this weekend. I assume you enjoyed your stay.'

'Certainly beats the last time I were 'ere. But I'm lookin'

forward to some peace 'n' quiet. Off to Marbella for two weeks, I am. Now where's that cab? Need to get to the airport.' Fumbling around in his shirt pocket, he huffed out a sigh. 'Dropped my pocket watch somewhere. Reported it to Housekeeping, I did, but can you make sure they send it on if it turns up? Not as pricey as it looks, found it in a junk shop, but it's got sentimental value, you know?'

'Of course.' I made a note on my iPad. 'And remember, you're welcome back here at any time.'

Judging by Thomas's rueful expression before he left, I suspect he's unlikely to ever return.

'Very snazzy.' The black bar table wobbles as Lloyd lays his laptop bag down on top. He gazes up at the gazebo canopy flapping gently in the breeze. 'And very ... understated.'

I ignore the sarcasm in his voice and continue to browse the spreadsheet on my iPad: a list of this evening's guests. I'm trying to memorise their names and job titles and have been Googling their photographs, where available, so that I don't make a fool of myself.

This party tonight means a lot to Derek, more financially than emotionally I now realise. The hotel isn't struggling, far from it, but he's always looking for something bigger and better, a new project that will thrust Panbrook – and him – into the limelight yet again. And now, it seems, he has one.

'I wasn't expecting to find you here.' The table wobbles again as Lloyd unzips his bag and pulls out his laptop. 'I thought you'd be clucking around like a headless hen by now.'

I scrutinise the table's silver pedestal base as it rocks on uneven ground. Pete will need to fix this before the party. 'Headless hens can't cluck. And everything's going to plan, as far as I can tell. While you've been holidaying this afternoon, I've been busy working – in the kitchen, the office, Reception area, Housekeeping, a few guest rooms...'

I have left Rosalie confirming the timings for this evening

with the kitchen staff and band. The chef is currently in The Lock-Up putting the final touches to the prison-themed canapés and beverages. I tasted some samples after Ellie's departure, to make sure they'll meet Derek's high standards. My favourites were the 'Clink Cocktail', a lychee martini, and the 'Dungeon Doughnuts', filled with blood-red strawberry jam.

'I saw you talking to our resident ghost.' Lloyd chuckles as he removes his glasses from his shirt pocket and puts them on. 'She really is the spitting image. I actually thought she was Anna at first. I'm guessing Ellie couldn't stay away.'

My cheeks flush with warmth. 'I've sent her home. And Anna's ghost wouldn't be here. Don't ghosts haunt where they died?'

'Maybe some aren't quite so fussy. I'm not sure they follow a manual.'

'What happened with the ghost hunters that time?'

Colour drains from his face as he glances up at B wing. 'Nothing really ... I— I felt cold, like there was an icy wind, heard shuffling sounds, a woody smell in the room – the usual cliches ... The organisers must have set it all up for publicity.'

The cold draught ... the woody scent ... the rustling sounds ... Of course! Someone must have set it all up at the museum – and B wing too. I shake my head at the rogue thought stomping through my mind – that perhaps ghosts do exist after all.

Lloyd opens his laptop and switches it on, typing in his password to access the home screen. 'No evidence of this mysterious Pops so far.' He clicks open some photographs and shifts the screen to the left to move it out of the sun. 'Maybe he used to be a sailor. You ever watch *Popeye*?'

I roll my eyes as he sings the theme tune. 'Thomas said he was a prison officer. Assuming Pops is a nickname, he's unlikely to be listed under that in any staff records, but I'll double-check in the museum again tomorrow.' The firefighter warned against it, but I need to know if I've found the man I'm searching for. 'Maybe this Pops was responsible for framing Anna. Fiona muttered something about Pops after she fell, but I had no idea what – or who – she was talking about. Maybe he's come back to cause trouble this weekend and she saw him in the crowd. Maybe he's the mysterious person who wanted to meet with you.'

'That's a lot of maybes.' Lloyd pulls out his notebook from his laptop bag. 'I spoke to Dr Land earlier. He says he always suspected that Anna was up to something. She kept disappearing to the kitchen garden, even when she was on shift, claiming she needed some air. Some people speculated that she was bringing drugs in. What do you think?'

I switch off my iPad and picture that news cutting I found in B wing. Someone is certainly trying to link those men's deaths to drug dealing in the prison.

'As I said, I didn't know Anna that well. We only met a few times and didn't really talk much. But Nate always said Anna wouldn't have risked her job.'

'Maybe this Pops was forcing Anna to deal drugs – master-minding the whole thing.' Lloyd purses his lips together in thought. 'Maybe he's the one who killed those men, or he asked Anna to do it for him. It's strange though that Pops never came up when I originally explored the case.'

'Dr Land said he'd forgotten about him after all these years.'

'Maybe there's a lot the doctor has forgotten – and maybe being here will help to trigger those memories.' Lloyd opens his notebook and flicks through a few pages as if he's looking for something. 'So let's go with the theory that Anna was dealing drugs at The Brook. That's what the police were origi-nally investigating. I've been going through the Healthcare records to see if there's a pattern.'

'Pattern?'

'I've been looking to see which of those prisoners visited Anna the most, or regularly, in the couple of months leading up to the murders. It might indicate who she was dealing to, or who was involved. Maybe they had threatened to report her if she didn't keep up the supply.'

'Or maybe she wanted to get out of the arrangement.'

Lloyd pushes his notebook towards me and points at a tally chart. Then he begins to read out loud. 'Steven Fisher. He was the known drug addict of the five. Eight times to Dr Land – once a week. Mainly about medicines for his anxiety and depression, and claimed he had aches and pains. After what he did to Anna, he wasn't supposed to see her at all. Yet he ended up seeing her once before they died.'

'Does it say why?'

'Nothing's stated in the ledger. It's just something I was told when I was researching my book. Maybe Dr Land was away and Fisher was desperate. Maybe Anna didn't have a choice but to see him.' Lloyd turns to the next page. 'Now we have Jonathan Roach. Ten times to Anna. That's over once a week. All minor things, it seems. But he had a thing for her – the old librarian I spoke to said Roach would write her poetry and leave it lying around.'

As voices reach us from outside the gazebo, we both look up. Derek and his entourage have moved closer. He's pointing out a stretch of the courtyard that's believed to be an old burial ground, the last resting place of executed prisoners. This area remains undisturbed, as not even my boss – in his quest for further renovations – is prepared to exhume the dead.

'Assuming the rumours were right,' Lloyd continues more quietly, 'Roach was thought to be involved in getting drugs in here. So maybe this whole Anna obsession was a cover-up between them.'

'From what I heard, she didn't like him at all. But then no

one really did. Are you suggesting it could be Pops, Anna and Roach working together?'

'I don't know. I'm just surmising. Then we have William Owen.' When Lloyd pokes his finger at the scribbled writing in his notebook, the table wobbles again. 'He saw Anna a lot at first, mainly for gardening injuries. Then stopped coming into Healthcare when Anna was on maternity leave, and mainly saw Dr Land once she was back. She didn't want him to work in Healthcare, which led to clashes between them. Maybe Anna was worried that Owen would discover her little drugs empire if he hung around too much, especially with his pharmacy background.'

'Yet eventually he did work in Healthcare, didn't he? Fiona let him in. But surely Dr Land and the head nurse – Kellie Wyndham – would have noticed if Anna was dealing drugs to prisoners. Though Anna could be quite devious, to be fair.'

Lloyd raises his eyebrows, clearly expecting me to elaborate, but instead I tear a corner off his open notebook page and fold it up to create a wedge. He scowls at me as if I have destroyed his favourite toy.

'It's a shame Fiona isn't still here as we could have asked her.' Lloyd gives a tight smile. 'Unless Anna wasn't passing drugs through Healthcare. Maybe there was another route – there was talk of the kitchen garden. Which brings us to Raziq Ahmed. Looks like he went to Anna six times. She used to supervise him in the garden, even though she wasn't an officer. Perhaps he had something going on with her and it was an excuse to see each other. Did she ever mention him?'

'Not to me.' I conjure up an image of Raziq in my mind. His dark eyes, angular face and brown skin. 'I can't say whether or not he was Anna's type as I never knew her type. I didn't meet my sister-in-law until just after Ellie was born. We never met Ellie's father; originally she claimed he was a one-night stand she met in a club. There may have been several of those, for all we know – she was bubbly, pretty...'

An image of Nate replaces Raziq's, a disapproving look on his face, reminding me that I'm referring to his sister. *Anna was no slut*, he often spluttered when he read anything in the media suggesting she was.

'Ahmed had lots of gardening injuries too.' Lloyd taps the table with his finger. 'Cuts and scrapes, nothing major, but I assume they all needed attention, including that time he was beaten up by other inmates.'

'Gardening can be dangerous business – rose thorns, backache, trips and falls, all those tools lying around...' I bend down and push the paper wedge under my side of the table base. 'What about Lucas Somers?'

When I attempt to wobble the pedestal again, this time it doesn't budge.

'He saw Dr Land every week, sometimes more, but no details. Didn't seem to see Anna at all. Maybe he was too busy grassing on everyone to the doctor and prison governor. Maybe he was going to grass on Anna too, so she killed him.'

'But—'

A throaty cooing sound interrupts me. A grey pigeon is observing us from the top of the next bar table, his sleek head cocked to the side in concentration.

I wave my hand to shush him away before he soils the tabletop. 'But we still don't have anything concrete to prove the drugs theory. It's not getting us anywhere.'

'I'm guessing the police must have found some evidence. It would have come out in court eventually if she had gone on trial.'

He opens up a photograph on his laptop and turns to another page in his notebook, this one covered in black handwriting. 'Actually, there's a discrepancy here. I took some photos of the displays in the museum earlier, before we had to leave – some printouts of the computerised Healthcare records – and also made notes of times and dates of appointments and cell checks that were written in the Healthcare ledgers.' He points at the screen. 'Looking now, some of these aren't logged in the computer system. That could be something. Dr Land once told me that Anna used to type up his appointments and notes. Maybe she was deliberately fiddling the books.'

'Or maybe you're just reading too much into it. Computers were so new, especially in prisons, so lots of things probably wouldn't have been transferred over. And remember how often computers used to crash in those days?'

'Yes, maybe you're right. I just want to find something – something useful.' He closes his laptop down and snaps it shut. 'Anyway, drugs money would explain her sudden riches. She bought a big house, a fancy car...'

'Sudden riches?' I press my hand against my lips to stifle a laugh. 'That's easily explained. Anna said Ellie's dad – Lucy's – had suddenly decided to cough up and help her out. Ellie was getting sick from mould and damp in their flat, so Anna finally contacted him. It meant she could buy a house and put Ellie in a nursery.'

'I thought you just said he was a one-night stand.'

'He was. Or at least that's what she told us at first. But that doesn't mean they weren't in contact at all.'

Lloyd removes his glasses and rubs his eyes. 'I don't understand why Anna wouldn't tell her family who Ellie's father was.'

'Nate always suspected he was married or much older than her.' More cooing comes from beside me – our avian spy is back. 'I've always assumed he was working here – one of the prison officers.'

'He must have been a rich one to buy her a house and pay for the nursery. I can't see prison officer wages covering that.

Which brings us to Jonathan Roach. Wealthier prisoners were known to try to bribe prison staff.'

'But I read in your book that his father cut him off after he was arrested. Are you saying that's not true?'

'Of course it's true. I spent years researching my book.' He gently taps his glasses against his laptop case. 'But Jonathan Roach had some unscrupulous contacts and was probably savvy enough to have money squirrelled away somewhere for when he was released.'

The pigeon hops onto the bar table again. I shake my head at him but don't bother to wave my arms this time. There's no point if he has taken a shine to that table – or to us. House-keeping will need to give every surface a thorough clean before the party begins. The pigeon eyes me with a conceited expression as if he knows he's won.

'That still doesn't mean Anna wasn't involved in some-thing. Maybe Ellie's father was too.' Lloyd's gaze shifts to the red acer, where the VIPs have gathered around two serving trolleys laden with sandwiches, rolls and pastries. The lottery winners spill out of A wing to join them for a late tea before the party tonight.

The journalist clears his throat nervously and gives me an uncomfortable smile. 'Ever since our conversation this morn-ing, I've been thinking about something ... Why didn't Nate want to talk to me all those years ago? I would have quoted him accurately. Maybe dispelled some of the rumours about Anna.'

'Nate didn't trust anyone. The whole world seemed to be against his sister. He certainly didn't trust *you*.'

Lloyd raises his eyebrows. 'Do you?'

'The jury's still out.'

I fish my phone out of my trouser pocket. No notifica-tions from Ellie. I tap out a message – *Hope you arrived OK. Love you* – and press send.

I look at the journalist again. 'That note you found in your room during the reception ... If someone knows Anna's innocent, why didn't they come forward when she was arrested?'

'So many people didn't want to go on record but still had something to say about Anna, those men and what happened that night. I referred to them as anonymous sources in my book.' He stares at a waiter setting up the bar area in the corner of the gazebo, carefully lining up the wine glasses like soldiers on parade. 'I reckon they were all former prisoners, or officers who were probably here at the party. They slowly crawled out of the woodwork, but it seemed like something was holding them back. One woman who wouldn't leave her name insisted that Anna was innocent but refused to give me more details.'

'Maybe someone was threatening her. Maybe someone still is.' Thomas, Fiona and Bryan have different memories of Panbrook, and they've all been hiding something this weekend, but there was one name they all shared. 'Sounds like we need to find this Pops.'

'Madeleine.' Derek is striding towards us, his face flushed. 'Can I have a word – NOW.'

31

MADDIE

NOW

SATURDAY
6.30 p.m.

Derek leads me towards Room A50, where Stella is sleeping over the weekend, opposite my room on the parallel walkway. He has remained silent since the courtyard, ignoring my questions. He unlocks Stella's door, glances around the landing, and beckons me inside.

The small window is ajar, letting in fresh air and the sound of the band rehearsing in the courtyard below us. The female singer is currently belting out 'Jailhouse Rock'.

Stella is lying on the bed, propped up on pillows, the covers scrunched up beneath her. Her black skirt rides slightly up her pale thin thighs, and her white shirt is open at the neck, revealing prominent collarbones and her O-shaped pendant. Her eyes are closed, and her hands are resting by her sides.

I take a step forwards. 'Stella?' She doesn't stir. As the

room spins around me, I lean against the wall to steady myself. 'Derek, what's going on?'

He rakes his fingers through his hair – a stark contrast to the relaxed man I was watching in the courtyard only a few minutes ago. 'Another guest reported some missing jewellery. I tried to contact Stella – to make sure it wasn't picked up by Housekeeping when they cleaned the room – but she didn't respond to my messages or calls.'

'So you came up here?'

'Rosalie said Stella was having a lie down, so yes, I came up to find her. With the party tonight, this was *not* the time for her to have a lie down. She didn't reply so I let myself in with the master key card. When I found her like this, I came to find you.'

I take another step towards the bed. Stella's mobile phone lies on the bedside table next to a box of paracetamol tablets and a glass bottle of water. An open doctor's bag sits on the floor under the window.

Bryan strolls out of the bathroom, wiping his hands on a white handkerchief. When he spots me, he stuffs the handkerchief into his trouser pocket.

I turn back to Derek. 'What's he doing here?'

'I called him as soon as I found her. I was hoping there was something he could do, but unfortunately not.'

'Are you ... are you sure she's...' I can't say the word out loud, although it resonates in my head.

Dead.

Stella's face seems more relaxed than when I saw her last, as if several years were washed away with her last breath. When *did* I see her last? In the courtyard garden? After Fiona fell? I can't even remember – the last few hours seem to have blurred in my mind.

'I've checked for a pulse.' Bryan shakes his head at Derek.

'She's definitely gone. I can't say for sure, but I suspect a heart attack.'

Despair washes over me, and tears prickle the corners of my eyes. Stella. Is. Dead. We weren't friends, by any means. But this? Fiona, now Stella. The writing on the mirror. The fire in the museum. This weekend seems to have been doomed from the start.

'What about those?' I point at the packet of painkillers. 'She could have taken an overdose by mistake. We need to call the police, even if an ambulance won't help.' I reach into my pocket for my mobile.

'No!' Derek clenches my wrist with a tight grip and a clammy palm. 'We can't— The party. *My* party. It will have to wait.'

'How can we have the party now?' I shake his hand off. 'And why are we even having this conversation? The police need to be told. It's a legal requirement. She's died in your hotel.'

He isn't thinking straight. Stella is his oldest employee, here from the start. I know he's a bastard to work for, but he must have some glimmer of a beating heart, surely.

'We don't need to get anyone else involved. Not yet.' Derek nods at the doctor. 'Bryan says there's nothing we can do, so we have our medical opinion. She can stay here for now.'

'But we don't know for certain it was a heart attack. Perhaps...' I trail off.

Perhaps what? Perhaps this wasn't a natural death? The paracetamol beside her could mean suicide, or even ... even what? How can I explain all of this to Derek, when I've told him nothing about my weekend antics, or the truth about me? I can't afford to lose this job, not until I have discovered the secrets of the past. I owe it to Nate, and to Ellie.

I turn to Bryan. 'Please, Doctor, please tell Derek this isn't wise. We can't just leave her in here.'

'Madeleine,' Derek grabs my arm with a vice-like grip, squeezing it so tightly that I drop my phone on the rug, 'I have important people coming tonight. Backers for the renovations ... local politicians and the planning department ... the local media. All potential sponsors for the building works and the festival. I need their support and I – *we* – have spent a lot of time, effort and money preparing for this party. This whole weekend, in fact.'

'But...' I pull away from him and reach down to pick up my phone. My arm throbs where he grabbed me.

'No time for buts.' Derek presses his lips tightly together. 'If we have the police all over the hotel now, we won't be able to hold the party. And I need this party. A few hours won't make any difference. We can do it later.' He wrinkles his nose. 'We just need to get our stories straight.'

I rub my arm gently, trying to excuse his behaviour in my head. *He's under stress. He's had too much to drink. He's in the early stages of dementia.*

'No, Derek, you need to report this. And other people will notice if Stella isn't around tonight. Rosalie. Radha.'

'As I said, the police can wait. This is my hotel – my rules. And Stella said she wasn't feeling well, which she did, didn't she?' Derek forces a smile. 'So tell Rosalie that Bryan told Stella to rest up and come down when she felt better. You'll have to manage without her.'

'But her family ... they need to know.'

I think of Nate's final moments. I stayed with him at the hospice, but what if I hadn't? I would have been even more devastated if he had died all alone in a hotel room.

'Stella didn't have any family, and she lived alone, and she was supposed to be here all weekend anyway.' Derek opens the door to the landing. 'Everything will be fine, Madeleine. Oh, and one more thing. I understand that Thomas Benson reported a lost pocket watch before he went home. I assume you're looking into all of this missing property?'

A nerve twitches at the back of my neck. Now isn't the right time to deal with this. 'Yes, well ... I was going to speak to you about Radha on Monday. Get the weekend over first. I have my suspicions and—'

'Speak to Housekeeping to make sure they haven't found any of the missing items. The rest can wait.' He flicks his hand into the air as if wafting away bad thoughts. 'Now let's get this party started. Just lock up this room on your way out. Coming, Dr Land?'

He saunters out of the room.

Bryan picks up his doctor's bag and gives me a sympathetic smile as he brushes past me. 'I'll see you in around an hour, Ms Batten. This isn't anyone's fault, and there really *is* nothing we can do for now. Just remind Derek to report it later.'

I stare at Stella, longing to rest my hand on hers for a moment, to reassure her that she isn't alone. But instead I clench my fists – I don't want my fingerprints over a potential crime scene.

Before I leave, I turn up the air conditioning as high as it will go and shiver in the icy draught. *Hopefully that will* ... I shake my head, not bearing to think about this situation any longer, and close the door, locking it with my master key card.

I return to Reception and message Radha, asking her to clean the tables outside while I go upstairs to freshen up and change my clothes.

I'm sticking to the story that Derek has fabricated, all in the name of his success and finances and public show.

This damn party had better be worth it.

ANNA

NOVEMBER 1997

Kellie peers into the Healthcare office. 'Seen Dr Land?'

'Morning, Miss.' Ahmed brushes past her on his way out.

She stares at me with a glimmer of a frown. 'What's he doing in here? And why isn't he in the consult room? Couldn't it wait 'til clinic later?'

'He wanted to know whether to cut back the climbing roses again. Takes his job very seriously. I told Estie to let him through.' I push the computer keyboard away from me, welcoming the chance to give my eyes a break from the screen. 'Bry's in B wing. Said he needed to check on a couple of prisoners.'

'I've hardly seen him in Healthcare all week, apart from sick parade.' Kellie pouts with disappointment. 'Maybe he's avoiding me.'

'Who's avoiding you?' Bryan nudges her arm. 'What have I missed?'

'Nothing.' Her cheeks redden as she steps to the left to let him through. 'But Somers was looking for you. And Eric.'

Bryan puts his medical bag on the desk next to my mug of steaming tea. 'Any idea why?'

Kellie straightens her jacket collar and smooths down her skirt. 'Somers looked worried as usual. And Eric muttered something about you checking in on Mance. I'd go, but I'm clocking off in a half-hour.'

'That's an early one.' Bryan unlocks a storage cabinet and grabs a wad of sugar packets from the top shelf. 'Going somewhere nice?'

Kellie chuckles. 'If only. Taking my car to the garage. It makes a funny noise when I put it in reverse. So, Bry ... about Mance.'

Bryan shakes his head, looking at his watch. 'Sorry, but I need to head to C wing for some cell checks before clinic this afternoon. I know ... always in a rush.'

I eye the Healthcare ledgers on the desk. 'Before you go, I need to confirm some of those notes with you, Bry. They don't—'

'We can do that later.' He stuffs the sugar packets into his bag, before brushing past Kellie on his way into the corridor.

She stares at his retreating back. 'See...'

'You're imagining it.' I pick up my mug and wrap my cold hands around it. There's a chill in the office today as the heating's broken again. 'It's more likely to be me he's annoyed with. He keeps offering to help me and Lucy out, so we can move into somewhere fancy.'

'Give you money, you mean?'

'I ... I guess so.'

'So why don't you just say yes?' Kellie's frown is back. 'This is your chance to give Lucy a better life. You can always pay him back one day.'

'Yeah ... maybe. I said I'd think about it.' I put my mug down and pick up the next IMR file. 'Better get on and log these. Maybe one day Bry'll get used to technology. And then I'd better take some of his new booklets to the library.'

'Your lucky day ... getting to see Roach again.' Kellie peers back into the corridor, comes inside and pushes the door shut. 'How's little Lucy doing? I assume everyone here knows?'

'Most of the staff do, and a few of the prisoners. Word gets around.' I reach into the top desk drawer, pull out a photo and pass it to her. 'She's started babbling a lot. No idea what she's saying but Dad thinks she's a genius.'

Kellie grins at Lucy's picture and hands it back. 'She's so cute.'

'Dad took it at his place last week.' In the photo, Lucy's sitting in a highchair, chewing on a teething ring. Her blonde hair's starting to curl. 'Nate can't believe how much she's grown. Says she's the spitting image of me.'

'He's back then?'

'Just for a few days.' I shove the photo into my trouser pocket.

'Still with that hotel manager?'

I squeeze my hands together. 'Unfortunately.'

'Why don't you like her?' Kellie leans against the desk.

'She irritates me. There's just something about her. Nate deserves better.'

'Nothing to do with her taking your big brother away from you and your dad, is it? You've said they spend a lot of time in Spain.' She gives me a knowing look.

I stand up and stretch my legs, unlock the storage cupboard and take out my medical bag. 'Time for me to go and see Mance.'

'But am I right?' Kellie calls as I leave the room.

'Gov Trayton.'

She startles at my voice, pushes her drawer shut and rests her hands on the desk. 'Nurse Kendall, what can I do for you today?'

I sit down in the spare chair and place an IMR file in front of her. 'It's about Mance. I've just been to see him. He's lying in bed and can't move.'

'Oh, how I've missed you, Nurse Kendall. It was so quiet here while you were on compassionate leave.' Her eyes light up with amusement. It's the first time I've ever seen her smile.

'He needs another scan. He can't walk at all now.'

She grimaces and picks up a pen. 'There's no funding and no escort staff to take him. And this time I don't want to hear your threats, Nurse Kendall. My answer is no.'

'He could be dying for all you know.' My skin prickles with frustration. 'And he's in so much pain. If you won't accept my professional opinion, I may as well not be here. Don't you even care?'

'Of course I care. But there's nothing I can do.'

'Well, I'm not prepared to put my reg on the line if something happens to that patient on my watch.' I jab my finger at Mance's file. 'I'll write in here that you're taking full clinical responsibility for his health, then you can sign it. So if we end up in the coroner's court...'

'That approach may have worked once with Benson, but it won't happen again. You can't threaten me or blackmail me. It's to do with budgets, remember?' Gov Trayton nods towards the door. 'Have a good day, Nurse Kendall.'

'Knock knock. Got a minute?' Estie pushes open the consult-room door and steps to the side. 'Brought someone to see you. Told him to wait 'til Bryan's on clinic, but says he can't.'

'Ahmed again?' I finish locking up the storage cupboard. 'He'll need to be quick. Clinic closes at three.'

'Cheers, ma'am.' The patient salutes Estie as he saunters

inside and sits down on the couch, crinkling the fresh blue tissue paper. It's not Ahmed – it's Owen.

Estie hovers in the doorway, glancing from me to him and back again, gripping the door tightly. 'Want me to stay?'

Ever since I came back from compassionate leave, she's been extra cautious, still worrying over what happened with Fisher. I've told her I'm fine and it wasn't her fault, but I don't think she believes me.

'No,' I stare at the patient, 'this one won't be any trouble.'

Estie raises her eyebrows and fingers the baton on her belt. 'Pills, you'd better behave yourself. I'll be outside.'

'Always behave myself in here.' Owen winks at me, then at Estie. 'I'm saving myself for you, ma'am.'

Estie rolls her eyes and closes the door behind her.

I pull out his brown folder from the cabinet. 'So how can I help?'

'I've got a bad headache. Another two paracetamol should do it. Unless you can give me something stronger.'

I flick through his IMR until I reach the meds chart. It's not easy dealing with a patient who knows just as much about medicines as you do, maybe more. 'You had some this morning from Nurse Wyndham, so you can't have any now. We've told you it's stress; taking extra painkillers won't help.'

'Oh, come on, Nurse Kendall, give a guy a break.' Tears well up in his eyes, and his shoulders shudder. 'I can't sleep. Can't concentrate on anything. I ... I keep thinking about my little Jessie.'

'How's she doing?'

'The doctors don't know yet if the treatment's working. I should be with them. She needs me. They—' His voice breaks as he wipes his eyes with the back of his hand. 'They all do.'

I want to comfort him, but I'm not working in a hospital now. Here, I can't be seen getting close to the patients. 'Do you think you might be depressed? I can prescribe something for that. Or I could get you some lavender from the garden. That's good for stress, a little bird once told me.'

'Next, you'll be telling me to meditate or something. We both know that's bullshit.' He glances at the door. 'Just heard Trayton's granted me Cat D and is transferring me to Egdon Open. Can you fucking believe it?' As he shuffles a little closer to me, his blue-and-white shirt gapes, revealing a rose tattoo on his chest.

I catch a whiff of his woody-scented deodorant. Must cost him a fortune, buying it from the canteen list. 'That's crazy. You need to be nearer your girls, not further away.'

'That's why you need to help me. Please.' He grabs my arm and stares into my eyes. Lowers his voice. 'Talk to the gov for me. She listens to you.'

My tummy lurches as I wriggle out of his grasp. 'You've got to be joking, right? Trayton doesn't listen to me.' Footsteps sound in the distance. 'What happened with Benson that time was a one-off. She wouldn't even get an ambulance for Mance earlier. I'm sorry, but there's nothing I can do.'

Owen reaches down and picks up a photo from the floor.

I shove my hand into my empty trouser pocket.

'Getting big, isn't she?' He runs his finger over Lucy's face. Another tear trickles down his cheek. 'Reminds me of my twins at that age. Imagine if you couldn't see her 'cos you were locked up? Or even worse, if something happened to her. Please help me. Come on, you know you want to.'

'No, I can't.' I keep my voice steady as I glance at the closed door. A shadow passes across the window. 'And give that back.' I snatch the photo out of his hand and shove it into my pocket. 'Remember, Estie's out there.'

The footsteps in the corridor are getting closer. Then they stop outside.

'You gotta help, please, Nurse Kendall.' He takes a step

back as the door handle turns. 'Just some painkillers then. For fuck's sake, that's all I—'

'Pills, that's enough.' Bryan walks in and stands between us. 'Step away from her or I'll call Estie in. She'll send you to seg if you don't behave.'

Owen scowls and slopes out of the consult room.

Bryan puts his arm around me. 'You okay? He'll be out of here soon – Trayton's transferring him so you won't need to worry.'

'Yeah, Owen said. Not the best timing. He's a right mess. It's all he could talk about.'

'He opened up to you? That's astonishing. Kellie will be so relieved. Some of the officers are worried he's getting unpredictable – aggressive, even.'

Bryan puts his radio on the countertop. He pulls out some of the sugar packets from his medical bag and hands them to me. 'Pills and Roach had a big bust up yesterday – Roach was covered in bruises so Trayton moved Pills to a different landing. That may be why she's moving him on.'

'That's weird. Owen didn't mention it.' I unlock the storage cabinet and stuff the packets into the jar on the top shelf, then lock it back up.

'Why would he?' Bryan blinks at me. 'There's a rumour that Roach and his poetry did it – his obsession with yours truly. He told Pills you and he are having a thing, and Pills said it was bullshit. They had a fight, and three officers had to break it up.'

'That's gross.' My skin prickles with goosebumps. 'Everyone knows Roach talks a load of shit.'

'Sure he does. But I'm guessing Pills has a thing for you too, or why would it get to him so much? You know he has an eye for the ladies. Annie, make sure he's not trying to sweet-talk you to get what he wants.'

'To be fair, Roach comes in more with his bloody

poems. And since I've started delivering some of your booklets to the library, I'm seeing even more of him. There's no
escape.'

'I'll let you blame that one on me, though you agreed to
do it.' Bryan's eyes crinkle in the corners. 'Feel sorry for Pills,
mind, not seeing his wife and little girls. I'd be devastated if I
couldn't see my Faye when she's having a bad turn.'

'Egdon's miles away.' I scrunch up the blue tissue paper
from the couch and throw it in the bin. 'His family need him
close by. And I'm worried about his mental health.'

'It's probably the only suitable prison with space for him,
and he'll be released in a few months. Anyhow, the move
would be better for all of us.'

'What do you mean?' I reach for the fresh roll and spread
the new tissue along the couch.

'He's been pressuring Trayton to let him come back to
Healthcare again. Says working in here would take his mind
off things. I've told the gov it's not appropriate, obviously.
Who knows what he'd get up to. Which reminds me ... Did
you go and see Mance earlier? When I popped in there, his
cellmate said you'd already been.'

'Yeah, I gave him some extra painkillers. Not much else I
could do.'

Our radios crackle. *Code Blue. Code Blue on C wing.*

I peer into Gov Trayton's office and watch her shove a hip
flask into her desk drawer. She pulls out a small bottle of
breath freshener and sprays it into her mouth.

I knock loudly, then storm in without waiting for an
answer. 'Gov.'

A scowl spreads across her face. 'You again. What now,
Nurse Kendall?'

'Mance died this afternoon, as I'm sure you've heard. He needed that hospital scan today, I told you.'

'That prisoner overdosed on cocaine, Nurse Kendall.' She taps her fingers on the desk. 'The officers found a bag of it in his cell. It was nothing to do with his medical condition.'

'He told me earlier he couldn't live with the pain. Felt like we'd all abandoned him. I guess he took action into his own hands and asked one of the other prisoners to get him something. It's your fault for not listening to me. Maybe you're not as focused on your job as you should be.' I nod towards her drawer and mime slugging from a bottle.

'I don't know what you're insinuating.' Her hand shakes as she slams it on the desk. 'Once I get the full briefing, *my* job will be to find out where he got the drugs from. *Your* job is to treat the prisoners.' The corners of her mouth twitch, as if something has amused her. 'I understand you gave him some morphine? I assume you checked the bottle carefully, and the dose. We've had a few unexpected deaths in recent months. Maybe I should be investigating Healthcare.'

'That's a ridiculous accusation, and you know it. Anyway, how am I supposed to do my job properly when everything revolves around your teeny budgets?' I clench my fists and take several deep breaths to calm my racing heart. 'Oh, and while I'm here, I hear William Owen is moving on.'

'I don't think that's any of your business.'

'Or maybe it is.' I nod towards her drawer.

'Nurse Kendall, Owen belongs in Cat D. I've been waiting for a suitable transfer placement for months so I'm not going to turn this down. We need the space here, and he'll have more freedom there.'

'Except Kent isn't where he wants to be, is it? He came into Healthcare earlier in a right state. One of his little girls is seriously ill and he needs to be near them – by staying at The Brook. Be better for his mental health, and theirs.'

Surely the Tin Man must have a heart.

'You're a nurse, not in charge of transfers. You do your job, and I'll do mine.'

Clearly she doesn't.

'But you don't let me do my job properly, do you? How many more prisoners are going to die in here? Their mental health is important. What needs to happen for you to take action?'

The governor stands up and takes a step towards me, a stony expression clouding her features. 'That's enough, Nurse Kendall.'

'Maybe you should be moving Roach on instead. But I guess money talks in this place.'

I slam the door on my way out.

**Excerpts from the 'Meet victim #4 – William "Pills" Owen'
chapter in *Panbrook Prisongate* by Lloyd Palmer – published
by Spotlight Books, August 2009**

*NOTE: William Owen's wife asked not to be named or quoted in
this book. She remarried a few years after he died and preferred
to keep their daughter out of the public eye, so I have respected
her wishes.*

"Will's dad packed his bags one night and fucked off.
Abandoned his five-year-old son for a French whore.
The bastard. I made sure Will never went without.
Worked long hours to keep a roof over our heads.
Wanted to make sure he was nothing like his dad. For all
the good that did."

— PAULA OWEN, WILLIAM'S MOTHER

"William started working here after he qualified as a
pharmacist. He had big ambitions – save up to buy his
own pharmacy, then expand to his own chain. He was a
valued member of the team, until we discovered he'd
been stealing from us."

— BEN HART, FORMER
SUPERINTENDENT PHARMACIST AT
BELL'S PHARMACY IN CHELMSFORD

"Like father, like son. Will had a lovely wife and two little
girls, big house, cushy lifestyle. But he was having it off
with a local GP. After everything we'd been through

together – as if I'd taught him nothing about respect – he threw it all back in my face. He needed to learn the hard way. So yes, I was the one who told his wife. And then the stupid cow forgave him."

— **PAULA OWEN**

"I was working in the pharmacy late one night catching up on paperwork. I could smell smoke and petrol so went down to investigate. The dispensary was on fire. I managed to get out the back and dial 999. If I hadn't been there, the whole pharmacy would have gone up in flames. If I'd gone down any later, I'd have gone up in flames too. A dog-walker saw William running away from the scene."

— **BEN HART**

"William Owen was a model prisoner at The Brook, keeping himself out of trouble, working in the prison garden. But his mental health began to deteriorate when his daughter fell ill. When he was recategorised to Category D, this gave him more freedom than the other prisoners and involved a move to Egdon Open. I thought the change would be good for him."

— **FIONA TRAYTON, FORMER PANBROOK PRISON GOVERNOR**

"One of my granddaughters got sick, *really* sick – leukaemia – and I wanted to help. But my son and his wife still wouldn't let me see her. She was so little – only three. They wanted to punish *me* because *he* couldn't keep his hands to himself."

— PAULA OWEN

"Due to pressure from Owen's family members and prison staff, I eventually permitted him to remain at The Brook. His lawyer insisted that I also allow extra family visits to enable Owen to see his daughters more often. Since he was now Category D, I also decided to move him from gardening to Healthcare, subject to certain conditions."

— FIONA TRAYTON

"Pills worked hard, but he and Anna clashed. I complained to Trayton but she wouldn't move him out of Healthcare. Anna was so much more relaxed when he was on day release. Pills worked at a small shop in Astonbury one day a week, and at a local market on Saturday mornings, selling the prison's herbs and spices."

— DR BRYAN LAND

"Will changed after his little girl died. He even got in touch with me. Apologised for everything that happened. When he started working outside the prison, we met up a few times. He said he was saving for his release and a fresh start. But part of me was waiting for him to screw up. He still had an eye for the ladies, you see – a right charmer, just like his dad. And then that little minx killed him. He must have found out she was up to something in Healthcare."

— PAULA OWEN

34

MADDIE

NOW

SATURDAY
8.00 p.m.

Tears prickle my eyes as I hover in the doorway to the courtyard garden, greeting the guests. It may be party time, but how can I socialise with Stella gone? And how long will it be before someone starts asking questions, noticing her absence?

I fake a smile as the local mayor poses in the pillory for the photographer. Her hands and head are poking through the holes, and her long auburn hair spirals down. She distorts her face into an exaggerated expression of pain and suffering.

Her dress is similar to mine, with its hem just above the knee, nipped-in waist and diamanté crystals scattered over the soft fabric. But hers is pale blue to match her eyes, whereas mine is burgundy, and she wears an expensive-looking chunky gold chain around her neck.

As soon as the mayor exits the pillory, another guest takes

her place. He hands his navy suit jacket to a female companion so it doesn't get crumpled.

It's reassuring to finally see our plans for this evening come to fruition, with all of the guests appreciating the minute details that make tonight unique. Canapés are served on silver mess trays, the bar staff are wearing orange boiler suits, and the cocktail glasses have handcuff charms around their stems. At the centre of the gazebo, a large serving trolley carries a stunning brown-and-beige cake, an exact replica of the prison created by a talented local patisserie I found online.

My hand trembles as I smooth out the wrinkles in the tablecloth. *Perhaps some food will steady my nerves.* I snatch a 'Blini and Locks' canapé – my own play on words – from a passing waiter. His striped clothing reflects light from the stake lantern beside us.

As the tiny pancake topped with soft smoked salmon melts in my mouth, I sense a stray bobble of sour cream trickling down my chin. The waiter coughs politely and hands me a silver-coloured cotton napkin, which I dab gently against my face.

Music drifts over from the far end of the gazebo, along with claps and cheers. The band suits the venue and occasion perfectly. Prison Rocks specialises in crime-themed songs and, Derek told me, performs at crime fiction festivals around the world. The male guitarist and keyboard player are both wearing black prison-guard uniforms tonight; the blue-haired singer in the centre is wearing a skimpy, striped convict dress. She's currently singing a cover version of Cyndi Lauper's 'Time after Time', her deep, husky voice whipping up a frenzy among her audience.

As I wander around the party, speaking to all of the guests, my memory game from earlier proves its worth. Derek takes centre stage, showing off his plans for B wing and the excitement that lies ahead. Journalists are taking notes, and councillors are asking questions. Architects and lawyers are networking with local builders and business owners. Lottery winners and journalists wander among them, taking photographs and revelling in the occasion, and yet again I wonder why Oliver Hodgson never arrived. Why would anyone turn down the opportunity to share such a prestigious occasion in the history of the prison, particularly when they applied for a limited-edition 'golden ticket' in the first place?

I have hardly spoken to Lloyd this evening. He brought me a 'Prisoner's Punch' earlier, extolling the refreshing virtues of the cranberry juice, fresh mint and lemonade blend. Since then, he has been busy chatting to some of his old work colleagues, not only from *Herts Life* but also from the national press, and he's been inundated with enquiries about his *Panbrook Prisongate* book update. He also spent a while chatting to Flint from Reception again. I hope he isn't having a problem with the new key card.

'Pretty bracelet.' Rosalie nudges my arm, taking care not to spill her lychee martini. Her hair is pushed back with a purple Alice band, emphasising the smoky make-up framing her eyes. She has scrubbed up well tonight. My rushed effort is little more than a dash of brown eyeliner and a smear of burgundy lipstick to match my dress.

'Where's it from?' She fingers one of the silver heart-shaped charms on the chain around my wrist.

'I can't remember exactly,' the bracelet jangles as I flex my fingers, 'but I've had it for years. Fell in love with it as soon as I saw it and knew it was destined to be mine.'

'Not surprised. A posh party in a top-notch hotel is the perfect place to wear it.' She squints up at B-wing, her eyes gleaming under the LED fairy lights. 'It's easy to forget anyone was murdered in there, isn't it? With all this fancy food and music going on.' She glances at her watch. 'Do you think I should check on Stella? She's missing all the fun.'

'No, you don't need to. I've just popped up there. She's fine – just a bit tired. You go and enjoy yourself.'

'Stella's been working so hard, maybe it's too much for her.' Rosalie's hand shakes, jiggling her glass. 'She's started taking sleeping pills, she told me, as she's always up half the night. She's going to be seventy next month, you know. I told her she needs to retire.'

'And I told her to have a lie down, so you don't need to disturb her. She's probably fallen asleep by now.' I attempt to keep my tone flat. This woman – barely more than a girl – clearly doesn't take a hint. We're surrounded by several guests, including inquisitive journalists searching for a scoop. Imagine the fun they'd have with this. 'I'll go up later to see how she feels and take her something to eat.'

Rosalie sips her drink. Her lipstick leaves a faint rose-coloured smudge on the frosted glass. 'Ooh, this is so good. Maybe take her one of these.'

A muscle twitches in my jaw. 'So, tell me more about yourself. Where did you work before here?'

'A property management agency in London. When clients relocated abroad for work, we looked after their homes. But it was nothing special.' She sways a little, her eyes not quite in focus. 'Not like working here.'

'What made you decide to apply to the hotel?'

'This sounds like another job interview.' Rosalie giggles and slugs down the remainder of her cocktail. 'The truth is, I saw the job advertised and realised I needed to try something new.'

She stares into her empty glass, her cheeks flushing. 'I think I'd better eat something to soak that up.'

While watching her sway over to the canapés, I spot Dr Land hovering in a far corner of the gazebo near the bar. He's observing everyone around him and listening to conversations, but seems rather out of place tonight, overwhelmed perhaps, despite Panbrook being more of a natural environment for him than anyone else. Perhaps he would have felt more at home if Fiona had been able to join him, or perhaps he just isn't a party person. Perhaps this is the real reason why he never attended Eric Martin's leaving party twenty years ago.

'Enjoying yourself?' I grab one of the desserts off a mess tray on the bar counter. 'Here, try this. It's a "Rhubarb and Custody".'

He laughs as I hand over the small glass pot and silver spoon. 'Good one. You've certainly had fun arranging all of this. That ghost of yours was particularly impressive.'

Ellie...

I still haven't heard from her. No doubt she's sulking over my refusal to allow her to hold her wedding party here.

'It's amazing what you can source online if you search for long enough. It took me a while to find the right person.'

'Well, you certainly did.' Dr Land dips the spoon into the glass pot. 'I'm heading home straight after the party so I hope I'm not missing much tomorrow.'

'Everyone will be checking out by ten, and we'll get the hotel cleaned and tidied for afternoon check-in. So, no, you won't miss anything.'

'That's good. It's been an excellent weekend. Great planning. You must be very proud of yourself, Ms Batten.' He stuffs some of the crumble mixture into his mouth.

'Apart from the few unexpected hiccups.' I look around to make sure we're alone, and lower my voice. 'Fiona ... Stella...'

'Having worked in a prison for so long, nothing surprises me. Hazards of the job, you could say, or maybe it's just The Brook.' Dr Land finishes his crumble and licks his lips. 'Mmmm, I fancy another one of those. There was nothing you could have done to help Stella, so please don't blame yourself.'

My phone vibrates in my bag. I pull it out and check the screen.

A message from Viv: *Tell Ells to call!*

'Excuse me. I need to reply to this.' I step to the side and type out my response.

She's at work.

Viv replies straightaway: *Shift changed to 9.30. Tracked her phone. She's still at hotel.*

My heart pounds as my fingers tap my phone keys: *She can't be.*

Viv messages me a screenshot of her Find My app, proving that Ellie – or at least her phone, which she's never without – is still here.

I call my daughter's phone, but there's no answer. I send a message, but she doesn't respond.

'Everything okay, Ms Batten?' Dr Land raises his eyebrows at me.

I force back a smile as though everything is fine. Yet my world appears to be falling apart.

35

MADDIE

NOW

**SATURDAY
9.00 p.m.**

My parental panic mode has switched on. Hundreds of worst-case scenarios flash through my mind, each one vivid and plausible as memories stir.

Ellie first went missing in a supermarket for twenty minutes when she was five, on Christmas Eve. We had come back to England for a last-minute festive break. 'Jingle Bells' was blasting through the shop's tannoy as we rushed inside for a pint of milk. Shoppers were ramming each other with overflowing trolleys, stripping the shelves of Brussels sprouts, Christmas puddings and cranberry sauce, and coming to blows over oversized turkeys as if their lives depended on it.

I still recall the dread creeping down my spine, the rapid thumping of my heart and nausea clogging my throat when I realised that Ellie was no longer clutching my hand. There were plenty of places for a young child to hide, and plenty of opportunities for someone to grab her. Yet I was convinced that Anna had risen from her grave and snatched her daughter back.

These are my exact feelings now, my imagination playing havoc yet again. Along with pangs of disappointment that Ellie lied to me when she insisted she was leaving the hotel straightaway.

I head to the obvious places first, beginning with the restroom where I saw her last. I push open the door with a trembling hand, concerned that I will find her in a lifeless heap on the floor tiles.

I don't know whether to laugh or cry when I discover all four toilet cubicles are empty.

I stumble into The Lock-Up, asking the catering staff if they have seen her, trying – and failing – to describe her blonde curls, petite frame and nurse's uniform as my anxious brain melts into slush.

I long to discover Ellie slumbering under a giant teddy bear in the supermarket's toy section, as I did when she was five. Or knocking back vodka in the hotel bar. Or sneaking off as a teenager with bottles of sangria crammed into her schoolbag to guzzle with her friends in the hotel grounds.

But everyone I speak to shakes their head and I leave empty handed.

I check the landing outside my room, and peer down to the empty floors below, before heading outside. Behind the museum, the dark, empty path is lit by the torch app on my phone and the twinkling disco lights in the distance. While I search the gloomy kitchen garden, nearby trees whisper as if calling her name.

I return to A wing and quiz the security guards at the hotel gates – no, they didn't see her leave, but then they didn't see her arrive either.

There's no sign of my daughter anywhere, as if Ellie was merely an apparition after all.

By the time I return to the courtyard, my hands are shaking and my head throbs. Every step seems heavier as if my feet are encased in concrete. I want to shout above the clamour of the crowd to break up the party. But how can I enquire about someone who shouldn't even be here.

Eventually I give in and pull Derek to one side, dragging him away from an in-depth discussion with Bryan about the prison healthcare system.

'That young woman earlier – the lookalike ghost I arranged...' If Derek is prepared to lie to me, then I'll lie to him too. 'Have you seen her tonight?'

Derek tuts at the interruption, his scowl accentuating the lines on his face. 'Why would she still be here? That was hours ago.'

Yes, hours ago indeed. So where is my daughter?

'Her office hasn't heard from her.' I clench my fists to conceal yet another lie. 'They just want to confirm she's not here.'

'I haven't seen her, no.'

He returns to the core of the crowd, mingling with the guests, seizing another cocktail off a tray and snorting at Bryan's joke. Because Ellie means nothing to him, and he has no concept of what she means to me.

Next, I speak to the VIP guests, the lottery winners, the surveyors and the lawyers, the band and the bar staff, while avoiding the journalists who will ask too many questions. I resist the urge to show them all Ellie's photograph on my phone.

And each time I ask if they have seen a young woman with blonde curls and a nurse's uniform, I receive a shake of a head in return.

I message Viv: *She's not here*

She replies immediately: *But her phone is!!!!*

My head tells me that Viv is wrong and Ellie left the premises – perhaps she dropped her phone. Yet my heart tells me otherwise.

I scrutinise the bar area, the throng of figures under the gazebo, searching for Lloyd with no success. The disco lights dazzle me, and music pulses in my ears.

Ellie should never have stepped foot on these premises this weekend, stirring up the past. She doesn't belong here – she never has.

And then I see a woman with long blonde curls, in blue and white, clutching an orange rucksack, skulking around the side of B wing.

'Where the hell have you been?' My voice is barely more than a whisper, but rage burns my throat. 'Viv and I, we've been worried. We thought something had happened.'

'Mum, I'm fine.'

'You've been gone for hours. *Hours.*'

I tap out a quick message to Viv: *Found her. All fine.*

Though Ellie's red-rimmed eyes prove she's far from fine.

She leans against B wing's stone wall. 'I just ... I just wandered around. Wanted to see the place on my own.'

'You didn't think to tell us?' I stare at her shaking hands. 'Have you been drinking? You need to drive to work.'

'No, I haven't been drinking.' Her eyes flash with anger. 'You're treating me like a child again. I simply forgot the time.'

'So why are you still here?' I flinch at a crunch of gravel nearby, deep voices and a clink of glasses, Derek greeting more guests.

'Because I wanted to be part of a history that was hers.' Her voice softens, and tears glisten in her eyes. 'Be somewhere she'd loved, whatever everyone thinks. It's where I wanted to be this weekend.'

And now I realise what Ellie is trying to tell me. What she

has been trying to tell me for weeks. That I should have asked her if she wanted to be here, either as Anna's daughter or as mine. It was never my decision to make.

'Ellie, I—'

She shrugs my words away. 'I have to get to work, Mum. They didn't need me so early after all, but I said I'd take the night shift.'

By ten o'clock, the relentless beat of the band pounds in my head. I'm desperate for a few moments of quiet, so I make my way down the side of B wing. When I reach the kitchen garden, I sit down on one of the three teak banana benches installed by Derek when he redeveloped the premises.

Most of the kitchen garden remains as it was twenty years ago. At first glance, it appears to be a haphazard scattering of vegetation and flowers, with no structure, rhyme or reason. But if guests look more closely, they'll spot the handwritten labels of plants that became the basis of Panbrook's cottage industry: strawberries and gooseberries, tomatoes and squashes, lavender and basil, coriander and fennel.

This evening, cigarette stubs and bird droppings are scattered around the bench bases. One of the stubs is still glowing so I stamp it out with my heel. Derek would be furious to hear that Housekeeping standards are slipping. Stella drifts into my thoughts yet again, and I wipe away a tear that has trickled down my cheek.

Leaves rustle nearby. I grip the bench seat tightly as a dark shadow emerges from between two bushes.

'Sorry, I didn't mean to disturb you.' Lloyd sits down beside me, clutching a cigarette and a blue lighter. He places his notebook between us. His black suit jacket is open, exposing his unravelled green tie.

I scrutinise the journalist. 'I saw you talking to Flint from

Reception earlier. Is there another problem with your key card?'

'No, that's working just fine. I was asking him where to find the head of Housekeeping.'

'Stella? She wasn't feeling well so she's having a rest.' The lie sticks in my throat, and I cough to clear it. 'Anything I can help with?'

'No, it's fine. It can wait.'

I point at the contents of his hand. 'We have a no smoking policy here – and I'm not afraid to enforce it.'

He laughs and shoves the cigarette and lighter into his jacket pocket. 'I've never been good at sticking to rules, but I'd better behave myself. Wouldn't want to get chucked out of a prison.' He leans back on the bench. 'So how long has Stella worked here?'

'Since the hotel opened, I believe.'

'A Panbrook hotel veteran. It would be interesting to know how it's changed over the years. I was thinking of adding something into my book's next edition. Hopefully I can speak to her in the morning before I leave.'

A nerve sparks in my ankle as I stare at the vegetable patch in front of us, where clusters of green shoots are poking through the soil. New life thriving in a venue more renowned for death.

'Did you know it's rumoured that executed prisoners were once buried in this garden. Minerals from their rotting bodies are believed to enrich the soil.' I chuckle at the look of horror on his face. 'Don't worry, two hundred years ago, not twenty years ago. And it's only a rumour anyway.'

'Well, everything certainly seems to thrive here.' His eyes light up as he sniffs the air. 'It looks and smells amazing. Who cares for the garden these days?'

'We have a group of volunteers, but Stella – and Pete our caretaker – are often out here organising them.'

'They certainly seem to know what they're doing. I can see why prisoners used to like working out here, especially with the leftover herbs and spices going into their evening meals.'

'That was only the Enhanced prisoners – the ones with special privileges – and only on a Friday night if they'd behaved all week. The rest of the prisoners had to slum it with bog-standard bland prison food, as Thomas said earlier.' A pigeon coos nearby. I glance around but can't spot it anywhere. 'Derek's kept up the tradition of using the herbs and spices in the hotel kitchen.'

'Hopefully not every tradition.' He points at the section devoted to medicinal and toxic plants.

I laugh at the fake worried expression on his face. 'That was also Derek's idea. He thought it would be amusing to have poisonous plants growing here. Belladonna and monkshood, foxglove – even hemlock. It certainly intrigues our guests – growing plants that can kill in a former gathering of killers.'

'The police never discovered where the hemlock came from that night.' Lloyd stares at the clusters of pigeon droppings along the pathways. 'Those birds get everywhere, don't they?'

'Derek says he tried everything over the years, but the pests kept coming back so he's now given up. I guess there's an endless supply of food. They tend to roost over there.' I point towards the storage sheds.

Lloyd stands up and smooths down his trousers. He picks up his notebook and stuffs it under his arm. 'I'd better head off. I'm meeting a journalist for an interview soon. Maybe you and I can catch up after the fireworks?'

'Yes, of course.' I rub my finger over my watch-face. Half an hour until the end of the party. 'I'd better get back anyway. I'm here to speak to *all* the guests, according to my orders for the evening.'

As if on cue, my phone buzzes with a message from Derek.

Where are you? Come to the gazebo NOW!

I give a weary sigh as I stand up and straighten my dress, ready to face my boss's latest drama.

Herts Life: Your local news and views

21 June 2019, 21:30

TALKING POINT: Is Panbrook Prison haunted or cursed?

By news editor Amita Singh

The Panbrook Prison Hotel turned ten this weekend. Many have wondered over the years whether the former prison is haunted. But is it possible that the premises may be cursed?

I was emailed earlier by Oliver Hodgson, who was fortunate enough to win a golden lottery ticket to attend the hotel's celebrations this weekend and to witness a not-so-welcome return to a controversial past. He described the party this evening as a rather tacky affair and a thoughtless insult to the memories of the five prisoners who were murdered there in June 1999.

Twenty years ago, prison nurse Anna Kendall was arrested for the poisoning of the five remaining prisoners on site that weekend. A few weeks later, she took her own life while she was being held on remand. The police subsequently archived the case, and the full details of the evidence against her were never revealed. Her motives for the murders remain unknown, although there has been much speculation. The mystery of the Panbrook Prison poisonings drives thousands of visitors to the hotel each year and continues to create division among the guests.

On Friday afternoon, as guests were arriving, Mr Hodgson claims he discovered a blood-red handwritten message on an internal lift mirror: 'Anna Kendall was guilty.' When he returned to the lift a few minutes later, the writing was gone.

Former prison governor, Fiona Trayton, fractured her hip during a fall late on Friday. I contacted the hospital this evening — she is still in critical condition in ICU.

On Saturday morning, a fire alarm went off at the hotel's museum while it was open to guests. Smoke was seen billowing out from the back room where the Anna Kendall case archives are kept. No guests were injured, no property was damaged, and the incident was soon resolved.

Mr Hodgson told me that an Anna Kendall lookalike went missing this evening, and a member of the hotel staff is resting after being taken ill. Is history repeating itself?

Mr Hodgson also informed me in his email that during his stay this weekend he has heard strange noises and experienced things that he is unable to explain, but he did not elaborate further.

Over ten years ago, disturbing events took place during the hotel's renovation works. One of the workmen claimed that he spotted eerie shadows in the corridors, and another claimed that he heard knocking sounds coming from within the prison walls.

Lloyd Palmer, author of *Panbrook Prisongate* (published by Spotlight Books, August 2009), who is considered to be the unofficial authority on the Anna Kendall case, was present during paranormal investigations in 2008. In news reports afterwards, the former *Herts Life* journalist vowed that he would never return to the prison premises.

Yet something — or someone — must have changed his mind, because Mr Palmer has been staying at The Panbrook Prison Hotel this weekend to re-evaluate the evidence for a second edition of his book. He and Derek Taylor, owner of the hotel, have announced plans to launch PrisonFest, a true crime festival, in 2021.

I can't confirm whether or not Mr Hodgson's account of this weekend's events are accurate. But it seems that twenty years on, tragedy and drama continue to plague the prison premises and that someone — or something — has been restless this weekend.

When I contacted The Panbrook Prison Hotel before publishing this article, Mr Taylor wasn't available for comment. I was informed, however, that although Oliver

Hodgson was on the guest list this weekend, he never arrived, and no one at the hotel has been able to contact him.

So there is yet another Panbrook mystery to solve — does Oliver Hodgson even exist?

MADDIE

NOW

SUNDAY
11.30 p.m.

The hotel is finally quiet. The party crowd have left the premises, and the overnight guests should hopefully be asleep. Despite my body being eager to recharge, my mind is too restless to relax so instead I am making efficient use of my time, relying on a strong cup of espresso in The Lock-Up to keep me awake.

When I returned to the gazebo from the kitchen garden, Derek showed me Amita Singh's article on the *Herts Life* website. He discovered it through a Google Alert notification on his phone. His hands were trembling with fury, and who could blame him. I read the article three times to make sure my eyes weren't deceiving me. It reads like sabotage, fuelled by an undercurrent of bitterness and sarcasm in the details that Oliver Hodgson supplied.

Derek called the newspaper and asked them to take the

article offline, but they refused, citing 'Freedom of the press'. We had to maintain our smiles and small talk with guests for another half an hour, before watching an impressive fireworks display. Then we waited not-so-patiently for the band and caterer to pack away their equipment once the party had ended. Finally, we waved Dr Land off in a taxi – after he had thanked us profusely for such an entertaining experience.

Once we were alone, Derek had a major meltdown, cursing Amita Singh and Oliver Hodgson with all manner of ills. He told me that I need to find this man and get a full explanation, as if I'm a modern-day Miss Marple.

But where do I begin?

I emailed Amita Singh, assuming she would respond on Monday morning, but instead her curt reply arrived almost straightaway. She couldn't – or wouldn't – tell me anything more about this mysterious man. All of their dealings had been conducted through emails this evening, she revealed, with no conversations over the phone, and she wouldn't supply his email address.

So here I am, none the wiser. All I know is that Oliver Hodgson is causing trouble on a grand scale, and that he must have been here all weekend. He knew about Fiona's fall, the fire in the museum, the launch of PrisonFest, Stella being taken ill … And, most importantly, he knew about the writing that appeared on the lift mirror, so he must have been here from the start.

I tried to find Lloyd for the catch-up he promised, and to ask him if he knew Amita Singh personally, but couldn't find him anywhere. So I gave up on my search and returned to my room to grab a notebook and pen and my iPad. It's fortunate that I did, as my phone gave up the ghost a short while ago, and I don't have a charger with me in The Lock-Up.

I have put together a list of everyone who has been staying and working at the hotel over the weekend, but have still drawn a blank. This Oliver Hodgson seems to be everywhere but nowhere. Judging by the critical content of the article, perhaps this isn't about the Anna Kendall case at all, or even about Panbrook Prison. Perhaps this is about Derek: a hotel rival determined to crush his success, or one of his disgruntled ex-employees.

I tap my pen against the pad of paper. When I Googled Oliver Hodgson again, all I could find was that same lawyer registered to a London office address. So who is he?

Rosalie spoke to him yesterday, but perhaps he was lying about his whereabouts during their conversation, or perhaps that wasn't even him answering the call. I try his mobile again, even though it's late in the evening, but there's still no response. I search for his Facebook profile and send a message asking him to get in touch as soon as it's convenient.

As I push my notepad away from me, disappointment swirls in the pit of my gut. Another dead end. The anniversary weekend is over, and I haven't achieved anything. None of the VIP guests could tell me about Ellie's father or provide new information about the events of that night in 1999.

The lights above me flicker with another power surge, casting strobing shadows across the restaurant. Imaginary whispers fill my ears as a faint, sweet woody scent hovers around me. I pick up my coffee cup and drain it, requiring that extra caffeine boost to keep me awake.

Footsteps head in my direction, slow and heavy like a death march. My neck muscles tense, then relax again when Derek walks in holding a couple of A4 files.

'I messaged you.' His eyes are framed with dark rings, and his cheeks are pale. 'You didn't respond.'

'I ran out of juice.' I jut my chin towards my phone. 'I'll put it on to charge later. I can't sleep anyway. My mind's on too many things. It's been one hell of a weekend.'

'You could say that.'

'So,' a nerve twitches in my shoulder, 'when are you planning on calling the police about—?'

'Once all the guests have gone.' Derek places the files down on the table in front of me. 'I told you that last night. As soon as the final guests leave.'

'But...' I trail off as my words stick in my throat.

My boss of principles seems to have lost his principles. The hotel clearly means more to him than common decency, or perhaps there's something else he's trying to hide. I realise now how little I really know about him and his past.

'I'm going back upstairs to get some kip for a couple of hours. I'll leave you holding the fort.' Derek nods towards the files. 'Put those in the desk in my office. Save me going in there again.'

'I can't get into your office, remember? You keep it locked, and the master key doesn't cover it.'

He pulls his office key out from his trouser pocket and hands it to me. 'I'll get that off you in the morning, so in the meantime guard it with your life. And be up early, as I'm taking Lloyd Palmer into the museum at seven. You need to find out where this Hodgson man is. And did you ask Housekeeping about that missing jewellery and the pocket watch?'

I take a deep breath at the barrage of questions. 'Not yet.'

'Oh, and by the way. Sad news.' His eyes remain ice-cold. 'Fiona Trayton died last night. She suffered complications during surgery to repair her hip.'

A frosty finger trails its way down my spine.

While Derek marches towards the lift, I walk over to his office next to The Lock-Up. Once I have unlocked the door and entered the room, I place the files on his large oak desk and plug my phone into the charger on the shelf next to the light switch. A low hum of electricity permeates the air, and pipes clatter above me.

Derek's office is immaculate but chilly, just like the man it caters for. An oak filing cabinet and a broad metal bookcase sit opposite his desk, and a small black-and-white striped armchair faces the door. An A3-sized map of the prison hangs on the wall, along with a large calendar marked up with hotel events and special occasions. One of Derek's commissioned prison-themed paintings is displayed in here too, identical to the one outside Lloyd's room; a man watching the free world while he spends the remainder of his life behind bars.

I pull out the 'Panbrook Anniversary Weekend' folder from the filing cabinet and place it on the desk. Wriggling back in Derek's black leather chair to get comfortable, I flick through the lottery winners' section again. Did Derek miss something when he vetted them?

Could Oliver Hodgson be a family member of one of those prisoners, or even a true-crime fanatic? But why then didn't the private investigators spot that during their searches? He's the only entrant who didn't feature in his selfie; instead, he sent in a photograph of a playful Labrador puppy inside an open cage, wearing a police dog costume and holding a 'Winner' placard in its mouth. Derek told me he found this amusing, despite the entry bending his competition rules. For someone so fastidious, this seems out of character for my boss.

I find the lawyer's profile on LinkedIn. Fortunately, Oliver Hodgson has been lax about privacy settings. He's a senior partner at one of London's biggest law firms, which has sponsored several major UK crime writing festivals. In one of his recent posts, he recommended his five favourite true crime documentaries – at the top of his list was a Netflix series about the Panbrook Prisongate murders. At least I now know why Derek was so desperate for this man to be here this weekend, always on the lookout for new investors and sponsors.

Could Pops be the all-seeing, all-hearing mysterious Oliver Hodgson? Perhaps this lawyer has a prison past. Could he have somehow manipulated the lottery entries so that he obtained a golden ticket, but was then unable to take up his place? Or maybe he *is* here this weekend, lurking in the shadows.

I send a message through LinkedIn.

This is Madeleine Batten at The Panbrook Prison Hotel. You won one of our coveted anniversary weekend lottery places, but haven't arrived for the celebrations this weekend. I want to confirm that you received our invitation. I have left you several messages. Please can you contact me as soon as possible.

As I return the folder to the filing cabinet, my mobile flickers into action and pings with notifications. I stand up and stretch my limbs before checking my phone screen.

Viv has left a message asking me to call her. Ellie has probably told her about the events of last night, or perhaps she also wants to try to persuade me to book their wedding party here. Since I'm the hotel manager, they'll need my agreement, even if it isn't as mother of the bride. I'm relieved that it's now too late – or rather, too early in the morning – to return Viv's call. This isn't the time for wedding talk.

Lloyd sent me a message at 11.30 p.m.

I think Pops is here.

My spine tingles. The last time I saw the journalist he was walking further into the kitchen garden to meet a former colleague. If he has found something, why hasn't he been in touch with me?

I gather up my iPad, phone and notepad, and pull out some of the staff files from the cabinet. Derek won't notice if these go missing for a few hours. I can put them back before I return his key. Stella's file is in the pile, and I want to see if she has a next of kin.

While hotel employees are on my mind, I visit Housekeeping. Fortunately it's empty, so I don't have to explain myself to anyone. I pull on a pair of vinyl gloves, search the cupboards and shelves and flick through the towels and bedding – the grimy unwashed ones and the folded clean ones. I don't find any missing jewellery, but I didn't expect to, no matter how easy it is for a necklace or bracelet to be displaced.

I unlock Radha's locker with my master key and look inside that as well. She always keeps a small bag in there, containing a change of clothes and some make-up. My gut fizzes with anger as I pull out an open packet of Marlboro Gold cigarettes. I scrunch them up and throw them into the waste bin.

I unlock my locker next and retrieve my purple toiletry bag. A few essentials spill out when I unzip it – my spare inhaler, emergency antihistamine tablets, a small packet of tissues ... I spritz the rose-and-cassis body spray under my arms and inhale the sweet scent. After repacking my bag, I riffle through Radha's locker one more time, shut both metal doors and use my master key to secure them again. Another job ticked off my virtual 'to do' list.

When I reach Lloyd's room, the door is ajar. A cacophony of voices and laughter greet me as I peer into the darkness. I open the door more widely and call his name. He doesn't reply but the voices continue, some high-pitched, others low, all deep in conversation. A sweet, spicy aroma drifts through the open doorway. Spotting a motionless mound on the bed, I call his name more loudly and insistently, but he still doesn't respond. The voices fade away for a moment, then start up again, but not one of them belongs to Lloyd.

I switch on the main light to discover the voices are coming from the radio. I press the 'Off' button and assess my surroundings.

The last time I was in here, it certainly wasn't neat and tidy – Lloyd was scurrying around in embarrassment, trying to make it look presentable – but this room seems to have been ransacked. The wardrobe doors and drawers are all hanging open, and Lloyd's overnight bag is lying on the bed with its contents exposed. A white shirt and navy jumper have been flung over the desk chair. An open bottle of aftershave has tipped over on the chest of drawers, and pyjama bottoms are scrunched up on the floor. The sheets and blankets have been pulled off the mattress and trail down the side of the bed.

A shard of fear lodges in my gut. Someone has been searching in here for something. Who the hell was it?

And where on earth can Lloyd be?

ANNA

SEPTEMBER 1998

'Mama.' Lucy toddles over to me, holding out a chewed carrot stick. She coughs loudly and loses her balance, landing on her bum with a thud. Her sharp cry pierces my heart as her gaze shifts to the empty rocking chair. 'Gapa. Gapa.'

Grandpa. Grandpa.

Tears well up in my eyes as I pick her up and sit her on my lap. I rub her back gently as she coughs again. She's not the only one who wishes Dad was still here.

He was alone in the house when he had his heart attack. No one was there to call for help, and I didn't even get to say goodbye. For weeks, I've been shouting and screaming at everyone at work in grief and anger, but I realise it won't bring him back.

'What are we doing with these?' Nate walks in carrying a stack of dusty books and sticks them on the kitchen counter. 'I found them in your car.'

'I'll take them to the charity shop next week. I had to sort through everything on my own, since you were love-shacked up in Spain.'

I place Mum's silver charm bracelet into the box and gaze around the room at the mess. We had to sell Dad's house to pay off his debts – debts he'd kept hidden from us – and now only a few treasures remain. Some silver cufflinks he wanted Nate to have, and Mum's jewellery for me. I've hidden her old gardening tools in my wardrobe away from Lucy.

'Down.' Lucy wriggles off my lap. She wipes her eyes and shoves the rest of the carrot in her mouth, then holds her hand out to Nate. 'More.'

He opens the fridge, pulls out the packet and hands her a fresh one.

'Ta.' Lucy toddles over to the toy garage and picks up a red car with her other hand. 'Brum. Brum.' As she coughs again, little chunks of carrot spatter over the carpet.

Bloody hell. Not again. I stand up and grab a damp cloth from the kitchen counter. Work tomorrow will seem like a rest.

Nate stares at her, his eyes crinkling with worry. 'She still has that cough?'

'The GP says it's an allergy. The nebuliser's helping, but it won't get better until we get away from that.' I point at the black smudges of mould along the wall under the window. 'Just as well we're moving out next weekend.'

'I still don't understand how you can afford this new place – three bedrooms, a big garden, a nice driveway. If you're over-stretching yourself, I can—'

'Stop asking me.' I bend down and scrub the carrot chunks off the carpet. 'It's all sorted. I've been saving up.'

'But—'

'Hello?' A knock on the front door, and Maddie sweeps in, flicking her dark curls back off her face. 'Is the door meant to be open? It'll let in all the cold air. It's freezing outside.'

I'd hoped their relationship would fizzle out but it's still going strong. And the bitch still likes to remind me that she lives in a posh hotel in a sunny climate with a sea view, while I'm stuck in this shithole.

'I didn't know you were coming today.' I squeeze the cloth in my hand to keep my voice calm. Carrot-speckled water runs down my fingers.

'Nor did I, but Nate said he was coming here. I didn't think you'd mind.' Her fake smile turns into a grimace as she spots the mess on the floor. 'I bought Lucy a present. Cute, isn't it?'

She shoves a stuffed elephant in my face. Bright pink and threaded with silver strands, with a wonky trunk. Looks like she found it in a cheap Spanish market.

Lucy toddles over and grabs the toy out of her hands. 'Ellie.'

Maddie wipes the rocking chair seat with a white paper tissue before sitting down. 'Yes, that's right. Ellie for elephant. Shall we call her Ellie?'

'Ellie.'

'And look.' Maddie pulls a notebook and pen out of her bag and draws a letter L. 'Look, Lucy, this is the letter starting your name. L for Lucy. It sounds like El for elephant.'

'Ellie.' Lucy gives the elephant a hug and leans against Maddie's legs.

'Are you calling my daughter an elephant?'

Maddie scowls at me. 'Don't be ridiculous. But she may as well learn some letters. Get her ahead before she starts school.'

'For God's sake, she's only fifteen months.' I turn to my brother. 'Nate, she's —'

'Keep me out of it.' He raises his hands, palms facing me. 'And it was nice of Maddie to buy something for Lucy, wasn't it? ... Actually, Annie, can you help me get some more books out of your car?'

'But I need to—'

'I'll look after Lucy, don't you worry.' Maddie throws me another fake smile.

When we come back, Lucy's sitting on Maddie's lap hugging the elephant, while Maddie reads her a *Spot the Dog* book.

I start clearing up the mess before Miss Posh-Pants complains.

My head's buzzing from my chat with Nate just now. I didn't want to say anything at first, but I've explained that Lucy's dad – one of the prison officers – is finally coughing up regular cash, which is why we're able to buy the new place. He just can't move in yet as he works too far away. Then Nate started asking questions I can't answer, so I shut the conversation down.

I close the lid of the jewellery box, then open it again. 'You cow, you've taken it, haven't you?'

Maddie looks up. 'What? Taken what?'

Heat flushes through my cheeks. 'My mum's silver bracelet. It was in here when I left the room.'

Nate walks in with a pile of gardening books. 'I heard raised voices. What's going on?'

Maddie clutches Lucy to her chest. 'I think your sister's just accused me of theft.'

'Annie?' Nate stares at me. 'I know you're under stress, dealing with those prisoners and clashing with that governor you hate – Gov Trayton, is it? – and also getting ready to move. But that's no way to talk to Maddie.'

'I put that bracelet in the box. So where is it?'

The stuck-up bitch gazes at him, her eyes all wide and innocent. 'Lucy picked it up and showed it to me while you were both outside. I thought she'd put it back again like I told her to.'

'I don't believe you. Where is it?'

'Annie!' Nate steps between us as if *I'm* the threat.

Maddie starts looking around, checking the crevices of the rocking chair and then the floor.

'Ah, here it is.' She pulls the bracelet out from her open handbag. 'Lucy must have dropped it in there.'

Nate shakes his head at me. 'You owe Maddie an apology. And don't forget to thank her for the elephant.'

'Ellie.' As Lucy holds up the stuffed animal, all I can think of is how quickly I can dump it in the bin once they leave.

'Heard you nearly killed some blokes last night. Guess some of them got their own back.' I dowse the swab in antiseptic and press it against Ahmed's bloody lip. He winces when I press harder. 'Don't be such a wuss.'

'The fuckers jumped me in the shower this morning.' He shuffles forwards on the couch, squinting at me through red, swollen eyes. 'Won't be picking mushrooms for the kitchen again. Just hope Tin Man doesn't move me off gardening.'

'Nah, you've got green fingers. She needs you out there.' I apply some tape to a larger cut on his cheek, though I doubt he'll be bothered if it leaves a scar. 'I've left some gardening books and tools in the big shed. Thought you'd find them useful. When I'm back in the garden later, I'll talk you through them.'

'You're a good teacher.' Ahmed tries to grin, but grimaces instead. 'I heard Pills is getting on your tits in here. If you need some of those mushrooms, I'll tell you where to find them.'

I fix my eyes on his. 'What the hell do you—?'

'Hulk said you can't stand Pills working in Healthcare. If you want him out your way for a while, those mushrooms would do it.'

I swallow sharply. 'Pills' little girl died last month, so have a little respect and keep your nose out of it. And don't believe everything Somers tells you, or I'll use this again.' I hold up the swab dripping with antiseptic. 'Anyway, all done. You can go now.'

He winces as he stands up. His ribs took a beating last night too. With all his tattoos and tough-guy act, you'd expect Ahmed to be as hard as a bedpost. But it's all for show.

A crooked smile crosses his lips. 'Don't I get special sugar for being such a good boy, Anna ... I mean, Nurse Kendall? My cellie says it's the best he's had.'

'No, you bloody don't. They're not for everyone, you know. Only the troublemakers.'

The consult room door opens and Owen walks in. He scowls when he sees my patient. 'You fuckin' twat. You—'

'That's enough, Owen.' I turn back to Ahmed. 'If you get any more bleeding, you'll have to come back in.'

'OK, boss. And have a good day, folks.' Ahmed raises an imaginary hat and winks at us.

I put the antiseptic bottle back in the medicine cabinet and lock it. When I turn round, Owen's flicking through an IMR file on the counter. He closes it, opens the healthcare ledger and runs his finger down the list of names.

'What the hell are you doing, William Owen?'

He startles and slams the healthcare ledger shut. 'Well, I was thinking I could do a stock-take, or go through patient medicines, since I'm a...'

'... pharmacist. Yeah, you tell us that twenty times a day.'

'But Nurse Kendall,' he rests his hand on mine, 'I'd like to help you out more in here. Anything you want. Maybe I can keep everything up-to-date on the computer. It would take my mind off things ... off Jessie.'

I pull my hand back. 'I wish I could make things better for you, but I can't. And I'm not going to lose my job just to keep you happy.'

He leans against the counter and nods towards the medicine cabinet. 'So when was the last time that had a sort out?'

'Yesterday.'

'Really?' He arches an eyebrow.

'Okay, maybe not yesterday, but you're here to assist with patients, do basic checks and keep the place clean. Not get your hands on any medicines.' I tut at him, shaking my head. 'Tell you what, you can go through the top store cupboard in the office – under my supervision. I threw out a pack of digestives dated 1986 the other day, but didn't have time to do the top shelf.'

'I don't want to do that crap.' Owen gives me a stony glare. Raises his voice. 'I want to do something useful. More useful than just being your skivvy.'

The door clicks open.

'Is he bothering you again?' Bryan saunters in and dumps his medical bag on the countertop. A flicker of anger crosses his face. 'I can have another word with the gov ... She'll send him back to gardening duty.'

Owen raises his hands and backs away from me quickly, as if a wasp has stung him on the nose.

I stifle a laugh. 'It's fine, Dr Land. Nothing I can't handle.'

'What can't you handle?' Kellie walks through the doorway and fixes her gaze on Owen. 'Oh, him. Well, we can always pressure the gov to transfer him to Egdon. I'm not sure why she changed her mind so suddenly anyway.'

'Tell you what.' Owen steps towards the counter. 'I can go through those booklets for you. Some of them are so old, none of the blokes will want them. And some of the pages are stuck together so they're no use to anyone. That way, I won't be near any medicines.'

'You can come with me on cell rounds instead. I'm sure Nurse Kendall can sort through the booklets while we're gone.' Bryan gives me a tight smile as he picks up his bag. 'I'm treating a fungal nail infection in half-an-hour, and I'll need someone to hold the patient steady. It won't be pleasant.'

Owen's face pales while Kellie and Bryan chuckle. He squints at me as if I'm going to rescue him.

I chuckle back. No chance.

Excerpts from the 'Meet victim #5 – Razlq "Razorhead" Ahmed' chapter in *Panbrook Prisongate* by Lloyd Palmer – published by Spotlight Books, August 2009

"My boy was first of our family to get a degree. So proud. Such a big thing. Gave him opportunities I never had when I came to this country. Such a kind boy – wanted to save the world. Wanted to save everyone."

— SYED AHMED, RAZIQ'S FATHER

"Raz was Mum and Dad's golden boy, but he was no angel. Decided he had to be my protector, 'cos he was four years older and I was a girl. Right pissed me off – I could take care of myself. But no one listened. Like, I couldn't look at a boy without Raz breathing down my neck. Went clubbing one night and a cute guy was hitting on me. Raz and his mates were there, off their heads as usual. It's all a blur. Too much to drink, you know. But then Raz was holding a blade, and the cute guy got it in the ribs. The cute guy died, and Raz was sent down."

— AALIYAH AHMED, RAZIQ'S YOUNGER SISTER

"That lucky bastard got a job in The Brook's kitchen garden right away. We all wanted that. He thought he were a big shot 'cos he had brains. Well, you ain't need no fancy degree in this place. Rubbed the big guns up the wrong way. Like all of us, Razorhead soon learnt to survive, mind. Worked out in the gym, tattooed up, toughened up."

— THOMAS BENSON, FORMER
PANBROOK PRISON INMATE

"Raziq was trying to make something of himself in prison so that nurse was teaching him gardening skills. We were very grateful. She even offered to give Raziq money for a small gardening business when he got out of prison. That was so kind of her."

— SYED AHMED

"Ahmed was Anna's little project, or maybe she was his, I'm not quite sure. I often saw them together in the shed at the back of the kitchen garden, discussing plants and seeds. I knew Anna loved gardening but it was all a bit OTT and took her out of Healthcare. She was a bloody nurse, for God's sake. She was in the garden even more after that mushroom incident, saying she'd teach Ahmed not to pick poisonous plants in future. Rumour was, it gave her ideas."

— DR BRYAN LAND, FORMER
PANBROOK PRISON DOCTOR

"Raz talked a lot about that nurse. Anna this, Anna that. Never Nurse Kendall. Like they were friends. It was weird. Like, how did a prison nurse get so close to him? Maybe he was suffocating her like he suffocated me, and she wanted to get rid of him so bumped him off."

— AALIYAH AHMED

40

MADDIE

NOW

SUNDAY
12.15 a.m.

I place the staff files, my iPad and notes on Lloyd's side table. My stomach churns as I stare at the unmade bed, the strewn clothes, the spilt aftershave ... Using the hotel intercom, I buzz through to the front gate.

'It's Madeleine Batten. Has anyone left the hotel since the party ended? One of the guests, I mean.'

'Nope.' Tonight's security guy jangles what sounds like a bunch of keys next to the phone. 'Nobody checked out or popped out. Gate's locked. Can guarantee that.' He jangles his keys for a second time.

'Okay, thanks.' I try Lloyd's phone again. It switches to voicemail.

As I gaze towards the closed bathroom door, goosebumps prickle along my arms. I pull a pair of vinyl gloves out from my pocket, slip them over my hands, then tiptoe over.

I push down the handle and nudge the door open.

Silence greets me.

The shower curtain is pulled taut across the bath. I hold my breath and gently pull it back, and exhale slowly with relief at the empty space.

I return to the sleeping area and search the wardrobe. Running my fingers around the pockets of his clothes and rummaging through his toiletries, I find nothing of any significance, other than he has expensive taste: Eton shirts and Armani trousers and Jo Malone cologne. No sign of those notes or the photo he showed me. His phone is also missing, along with his laptop and Moleskine notebook.

I check his overnight bag, under the bed, behind the curtains, and even the not-so-obvious places such as the narrow gap at the top of the wardrobe. But there's no sign of the missing items. I place his overnight bag under the window, out of my way, and begin to tidy up the rest of the chaos.

After shutting the wardrobe doors and drawers and straightening the bedding, I spot that the chest of drawers has been moved forwards slightly, edging onto the rug. I give it a nudge backwards but it doesn't budge, so I reach behind to see what's in the way – and pull out Lloyd's padlocked laptop case.

I sit down on the bed with the bag on my lap to contemplate my next move.

Lloyd told me we should combine forces, we shook hands on it, yet we now appear to be working individually. As hotel manager, I am responsible for everything that goes missing on the premises, including guests and employees.

Two minutes later, decision made, I rifle through his toiletry bag and grab the sharp pair of nail scissors that I had noticed earlier. I place his laptop bag on the bed and carefully stab the scissor blades through one of the fabric joins, ripping through the canvas until I create a large hole.

Reaching inside, I feel for the hard casing of his laptop and drag it out. I shove my hand in again and pull out his copy of *Panbrook Prisongate*. I lay these down carefully on the desk, side by side, and run my hand back through the bag to make sure his notebook isn't inside. Lloyd deliberately hid his laptop – did he expect someone to break into his room tonight? Or was he hiding it from me?

I open up the MacBook and switch it on. It needs a password to log in – of course it does. How on earth can I work it out? I barely know the man. But I have to try. It can't be anything too obvious, but has to be something he'll remember. So the password must mean something to him, a word or phrase he won't forget. He has no family that I know of, and I certainly can't imagine him using the name of his ex-wife. There's only one thing that I know Lloyd Palmer is obsessed with. He told me that himself. Something that has been on his mind for the last twenty years – and mine.

I take a gamble.

Panbrook. The laptop screen blinks at me, taunting me.

I try again.

Kendall.

Nothing ... I am stumbling in the dark. I don't know how many tries I'll have until I'm locked out.

I think back to yesterday, when we were sitting under the gazebo – when he switched on his laptop and fired it up. The long password he typed in – the movements of his fingers.

A password hint appears on the screen: *She did it in full*.

I take one last gamble as the final piece of the puzzle slots into place.

Anna Kendall

The laptop chimes and the screen springs to life.

It seems ironic that Anna, the heart of Lloyd's decades-long obsession, originally the woman he wanted to convict and now the woman he wants to set free, is also the key that has unlocked the heart of his laptop.

Once his home screen has loaded, I click open several folders labelled 'Panbrook Prisongate', 'Panbrook' and other variants. They contain earlier drafts of his book, files of his research, digital scans of newspaper articles, old prison photographs gathered over the years, and transcripts of interviews he conducted.

As much as these intrigue me, I don't have time to go through all of them now, so I take a few photographs of the recently opened files with my phone. Something tonight must have sparked Lloyd's message to me: *Pops is here.*

Could Pops be residing in the hotel grounds without us realising it? If he isn't this missing Oliver Hodgson, could he be one of the guests, or even one of the staff? I don't know everyone who works for Derek, and certainly not their names. I have only worked here for a few weeks myself, and various other people come and go when we require their services, employed through agencies – housekeeping, catering, security … And then there's Derek and his investors – all of whom could have had associations here at Panbrook before the hotel opened.

I gaze at the staff files on the bed, the ones I 'borrowed' from Derek's office, and bring them over to the desk. I browse through Radha's first. Before she arrived here, she was working for a cleaning agency in Luton, only for a couple of months. Her file doesn't say much more. Why did she leave? Is there some useful information I should know?

I search for Stella's file next and find it near the middle of the pile. No next of kin is listed, but as I skim through her previous employment details, excitement bubbles inside me.

Because Stella has been lying for all these years, or has at least omitted the truth.

Derek wasn't joking when he proclaimed that she was one

of the prison's fixtures and fittings. She has – or should that now be had? – lived alone in nearby Abingford for her whole adult life. She applied to work at the hotel as soon as it announced its opening date, hers being the first job application to arrive in the post.

My skin tingles with astonishment because that isn't all...

Stella has been so proficient at nurturing the kitchen garden since the hotel opened because she worked here before it closed, as one of the prison guards. Is this why she has been so elusive this weekend, worried that someone would recognise her? And what if someone did?

Perhaps Stella panicked. Did she have the strength to push Fiona over the safety screen? Did she set the fire in the museum, afraid that her past would be exposed?

This revelation means she must have known what happened that fateful night. Perhaps she knew the five men. Perhaps she knew Anna.

I think back to the questions Lloyd asked me when I last saw him in the kitchen garden, just before the party ended.

'So how long has Stella worked here?'

'Since the hotel opened, I believe.'

'A Panbrook veteran, then. It would be interesting to know how it's changed over the years.'

Has Lloyd worked out who Stella is?

Stella's room feels so frosty that I wish I was wearing my cardigan, but I don't want to turn off the air conditioning.

My footsteps shatter the silence as I creep past the mound on the bed. I try not to look too closely, but still catch a glimpse of her lying there. Her eyes are closed as though she's merely dreaming, as if she will spring back to life if I touch her.

Tears well up in my eyes as I take a step back towards the door. I have sneaked into many empty hotel rooms over the years, but how can I search one with a dead staff member inside? Someone I have worked with. Someone who sat on the bench with me just a few hours ago. And now guilt tugs at me, too. I never bothered to get to know Stella. What did I really know about her life? If I had shown some interest, would she have opened up to me, admitted her identity and told me what I needed to know?

I have spent my professional life overseas and never made any strong, long-lasting friendships. Ex-pats always came and went in Spain, and I often worked unsociable hours. I barely had enough time to spend with Ellie and Nate, let alone anyone else. Ellie made friends with other children at the English-language nursery, then at the international school, but I kept their mothers at a distance, too afraid that my secrets – our secrets – would sneak out and destroy our lives.

I peek at the bed again. I need to do this for Nate, for Ellie, and for me. And perhaps for Stella too. I reach into my pocket and pull out the fresh pair of gloves that I collected from my room on my way here.

I step into the bathroom, then explore her wardrobe. Stella didn't bring much for the weekend: a couple of changes of clothes, rose-scented body spray and shower gel, face cream, and a long pink, embroidered cotton nightdress. Everything is folded neatly in her overnight bag or hanging in the wardrobe (I put it back exactly where I find it) or is still lined up beside the bathroom sink as if waiting for her to return.

I inch closer to inspect the contents of the side table. Her phone is still lying beside the paracetamol packet and glass water bottle. I count the painkillers first. Most of the thirty-two are missing, which means I can't rule out an overdose, but she may not have taken them all in one go. I can't see the sleeping pills Rosalie mentioned. As I sniff the contents of the water bottle, I gag at the strong alcoholic odour.

My fingers twitch. I should be calling the police, asking

them to investigate, but Derek was right when he said a few hours won't make a difference. Stella is gone and won't be coming back. Meanwhile, I could be getting closer to the truth, to finding out the identity of Ellie's father – and this prison officer called Pops.

I pick up her phone, an ancient black Nokia that blinks to life when I switch it on. It's so old that it doesn't need a passcode and is still retaining some of its charge. Stella has no messages listed on there – to her, or from her – which seems a little strange. Maybe she really was a loner. I scroll down and make a note of her few contacts, just in case I need them – a doctor, a hairdresser, a dentist.

Opening the side table drawer reveals a few black pens and familiar-looking yellow notepaper. So Stella must have left that note for Lloyd, her words claiming Anna's innocence, and she must have also been the mystery person in B wing. Finally she wanted to tell him about the past, while avoiding him in person all weekend.

With her Panbrook Prison history, this would certainly be a reason why someone could want her dead.

41

MADDIE

NOW

SUNDAY
1.00 a.m.

Back in my own room, sitting at the desk, I'm browsing through the files on Lloyd's laptop. I have changed out of my party dress, relaxing in some casual trousers and a loose T-shirt. An unwrapped bar of nut-free dark chocolate sits beside me, along with a small mug of espresso as a caffeine boost to keep me awake and alert.

There must be a way of discovering the identity of Pops now that I know Stella's true identity. I scroll down the list of interview transcripts that Lloyd has conducted over the years, some over the phone and others face to face. Many made their way into the final version of his book. Edith Bell, former English teacher of Lucas Somers. Alisha Reddy, Steven Fisher's neighbour. Paula Owen, William Owen's mother. Daniel Ingleworth, Lucas Somers' former employer. Fiona Trayton. Bryan Land. Even Thomas Benson.

Looking down the list, I can see a few obvious gaps – some of the prison staff who would have known Anna and the prisoners best of all. No Kellie Wyndham. No Stella. Most of the officers who would have been here at the prison that night. Why did all of these people keep silent while Lloyd was gathering information for his book? And why has Stella kept quiet for all these years but now changed her mind?

Stifling a yawn, I reach for the chocolate and pop a piece in my mouth. A sugar rush floods my head as it dissolves slowly on my tongue. I wash away the bitter residue with a gulp of equally bitter coffee.

Continuing my research, I jot down a few pointers on my notepad, in case I fall asleep and forget my train of thought.

My heart quickens at a rustling sound outside my room. Gripping my phone tightly, I push my chair back and stand up, open my door a crack and peer out. The landing lights are always dimmed during the night to conserve electricity. Ghostly shadows flicker across the black-and-white striped carpet as moonlight pours in through the window at the end of the walkway.

I peep at Stella's room. Her door remains closed. Then I peer over the handrail to confirm the landings below are empty.

My right calf muscle twinges – I've been sitting still for too long. Fumbling in my pocket to make sure I have my keys and key card, I shut my bedroom door behind me. As I pace along the landing towards the window overlooking the car park, gripping my phone, Nate's last words replay in my mind.

I won't be here to see Ellie live her life. Maybe – just maybe – when she gets married, her real dad, her birth father, could be there. See if you can make that happen, Maddie. Annie told me he'd started supporting her and Lucy, but wouldn't tell me who he was. See if you can find him or his family. For me and for her. And for Annie's sake – please do it for my sister, too.

Ellie's wedding is in two months, and this weekend may be my only chance to fulfil Nate's final wish. Not that I truly want to. For if I find Ellie's birth father, this will reveal my daughter's identity. And if we dredge up the past, her life will never be the same again. *My* life will never be the same again.

When I reach the end of the walkway, I peer out of the window. In the distance, the sycamore trees are swaying in a strong breeze.

In a few hours, dawn will break, and this anniversary weekend will be over. If I don't fulfil Nate's final wish, will this make me a bad wife and a failed mother? Ellie may have been Anna's once, but she has been mine for twenty years. I have cared for her and looked after her for all this time, just as a mother would. Cuddled her when she woke up screaming because there were monsters under her bed. Treated her cuts and grazes when she tripped over in the park. Helped her with homework and revision for exams. Bought her first bra when she was twelve. Dried her tears when her first girlfriend broke her heart. Taught her how to cook Spanish paella the way she likes it. Grieved with her when we said goodbye to Nate.

Yet how can I refuse my husband's last wish? If I do, guilt will continue to burn and stab at me. It could fracture my relationship with Ellie, and I have never let my daughter down.

Because Nate also told Ellie what he wanted me to do, and now she wants to know more about her roots.

A hand taps my shoulder. I drop my phone and swallow back a scream as I swivel around.

'Alright?' Pete peers at me with concern etched in his eyes. He reaches down, picks up my phone and hands it to me. 'Didn't mean to scare you, but you didn't hear me calling. Whatcha up to?'

'I couldn't sleep. Thought I heard a noise out here. What are you doing up so late?' I tap my watch face.

'Don't sleep much either. Too much going on. All those

knocks, whispers, rustling, flickering lights ... Always figured this place is haunted. I bet the ghosts have lots of stories to tell.'

I roll my eyes. *As if ghosts actually exist.* 'I don't suppose you saw Lloyd Palmer after the party?'

'Not in his room?'

'No, I guess he must have gone for a walk. He said he was looking for someone.'

The name *Stella* rings in my head.

'Maybe he's chatting to some ghosts.' Pete chuckles. 'Well, if I see him, I'll let you know. Looks like everything's quiet here. Best get back to my office – try to get some kip. You too, eh?' He grins at me, before strolling towards the lift.

Back in my room, I open up my bag and pull out the newspaper cutting I found in Jonathan Roach's cell. Pete is right; someone needs to listen to the prison ghosts, real or not.

This cutting is from one of the national papers in 2010, containing more speculation about Anna. I missed the original, probably because I was busy looking after Ellie in Spain.

I skim through each paragraph, trying to work out why someone left this particular cutting for Lloyd – Stella, I now assume.

Did dead pigeons and drug smuggling lead to the downfall of Anna Kendall?

New evidence suggests that Anna Kendall, who was accused of the murders of five prisoners at Panbrook Prison eleven years ago, was involved in drug smuggling at HMP Panbrook. The prison nurse was often seen in the prison's kitchen garden, speaking

VICTORIA GOLDMAN

to the inmates and other prison
staff, even though she was based in
the Healthcare department. It is now
believed that drugs were coming into
the prison through this route and
that she was likely to have been
involved.

Jail chiefs have estimated that £1m
of drugs were smuggled into HMP
Panbrook during 1999. It was originally thought that the drugs were
coming in through the prison library,
through Jonathan Roach, one of the
prisoners who was believed to have
been poisoned by Anna Kendall on that
Friday evening in June 1999. But new
sources have revealed that some
dealers were using homing pigeons to
deliver drugs in pouches strapped to
their chests. These birds landed in
the prison premises for inmates to
find. Other dealers were cutting open
dead pigeons and stuffing drugs
inside, then sewing them up or
sealing them with glue. They would
throw the carcasses over the stone
perimeter wall into the kitchen
garden. Prison staff didn't inspect
the dead birds — these were stuffed
into the bins as soon as they were
found — and prisoners would open them
up later on to retrieve the contents.

My hands itch, and bile rises in my throat, as I think back to the dead pigeon I found in B wing. I stick another piece of chocolate in my mouth to mask the sour taste before reading on.

Police claim that Anna Kendall killed one or more of the five men to silence them. Traces of water hemlock were found in cake crumbs in those prisoners' cells. Anna was seen carrying cakes to their cells earlier that day. Two of those poisoned men — Raziq Ahmed and William Owen — worked in the kitchen garden, although Owen had more recently been working in Healthcare. Were these men her intended targets?

Anna Kendall was held on remand at HMP Clayton following her arrest but died before her trial, so her case never reached the courts. She was discovered one evening by a prison guard during a routine flap check, having overdosed on heroin. The prison doctor was unable to resuscitate her. It is believed that Anna turned to drugs in response to negative media attention. Whether or not she intended to take her own life is unclear. In the 1990s, one in seven prisoners at HMP Clayton was reported to develop a drug problem behind bars.

I push the newspaper cutting away from me and rub the back of my neck. So the murders were about drugs after all? Perhaps this is what Stella had been trying to tell Lloyd Palmer. But then why, in that note she left him, did she claim Anna was innocent?

Nate was adamant that Anna would never have taken drugs, let alone overdose. She would never have put Ellie's future at risk, he said. He believed someone killed his sister to silence her. Nate also claimed Anna was framed – that she would never have been involved in drug smuggling into the prison, let alone kill those five men. Yet the poison was in the cakes she baked for them, so she must have been responsible. Perhaps my husband was wrong on both counts. After all, I don't believe this was the first time my sister-in-law tried to kill someone.

I log back in to Lloyd's laptop and browse the recently viewed files. Lloyd is so meticulous that he has labelled everything with the time and date he found them. I pause at some photographs of the museum before the fire – the ones he took of the displays and the walls. Because now I can spot what was in that gap. The gap that firefighter convinced me didn't exist. I have passed that wall so many times, yet never really looked, making a beeline instead for the photographs and records in the *Panbrook Prisongate* collection. Whoever set that fire in the museum must have removed this photograph on their way out.

The faded picture features a cluster of prison staff, many of them holding cans of Coke or bottles of beer. One woman holds a vodka bottle and some plastic shot glasses. An older man sits on a chair under a 'Good Luck, Eric' banner. This must be Eric Martin at his retirement party.

Few of the people are facing the camera, so the photographer must have caught them off guard. Most faces are blurred or too small to see clearly. None of them are in uniform.

Once I zoom in slowly, I recognise Anna standing on the right-hand side, holding a small plastic cup; her eyes are like Ellie's, her smile is like Nate's. I spot a younger Stella beside her, from the O-shaped pendant around her neck. A tear trickles down my cheek, and I wipe it away with my finger. A blurred hand is on the far left of the photo, the rest of the figure just out of the shot.

Fiona is crouching beside Eric at the front, clutching a large wine glass, her eyes possibly a little glazed. She clearly stayed at the party for longer than she told me. A large, stocky man behind her stares in the direction of the camera, a faint smile on his lips. His rounded face seems familiar but I can't quite place it. His shirt sleeves are scrunched up, exposing a black-and-white tattoo on his upper arm.

When I zoom in even closer, the *Popeye* theme tune rings in my ears.

The tattoo is a ship's anchor.

I look back at the journalist's laptop bag, still with his copy of *Panbrook Prisongate* inside it. I pull the book out and browse the pages he has flagged up with colourful Post-it notes. All are chapters about the prisoners and Anna, most containing interviews with family members, old friends and former prison staff or inmates. Could one of them be Pops?

I pause when I reach the centre of the book. Here, Lloyd has stored the handwritten note on lined yellow paper. The note I now assume Stella left for him, along with an odour of cigarette smoke in his room. He has circled three of the words in red: *...find the pigeon*

Tucked behind it is an empty hotel key card holder enve-lope. Three words have been handwritten on the back in black ink: *Follow the pigeons.* Lloyd has added a time and date. This is the key card that Flint handed to Lloyd. Did Stella put him up to it, or is Flint involved too?

As if on cue, a grey pigeon lands on the narrow ledge

outside the window. It coos at me and cocks its head. A small blue plastic tag is wrapped around its leg. I don't know much about pigeons, but surely it should be fast asleep by now.

The note Lloyd received. The dismembered pigeon I found in B wing. The article about pigeons, drugs and Anna. And now this envelope.

Follow the pigeons.

Stella may be dead, but I know what she wanted Lloyd to do. And now it seems to be my turn to follow her instructions – before the guests and staff wake up, ready to leave the premises, like prisoners desperate for release day.

42

MADDIE

NOW

SUNDAY
1.40 a.m.

Light glints off B wing's windows as I stroll across the courtyard, with sycamore leaves dancing around my feet in the breeze.

That pigeon cooing at me on the windowsill was wearing a tag and seemed well groomed and well fed. I hadn't noticed the pigeon tags until this weekend, but sometimes you only see what's in front of you when you really take time to look.

'*Follow the pigeons*,' said the words on the back of the envelope – perhaps it isn't a wild one I need to find.

A faint tapping sound comes from the museum entrance. It stops, then starts, then stops again. I draw to a halt as a small, dark shadow glides towards me across the gravel.

The tapping sound returns, and the shadow morphs into a grey pigeon, its sleek iridescent neck plumage shimmering in the moonlight. He struts towards me and bobs his head in greeting, as if he's in charge of this hotel rather than me. Lowering his head, he pecks at the dirt, inspecting for grubs or seeds or whatever it is that pigeons prefer to eat, and gazes up at me again in curiosity.

A gust of wind rattles the museum door. The pigeon stretches out his wings, ready to take flight. As he launches himself into the air and flies over B wing towards the kitchen garden, I glimpse stick-thin legs with a blue metal tag.

I wind my way around the side of the building, stretching my cardigan across my chest to ward off the early-morning chill.

The banana benches are still spattered with pigeon droppings. A few cigarette butts are scattered around the bases, remnants from last night's party no doubt, or perhaps Lloyd was here earlier having a sneaky smoke. Housekeeping will need to clean this up before the next cohort of hotel guests arrives.

A tapping sound comes from the far end of the garden. I swivel my gaze towards the shadows, expecting to spot another pecking pigeon, but instead glimpse a trail of smoke drifting into the sky.

Lloyd?

I stroll past the herb and spice beds, the 'Do Not Enter' sign, and the small greenhouse that houses the vegetables, until the two sheds loom ahead of me, flanked by sweet-smelling jasmine and fuchsia and lavender bushes.

I call these buildings 'sheds' but they're actually much larger, more like timber warehouses. The smaller of the two is where our tools and seeds are stored. The second one holds the dehydrators for drying the herbs and spices, which are then packaged neatly into jars and bags and boxes, ready to be sold as Panbrook gifts and souvenirs.

The door to the smaller shed is ajar, with a glimmer of light winking at me through the gap. I push it open and tiptoe inside.

A thin foam mattress is leaning against the wall by the door, behind a small wooden table topped with empty crisp packets. A refrigerator hums gently, and metal dumbbells, a weight bench and a skipping rope are stacked up neatly in the corner. Threadbare cushions on a pine rocking chair suggest that someone has made themselves at home here – and very comfortably.

Lloyd's last message to me: *I think Pops is here*.

Is this where Pops has been staying unnoticed? Did Stella know?

I walk past metal racks housing spades and hoes and rakes, then zigzag around shelving units stacked with compost bags and seed packets, until I reach a metal door at the back. The padlock is open, and a small key pokes out of the hole.

Curiosity stirs in my chest as I yank the door open. I find myself facing the prison's tall perimeter wall, with the original barbed wire draped high over the top. A large gap indicates where a prisoner once cut through it trying to escape. The summer breeze rustles the broad sycamore leaves on the branches drooping over the brickwork. The trees are whispering, warning me back – the last sentries between the prison and the outside world.

I step forwards into the shade of the wall, tugging my cardigan across me as the breeze picks up yet again. Under the branches stands a large wooden pigeon loft. A solitary pigeon – a blue metal tag around its leg – pecks at seeds sprinkled on the ground. Others are sleeping in open nesting boxes, amid perches and traps with landing boards. A few grunt and fan their tails at the sudden interruption.

Follow the pigeons.

'Well ... I found you. But now what?'

A grating sound comes from nearby: a shutter closing. I detect a flicker of movement, too large to be that of another pigeon.

I take a step backwards. My hands curl into fists and my cheeks burn, as adrenaline courses through my veins. I regret not grabbing one of the garden tools on my way through.

'Took your time.' A man emerges from the shadows and strolls down the side of the pigeon loft. He's clutching a screwdriver and ragged pieces of chicken wire. His beard is speckled with dust and grit, and his jeans are covered in grease.

His eyes widen when he reaches me. 'Oh, I thought ... Never mind...' Pete places the screwdriver and wire down on one of the landing boards and wipes his hands on his jeans.

'I'm still looking for Mr Palmer.' Disappointment swirls in my gut, mixed with a sigh of relief. I have found the hotel's caretaker, not some madman camping out in the former prison grounds. 'I thought I saw the journalist heading this way last night.'

'Guests aren't allowed near the sheds, you know that. And why are you here? Need me for something?'

'I thought I'd "follow the pigeons".' I study Pete's face as I recite the words. He remains composed. 'Who do these ones belong to? They're certainly not wild.'

'They're mine.'

'Does Derek know? He's never mentioned them.' Pete gives a nonchalant shrug, so I continue. 'I saw the bed inside. It wasn't there when Derek gave me a tour on my first day. Do you sleep here?'

'I do sometimes. Saves me getting here early some days. Clear it up if someone's coming to visit, but no one usually does.' He glances at his watch, then towards the entrance into the shed. 'Don't suppose you saw Stella last night, did you? I knocked on her door but she didn't answer. Thought you were her.'

I flinch as guilt pokes my spine. 'She wasn't feeling well. I'll check on her again in the morning.'

'Due to storm again tonight. You'll want to get back to bed before it does.' As he wipes his forehead with the back of his hand, his rolled-up shirt sleeve gapes, revealing large, well-toned muscles.

Sharp pains stab my ribs as I pull my phone out from my pocket and launch one of the apps. Earlier, I had emailed myself Lloyd's photograph of the prison staff picture – the one that went missing from the museum wall.

The trees behind Pete are still swaying, still whispering, and now I'm whispering too. 'Is it time, Nate? What if I don't want to know the truth?'

'What did you say?' Pete stares at me and scratches his beard. 'What truth?'

'Did you know Stella used to work here? Her full name's Estelle. She's in this old photo. I recognised her necklace.' I hold my screen up in front of Pete's eyes and zoom in to enlarge her O-pendant and then her face. 'And you must have worked here, too.'

He fidgets on his feet, his face draining of colour. 'No, I—'

'Liar.'

I point at his upper arm, at the black-and-white tattoo that flexes over his skin, the Popeye name on the anchor much more prominent in the flesh.

'You must have set that fire in the museum in a panic to remove the original photograph. Maybe you hadn't noticed it until this weekend and realised it would identify your tattoo. No wonder you always cover your arms.'

'No, I— Why would I set fire to the museum? I can get in there any time I want.' His eyes lock with mine as I cross my arms and press my lips together tightly. 'Okay, okay ... I worked here at the prison many years ago. It's just not something I like to talk about.'

'Well, maybe it's about time you did.'

Nausea swirls in my throat as I realise what this means. *See if you can make that happen, Maddie. See if you can find him.*

Now I've found Pops, have I found Ellie's father? And if Pete doesn't have that photograph, who does?

43

MADDIE

NOW

A pigeon stirs in the nesting box, then another, and another. Their beady eyes gaze at us.

'Let's go back through. Don't want to wake the troops.' Pete's arm muscles flex as he picks up his screwdriver and the chicken wire.

My heart thumps rapidly as he pushes past me. Pete is strong, agile for his age. If he turns on me, I wouldn't have a chance. Yet he's a stark contrast to the way Thomas and Bryan both described him.

'Tough bloke, big ... kept everyone in check.'

'Bent as a nine-bob-note.'

Who should I believe?

'Coming, Madeleine?' Pete points towards the door, the only route out of here.

I nod reluctantly and follow him back into the storage shed, past the tools and the seeds and the compost bags, until we reach the front area. He pulls out two green camping chairs from behind the folding bed and opens them.

'Take a seat...' He gestures towards the nearest chair. 'Welcome to my office.'

The canvas sags under my weight when I sit down and drop my phone into my lap.

I stare at the dumbbells, then back at the man in front of me. 'You've changed a lot over the years – lost weight, muscled up, grown a beard. But that,' I point at his tattoo, 'that's still the same. The last thing Fiona Trayton said to me before the paramedics took her away was "Pops". Now I know that's you.'

'Those days, everyone called me that. Officers, inmates ... even the gov. Only started using "Pete" again when I took this job. Though not Annie. She never called me "Pops".'

'What did she call you?'

He chuckles softly, and his eyes light up with affection. '"Owl Face". That were her first impression of me on her first day, while I thought she looked like a wee lamb going to slaughter. It were our little joke – anything to lighten things up in here. I looked quite different then, as you can see in that photo.'

'Did anyone else recognise you this weekend? Fiona Trayton? Bryan Land? Thomas Benson?'

'Don't think so.' He slumps forwards, resting his forearms on his knees. 'Kept away from them, much as I could.'

'Yet Fiona said "Pops", so she must have seen you here somewhere.' I take a deep breath to steady my nerves. 'I heard her arguing with someone before she fell. Did you push her off the landing to keep her quiet?'

'No, I'd never!' Pete slides his chair backwards, scraping the steel legs against the wooden floor. His eyes flash with anger. 'I'd never—'

I grab my phone and stand up, assessing the distance between me and the door.

'Sorry, I...' He nudges his chair forwards and gazes at the floor sheepishly. 'Look, if the gov were pushed, it weren't by me. Never liked her, but no, I'd never do that. Honest.'

I sit back down, recalling the staff meeting after Fiona's fall, when Pete also wanted to call the police. He wouldn't have made that suggestion if he was guilty, surely? Did Stella stop him getting the police involved to avoid their identities being discovered?

'After she fell, you were on the landing upstairs inspecting the safety screen. Someone could have spotted you then.'

'Had to do my job – Derek didn't give me a choice. But as you say, I've changed lots over the years. Stella has too. She went by Estie in those days – but after what happened she wanted to start afresh. We both did.'

I think of Stella lying in her cell. Was it overdose or murder? For years, she's been taking a huge risk working at Panbrook, hiding in plain sight – both of them have.

'Why have you kept quiet about your identities for all this time?'

'If you're going to keep asking questions, I need a drink.' Pete leans over and opens the fridge. 'Want one?' He pulls out a bottle of beer. 'Or a can of Coke?'

I shake my head. He nudges the door shut and gives it a final push for good measure to seal it. 'Why are you and Stella still working here – after what happened?'

'We both drifted in and out of jobs when the prison closed. Found it hard to settle. We'd worked here for so long, it's what we knew.' He pulls out a folded Swiss Army knife from his jeans pocket and removes the beer's metal cap with the bottle opener. 'Once the police shipped out, we came back most weeks.'

'But someone must have changed the locks, surely.'

'When you work in a prison, you know how prisoners are gonna try to break out, so you also know how to break in. Ladders over the wall. Snipped the wire. Plus, we still had some keys. No one thought to change the locks on every side gate.'

'Not even Derek when he turned Panbrook into a hotel? He must have known you both used to work here.'

'He did.' The caretaker gives a smug smile. 'But guess he's not as thorough as he thinks. When we got jobs here, it felt like we were coming home. We could keep the garden going. Didn't want to waste all that hard work ... all Annie's work.' His face softens as he says her name. 'Felt we owed her.'

The shed door slams open, propelled by a sharp lavender-scented gust of wind. Pete stands up and stretches his legs. He strides over to the doorway and peers out before pushing the door shut. He gives it a final shove with his shoulder for good measure, just as he did with the fridge, then returns to his seat.

'I still don't understand why you've kept quiet for all this time.' And then I wince as the truth stabs at me, like a knife twisting into my side. 'You were the officers on duty that night.'

A wistful expression darkens his eyes. 'Not officially. There weren't a duty roster over that weekend – no one expected prisoners to still be here. Tin Man were so pissed by then, she didn't even think of it. Stella and I drew the short straws. But we were drinking and forgot the time – forgot to check on them. And when we did...' he grimaces, '...it were too late.'

'You said you owed Anna.' I lean forwards. 'Did Anna kill those men, and then you tried to cover it up? Or maybe it was you. Is this why you owed her – for taking the blame, for covering up what you and Stella did?'

'Course not.'

'Perhaps you were involved in drug trafficking here. Both Bryan and Thomas suggested you were involved in something.'

'They're lying.'

'But why would they lie?' I draw in a deep breath as more questions fill my head. 'What happened to Kellie Wyndham after the prison closed? She seems to have disappeared.'

'I don't know. The last time I saw her were at that party. Stella and I tried to find her for years.'

The door flies open again. Sycamore leaves swirl inside as if they're being pulled by invisible strings, and a sickly scent of jasmine permeates through the air.

Pete stands up and peers out, his hands gripping the wooden doorframe.

A small, tagged pigeon wanders through the open door-way, bobbing its head and cooing softly.

I nod towards it. 'How long have you kept pigeons here?'

'Good few years.' Pete pushes the door closed. The bird ruffles its feathers but doesn't seem perturbed about being trapped inside. 'Used to race them, but now we're all getting on a bit. This one's like me – don't like to sleep much.'

'I found a dead one,' my hands flinch at the memory of scrubbing my skin free of pigeon blood, 'in a box in B wing. Stella put it there, didn't she? And she left a newspaper cutting about how pigeons were used to get drugs in here, tying it back to Anna. She had planned to meet Lloyd Palmer that night but I was there instead. She'd left a note in his room.'

'I left that for him. It were a wild pigeon, already dead when we – when Stella – found it by the bins. Thought it would attract his attention.' A faint frown passes across his face. 'Except you turned up. So she had to send him another note on a key card through Reception.'

Follow the pigeons

The pigeon coos again. Pete wanders over to the metal shelving unit behind him and reaches for a small tub of bird-seed on the top. He pulls off the lid, pours some seeds into his cupped hand and crouches down. The pigeon pecks at the contents of his palm.

'But why do all of this? Why go to so much effort?'

'Stella and me, we wanted to get Mr Palmer's attention,

but we didn't want to be seen doing it.' Pete stands up and rubs his hands together. The remaining seeds scatter over the floor, a few sticking to his trainers and others tumbling into the wooden grooves.

'We wanted him to look back at the case and work out what were really going on in here all them years ago. Since he's updating that book of his.' He snaps the tub's lid closed and returns it to the top shelf.

'But why not just tell him everything you know?' I clench my fists in frustration. I have finally found someone who was in the prison that night and he's refusing to reveal anything about the past. 'You must know who poisoned those men if it wasn't Anna. Why didn't you and Stella just tell the truth at the time.'

'Because he...' He sits back down in his chair, his shoulders slumped forwards. 'Because she were in over her head.'

'Who? Stella?'

'No ... Annie.'

'Anna?' I shake my head. 'What do you mean?'

'Someone set her up. She were framed. She couldn't have baked those cakes that day. We thought the police would realise when they investigated, but then she...' Pete wrings his hands together. 'After that, we just wanted the whole thing to go away. We didn't want attention, and it wouldn't bring Annie back. We didn't want to get involved anymore.'

He shakes his head at his watch with a sigh. 'Stella should be here by now. Where is she?'

'Did Lloyd guess Stella's identity – and yours too?'

'Not that I know of. Though I think I heard him asking Flint about her.'

And now Stella's dead, and Lloyd's missing. My stomach churns.

I pick up my phone to check for notifications, but this

shed is an internet dead zone. As I lie it back on my lap, the screen flickers to life.

'Figured who you were soon as you turned up. Stella did too.' He jerks his beer bottle towards me. 'Never said nothing, mind, thought you had your reasons. Little Lucy, all grown up.'

'She's getting married in a few weeks.'

'I know ... she told me.' A smile spreads across his face.

'She told you?' My hands begin to tremble.

'Sure, when she were in here before. No...' he shakes his head, '...not before ... It were last night. Saw her out there. Crying, she was, during the party. Gave me a right fright in that nurse outfit. Thought she were Annie at first, come back from the dead. Brought her in here for a drink to calm her down.'

'She ... she told you who she was?' My words come out in a whisper as saliva drains from my mouth. My shoulder muscles stiffen.

'Nah, I figured it out. When she were talking about her mum, and her step-mum, and this place...'

I slump back in the chair. Everything I had warned Ellie about for years could have been crushed in that one foolish moment of curiosity.

'Wants to get married here, she said.' Pete picks up his beer and raises it in the air. 'Lucky bloke, the groom.' Ellie clearly didn't tell him everything. 'Annie woulda been so proud. Lucy's dad too.'

'Her dad?' My stomach fizzes with a combination of intrigue and dread. 'You're not...?'

Pete roars with laughter. 'You thought...? Really? I'm old enough to be her grandad.'

'I just— He was a prison officer – that's what Anna told Nate. So who is he?'

Pete reaches into his shirt pocket and pulls out a small

open packet and lighter. He draws out a cigarette and ignites it. 'Annie never liked you. Called you a stuck-up bitch, you know. Never trusted you. Thought you were trouble. She'd never have wanted you to have Lucy, though looks like you've done a good job there. Can't fault you on that.'

I stifle a cough as smoke curls its way into my lungs, and unzip my medicines pouch around my waist in case I need my inhaler. I know my sister-in-law never liked me – she made that very clear. Too clear by the end. And I was never allowed to call her Annie. 'You said Anna was framed. Yet the police seemed to have evidence against her ... and she brought those cakes in.'

'Even if Annie gave them the cakes, she can't have put that poison in.' Pete lets out a sorrowful laugh. 'She would never have killed him.'

'Killed who? Raziq Ahmed? Because they got on so well? Her gardening protégé?'

'No ... not him. The one who wanted to be near his girls – *all* his girls. Sad, it was.' He takes another drag of his cigarette and breathes out gently. Rings of smoke drift upwards.

Only one man fits that description. I lean forwards and whisper the words, not quite believing them to be true. Though it would explain so much. 'Are you saying that William Owen and Anna were— Was *he* Lucy's father?' Pete raises an eyebrow as I calculate some dates in my head. 'But I heard they bickered all the time because he wanted to do more in Healthcare. They hated each other.'

'Wanted everyone to think that, and it worked. I let them meet in here sometimes on the quiet.'

So that's why Anna spent so much time in these gardens. It was nothing to do with drugs after all.

I frown as I recall the information in Lloyd's book. 'William Owen told his family he was going back to them when he was released.'

'Not what he told Annie.' Pete shakes his head. 'She were all ready for him to live with her and Lucy when he got out. Was getting the house all nice. She were so happy.'

Or was William spinning Anna a web of lies?

I zip my medicines pouch back up. 'Why are you really hiding here at Panbrook, Pete?'

He gazes at his beer bottle, unable to meet my eyes.

Now I see the storage shed in a different light. Not so long ago I thought someone had made it homely, but now it seems stark and cold, a prison within a prison.

I stand up, grab my phone and back away from him towards the door. 'What are you so afraid of?'

44

ANNA

JANUARY 1999

Bryan's reaching into the supplies cupboard when I stroll into the consult room carrying a stack of counselling booklets. As he moves forwards, he bangs his forehead on the top shelf. 'Damn it.'

'Morning! I picked these up from your new supplier last night, just as you asked. Where do you want them?'

'Stick them on the desk and we'll sort through them later. Thanks for doing that – I couldn't leave my Faye on her own. She had another funny turn.'

I put the booklets down. 'Did you hear that rumour about The Brook...?' I trail off as I catch sight of the time on the wall clock. 'Hey, where's Kellie? She's doing clinic at ten.'

'Annie, she— Kellie's in with Tin Man this morning. You'll have to do it instead.' He rubs his forehead. Must have been some whack as there's already a bruise forming.

'What's going on?'

Bryan stuffs some sugar packets into his bag, closes the cupboard and locks it. 'With those new Prison Rules coming in next month, Trayton wants to make sure the men are getting all the healthcare they're entitled to – the same care as outside. If not, she wants to come up with a plan to introduce a wellbeing programme for them, tying in with the NHS.'

'A bit late for that, surely?' I heave my bag off the chair, feeling the weight of the Tupperware box inside it. 'I heard a rumour this place might close later in the year. Some of the officers were talking about it on my way in. Why would Trayton want to make changes now?'

'A last-ditch attempt to stop it closing and keep her job, I reckon.' He stretches his legs, jangling the keys on his belt. 'If she runs this place more efficiently, there's less chance The Brook will be on the closure list. As if prison budgets will allow that.'

'Guess we'll be handing out more of those then.' I point at the booklets and grin at him. 'Maybe the gov will fork up some cash to pay for them. That'll be handy. Ironic too, after all our hard work. Maybe she should stop drinking so much and focus on this place. I certainly can't afford to lose my job. The bigger Lucy gets, the more cash I need.'

He chuckles, but then his grin turns into a frown.

'Bry, what's up?'

'I wasn't sure whether to say anything, but better to warn you now.' His eyes harden. 'Trayton's been looking into recent prisoner deaths. Apparently they've been rising. She's speaking to Kellie about it.'

My tummy somersaults. I've wanted today to be so special, all about the good stuff, and it's going downhill rapidly.

'Surely all deaths are suspicious in here – drugs, suicides, fights ... and the lack of medicines and procedures.' My voice catches in my throat. 'Let me guess, she's putting the blame on Healthcare. Now why doesn't that surprise me. If there's anything going on, I reckon it's one of the officers. Most of them can't stand the prisoners. Have you seen how they treat them?'

'Talking of prisoners,' Bry rests his hand on my shoulder,

'I caught Pills flicking through the Healthcare ledgers yesterday. Any idea why?'

I tense as he squeezes gently. 'How would I know?'

'Well, you spend a lot of time with him in here, don't you? Sick parade, clinic, cleaning, tidying ... Far more than me and Kellie. So you might have seen what he's up to.'

A door slams in the corridor, followed by footsteps and a jangle of keys. Whoever it is walks past without stopping.

I shake Bryan off. 'I haven't seen Owen up to anything. I'd prefer it if he wasn't in here at all, you know that. He even offered to log all our records on the computer and do a stock take – said it's something less for us to do.'

He clenches his jaw. 'You haven't let him, have you?'

'Course not. He's not allowed near medicines, and that includes the stock list. I told him he's mainly here to keep this place clean.' My gaze drifts towards the desk stacked with paperwork and booklets, and Kellie's blue jumper scrunched up on the chair. 'Maybe I'll have a quick tidy before clinic.'

Bry peers inside his medical bag and fastens it. 'Better make sure all our records are up to date, Annie. I'm sure Trayton will want to look through them at some point. And make sure Owen's not causing any trouble this afternoon. I'll speak to the gov if he is. This might be a good reason to get him out of here.'

'I can't watch him today. He's on day release, remember?' I glance at my bulging bag, then at the clock. 'And I'm leaving early.'

'In that case I'll go through the records myself when I get back.' He laughs when I raise my eyebrows. 'I'm sure I can use the computer without you, Annie – if not, I'll find someone to ask. Where are you off to again?'

'I'm picking Lucy up from nursery at twelve, and we're heading to a friend's birthday party. I did tell you.'

'Sorry, had a lot to think about, with my Faye and all. Hope you've baked some cakes for your friend.'

'Of course! Can't have a birthday party without cakes.'

Bryan laughs. 'Maybe you should bake a batch for Owen. Isn't it his birthday later this week? Any excuse for cakes in Healthcare.'

I shake my head. 'Wouldn't waste my time. I'll tell you what though ... If The Brook ever closes, I'll make a special batch of leaving cakes for some of the prisoners – the ones we see the most. A "goodbye gift". Or maybe a "good riddance" gift for those we don't like.'

'Sounds like an excellent plan. So, where's the party today?'

'It's a secret.' I look up at the wall clock again – I can't risk being late. 'So secret, I'm not even telling you. Not told anyone. I don't even want Lucy to know until it happens.'

After he leaves the room, I unlock the medicines cupboard and line everything up neatly on the shelves. I tidy the desk drawers, fold Kellie's jumper, and leave Bryan's stuff for Somers near the door so it's within easy reach.

The storage cupboard in the office is already tidy as Bryan and Kellie went through it the other day, but I still find a squashed digestive biscuit and a couple of Bryan's sugar packets stuck to the back. I pull them out and shove them into the medical waste bin, which is being collected at lunchtime.

I stare at the booklets on the desk. I'd better gather a stack for Somers and another one for the library. I can deliver those on my way out.

Bryan's right – there's not much else I can do right now. But at least I feel like I've done something useful in case Trayton arrives.

Will bounces Lucy on his lap. He's been given an hour for lunch, so we're sitting on a bench having a sandwich and a Coke. It feels like we're a proper couple – finally. It's a bit chilly, but it's nice being outside rather than stuck in Healthcare. And the sun's shining, so that's a bonus.

'Mmm, this is the best spread I've had in years.' Will laughs as Lucy blows me a kiss, clutching that bloody elephant as always. 'And I've got birthday cakes, even if it *is* nearly a week early. I almost feel like a normal bloke again. In civvies. No locked doors. No screw looking over me. Except I've my prison ID card in my pocket and I'll soon be banged up again until next time.'

'Don't miss the bus. It's at five, remember? They'll call a search party if you're late.' I tickle Lucy under the chin and laugh when she giggles back at me. 'By the way, what do you know about The Brook closing?'

Will draws in a breath. 'What would I know?'

'But you heard about it, right?'

'Course. Talk of the landing before I left this morning.'

'The gov wants to introduce a new healthcare programme to make it look like she can do her job properly.' Tears spring into my eyes as I remember my conversation with Bry. I wipe them away.

'What's up?'

'Trayton's looking into some deaths at the prison, Dr Land said. That's crazy. Men die all the time in there, usually from drugs. I guess she's just trying to cover herself – wanting to make sure The Brook doesn't get put on the closure list. And she's trying to blame us. She hasn't been sticking her nose in, has she? Asking you about Healthcare? Bry said you've been looking through our notes again.'

'Are you calling me a grass?' As his voice rises, Lucy starts to whimper.

'Shush, you're scaring her.' I take her from him and give her a cuddle. 'I'm just worried, that's all. Trayton's been gunning for me for years. She once accused me of killing patients just because she wouldn't authorise the tests they needed.'

'If anything odd happens, I'll tell you, babe. Sure I will. I certainly wouldn't talk to Tin Man.' Will tickles Lucy's cheek, screws up his face and pokes out his tongue. She gives him a faint smile. 'And I look through the notes because I'm interested, that's all. It's my pharmacy training. Can't help myself.'

'Well, in future, don't. Or Bry will get you moved out of Healthcare and we won't see each other so much. He thinks Tin Man moved you from gardening to annoy me. Maybe she did.' I nudge his arm as he lets out a laugh.

'More. More.' Lucy hugs her elephant again. She won't go anywhere without that bloody thing. If I forget to take it out with us, she screams, and she won't go to sleep unless it's tucked in next to her. We'd better not lose it as I can't buy a spare. Certainly not asking the stuck-up bitch for one.

I sit Lucy down between us. It's nice to be away from the prison this afternoon, especially with Will. A bit risky out in the open, but we're shaded by the trees. And we deliberately met near his work as it's out of the way. 'So, when you're released, you're coming to live at our place, yes? You did promise.'

'Course, babe.' He leans back and closes his eyes for a moment, his face more relaxed than it's been for months. 'Can't wait.'

'And they'll let you stay somewhere overnight nearer your release date. So I was thinking...'

'You know I can't yet.' He rests his hand on my knee and rubs it gently. 'Need to keep all this quiet for now, yeah? 'Til we're settled.'

My heart sinks. I know he's right – we can't risk it – but I hate having to pretend all the time.

'Look, babe, once I've made my fortune, I'll buy you the world and everyone will know about us.'

I gaze at the row of shops nearest the green, with their matching yellow canopies. A woman creeps out the furthest doorway and tugs the door shut behind her. She shoves her hand in her pocket and pulls her hood over her head. 'Well, I did see a gorgeous silver bracelet in Jennifer's Jewellers earlier – it was two-hundred quid. That can be my first present.'

Will caresses my hair. 'Anything you want, babe. And I'll buy a matching one for Lucy.'

Holding our drink cans and sandwich wrappers, I stand up and stretch my legs. 'Watch her for a mo, will you?'

I stroll over to the bin by the path. As I drop the packaging inside, a woman scurries past me. It's the woman who's just come out of the fancy jewellers. Her hood's covering her hair, but something about her looks familiar. Maybe it's the way she walks or...

Something sparkly falls out of her pocket into the long grass. I sprint over and pick it up. She startles when I grab her arm to attract her attention.

'Hi, you dropped—' My heart thumps in my chest. I move to the side so she can't see Lucy with Will in the distance. 'Does Nate know you're back?'

'No, I ... I came back last night.' Maddie clutches her bag to her chest. 'Spur-of-the-moment work thing. I haven't called him yet.' She eyes me with suspicion. 'You normally work on a Tuesday, don't you? This is well out of your way.'

'I could say the same thing about you. It's not exactly buzzing round here. No swanky hotels in sight.'

She swallows sharply, her cheeks reddening. 'I fancied a change.'

I hold up the silver bracelet that fell out of her pocket and finger one of the heart-shaped charms. 'Saw you drop this when you rushed out the jewellers. Looks pretty. Expensive too. New, is it?'

She snatches the bracelet out of my hand and opens her bag. 'Yes, I decided to give myself a treat. Must have a faulty catch. I'll need to get that fixed.' She squints past me. 'Is that Lucy? Who's she—?'

'Just an old friend. Haven't seen him for years. We're having a catch-up.'

'Maybe I should come over and say hello.' She takes a step forwards.

As I grab her arm to hold her back, her allergy pendant glints in the sun. 'Lucy needs a sleep and he needs to get back to work. But look, Nate's coming over for something to eat later, so why don't you come, too? Around six-thirty?'

When I get back to Will and Lucy, he's peering into the distance. 'Who was that?'

'Nate's Maddie. I told her to come over later to see Lucy.'

'But you don't like her.'

'True. Can't stand the woman.' I stare at my little girl cuddling that bloody elephant. 'But I'm doing this for Nate. And for us.'

Maddie eyes my oak furniture and black leather sofas as she hands me a bunch of pink and yellow tulips and a picture book for Lucy. 'Love what you've done with this place. Much more space.' She gives me a knowing smile. 'Did you enjoy the rest of your lunch with your friend?'

'It was fun catching up.' I stare pointedly at her wrist. 'Good to see you didn't lose your new bracelet again. Though I guess you'll just replace it if you do.'

'Saw this in a toy-shop window last week and thought

Lucy would love it.' Nate wheels in a wooden play kitchen. There's a cooker in the middle, cupboards on both sides, and a hob on top. 'Hey, did I hear you say you saw each other today? You didn't tell me, Maddie. Where were you?'

Wrapping her arm around Nate, she shoots me a glare. 'In town. We just waved from afar.'

I raise my eyebrows at her lie. Secrets between them already. It's just as well they're not going to last.

Lucy toddles over with a plastic stethoscope around her neck, sucking her thumb in her cute way. She picks up one of the wooden pots and puts it in the pretend oven. 'Cake. Yummy.'

She pulls the pot out and hands it to me. I ruffle her blonde curls, tied up today with a pink bow. 'Ellie. Maddie. Want up.'

Maddie picks her up and sits down on the settee so Lucy can show her the stethoscope. Gotta admit it, she's good with my little girl. And Lucy loves her. It's just a shame I don't. Nate could do so much better.

My oven's beeping so I head into the kitchen and pull on some oven gloves. Dinner certainly smells good. Let's hope it tastes good too. I open the oven door, remove the pasta dish and bring it to the table. 'Everyone come over. Dinner's ready.'

Nate helps Lucy into her high chair, while Maddie sits down next to her, placing her handbag on the floor. There's an empty chair at the head of the table as none of us can bear to sit in it. I blink away the threat of tears. It's so quiet here without Dad.

Maddie sniffs the pasta dish, crinkling her nose. 'What's in it?'

'Pasta, basil, oil, garlic, onion, seasoning...' I spoon a large portion onto her plate. 'Enjoy.'

She sniffs again and picks up her fork. Then stuffs a large

mound of pasta into her mouth and swallows. 'This is really good.' She picks up another forkful.

I spoon out some pasta for Nate, and a tiny portion for Lucy. 'Well, there's plenty more if you want it.'

'What the—' Maddie pushes her chair back, pressing her hand against her lips. She reaches down to her handbag, pulls out a strip of pills, pops one out and stuffs it in her mouth. 'You lied. You little...' She glances at Lucy. 'That's got nuts in it. My mouth's all itchy, and I can't—'

'Annie, what have you done?'

I look at Nate, my kind, sweet older brother who deserves someone so much better, and fake a horrified expression. 'Oh God, I'm so sorry, Nate. I totally forgot about the crushed pine nuts. I made it last night when Maddie wasn't coming, and I didn't think, and then—'

'Are you okay, honey?' Nate gently rubs Maddie's back. 'Do we need to call a doctor, or an ambulance?'

I nudge his arm. 'For God's sake, I'm a nurse. I can deal with her.'

'Don't let her anywhere near me.' Maddie presses her hands against her red cheeks. 'She just tried to kill me.'

'It was a mistake.' Nate glares at me. 'A *stupid* mistake.'

Maddie pulls out her Epipens and puts them on her lap. 'I didn't have too much pasta – thank God – so hopefully I won't need these. The antihistamine should start kicking in.' Her voice sounds nasally and croaky already. 'Is there some ice cream in the freezer? That sometimes helps with the itching.'

Nate puts his arm around her. 'Annie – can you get some?'

Maddie grips the Epipens tightly. 'Just in case it gets worse ... you remember how to use these, Nate, like I showed you?'

'Of course I do, honey. You've shown me a few times. I stab them into your leg just here.' He rubs her thigh gently.

I grin at my brother. 'Well, if you don't know where to stab her, I do.'

Nate scowls. 'Annie, ice cream ... now.'

I fake a smile while my tummy swirls with disappointment. Brushing past Maddie to get to the freezer, I whisper softly into her ear. 'Next time I'll do it properly.'

Excerpts from the 'Meet the suspect – Anna Kendall' chapter in *Panbrook Prisongate* by Lloyd Palmer – published by Spotlight Books, August 2009

"Nate was the quiet one – always with his head in a book – and Annie didn't stop talking. Bright little thing she was. Annie would cluck round him like a right mother hen every time he fell over or didn't feel well. Always patching up her dolls like they were real babies. Shoulda guessed she'd be a nurse one day."

— MICK MORGAN, OLD FRIEND OF THE KENDALL FAMILY

"Anna and I were at nursing school together and shared a flat for a while. She was one of the top students in the year, but also loved a good time. She was often bringing junior doctors home. Guess it was her way of winding down after a long shift."

— JENNIFER DURHAM, CLINICAL NURSE AT THE ROYAL MARSDEN HOSPITAL

"When Annie said she was after a job at The Brook, we thought she was having a laugh. Eddie didn't like the idea, but Annie was stubborn, independent, always had been, and applied anyway When Eddie died, Nate was away so poor Annie was dealing with everything on her own, juggling Lucy too. It was a hard time for her."

— **MICK MORGAN**

"Anna didn't take any nonsense from the prisoners, but cared a lot – too much, maybe. It wasn't easy at The Brook – we all saw things that made our toes curl, that made us want to pack it in at times. But Anna … she generally shook off all the bad stuff. Or so I thought. I guess it all just got too much for her."

— **DR BRYAN LAND, FORMER PANBROOK PRISON DOCTOR**

"I like to think Anna and I were friends, more than just work colleagues. But after what happened, maybe I didn't know her at all. If only she'd talked to me about how she felt, perhaps I could have saved those men. And saved her."

— **DR BRYAN LAND**

"Drugs were always an issue in the prisons so The Brook wasn't unusual. There had been a rise in drug-related deaths, and Dr Land suspected one of the prison officers. When those five prisoners died, and the police suspected it was Anna, it made me wonder what she'd been up to."

— **FIONA TRAYTON**

"I'd heard rumours about Anna and drugs but always dismissed them. As I said, we were friends. I'm sure I would have noticed. But maybe she was up to some-thing else in Healthcare. Maybe she and Kellie were in it together. Maybe it was her and Owen. Even her and Roach. The police clearly had evidence against Anna."

— DR BRYAN LAND

"Anna was a lovely girl. She didn't kill them, I'm sure of it. She was good at her job and the prisoners liked her and respected her. The officers too. Drugs were coming into the prison but not the way they thought – if the police had done some digging, they'd have found out how. She'd never have killed those men. Anna was inno-cent – she was framed."

— ANONYMOUS FEMALE OVER THE
PHONE

MADDIE

NOW

SUNDAY
2.30 a.m.

I stride back towards the prison buildings, leaving Pete wracked with guilt, drowning his sorrows in a second bottle of beer.

The banana benches are bathed in a soft halo from lamp-light when I reach them, a golden oasis amid the muted browns and greens of the surrounding vegetation. I perch on the edge of the nearest bench, the same one that I sat on with Lloyd, and survey the kitchen garden. Anna's hard work, Pete called it. Her legacy to Panbrook, just as Ellie is her legacy to me.

A lump swells in my throat. Ellie's father certainly won't be coming to her wedding – I will have to break it to her gently – but I could search for his family. His other daughter, a half-sister for Ellie, the sibling she has always longed for. That is what Nate would want me to do. Yet with the wedding in just a few weeks, I don't really have time – or maybe that's just my excuse. Assuming Anna killed William Owen, with any luck his family won't want to know us anyway.

My phone vibrates in my pocket. I pull it out to catch up on notifications.

Went to explore. Going to sleep. LP

I send a reply: *OK, see you at breakfast*

So Lloyd really did just go for a wander, as Pete suspected. But where has the journalist been for all this time?

I rub my forehead with the palm of my hand as I realise there's something else I should have asked our caretaker. Where could this elusive Oliver Hodgson be?

I also have three messages from Viv, all repeating the same thing: *Call me! Whatever time!*

I ring her mobile.

'Hey, it's Maddie.' My words echo in the silence. 'Everything okay?'

'Is Ells with you?' Her voice sounds distant, as if through a speakerphone.

'No, she was going to work. They were a nurse down, she said. Perhaps she pulled an all-nighter, knowing you're not around.'

'She never arrived.' Viv's voice is high-pitched, wavering, not like her usual calm self. 'She messaged them to say she didn't feel well. I tried to call her at work about something, that's when they told me.'

'No, that can't be right.' My hands feel clammy as I grip my phone more tightly. Ellie lied about where she had been during the party. She wouldn't have lied to me again, would she? 'She's probably just asleep at home, Viv, and hasn't even heard her phone. Have you tracked it?'

'Nothing's showing up. I'm on my way home now.' A car hoots in the background. 'Be another half-hour.'

I stand up and pace in the direction of A wing. Fine drizzle hovers in the air, along with an earthy scent in the breeze ruffling my trousers. A faint sheen of moisture coats my cardigan. 'Have you called the police?'

'No, I wanted to speak to you first, and check at home. She'd kill me if I was making a fuss unnecessarily.'

'She told me she was definitely leaving for work. I'll meet you at your place.' My heart hammers in my chest as I end the call.

I don't have time to pack a bag. I can leave everything behind. But I'll need to message Derek, explaining why I have to abandon my post. My daughter always comes first.

As I head back around B wing towards the courtyard, a flash of colour catches my eye. An orange backpack, lying on the ground near the main doors.

'Ellie?' Her name echoes around me as I peer through a B-wing window into the darkness. My reflection stares back.

'Ellie?' I bang on the door with my fist. Kick it with my foot.

No answer, and the door doesn't budge.

I gaze around the empty courtyard. My daughter is nearby, I can feel it in my heart. I walk towards the main hotel building clutching her bag, inhaling her perfume in the fabric, imagining I am hugging Ellie herself.

The museum door rattles as I pass it. A broken padlock lies on the ground.

She wouldn't have, would she?

I push the door open and step inside. 'Ellie?'

The smoky stench from the fire still lingers in the air. But that isn't all I can smell as I creep into the room. Stale sweat ... a whiff of sweet aftershave...

As I walk further into Room One, my left shoe kicks a small object peeking out from under the front desk. I crouch down and pull out a familiar framed photograph. How did the firefighter miss this when he checked the room?

Scrutinising the picture away from the glare of a computer screen, I can see the faces more clearly – Anna's, Pete's, Stella's, Fiona's – along with that hand at the front, belonging to someone who was moving away from the camera.

Someone who didn't want to be seen ... and now I know why.

A muscle twinges in my cheek. I need to get out of here. I need to find Lloyd, because everything is clear. We have all been wrong for all these years – the police, the media, Lloyd, me...

Turning towards the door, a wayward floorboard creaks under my shoe. A grating noise comes from behind me, something heavy scraping across the floor, and a hard, narrow object whacks the side of my head.

The picture tumbles from my hand as I slump forwards. Clutching the corner of the desk to steady myself, my hearing dulls as blood rushes through my ears. My vision fogs over as my legs give way and I hurtle towards the ground, landing on my side.

The last thing I see is a blurry face hovering in front of me, and a bright light shining in my eyes.

47

MADDIE

NOW

When I open my eyes, I feel as though I'm on a turbulent sea voyage. The world appears to be spinning, and nausea clogs my throat until I swallow it back. My thoughts remain jumbled, and it takes me a few moments to shuffle recent events into a logical order. My discussion with Pete. Viv's message. Ellie's disappearance. Her bag near B wing. The blow to my head.

And then I see Lloyd, or imagine I see him. For it can't be him, can it? He sent me that message to say he was going back to his room. Yet when I take a closer look at the man on my left, I realise it *is* him – just nothing like I saw him last.

His pale face, turned towards me, is lit by the soft glow of the museum's floor lights. He gazes at me with pleading eyes as he slumps against the wall, his hands bound together behind his back. His wire glasses lie broken on the floor beside him. One side arm has snapped off at its hinge, as if someone stepped on it, and the lenses have shattered.

'Lloyd...' As I reach forwards, rough rope fibres dig into my wrists. My shoulder aches and a whooshing sound fills my ears. I rest my hands back on my lap and lean against the cool stone wall behind me.

'Hello, Ms Batten.' A torch beam shines on my face.

'But ... but you went home. I watched you get into a cab ... I waved you off.'

A cold, deep laugh. 'I asked the driver to drop me off up the road, then slipped past security when the guard went out for a smoke.'

So much for the guard rattling keys down the phone at me.

'But how did you get in here. Wasn't the door locked?'

The light drifts towards me and a man steps into my field of vision. His white shirt looks grey in the dim lighting. He carries a torch in one hand and a small handgun in the other, both pointing in my direction. His hands are sheathed in surgical gloves.

'When you work in a prison for years, there's always someone to teach you how to pick a lock.' Bryan gives me a smug smile. 'And it's been useful to keep a few contacts.'

The back of my head throbs as I take a deep breath, ready to—

'If you're thinking of calling for help, don't.' He trails the beam of his torch along the opposite wall, revealing a petite figure curled up on a grey prison blanket, motionless. Her hands are bound together, a scarf tied across her mouth, and her orange backpack is now beside her.

Ellie

My gut twists into knots as I stare at my daughter. Tears well up in my eyes. 'What have you done to her?'

'She's fine. Just a sleeping tablet.' The doctor prods her gently with the torch. 'She looks so much like Annie, doesn't she? Astoundingly so.' He gazes up at Anna's photo on the wall, then shifts his focus back to me. 'I know who she is, by the way – and I worked out who *you* are. That look on your face last night when you realised she was missing ... and then, when Derek was introducing me to other guests, I spotted the two of you together near B wing.' His eyes crinkle with tenderness. 'Little Lucy. It's hard to believe it.'

The outside door rattles in a sharp gust of wind, hitting something large and sturdy. Squinting into the distance, through the narrow doorways, my eyes pick up the faint outline of the Isaac Cane mannequin lying on his side.

'So ... where was I? Oh yes.' Bryan raises the torch as if he's hailing a taxi on a London street. 'Ms Batten, let me bring you up to speed. Did you know Mr Palmer now thinks Annie may be innocent. Quite a turnaround, wouldn't you say?'

The doctor shoves the gun into his trouser waistband and rests the torch on a nearby cabinet, next to his battered doctor's bag and the broken photo frame. Pulling a phone out from his rear trouser pocket, he holds it against Lloyd's thumb to unlock the screen.

Doubt nags at me over who really sent the journalist's message earlier. And Ellie's message to Viv.

The doctor scrolls down with his finger and begins to read aloud. 'When I wrote *Panbrook Prisongate* ten years ago, I never expected to write an update...' He shoves the phone back into his pocket. 'Well, the original is certainly a pile of horseshit, isn't it, Mr Palmer? The contents of this, too.' He holds up Lloyd's notebook. 'Ms Batten, I've been trying to persuade him otherwise, but he won't listen. So he's forced me to take drastic measures. I just had to wait an age for him to come round after—'

'He hit me with something. Knocked me out for a while,' Lloyd winces with each whispered word. A trail of blood trickles down his forehead from a deep gash on his head. 'He was at the party that night the men died.'

Bryan gives a sarcastic laugh. 'How could I miss the finale – a "good riddance gift", as Annie once called it.'

He picks up the broken photo frame and whacks it against the corner of the cabinet. Shards of glass scatter across the wooden floorboards, glimmering in the half-light. The cabinet's frontage shatters too, and the contents spill out towards us – prison bedding, plastic cutlery, counselling booklets, old prison memorabilia, gardening tools – whipping up clouds of dust on the floor.

A stray sugar sachet lands on my shoe. I twitch my foot to flick it away.

'For years, I've manipulated the truth.' Bryan rips the photograph from the frame. 'Or thought I had until now.'

Lloyd twists to the side, grimacing in pain as he straightens his back against the wall. 'But you're not in that picture. I checked.'

'His hand is.' I jut my chin towards Bryan. 'I recognised his signet ring.'

'That's very observant of you, Ms Batten.' Bryan shoves the photograph into the waste bin.

'I get that from my mother.'

He reaches into his doctor's bag and brings out a packet of Mayfair Green menthol cigarettes. He lights one and tosses it onto the photo. The paper catches alight. The sides furl, each face blackening one by one. Anna. Stella. Fiona. Until only Pete and Bryan's hand are visible, and then they're gone too.

The doctor throws a grey prison-issued towel into the bin to smother the flames.

Residual smoke spirals towards the ceiling.

My chest tightens as if someone is sitting on me, sucking out all the air. I press my hands against my trouser waistband, searching fruitlessly for my medicines pouch. My stomach lurches, my breathing quickens, and a cough stirs in my throat.

Sitting up straighter, taller, I take slow, deep breaths to

calm down my airways, as my asthma nurse taught me, to get more oxygen into my lungs. I focus on the dust motes frolicking in the beams of the low floor lighting – breathing in and out, in and out – to prevent a full-blown coughing attack.

Lloyd nudges my legs with his feet and gazes at me with concern when I turn towards him. Giving me a reassuring smile, he returns his attention to Bryan. 'So that photo is why you came back tonight?'

Reaching down to the floor, Bryan gathers up the counselling booklets and stuffs them into his doctor's bag. 'I came back to The Brook to tie up loose ends.'

'You mean Fiona Trayton?' As I force my words out, the tightness in my chest returns.

He snorts with laughter. 'But that was an accident, Ms Batten. It's so easy to fall from a landing, especially if you've had too much to drink.'

'And what about Stella? Was she an accident too?'

Lloyd gapes at me. 'Stella from Housekeeping?'

'Yes, she's...' I shake my head, still unable to say it out loud, ...*dead*. 'She was a prison guard here at The Brook until it closed.'

A smile flickers across Bryan's lips. 'Never expected to see Estelle talking to you on that bench in the courtyard the other day. After all these years ... and still wearing that necklace. When I tracked her down in her room yesterday, she threatened to go to the police.'

My breath snags in my throat. 'So what did you do to her?'

Dr Land holds up his open bag and shakes it gently, rattling the contents. 'Take this everywhere I go. Never know when I might need what's inside. Just as well security's always been lax around here.' He bends down, picks up some sugar sachets and stuffs them inside his bag. 'I did say there was nothing you could have done.'

His words jab at my forehead as Stella's face thrusts itself into my mind. I stare at his open bag, bulging with everything inside it, and at the gun in his waistband, thinking back to the article she wanted Lloyd to find – the one accusing Anna of smuggling drugs into the prison, despite insisting that Anna was innocent.

And now the truth begins to dawn on me.

48

MADDIE

NOW

'It was you.' My voice rises in a mixture of anger and excitement. 'You were bringing drugs into Panbrook in plain sight through Healthcare. Doctors and nurses wouldn't have been searched going in and out.'

The museum door's hinges squeak as it clatters against Isaac Cane. Wind moans through the gaps in the window frames, and rain patters against the glass.

'Was Anna part of it?' Lloyd shifts uncomfortably against the wall. His shirt is damp with sweat.

The doctor smirks. 'There was so much people didn't know about their favourite prison nurse. To be fair, I sucked her into my enterprise from the start. I needed more hands on deck.'

A chilly draught creeps across the wooden planks, seeping through my clothes. Goosebumps spread along my arms. 'But you were chief medical officer here. Why did you need to deal drugs?'

'My Faye was so ill.' The doctor rubs his eyes and takes a deep breath to steady himself. 'The NHS wouldn't pay for the medicines, can you believe it? I'd given so much of my life to saving patients, and that's all the thanks I got.' His voice drips with resentment. 'My wife was worth every penny, and more, but it was so expensive to get her medicines privately, so I had to do whatever I could to make ends meet.'

'Were all five men involved?' Beads of sweat glisten on Lloyd's forehead, despite the cool air, and his right shoulder is shaking. Sitting with his hands tied behind his back for so long must be taking its toll.

'Of course. People always did as I asked.' The doctor grabs the remaining sugar sachets and shoves them into his bag. 'One of the best lessons I learnt at The Brook was how to keep everyone in line – cons, screws, staff ... We all played the game. A threat here, another there. Secrets in prison are gold dust.'

'So why kill them?'

'When the prison was closing, Ms Batten, I had to take action. I couldn't risk anyone revealing my secrets elsewhere. And then Annie said she wanted out.' His face reddens in anger. 'After everything I'd done for her and Lucy to give them a better life.'

Lloyd mouths something at me as he wiggles his shoulder again. His eyes focus on the smashed cabinet glass, then he nods at the contents of the floor: the prison bedding, the gardening books...

I shake my head at him and shrug. 'Why didn't Anna reveal the truth afterwards, once she'd been arrested?'

'She needed to protect Lucy.' The doctor glances at Ellie. 'But Annie was certainly not innocent. Maybe she was when we first met, but then I realised she'd been getting up to no good in here. With him.'

William Owen...

A muscle twinges in my jaw. 'Yet you didn't dob her in.'

'As I said, I liked to play the game.' Bryan laughs. 'Secrecy, bribery and corruption. A prison nurse caught having sex with a prisoner was a sackable offence, gross misconduct. And having a daughter together was—'

'You said you didn't know who Lucy's father was.'

'You asked me if Annie *told* me who he was. She didn't but I guessed. I saw them together far too often, and far too close, even more so when he transferred to Healthcare. Kellie and I never understood why Trayton kept Pills here. Until I realised he'd been sent to spy on us. Prison deaths had been rising, and the gov was convinced we were up to something in Healthcare.'

Bryan flinches at a loud crash of thunder. Lightning flashes through the mesh windows, strobing the room. The museum door rattles, accompanied by a faint crunch of gravel outside.

The doctor pulls the gun from his waistband and trains it on Lloyd, then on me.

'Don't move,' he whispers, jerking his chin towards Ellie.'

'Please ... don't do this.' I gaze at Ellie, her soft blonde curls framing her face, still in a drug-fuelled slumber. Hopefully unaware of the conversations around her. 'Please let my daughter go. She doesn't belong here.'

Bryan sniggers. 'Don't you mean Annie's daughter? But no need to worry about her. She'll be coming with me.' He raises the gun. 'Now I've got your hotel keys, I'll just wait for the security guard to pop out for another smoke.'

Another flash of lightning and the floor lights flicker. The room plunges into semi-darkness, lit only by the faint glow of the torch.

The journalist springs to life, flinging rusty gardening secateurs onto the floor. Ripping frayed rope from his wrists, he throws himself at Bryan, rugby-tackling him to the ground. 'You bastard.'

The two men thrash around on the walkway. The journalist on top, then the doctor, then the journalist again.

Lloyd trying to grab the gun, the doctor holding it out of his way.

Bryan's foot catches the corner of a nearby cabinet. The wooden unit wobbles precariously, then crashes onto its side. The front panel of glass shatters, and healthcare ledgers and IMR files spill out onto the floorboards.

As Lloyd pins Bryan down, the gun slips out of the doctor's grasp and slides towards Ellie. The journalist wraps his hands around Bryan's neck and begins to squeeze.

Shards of glass stick to my trousers and pierce my skin as I shuffle towards Ellie, towards the gun. Stabbing pains ripple along my legs.

Bryan squirms and flings out his arms, grappling around on the floor. Then he drives his arm upwards.

Lloyd screams in pain as the doctor pushes him away. Blood drips down the journalist's side, a large shard of glass piercing his shirt.

The doctor crawls towards Ellie, glass crunching under his hands.

Lloyd grabs his ankle, yanking him back just as I reach for the gun.

But it's too late.

Bryan's hand is already wrapped around the grip. He arches his arm and cracks the muzzle against Lloyd's head.

The journalist goes rigid, then slumps to the floor.

Bryan creaks himself up on one knee, then the other, keeping the gun trained on Ellie but his eyes focused on me. 'If you try anything...'

Scowling, he nudges the secateurs and stray shards of glass away from me with his shoe. 'If you hadn't shown up, this would've all be over by now.' He spits out his words. Then shoving the gun back into his trouser waistband, he lashes my ankles together and checks the rope around my wrists.

A sharp pain in my hip sends a rush of blood to my head. I

suck in a lungful of air. 'Everything nearly backfired twenty years ago too, when William Owen didn't die straightaway. It was just as well you had a backup plan.'

'You're more astute than you look, Ms Batten. But you've got one thing wrong...' Bryan's eyes flash with amusement. 'I never had a backup plan. Annie finished him off, not me.'

I shiver at a sudden chill in the room. *Was I right all along? Does this mean Anna was guilty?*

I flinch as I sense Nate's disapproval at my thoughts. The doctor is playing with my mind, still trying to lay the blame on Anna as he did in the past.

Yet I have always believed my sister-in-law was capable of murder. She tried to kill me once, after all.

I shudder as I recall her whispered words in my ear on the night she deliberately fed me pine nuts in her pasta dish: '*Next time I'll do it properly.*'

Her words hung between us – and only us – as no one else would ever have believed me. Certainly not Nate. If Anna had lived, I'm sure she would have killed me eventually.

The doctor ties up Lloyd's hands and feet with fresh rope, using more force than required. The journalist groans and grimaces, but his eyes remain closed.

Anger burns in my chest as my gaze meets the doctor's. 'So you're now going to shoot us?'

'Shoot you?' He smirks. 'Guns attract far too much attention. I only brought it to keep Mr Palmer in line if I needed to.' He pulls out the gun from his waistband and places it on a tall cabinet. 'I have other plans. Just as well I brought spares.'

Goosebumps prickle my skin as he removes two syringes and two glass vials from his bag. 'But they'll know it was you. They'll work it out.'

He pulls out Lloyd's phone from his trouser pocket and stamps on it, smashing the glass. Then he fishes out a gold fob watch from his other pocket and waves it in front of me. 'Not when they see this. There's always someone to blame.'

He chooses one of the syringes and fills it with a clear, colourless fluid from one of the vials. Pacing over to Lloyd, he grabs the journalist's arm and searches for a vein. Then, with a medic's precision, pierces the skin with the needle and injects the syringe's contents.

Lloyd's eyes snap open, as if sensing the extra fluid flushing through him. His pupils contract as his breathing slows down.

'Lloyd...' Nausea bubbles in my throat as his eyes close again. 'Lloyd ... please.'

Bryan grabs another syringe and fills it from a fresh vial. He strolls over to me with a ruthless glint in his eyes.

Warm sweat pools at the base of my spine.

The museum door rattles in the wind. Its hinges squeal. A sweet woody scent drifts in my direction, and an icy draft glides across my arms. The rope around my wrists seems to slacken as my imagination goes into overdrive.

Bryan tugs at his shirt collar and stumbles. As he rights himself, the syringe flies out of his hand and rolls under the toppled-over cabinet. He bends down and reaches underneath, his arm searching in all directions. 'Where the hell are you?'

Wriggling my wrists to loosen the rope even more, I will the syringe to roll further away from him, but fortune isn't on my side. Bryan lets out a quiet whoop of triumph and pulls his hand out. Clutching the syringe, he stands up and pivots towards me.

A chill smothers my skin when I glance at Lloyd. He has now slumped to the right, his face turning an alarming shade of grey. Tears brim in my eyes as I swivel my gaze to Ellie, whose eyelids are fluttering as she gradually stirs.

'Please help us! Please!' I back up against the wall, shrinking into myself, hoping someone can hear me. I have no intention of joining the prison's cohort of legendary ghosts tonight.

A door behind me slams and a dark figure rushes past. It barrels into Bryan, knocking him to the ground, and thumps him in the face. A large anchor tattoo flexes over beefy arm muscles. 'Should have done this years ago. This is for Annie.'

The syringe falls from the doctor's grasp. Blood pours from his nose. His jaw drops and his eyes widen as he croaks, 'Pops?'

Thursday, August 5, 1999
Published at 22:30 GMT

[FRONT PAGE]

Panbrook poisoner found dead

Anna Kendall, 27, a prison nurse from
Abingford, Hertfordshire, has been found
dead in her cell at HMP Clayton in Bedford-
shire. She was being held on remand for the
murder of five prisoners at HMP Panbrook on
Friday 18 June 1999.

More to follow.

50

MADDIE

NOW

SUNDAY
3.30 a.m.

I insert the end of my inhaler into my mouth, wrap my lips around the cold plastic and take a deep breath. The steroid spirals into my lungs, easing the wheezing from the residual smoke that still lingers inside me. After a few seconds, I place the inhaler down on the table and gently press a cold pack against the back of my head.

Pete watches me from the doorway, concern etched in his eyes.

Derek is chatting to the police at a nearby table about Bryan's possible involvement in Fiona's fall and Stella's death, which my boss 'conveniently discovered' just before they arrived.

The back of my head throbs as I put the cold pack down and grab a paper tissue from a cardboard box in front of me. I gently blow my nose, trying to remove the stench of smoke, and use another tissue to dry my eyes, patting them carefully one at a time.

The paramedic suspected I may have mild concussion, but I couldn't fit into the solitary ambulance that arrived. While Lloyd and Ellie were being transferred to the hospital, I watched the police handcuff the doctor and drag him away, savouring that moment. They found his car hidden under some trees near the hotel gates. That must have been how he intended to smuggle Ellie out.

Viv has been messaging me constantly with updates, reassuring me that Ellie will be fine. Bryan had told the truth when he said it was just a mild sedative. The police found Stella's sleeping tablets in his bag. Lloyd's wounds are being dressed and he's being treated for hypoglycaemia triggered by an insulin overdose.

Viv called the hotel when I stopped replying to her messages. Reception sent Pete to find me and he noticed the museum lights were on. Since the front door was blocked, he used his alternative route, through the outside storeroom. The inner storeroom key has never been lost – it was just never given to Derek. Pete has been using that museum entrance as a shortcut for years.

My phone vibrates with a message.

What anniversary weekend? I never received an invitation. Please contact me on this number. Oliver Hodgson.

I call the phone number on the screen, keeping my voice as low as possible. When the call ends, excitement rumbles in my gut.

'Here.' Someone places a glass full of water on the table next to my hand. 'I thought you could do with another drink before I head home.'

I look up at the young woman in front of me. Rosalie is clutching the handle of a cabin-sized yellow wheelie case.

Perfect timing.

'Thanks.' I pick up the glass and sip the cold water to ease the dryness. 'What's going on over there?' I jut my chin towards Radha, who is standing in the doorway with a female police officer at her side.

'They've just searched her locker and found a necklace with a pearl pendant. One of the guests reported it missing on Friday – it looks like Radha has been stealing from guest rooms.'

I rub at my bare wrist. 'What about that other woman who lost her bracelet? Mrs Etherton.'

Rosalie shakes her head. 'Maybe she dropped it in the hotel grounds, as she thought, or maybe Radha hid it somewhere to collect at a later date. The Ethertons moved house last week, so I've written down their new address.'

She reaches into the small front pocket of her wheelie case, pulls out a piece of lined A4 paper and hands it to me. 'Sorry about the pen colour – it's the only one I could find.'

I stare at Rosalie's neat red handwriting, the swirls of the a's and slants of the n's. My chest tightens.

'It was you...' I shake the paper in her direction. 'You wrote that message on the lift mirror: "*Anna Kendall was guilty*". But why?'

Rosalie looks across at Derek. 'It was a message for Lloyd Palmer but you saw it instead.' Her voice is barely more than a whisper as she gives me an apologetic smile. 'I saw you scrubbing it off. Sorry to waste your time. It was a mad, angry moment.'

'Well, you're wrong. Anna wasn't guilty. The doctor admitted he ... he killed all ... all five men.' I stumble over these words as if nothing else the doctor said mattered. 'Anna didn't do it.'

'Believe what you want.' Rosalie's voice cracks, tears welling up in her eyes. 'But Anna was no angel.'

As I gaze at her distraught face, I realise these are more

than just the heartfelt emotions of a stranger. These are personal, concealed for so long deep in her heart.

So this is why she has seemed so familiar.

I gesture for her to sit down in the chair next to mine. 'You have his eyes, his jaw ... You're William Owen's daughter.' There's a hint of Ellie in her features too.

Rosalie grips her hands together to stop them shaking. 'I cried during Derek's welcome speech and again in the museum when I saw my dad's photo on the wall. I'd shut him out of my thoughts for so long.'

'You and your mum disappeared after the murders.'

'Yes, we...' She looks around the room, her eyes resting briefly on the library books. 'You know, I always hated this place. I remember coming to visit. All those scary men. I was so little at the time.' Tears begin to flood down her cheeks.

'My dad promised he'd be home one day. I didn't understand why he was locked up in here. And then Jessie died,' she wipes her eyes with the back of her hand, 'and Dad still didn't come back. I thought he hated us. Mum made us move away after that. I lost my sister, my dad, my friends...' Rosalie sniffs loudly. 'Mum remarried, our surname changed, and I hated this place even more.'

I rest my hand on her arm, realising what it has taken for this young woman to be here. 'Yet you still chose to come back.'

She grabs a tissue from the box and wipes her face. 'This place has been hanging over me for twenty years, nearly my whole life. I wanted – needed – to be here this weekend for closure.'

Ellie's face flashes into my vision. *Maybe you're not the only one...*

'So why didn't you just email to ask if you could come as a guest?'

313

'Because I didn't want to be here as the grieving daughter, that's why.'

As her voice rises, Pete takes a step towards me. I shake my head at him, prompting him to take a step back. Neither of us has mentioned my family's past or who Ellie is. If I need to tell the police, I will do this privately in my own time and on my own terms with a lawyer in tow.

'I didn't want everyone's pity,' Rosalie continues. 'When the job came up, I applied on the off-chance ... Figured if the universe wanted it to happen, for me to be here, it would.'

'But that's not all you did, is it,' – I pause for dramatic effect – 'Oliver?'

Her cheeks flush and her hands shake. 'How did you find out?'

'The real Mr Hodgson finally messaged me through LinkedIn. The phone number he gave me is different to the one on our system. I've just spoken to him. He's one of your work clients.'

She gives me a half-smile and wipes her eyes. 'When I realised how much I wanted to be here, I applied for the lottery. Figured I'd up my chances if I applied from several names and addresses. I used my work client list, around forty of them, and bought a new phone. The clients were all away so they didn't know. I was paid to gather their post and look after their homes. Oliver Hodgson's name and address got lucky. I haven't left my job – I'm officially on a work break right now.'

'They gave you a job reference. I saw it in the file.'

Rosalie blushes. 'I typed it out myself on the House-Holders letterhead when I was alone in the office one day.'

I can't admit it out loud, but I'm impressed with her resourcefulness.

Everything she says ties in with my phone call. Mr Hodgson told me he's currently working in Australia, with Rosalie Masters at HouseHolders responsible for his property in London. This explains why he, or rather *she*, entered our lottery with a picture of a cute puppy rather than of the man himself.

'But then you got the job here.'

'Yes. When I saw it advertised, I applied for the hell of it, not expecting to actually get it. So I had an exclusive lottery ticket I didn't even need.'

The police officers stand up, shake hands with Derek and stride towards the door, with Radha between them.

My wrist throbs as I watch them leave. 'Why did you email the newspaper last night as Oliver Hodgson?'

She glares at Derek. 'God, he can be a bastard to work for, can't he?' She grabs a fresh tissue and scrunches it up with shaking hands. 'I've had to be so restrained. But I was drunk ... angry. All these celebrations going on when those men – my dad – died in here, and no one cared. Funny though, as I don't really remember him. He's just a face, not much more, and he betrayed us...' she scowls '...with *her*. Anna Bloody Kendall.'

A tingle of warmth flushes my cheeks. 'You knew? About him and Anna?'

She nods. 'He'd told Mum before Jessie got sick that he was leaving us for her when he got out. But then he changed his mind – said she was up to something in here – and Mum agreed to take him back. Give our family another chance.'

Rosalie's tears spill out again. As she tries to use the mangled tissue to wipe her eyes, it breaks apart in her hand. I hand her a fresh one from the box.

'You know, it's weird being back here – almost like my memory's been playing tricks on me.'

My skin prickles. 'What do you mean?'

'I thought I could smell my dad's prison deodorant the other night.' Her nostrils flare. 'It always reminded me of apple trees near our house. It's probably the only thing I've never truly forgotten about him.'

51

ANNA

18 JUNE 1999

'Here. Take this.' Bryan shoves a small Tupperware box into my hands.

'Ew.' I point at his surgical gloves.

'Don't panic.' He pulls them off and chucks them into the medical waste bin. 'I stuck them on at the end of sick parade but didn't need them after all.'

I peel off the Tupperware lid. The sweet, yeasty aroma of freshly baked cakes wafts around me. 'Ooh, these smell yummy.'

Inside are five little fairy cakes with swirly yellow icing sprinkled with silver balls, just like I make them.

'Where did you get these? And why are they all wrapped in cling film? That looks a bit weird.' I reach in to take one.

'Hands off!' Bryan pushes my fingers away from the box. 'They're not for you. I'm keeping them wrapped so they stay fresh. It's warm in here so don't start fingering them or the icing will melt.'

'Who are they for?'

'Since your new kitchen's still not finished, I got my Faye to bake a big batch for the party on your behalf.' He points at a large, square Tupperware box on his desk. 'These five are wrapped up to make it easier to hand them through the cell flap. Say they're from you.'

'Why from me?'

'Eric was so looking forward to the birthday cakes you promised, and I heard you telling Pills that even prisoners deserve a leaving surprise on their last night. I know it means seeing Fingerling again – after you saw him in clinic last week – but you can just shove the wrapped cake through the viewing flap. You don't have to say anything. You wouldn't want to let Pills down, would you?' He gives me a bemused smile.

I draw in a sharp breath. 'Well, it's not like I'll be seeing him after today.'

I gaze around the office. Most things have already been removed, and the furniture will be going after the weekend once the prison's officially closed. 'Are you still taking that SMO job at Clayton?'

'I have good contacts there, so maybe. Want to join me? Start up somewhere else?'

I stare at the booklets with the stuck-together pages, and at the sugar packets on the desk. That's what Steven Fisher was looking for when he locked us in the consult room that time.

Our little secret, Bryan once called it, after he handed me a wad of cash, told me to buy some new clothes for Lucy and start contacting local estate agents. I've been keeping his secret for all this time, even becoming part of it, finally able to give Lucy the proper home she deserves. But now The Brook closing could give me a fresh start.

'I still want out,' I whisper. 'I told you I don't want to do this anymore. You pushed me into it in the first place. Making me log fake appointments and change your records so you could pass your "special sugar treats" to the prisoners. And deliver those booklets to Roach in the library. I never had a choice.'

'There's always a choice, Annie.' Bryan pushes his hair away from his face. 'You *chose* this. You needed the money to get out of that flat.'

'Yes, I wanted to give Lucy a better life – but not one with a criminal for a mum.'

'And her dad? It's not like he was ever going to help you out, whatever you told your family. He's been stringing you along all this time.'

An acid taste swirls in my mouth. 'What do you mean, Bry?'

'You know exactly what I mean. *Who* I mean.' He stands up. Wrings his hands together. 'Look, we can talk about all of this after the weekend once The Brook's closed. You don't need to worry about anything. Today's a celebration – and I need to get home to my Faye.'

'You're not coming to the party? Everyone will be there. It's our last night.'

Our last night. I still remember my first day here as if it was yesterday. All that talk about hiding files in cakes, and all those new-girl nerves. So much has happened since then, so much that no one else needs to know about.

'My Faye wasn't too good this morning so I don't want to leave her on her own. I only came in to tie up a few loose ends before this place closes and say a few goodbyes.' He points at the Tupperware box. 'Just don't forget to give out those cakes. Wouldn't want all her efforts going to waste. And don't forget the men's ones – I've added extra lemon icing to those as a treat. Makes them taste even better.'

'Why are you being so nice to the prisoners today?'

'I'm always nice, aren't I? Anyway, I'm doing this for you, not them.' He cups my chin with his hands, then picks up his medical bag. 'Just make sure this stays between us, Annie?

Remember they're from you. I don't want the prisoners thinking I'm getting soft.'

I open the shed door and peer in. 'On your own? Need any healthcare?'

'Sure do. I've got this odd craving, Nurse Kendall.' Will nudges the door closed behind me and pushes me up against the wall. His hand reaches under my skirt.

Despite the stir of longing inching up my thighs, I push him away. 'Not now ... Pops is out there.'

'He'll be fine with it. You know he is. Now give me my last-day treat.' He pulls me towards him again. 'I'm glad transport was delayed.'

'I'll be giving all of you that leaving treat I promised.' I laugh as he sticks out his tongue. 'No, not that. Bry, he— I've baked a little cake for all of you. Better than the muck you'll get from the kitchen. I'll drop them into Enhanced later.'

'Forget the cake. I've got another leaving treat in mind.' He kisses my lips gently and nuzzles my neck. 'I love you, babe. You know that, right?'

'Will, I don't have long ... and if Pops comes in...'

'He won't. He's gone for a slash. Said he trusted me not to do anything stupid – and Estie's out there. I'm Cat D, remember, allowed out on my own. And I'm getting out soon so Tin Man knows I'm not going to take any risks.'

I begin to unzip my skirt – slowly and carefully so I don't catch the little flap of fabric in the metal teeth. 'I've finally told Lucy her daddy will be coming to live with us very soon. She's so excited.' I pause as the shed door rattles. 'What was that?'

'Nothing. Just the wind as usual. Relax.' Will takes my hand and kisses it. He slides my skirt down over my hips until it gathers around my ankles. 'Now ... where were we? Ah, yes

... just here.' He kisses my neck, then starts to unbutton my shirt. 'Lockdown's not for another hour...'

Ahmed's hoisting a dead pigeon into a wheelbarrow when I get back to the kitchen garden. Sweat is streaking down the back of his shirt. Estie is watching him closely, even though he doesn't need much supervision.

Like Will, he'll be released soon. He told me he's been so motivated by his time at The Brook that his parents are going to set him up with a gardening business.

'Hard to believe this is our last day,' Estie says when I sit down next to her. 'I'll miss this place. Spend so much time here ... far more than home.'

As I glance around at the garden, sadness rumbles in my tummy. The sun shines down on the pathways and highlights the vivid reds and pinks of the roses. What will happen to our hard work once we're gone?

'Seen Pills?' Ahmed's deep voice breaks the silence. He hands us both a sprig of lavender.

My cheeks grow warm as I inhale the floral scent. 'Only in passing. I think he's in the shed. Why?'

'He didn't tell you his news?'

'No, what have I missed?'

Estie leans back against the bench. 'Gov Trayton has granted him early release. Not sure why, but he's getting out soon after he gets to the next place.'

'But—'

'His missus must be so excited.' Ahmed grins at me. 'Pills said she's arranging a party for all their mates and their little one. What's his kid's name? She can't be much older than your Lucy.'

I pick up my medical bag and a nearby shovel. 'I'll put this away before I head back to Healthcare.'

When I reach the shed, I slam the door open and hang the shovel on a hook.

'Thought you were Pops. I'm not sure there's enough time to—' Will gazes at my frown. 'What's up, babe?'

'What's up? Ahmed just said you're getting out next week and going back to Tina and Rosie. Why did you lie to me?'

He looks down at the floor. Shuffles his feet. 'She's insisting. What can I do? I can't tell her about us, can I? If the gov finds out, you won't get another job.'

'You promised me. Even just now.' I press my hand against his chest and give him a gentle shove. 'After you fucked me in here.'

Will grabs my wrist, tightening his grip as he pulls me towards him. 'I love you, babe, but Tina needs me.' He runs his fingers over my cheek. 'I can't just leave her, not after what happened with Jessie. Rosie thinks I hate her because I've been gone for so long. I need to fix things. I'll come and see you when Tina's not around.'

'You're kidding, right? You've another little girl, remember? You said you loved me – loved *us* – and you'd move in when you got out. I've been getting the house all ready. Lucy's so excited. We both are.'

'So we can still see each other, can't we? Tina doesn't need to know.'

'Don't treat me like a whore. Don't mess with me, Will. It's Tina or me. You can't have it all.'

'And you don't threaten me, Annie.' He grins, pointing to my medical bag. 'I know what you've been up to. Found those drugs inside some booklets. If you cause me trouble, I'll tell all to the gov. Tin Man only let me stay at The Brook to spy on things. To spy on *you*. That's why she insisted I worked in Healthcare. See if I could work out why there've been so many overdoses. I've kept quiet so far, but there's still time to have a chat.'

'A chat with Tin Man? You bastard.' The outside door creaks in the wind, and I take a step backwards. 'I'll tell them you forced yourself on me and blackmailed me to stay silent. I'll tell Trayton the drugs are down to you. Dr Land will back me up.'

'But, Babe—'

'Enough of your sweet-talk.' I push him away from me. 'You'll go back inside, you know that. Your word against mine. You're just a pathetic con. I'm the nurse here, remember. My word carries more weight. If you say anything, you'll regret it.'

Kellie's hitched up her skirt and is dancing on the table. Eric's smiling like he's reached seventh heaven, enjoying the view from his chair. Dirty old bugger.

I've just come back from taking Faye's fairy cakes to the prisoners. I wasn't going to bother, not after what happened with Will in the garden. But I wanted to see him one last time before this place closes. Try to get him to change his mind. Get him to apologise. But a fat lot of good that did.

My tummy seethes with anger. I love him, for God's sake, and I thought he loved me. I can't believe that bastard's picking them over us. If he says something to Tin Man, she's not going to believe him, is she?

Someone nudges my arm. I stare at them in confusion. 'Hey, Owl Face, where's your uniform. Aren't you on duty?'

'Not officially, Little Lamb. There's no roster.' Pops grins at me as he stubs out his ciggy and picks up a beer. 'Figure one drink won't hurt anyway. Who's gonna to tell? Not expecting any trouble. Fingerling's been ringing the cell bell, but he's just mucking about for attention.' He ducks as Tin Man looks our way.

'Want one, Annie?' Kellie wiggles a plastic cup and a half-full bottle of vodka in the air.

'I can't. What if there's a call for Healthcare? You're certainly too pissed to do it. One of us has to be responsible tonight.'

Estie nudges my arm. Raises a beer bottle in the air, her fancy O-pendant jangling around her bare neck. So much for guard duty tonight. 'Oh, come on, just a small one, Annie. Who's going to tell on you?'

Kellie points across the room. 'Hey, look, someone's taking photos. Quick, let's join in. Remember our last hours at The Brook.' She grabs our arms and drags us over.

A camera flashes, and lights speckle my vision.

Estie nods at Owl Face. 'Come on, Pops, best do our rounds, then we don't need to bother again. Annie, save us another drink.'

'What if Tin Man sees you?' I jut my chin towards Trayton. She's stuffing one of the fairy cakes into her mouth, holding a wine glass in her other hand. With any luck, she'll choke on it.

'Forget about the gov. She's beyond pissed.' Kellie giggles and sways and waves the vodka bottle in the air again. I wouldn't exactly call her sober either. 'Loosen up a bit tonight, Annie. You're usually always up for a drink. Come on.'

I stick my hands on my hips and give her a mock glare. 'Bry's not here. Someone needs to be on Healthcare duty.'

'Not here? But I thought he was...' Kellie's gaze shifts around the room. 'Oh, I must have imagined it.'

'See, you're hallucinating already.'

'Come on, just a little one.' Kellie hands me a plastic cup and pours out a shot. 'We've just five cons banged up in here. They're probably all asleep. Two guards is the best ratio we've ever had – even if they're pissed.'

Will's words jar in my head. '*I love you babe, but Tina needs me.*'

'Okay, okay, you've twisted my arm. I'll soak up the alcohol with one of those.' I drain the cup, then choose a fairy cake and stuff it in my mouth. My tongue tingles with a strong taste of lemon. I lick the sweet icing residue off my lips.

Kellie pours me another shot, or maybe it's a double. Guess if I drink enough I can forget about Will tonight. I drain the cup again and stuff another fairy cake in my mouth before joining her on the dance floor.

'Code Blue on B wing.' My radio crackles to life. *Bloody hell.*

I pull the walkie talkie off my belt and respond. 'This for real?'

Forget the radio codes tonight. Kellie's right – who's going to know?

'Annie? Is that you?' Owl Face's deep voice. 'Get over to Enhanced ... now!'

My footsteps echo on the empty landing. I munch another fairy cake on the way. Hopefully no one will notice I can't quite walk in a straight line. It can't be anything that serious as they haven't sounded the alarm.

'In here.' Estie peers out of Will's cell. 'What took you so long?'

'I had to pop to Healthcare. Grab my bag.' When I shake it in front of her, syringes and vials rattle inside. 'What the hell's happened?'

I crouch down beside Will. He's not moving, his eyes are closed and he's dribbling onto his bare chest. My nose wrinkles at the stink of vomit all over the bed and floor.

'Is he...?'

'He was still breathing when I checked, but barely. Pops is next door with Ahmed. Fingerling, Lucas and Roach are already dead.'

'Dead?' I feel all wobbly inside as I pull my gloves on and open up my bag. 'If we don't know what's wrong, I don't know how to treat him.'

'There must be something you can do.'

My head's all muddled from the vodka. 'It could be poison. Or something they've eaten. Or they've OD'd on something.'

'Ahmed's gone,' Owl Face shouts.

Estie shakes her head slowly and gives me a tight smile. 'It's not looking good for Pills then. I'm sorry, Annie. Just do what you can.'

I look down at the man lying on the bed. The man I've loved for years. The father of my precious little girl. *Will, you promised. And then you chose her over me.*

Will's words surface. *'I know what you've been up to ... If you cause me trouble, I'll tell all to the gov. I've kept quiet so far.'*

Maybe whoever poisoned these men has done me a favour.

'Okay, some saline will help rehydrate him.' My hands shake as I take out a syringe and a vial of insulin.

Owl Face calls for Estie, and she runs into the cell next door.

I carefully take off the syringe cap, fill it from the vial and push the needle into a vein in Will's arm, draining the contents. Then I pull out another syringe and vial and do the same.

He opens his eyes and tries to speak, but no words come. His eyes start to dull and then there's nothing.

'I'm sorry,' I whisper as I empty the syringe, a tear trickling down my cheek, 'but I warned you, Will. I warned you not to mess with me. I can't risk you blabbing. I won't risk losing my daughter. It's me and Lucy forever.'

Excerpts from the 'What happened that night?' chapter in
***Panbrook Prisongate* by Lloyd Palmer – published by**
Spotlight Books, August 2009

"It were a strange time. Eric's party had been planned for weeks. Never expected any prisoners to still be at The Brook, and in our heads our jobs were done. Looking back, we probably shoulda postponed the party when the transport were cancelled."

> — **ANDREW ELLIS, FORMER PRISON OFFICER**

"We were just having a few pints before The Brook closed. OK, so maybe it did get a bit raucous. More than usual. And I guess maybe none of us screws were as vigilant as we coulda been. But never coulda predicted what was going to happen. No one could."

> — **ANONYMOUS PRISON OFFICER OVER THE PHONE**

"The poison used that night was hemlock water-drop-wort, also known as 'dead man's fingers'. Its root looks a bit like a wild parsnip, and its leaves look and taste like parsley, so you do hear of accidental poisonings from time to time. You can find water hemlock in several places around Hertfordshire, including near Panbrook Prison. It's the most poisonous plant in the UK and gardeners are told to steer clear of it. Anna must have known that."

— DAVID WELSH, CLINICAL TOXICOLOGIST AT OXFORD UNIVERSITY

"Traces of the poison were identified in cake crumbs discovered in all five cells that evening. This can't have been accidental, as you wouldn't stick something looking like a parsnip in a cake, would you? Unfortunately, eating the plant causes symptoms rapidly – fever, vomiting, seizures, sweating, hallucinations – and there's no treatment."

— DAVID WELSH

"Anna was always making fairy cakes for birthdays, so no one thought anything of it. She showed me those cakes in the morning and said she'd made a separate batch to give the prisoners a leaving gift. I thought it a bit odd as she'd wrapped each of them in clingfilm, but it was none of my business."

— DR BRYAN LAND, FORMER PANBROOK PRISONER DOCTOR

"I thought it was so nice of Anna to make those cakes for my leaving do. I liked her, I really did, but guess there was a side we didn't see. Just as well she didn't poison *all* of us. That girl deserved everything she got."

— ERIC MARTIN

53

MADDIE

TWO MONTHS LATER

Ellie wanders among us like an angel, her golden curls spiralling down her back. The crystals on her ivory dress sparkle in the sunlight. So many wedding guests have commented on how much she looks like me, out of politeness obviously, for we share no DNA and my features are as dark as hers are pale.

When I look into her soft blue eyes, all I can see is Nate, her own flesh and blood. Or perhaps it is Anna I really see – the mother Ellie doesn't remember, the young woman who has haunted much of our lives, leaving a legacy I cherish as my own.

Ellie catches my eye and beams as Viv takes her hand and kisses it gently. I pull my phone out from my silver clutch bag and take a photograph of the happy couple; a memory that I'll savour forever. Their matching tiaras twinkle in the sunlight as they walk slowly over to the food table near the A-wing entrance. A tear trickles down my cheek, no doubt ruining my mascara. I wipe it away with my finger. These are the two people I care about most in the world, and I wish Nate was here to share this special moment.

A loud cheer comes from the bar area – one of Ellie's hospital colleagues raising a toast. I look over, half-expecting to see Lloyd Palmer drinking a Jack Daniels, but he's still recuperating at home.

He and I have emailed and messaged four or five times since then, perhaps more, any animosity on my part now ebbed away. I suspect there's some mutual attraction, our shared experiences tying us together in more ways than I would care to admit.

Ellie insists that it's time to live my life to the full and put the past behind us. But I'm not sure how Nate would feel about me letting into my life the man who threw Anna to the media lions. And I have no plans to share my life with anyone else ever again.

My daughter insisted on holding the wedding party here at Panbrook when we failed to find another suitable venue. I tried to discourage her, explaining that it could dredge up difficult memories of that night in the museum, but she insisted. She remembers Bryan offering her a drink – laced with one of Stella's sleeping tablets – but nothing after that, until she woke up in the hospital with Viv at her side.

There are no outward signs here of those traumatic events. Rose petals have been scattered around the courtyard, and four flower trees in peach and amber shades stand around the red acer like sentries on guard.

Yet unease still ripples over my skin.

I realised what Bryan Land had been doing twenty years ago when I saw him pushing the booklets and sugar packets into his empty doctor's bag. When Fiona Trayton fell from the landing, Rosalie asked him if he had checked her breathing and blood pressure. What respectable, experienced doctor wouldn't carry a stethoscope with him for emergencies?

The museum remains closed. The entrance is boarded up for forensic investigations, yet that building still haunts my dreams, or rather my nightmares, with Isaac Cane's beady eyes staring into mine.

I gaze up at B wing, now ready for the renovations next month. A glint of light catches my eye, a slight movement in a window, a shimmer of the sun – or perhaps William Owen is up there watching us and giving his daughter his blessing. A shiver inches its way down my spine.

Ellie is right, of course; the hotel's courtyard garden is the perfect size for our gathering, and Panbrook is an important part of her past, whether I like it or not. Derek hasn't charged us for the venue – probably to keep me quiet about events over that weekend – and even paid for the gazebo as we can't trust British summer weather.

A pigeon coos at me from a nearby table, a blue tag wrapped around one of its twig-thin legs. I look around for Pete, who is here today as Ellie's guest – the man who saved our lives and knew her birth mother best. I suspect that she's beginning to think of him as an eccentric grandfather figure.

He's standing at the edge of the gazebo, listening to the jazz band, stomping his feet in time to the music. His navy jacket flaps awkwardly around his waist. He and Ellie have spoken several times during the past few weeks, with Pete revealing more about Anna when Ellie asked questions I could never answer. If he's mourning Stella's demise, he doesn't show it – but I suspect there is a lot of sadness behind his smile.

The media has been having a field day, as new details about the case have been leaked and new evidence has been uncovered. The Facebook forums are buzzing again. New podcasts have been released. So far Ellie and I have remained anonymous – hopefully this will stay that way. Though twenty years on, it may be much more difficult for our identities to stay under the radar. I have a lawyer working on that.

Rumour has it that Bryan Land had encouraged Lucas Somers to become a Listener to counsel prisoners, and even staff, to find out their secrets. *'Secrets in prison are gold dust.'* His paper trail led back to Jonathan Roach, who put cocaine-filled booklets into library books to pass around the prison. Payment for drugs was arranged through prisoners' family members and paid into Faye's bank account. *'There's always someone to blame.'* Bryan Land bribed Fiona Trayton to make sure those five particular men remained at the prison on the final weekend. And he drove his wife to the phone box near Ellie's nursery so she could make the call to cancel the prison transport.

He had it all planned out then – and all planned out this weekend.

Those syringes in his bag contained large doses of insulin – enough to kill. He couldn't risk the police opening up the case again if the journalist believed Anna was innocent. Lloyd found his room ransacked, along with a note inviting him to the museum. Once inside, the doctor hit him with the photo frame and knocked him out. He had stolen Thomas Benson's pocket watch to frame the ex-prisoner for Lloyd's murder. Mine too. The police found a plane ticket to Spain at Bryan Land's home, along with more insulin supplies.

I wander over to the kitchen garden and sit down on a banana bench to rest my weary feet, which have been squeezed into uncomfortable silver slingbacks all day. It seems peaceful here, a brief respite from the music, and at this current moment in time, I can't imagine ever wanting to leave this job. But things will be different tomorrow, I am sure, once reality returns, along with a fresh start.

I came to Panbrook to see if I could find Ellie's father, to fulfil my promise to Nate, and now my quest is complete. I can't forgive Derek for the way he behaved during the anniversary weekend, when we found Stella in her room – how he put his hotel above the welfare of his employees. Though I haven't revealed details of his behaviour, not even to Ellie or Lloyd.

Hopefully Rosalie won't work out that Ellie is her half-sister. I certainly won't be mentioning this. I'm not prepared to share Ellie with anyone other than Viv. Rosalie quit her job here as soon as the anniversary weekend was over, citing stress and anxiety as the cause.

I'll also be handing in my own letter of resignation once this wedding is over. I already have a job lined up at a small boutique hotel in Knightsbridge, with no cells or murders or restless ghosts. I'm sure that Derek will give me an outstanding reference to keep me quiet.

I finger the silver bangle around my wrist – its diamanté sun and moon ends glinting in the sunshine. Once Celeste Etherton's special birthday gift, now it's mine. Secrets are funny things, aren't they? We all have something to hide – big or small – and will do anything to keep things under wraps.

Who knows what little trinkets I'll find among those wealthy guests in London, and who I can blame it on next time. Radha has already lost her job. I didn't spend much time with my mother over the years, but she still taught me a lot. She used to pocket guests' treasures too, but only if she believed they could afford to replace them. Searching guest rooms is very revealing.

My phone vibrates in my bag. I pull it out and find a WhatsApp message from Lloyd.

How's it going? Dance with any prison ghosts?

I laugh and reply with: *They're all stuck behind the bar(s).*

He responds straightaway: *At least Ellie had the best wedding present of all – that Anna really was innocent.*

I let out a long, slow sigh as the weight of yet more secrets continues to press heavily against my chest.

I'll never tell Ellie what I really learnt from Bryan Land after he knocked Lloyd out. Because then she will ask more questions.

And how can I tell her that – despite the official evidence – her birth mother was guilty after all?

BBC NEWS: Updated every minute of every day

Wednesday, September 18, 2019
Published at 11:35 GMT

[FRONT PAGE]

Panbrook Prisongate files reopened

A 69-year-old man has been charged with the murders of five prisoners at HMP Panbrook in June 1999, twenty years after the original investigation was closed.

Further enquiries are taking place to establish whether he was also involved in the death of Anna Kendall, the prison nurse who was accused of the prisoners' murders. Her death at HMP Clayton in August 1999 was originally believed to be suicide by a drug overdose, but new evidence suggests that this may, in fact, have been murder.

This man is also believed to be responsible for the death of a Panbrook Prison Hotel employee on the hotel premises in June 2019, and was possibly the perpetrator of the fall of a 72-year-old woman at the hotel on the same weekend. A police source has revealed that he may even have been responsible for the disappearance of Kellie Wyndham, the former head of Healthcare at Panbrook Prison, and the death of his wife in 2001.

More to follow.

ENJOYED LITTLE SECRETS?

Thank you so much for choosing to read *Little Secrets*. I hope you enjoyed reading it as much as I enjoyed writing it. If you have time, I would be very grateful if you could leave a rating and/or short, honest, spoiler-free review of *Little Secrets* on Amazon, Goodreads or wherever you bought this book. Your ratings and reviews help me reach new readers. And please recommend my book to your family and friends.

Have you read my Shanna Regan Mysteries?

The Redeemer

Threatening plaques, vigilante killings, a Jewish community in an English town – what's the link? The clock is ticking to the next murder.

The Redeemer was shortlisted for Best Debut Crime Novel of 2022 in the Crime Fiction Lover Awards 2022 and given an honourable mention in the Capital Crime/DHH Literary Agency New Voices Award 2019.

The Associate

A missing architect. An interfaith charity project. Vandalism and online threats. Can racist slogans lead to kidnap – or even murder?

The Associate was the Editor's Choice Winner of Best Indie Novel of 2023 in the Crime Fiction Lover Awards.

AFTERWORD AND ACKNOWLEDGEMENTS

Little Secrets was my lockdown book and I'm so excited to finally set it free. I began planning it in October 2019 after visiting the Malmaison Hotel in the former Oxford Prison, but I wrote most of the words in 2020 to 2021 when the world was going through the Covid-19 pandemic. My fictional prison-themed hotel is very different to the real-life version, but I loved the concept of a crime novel featuring a former prison that's now a luxury hotel. I would lock myself in my virtual prison-on-the-page to escape the global bad news. So it's not surprising that this book was known as 'my prison book' until I finally decided upon the title *Little Secrets* in March 2025.

When I began writing *Little Secrets*, I knew very little about prison life or life as a prison nurse. Special thanks go to former prison nurse, Annie Norman, who guided me through day-to-day prison life in the 1990s, specifically the healthcare department. I had already called my fictional prison nurse Anna/Annie, so our conversations were meant to be. Lynne Milford, fellow crime author, put me in touch with Annie through serendipity – sometimes life's coincidences can save the day (or, in this case, the book idea). Thank you, Lynne – and for your support in general. Thanks also go to Dan Rinsler for answering my questions about planning regulations for old and listed buildings while I was writing this book, and to Dr Jo Osborne for confirming a last-minute plot point. Any errors are mine alone.

This book hasn't reached the world without some professional help. Thank you, Sara Starbuck and Elinor Davies, for your excellent editorial advice and support (especially when challenges arose), and to Barbara Copperthwaite for her fabulous copyediting skills. Thanks also go to Mark Swan (kidethic) for his brilliant cover-design magic, and to Thomas Ziegel, talented graphic designer and illustrator, for hand-drawing the prison map that features in this book.

A big thank you to my early readers and supporters of *Little Secrets* (or parts of it) in its various forms over the years (in no particular order) – Kate, Steph, Tracy, Jen, Susi, Joy and Alexandra. Thank you to Sarah for our regular chats about the ups and downs of the publishing industry, to Linda for being on call for laughter and tears over the years, and to Marnie, Hilary and Victoria for solidarity over two of the most important things in life – books and bagels. Also a big thank you to my family, friends, supporters and readers. And finally, but certainly not least, my love goes to Richard, Samuel and Adam for being my biggest champions.

PLEASE KEEP IN TOUCH!

I'm a freelance journalist, editor, proofreader and author. I live in Hertfordshire with my husband and two sons.

If you would like to keep up to date with my latest book releases, you can join my Readers' Club for occasional news and exclusive giveaways. It's completely free, your email address will never be shared, and you can unsubscribe at any time.

vgoldmanbooks.com/join-my-readers-club/

You can also follow me on Amazon to be notified about my next book. To do this, find one of my books on Amazon. Click on my name to arrive on my Amazon page, and then click the Follow button.

You can connect with me in various ways too:

Facebook: www.facebook.com/VictoriaGoldmanBooks
Twitter/X: @VictoriaGoldma2

PLEASE KEEP IN TOUCH!

Instagram/Threads: @victoria_goldman_x
Bluesky: @victoriagoldman.bsky.social
Website: vgoldmanbooks.com